THE LIGHTLESS PROPHECY

BOOK ONE

DARKHAVEN

KEL E FOX

Darkhaven: Book 1 of The Lightless Prophecy

First paperback edition
ISBN: 978-1-922731-01-2

First published in Australia in December, 2021

Outfoxed Media (an imprint of Kel E Fox)
Perth, Western Australia
admin@outfoxedmedia.com.au

Cover design and interior formatting by Outfoxed Media
outfoxedmedia.com.au

kelefox.com

A catalogue record for this book is available from the National Library of Australia

For everyone who suspects that magic might be real

The Good Night

Lovely is the night!
A hiding place
Fit for the most beautiful dreams.
Lit by soft moonlight
And the glow of distant stars,
Harsh, bright giants
Far away so
They do naught
But dance for us
Across the inky blue.

Safe is the night.
A dwelling place
Where rivers flow
Unseen by prying eyes;
Chirps and rustlings go unheard
While tangled lovers lie.
Whispers between friends
Any man wants to know
But the night
Keeps her secrets.

Kind is the night.
A resting place,
Somewhere to let a weary head
Be exactly that.
The day pushes,
Relentless,
Urging us about our tasks,
Berating foot faults.
But wait for the night
And our salvation.

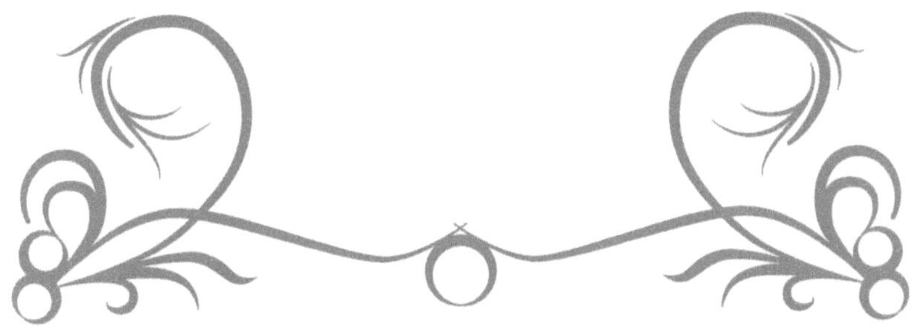

Gabby's Journal

November something. Exams, ugh

I don't know when I stopped believing in magic. But whenever it was, I also stopped making decisions, because what hand was worth keeping if magic wasn't in it?

Now? Now I don't know. The teachers say it's science, and they have the labs stuffed with gear and computers full of data, but still when I ask the question, it's like Year 10 biology all over again.

Why?

I get how *it works. That's like saying if you stack a bunch of books on top of each other you have a pile of books. It doesn't matter if you stacked them yourself or found them like that, the process is apparent. But why? Why are the books there in the first place? Why stack them in a pile? (I mean, why wouldn't you want a tower of books? But that's not the point.)*

Flamebeard talked in circles and still never answered the question.

For all our science, there's way more that we don't know. Saving lives and building cars and browsing the internet is great, but I no longer believe that science rules out magic.

Maybe it's just a matter of definition. Maybe this is the way to find out. If the answer is out there, Darkhaven has got to be a good starting point, right?

I just don't know if it's worth the cost.

CHAPTER ONE

A Chocolate Overdose Kind of Problem

I had imagined, age five, that an adult was something you suddenly became, probably around the same time you grew that monumental millimetre that made you taller than your parents. After that, you'd no longer be childlike, and you would know exactly what it was you were going to do with your life. By twelve, I figured adulthood mostly seemed to revolve around the concept of "bills". I thought, at the time, that it would be a sad day when an envelope sticking out of the letterbox would be something other than a birthday card or a parcel delivery notice.

Now, I was nearly seventeen. It was pretty clear that I was not going to be as tall as Dad, and my mother had died when I was a baby, so I had no idea if I'd reached adulthood by her vertical measurements. I'd complain while paying my mobile phone bill, feeling less like an adult and more like a disgruntled teenager stuck in a limbo of self-doubt and responsibility. I was starting to doubt that adulthood was even a thing. Perhaps adults were just children who no longer believed in magic.

Water ran through my dyed-black hair, slicking the strands down to my shoulders, swirling around my feet and gurgling down the drain. I grimaced at the epic purple bruise on my thigh from Friday's Phys Ed class – soccer was not my thing, unless stopping my own team's goals counted as a talent – and tipped my head back, rinsing away the last vestiges of sleep. Someone banged on the bathroom door.

'Gabby. You'll be late.' My uncle Alex. He and Dad worked in national security, which might be really cool – I wouldn't know, since it was all top secret. I'd spent my childhood shuttling between them as they each went on their undisclosed missions. I was the only reason they talked to each other. Except for similar career choices, they were a study in opposites. Dad was tall and thin and had been bald for as long as I could remember, which he claimed was by choice because he couldn't stand his untidy hair. Alex was short and muscular and kept his brown-with-grey locks neatly trimmed. Being short and somewhat stocky, I had more of my uncle's physique, although I definitely wasn't muscular, or even very fit. I loved Alex, but he was a pedant about punctuality and obsessed with health food, and I was supposed to get a hearty breakfast in before school.

I couldn't bring myself to turn off the tap. It was hard enough on any day in winter, or any Monday at all, but it was the beginning of July, and we were getting our TISC handbooks for university applications. It was time to make some decisions. Next year I would be eighteen, and apparently well on my way along the path of the rest of my life. I still had no idea which university or course to apply to. None. Well, not sports science.

The warm water flowed around me, unbothered that I didn't have an answer for The Question: what was I going to do? Or the even harder variant – what did I want to be? God knew. Except I was starting to doubt that God was a thing either.

'Gabby!'

I grumbled and got out of the shower, goosebumps prickling my skin. I didn't mind the cold. After all, it was Perth, Australia, which no one would admit was a desert masquerading as a temperate Mediterranean coastline. Perth was lovely for about two weeks in September. Then, for the next six months, it was like living on Mercury.

I dressed quickly, then reached for my makeup case and applied foundation, evening my skin tone with satisfaction. Cecelia, my best friend, said I should be happy in my own skin without cosmetics. I just told her right back that I wore makeup because I liked it. I did. I also liked that I didn't have to worry about a breakout at that time of the month, or the red blotchy patches on my cheeks when I got angry at someone. I liked having less-visible freckles on my nose and shading my cheeks to look slimmer. And I liked the idea that no one in the world except Dad, Alex and my two best friends had any idea what I looked like without sharp black eyeliner and dark red lipstick. I blotted my lips with a tissue and capped the tube.

'I'm leaving now!' Alex called from somewhere near the front door. I tucked a matching lip gloss into my jeans pocket, grabbed my not-quite-school-dress-code jacket, zipped on my favourite heeled, black ankle boots and ran out.

Cecelia's light blue eyes narrowed as I hurried into first-period English – two minutes after the bell – but she greeted me with a smile. She had her pale blonde hair pulled back in its usual tidy ponytail and a piece of apple skin wedged in her slightly askew front teeth. Obviously she hadn't skipped a wholesome breakfast in favour of makeup, which she never wore. I'd never seen so much as a single pimple on her. Cecelia Wilson, already taller than both her parents and definitely over the cusp of adult maturity, had been my best friend since pre-primary. On the first day of school, our untidy class of five-year-olds had sat in a circle on the mat for a sing-along, all holding hands – reluctantly, in my case, because on one side was the bossy, tone-deaf teacher aide who kept squeezing my fingers encouraging me to join in, and on the other some snotty boy who'd sneezed on me at recess. Directly opposite me was a long-limbed girl with her flyaway blonde hair in pigtail plaits and her face lit up with exuberant song. She beamed when our gazes met, and I decided then that we would be best friends. Probably the best decision I'd ever made. No doubt about her TISC applications: she intended to become the third Doctor Wilson in the family, like her dad and her older brother, Bryce.

I sank into the chair next to her just as Mrs Johnsen waddled in. I'd read some stupid fashion blog once that said you're either pear-shaped or apple-shaped, depending on your fat distribution. I had pear hips, for sure. Cecelia was a celery stick. Mrs Johnsen was not tall, but wide and round. She kept her thick hair in a tight bun and wore paisley patterns in varying shades from beige to brown, occasionally venturing into a brownish pink. She had missed the memo about bras being a thing again now that the sixties were over, and her unrestrained bosom swung from side to side with more enthusiasm than her shuffling gait warranted. Dark eyes, framed by heavy glasses, glittered ominously. Mrs Johnsen could almost physically poke you with nothing more than her gaze. I sat up straighter. Slightly.

She cleared her throat. 'Your mid-year assignments were abysmal. Whatever your plans are for next year, you will need the skills required to write a formal essay. Your next assignment will be an analysis of three poems of your choice, from one of the set texts.' She squeezed between desks, handing out the papers. Apparently she had tortured anguished souls at university during her postgraduate days, and she never lost an opportunity to tell us how unbelievably hard first-year uni was and how unprepared we all were.

'There will be a ten per cent per day late penalty. You will reference your answers. I don't want to read a single opinion unless it's from the mouth of the poet laureate.'

'But Miss, I'm not even taking English at uni!' Todd, a dick from way back, called out. Todd was uber-athletic and the object of most high school crushes. Not mine or Cecelia's – I'd never actually had a crush on anyone, to Dad's dismay, and Cecelia wouldn't look up from her textbooks for long enough to notice a boy or a girl.

Martin, an oily-haired slimeball who'd gained popularity by association, elbowed Todd. 'Hell, I'm not taking any humanities, let alone this girly subject. Unless there's a "partying one-oh-one"!' Another original knobhead.

Mrs Johnsen didn't reply, except to collect two battered copies of Gwen Harwood's *Selected Poems* from her desk and advance down the rows. She placed one in front of each boy and leaned her considerable bulk down towards them. Two wide-eyed faces pulled as far back from the unbridled breast display as they could.

'Then aren't you lucky you won't miss out. You' – she pointed a finger at Todd – 'read aloud. "Suburban Sonnet".'

Martin let a snigger out, a wild sound that threatened to escape and dance around on the tense atmosphere. Mrs Johnsen fixed her glare. She could catch an errant outburst with the bat of an eyelid.

'And you,' she said with malicious delight as she turned to Martin, 'will present a speech at the end of the week, enlightening us with your understanding of how a feminist might have felt living in a society of 1950s repression. Make sure you emphasise how *girly* it was.'

She straightened, looking around the room. Any other stray giggles were quickly leashed. Todd completed his reading in a speedy monotone and the class settled into soft whispers as Mrs Johnsen, barking an order to work on our essay plans, plonked down into her desk chair and stuffed her nose in a hefty book.

I doodled an intricate, pointless pattern of swirls and loops on my notebook and wondered if I would feel better about the world if I had an obvious talent, like sports, singing or drawing. Something resembling a pair of eyes emerged from my scribbles, and I spent the rest of the class attempting to turn it into a cat. I didn't even like cats. I'd always wanted a dog.

'Time to go,' Mrs Johnsen declared from her desk, without lifting her eyes from her novel. Cecelia packed up her pens and glanced over at my work, a confused frown crossing her face.

'What is that?'

I sighed, flipping my notebook shut. Clearly, I had zero talent with a pencil. I shoved my stuff in my bag and followed Cecelia out.

I mused all the way to Human Biology, thinking about how to solve my dilemma and nearly walking into a bunch of Year 8 kids gathered around a tablet in the hallway. My old method for choosing classes – picking a subject at random, changing my mind twenty times before the form was due, then rocking up in deputy principal Mr Cantwell's office in Week One to change it again – now seemed inappropriate. I took my seat next to Cecelia and realised I'd left my textbook in my locker. Oh well.

'Did you know,' began Mr Flancinbaum, a gangly, bearded man who insisted we all call him Sam, 'that lightning only kills ten per cent of the people it strikes? Ten per cent!'

He beamed around the room, hair sticking up above his ears in enthusiastic tufts. Most of the school called him Flamebeard, thanks to an unfortunate lab experiment involving a Bunsen burner – an incident that had become a cherished and well-embellished story among the students. Flamebeard turned on the projector to show a person with spiderwebs of red tracing over half their body.

'But you still don't want to take your chances. A bolt of lightning can be five times hotter than the surface of the sun, and – yes, Michaela?'

Michaela, another aspiring doctor and Cecelia's main competition for Dux of the school, had raised her hand. Next to the four different coloured highlighters, open textbook and red, blue and black pens laid before her was the course summary. 'Mr Flancinbaum, is any of this going to be in the exam?'

Flamebeard paused, crestfallen. 'Well, not specifically, but it is fascinating!'

In almost perfect unison, the class packed away their notebooks and pens. Not deterred, Flamebeard pressed on with his lecture on the effects of lightning strikes while my mind drifted. I couldn't concentrate on Australian poetry or bio-electrical systems with this career-defining, life-altering decision in my head. I was good at a lot of things, but none of them jumped out. I stared out the window, contemplating what fundamental human purpose I was missing, until the class ended.

'Where's Zenna?' Cecelia asked as we settled onto our usual patch of grass for lunch. Zenna was our other best friend. My other best friend, if I was honest; she and Cecelia were an unlikely match who were only connected through me, but we worked as a trio. The doctor, the artist, and whatever I was supposed to be.

'I think she has some film project due,' I replied. Cecelia complained about the English essay as we fished our lunches out of our bags. I commiserated, but I knew that once I dove into the project I wouldn't mind it. Cecelia was more of a science wizard, which was to say that while everywhere else she got near-perfect marks, in English she managed low-to-mid 90s.

'So,' she said, between carrot sticks, 'which uni are you going for?'

I sighed and bit into a muesli bar, the kind coated with yoghurt and full of chocolate bits. 'I don't know, Ceel. I have no idea what I want to do after school, and it's like if I don't make that choice now I'm doomed. I'm going to go home with this stupid thing' – I stabbed a finger at the TISC handbook poking out of my bag – 'and consume chocolate until I die and the whole problem goes away.'

Cecelia reached into her bag, her fingertips brushing the handbook I could see wedged between her subject files.

'Please don't,' I protested. 'I don't want to think about it now.'

She gave me a sly smile and withdrew two blocks of roasted almond milk chocolate. 'I thought you could come back to my house this afternoon and we could die of chocolate overdose together,' she offered.

I grinned. 'Sounds good. But don't expect me to have any great epiphanies.'

'You can always just go with UWA. Then we'll be on the same campus at least. I'm sure you could apply for a transfer if you changed your mind.'

The problem, I thought, was that I never made my mind up in the first place.

CHAPTER 2

Oil Over Velvet

Y ou don't need to make your mind up about much,' Zenna said, adjusting the settings on her digital camera. I didn't bother paying attention. I did the bare minimum I could get away with in Media Production, my non-ATAR elective, and I still hadn't learned how to use a proper camera. If anything, I was worse with a DSLR – I had no idea what the acronym stood for, and a DSLR didn't take care of everything for me like my trusty smartphone.

Zenna's multitude of silver rings glinted in the winter sun as she twisted dials with purple-polished fingertips. I'd met this petite girl with rainbow nails and glitter in her hair in Photography back in Year 9, and even though I'd sucked at it, I'd stayed in the class because I figured the next thing I chose might be just as bad, but without anyone fun to hang out with or help me with homework. Unlike me, Zenna Robinson had an eye for a great photo and the skills to take it. She wasn't doing ATAR, but she was planning to go into cinematography, and she was almost top of the class. At best, I could maybe pick out an interesting subject. I'd yet to get anything in focus.

'No,' I remarked, 'just how to go about the rest of my life. You know, the Question.'

Zenna pushed back her hair – this week, red with gold streaks – and sighed dramatically, putting on her best teacher voice. 'Gabby. What are you going to do?'

'Oh, I don't know, go home, take a long bath, order pizza.' I elbowed her.

'Hey, watch the camera! Be useful, go and lie on that bench. There's no better time to start your career as a photographic subject.'

I snorted. 'Ha. I am not model material.'

'I didn't say you'd be modelling. You add interest to my landscape.'

I sashayed to the bench, exaggerating the wiggle of my hips, and sat down, lingering on the shady end and hunching into my jacket.

'In the sun, please!' Zenna called, waving her hand at the other end, rings flashing in the sunlight.

'But it's glary,' I grumbled. I made a point of squinting in her general direction.

'It's not that bad. Just do it. Like your TISC thing. Just pick a university that you like the look of and do it.'

'Easy for you to say. What if I don't even get a high enough score?'

Zenna kept taking photos. 'Then you won't have to worry about having picked the wrong place.' She gestured to the camera on its tripod. 'Your turn.'

I pulled my phone out of my jacket pocket and started snapping. Zenna rolled her eyes and packed up the equipment.

Two minutes later, we wandered back to the computer lab.

'Did you even take any pictures?' she asked.

'Yes,' I replied, indignant. She raised one eyebrow.

'See.' I gestured as we logged into the computers. 'They've already uploaded to the cloud. Efficiency is an art form.'

Zenna frowned as she gave my meagre collection a short review. 'Efficiency is not art.'

We worked in silence. It took me about ten minutes to give up. I turned to Zenna. 'Can I please use some of yours?'

'Hmm,' she began, not taking her eyes off her screen, 'sounds like plagiarism. Why would I let you do that?'

I gave her my best mock-pleading face. 'Because it would be equally unethical to let your friend fail when you knew you could save her.'

Without pausing in her work, she passed me a USB drive. 'You forgot you also took these.'

I smiled, plugged the drive in and opened the folder. They were good, but not her usual standard. I knew I'd never get away with passing off anything she'd taken properly as mine. The last file was a video of me sashaying in front of the camera. I grimaced at the size of my bottom. 'Bitch,' I remarked.

Zenna smirked. 'You owe me.'

'Big time. But still a bitch.' We giggled, then lapsed into busy silence.

Ten minutes before the end of last period, a runner came in with a note summoning me to the deputy principal's office. I told the receptionist my name and waited in the corner next to a drooping potted fern and an old sofa that looked too hard for anyone's butt, trying not to read the career advice posters in abundant display on the wall. My eyes had just settled on a lacklustre advertisement about the school's drama production when a guy's voice sounded behind me.

'Don't go.' It wasn't just a voice. It was the sound of oil spreading over velvet. Water thundering over a cliff. But voices didn't sound like that, at least not that I'd ever heard. I turned.

He was roughly my age and all lanky limbs, with alarmingly scruffy black hair. He lounged on the rock-hard sofa as if he lived there, in black sandshoes, casually-on-purpose ripped black jeans and a white t-shirt. A delicate silver chain hung around his neck, disappearing under his shirt. He was wearing sunglasses, the black wrap-around kind with mirrored lenses so I could see only myself in them.

'Hello,' he said, in *that* voice. I could feel his gaze on me, even through the dark lenses.

'Um, what?' I sputtered.

He broke the gaze, looking down at the corner of the couch where a thread was torn loose.

'Sorry,' he said. Now he sounded normal. 'The play. It's terrible. Trust me, I saw the rehearsal.' He looked back up. Something was different about him from a moment ago, but I couldn't pick it.

'Ri-ight.' I drew the word out. 'Well, I wasn't going. I was ... '

'Not looking at career posters?'

I started. How had he known that? I glanced over the array of "Be at the cutting edge of biotech" and "Do you have what it takes to lead a team?" posters and shrugged, trying to sound as casual as his jeans looked. 'I just wish I could meet God or whoever it is up there and they could tell me what the hell I'm supposed to be doing.'

He looked at me. Sunglasses still on. 'Do you really wish you could meet this god of yours?'

I turned away from his intensity. 'I don't really believe in God. I'm here to see Mr Cantwell.'

The strange boy chuckled. 'That's probably about as close as most people get to the god of careers.'

I didn't get it. And I was miffed at his familiarity. 'How did you know I wasn't reading career posters anyway?'

His long fingers picked absently at the loose thread in the couch. 'Lucky guess. And you know, there's about twenty of them and you're deliberately staring at that one very dull drama PSA.'

Mr Cantwell opened his door and waved me in.

'Nice chatting,' the boy said, stretching his arms overhead and sticking his legs out like this was his living room or something.

'Whatever,' I muttered. I stepped over his feet, my toe catching the edge of his shoe. The boy grinned.

Mr Cantwell returned to his office chair and motioned for me to sit. He was a tall, angular man with a face full of features competing for dominance: prominent chin, long nose and dark, bushy eyebrows. He was gruff and blunt and feared by most of the school, but under the suit and tie and stiff exterior, he genuinely cared about the plights of indecisive students.

'Ah, Gabby. I thought I'd see how you were doing with your university choices.'

I gave him a "how-do-you-think" look – we were familiar enough – and plopped into one of the chairs in front of his desk.

'You've been in here every semester since you had to choose your Year 9 electives, trying to change your subjects.'

It was true. I folded my arms, trying not to betray my internal anguish. 'I don't think I can get this right.'

He leaned back in his chair. 'Did you meet with the career counsellor?'

I nodded. Fat lot of use that had been. The woman had looked at my records, then looked at me and asked if I had thought about having a baby. I'd walked out without a word. Mr Cantwell steepled his fingers and regarded me over his reading glasses. 'It's not about getting it right. Consider that a university degree isn't for everyone. I'm not saying you don't have the academic skill – you definitely do – but it isn't your only option. Just keep that in mind.'

'What else should I do?' Stupidly, I felt like crying. I pushed the feeling down and gritted my teeth.

'Well, I would suggest a gap year. Take some of the pressure off. My daughter took a year off, travelled a bit, worked, and she said it gave her a different perspective. Or you can look at TAFE options, if vocational training appeals more to your interests.'

I slumped. TAFE. Degrees. Gap years. Nothing felt right. 'But I still have to apply to somewhere now. I need an epiphany.' My voice cracked. Dammit.

Mr Cantwell smiled. 'Gabby, sometimes in life you just have to make a decision.'

An alarm beeped from his wrist. 'If you need anything, just let me know,' he offered, silencing the alarm as he stood to open the door. I smiled and thanked him, not meeting his eyes, in case he saw mine about to water, and hurried out of the room.

The strange boy was gone.

Heavy clouds were massing on the horizon when I came out of Cantwell's office. I took a deep breath of the electric air, letting it diffuse the feeling of panic. Frizzy hair be damned, I loved a good thunderstorm. Sure, I wasn't fond of the humidity that preceded one, but it was worth it for that feeling of pent-up excitement. Like being a kid, waiting at the gates of the Perth Royal Show, next in line for the turnstile.

Dad was back today and he picked me up in his black Calais – his inconspicuous drive, for when a chauffeured Mercedes was too theatrical. I had long ago stopped asking questions. When I was five, Alex had bought me a cubby house, turned it into my "special agent" office and told me that whatever I got up to in there, it would be top secret. Not even he could know. That way, we would both have our secret lives. Dad took a different tack. I had questioned him, once. Never again.

'How was school?' Dad asked as I slid into the warm front seat.

'It sucked.'

'Ah, today was the day the TISC handbooks were released from their cage to unleash terror on uncertain students. I'm in the know.' He tapped his nose.

I rolled my eyes.

'You know it's not the end of the world if you start the wrong major. You can always change it.'

'Who says I even want to go to uni?' I said, thinking about Mr Cantwell's comment.

'Well, you have some time to think about it. But it doesn't hurt to have a plan.'

I sat in stubborn silence. He shot me more than one concerned glance. It wasn't Dad I was mad at, but I was mad at something, and he was there.

Since Dad's house was in West Beach and I went to West Beach Senior High School, the drive home took less than ten minutes. West Beach was named, with an extraordinary leap of imagination, for the beach it incorporated, and being in Perth meant it faced west. Of course pretty much all beaches in WA faced west, but whatever. It was a quiet suburb, and both Cecelia and Zenna lived within a few minutes' drive, or a fifteen-minute walk if I couldn't get a lift. All the houses looked the same: beige, rendered four-by-twos with double garages and well-kept lawns at the front. Two-point-five dogs and a kid and all that. I loved Alex's little apartment in the city, where Italian pistachio gelato was only a short stroll away and the neighbourhood lawnmower brigade didn't wake me up every Saturday morning.

Alex spent most of his time in Canberra when he wasn't staying with me. Talk about being an imposition. I'd hassled him about it once, but he assured me that he loved hanging out with me, then grinned and said it was all about the water anyway, and when he wasn't working, he was rowing or water skiing or paddleboarding. Alex teased me about being the only person in the world who wore shoes and jeans and a long-sleeved shirt to the beach; I maintained that anything less than knee-high boots was inviting sand into my socks where it didn't belong. Beaches were pretty – in photos. And I had to admit they were kinda awesome in a thunderstorm. I had always had an urge to watch a thunderstorm roll in from the vantage point of a mountaintop. Sure it would be suicide-crazy, but still. Fantasies were supposed to be crazy.

Dad frowned as we drove down our street. By the time we pulled into the driveway, his expression was black, his mouth a thin line. A silver BMW waited in front of the garage door. I peered at it, curiosity twining with unease in my stomach.

We almost never had visitors, and definitely never unannounced.

Dad pulled up alongside the BMW and turned off the engine. 'Stay in the car.'

Before I could open my mouth to protest, his door shut behind him. A woman dressed in a pencil skirt and jacket stepped out of the back of the BMW. I leaned over and cracked Dad's window.

'You shouldn't have come here,' Dad said, the warning low in his throat.

'We can't all play happy families, *Jon*,' she said with a cold sneer. She handed him an envelope. 'Let me know what you want to do about it.'

Dad tucked the envelope in his jacket pocket and glowered after the BMW as it disappeared down the street. I grabbed my bag and followed him into the house, intrigued, but he vanished into his office without a word. Something to do with his work then. It was unusual that his co-workers would come to the house, but I'd long ago stopped worrying about furtive visits from people Dad worked with.

I slung my bag down in the hallway and headed for the kitchen as my phone buzzed – Cecelia, reminding me of our TISC book and chocolate date. If only there was a job for someone whose favourite thing to do was eat dessert. While I rummaged in the freezer, Dad's footsteps scuffed across the room and I straightened, ice cream tub in hand. 'Can I go over to Cecelia's? We're going to study.'

'Sure. But be back early, please. It's a school night.'

'Is it really?' I asked, mocking. 'Here I was thinking it was Friday.'

'Wishing, more like.' He had his wetsuit and beach bag in hand, ready to head back out and take advantage of the wind and storm swell, but not before he admonished me about eating some fruit. 'Apples, Gabby. The round red things in the bowl on the table. Or bananas. And it doesn't count if you eat it with syrup and ice cream!' Then he was gone.

I made myself a banana split, complete with two scoops of ice cream, chocolate sauce and maple syrup, and sat at the table with my TISC handbook. I flicked aimlessly through the pages, not really seeing them. The Question loomed over me. Cecelia was so sure of her path that, despite her efforts, she really couldn't understand my problem. Zenna was more sympathetic, but she didn't have any great advice either. She said I should just go to uni, which to her – a smart girl who had somehow never fit into academia or aspired to university study – was a magical world where clever people found their place.

Teachers were no help to me either. They had lamented my lack of application to my studies all year, ever since I realised that none of my subjects were inspiring me and stopped bothering. When I tried to explain that to Flamebeard, after he told me that I had an aptitude for biology and should pursue it with more vigour, he responded by launching into an impassioned talk about molecular genetics. I had stared, wondering at how the irony was lost on him. And that was the point: if I was destined to pursue the subject, if I really cared, I too would have forgotten what we'd been talking about and joined him in the genetics digression.

I wondered what my mum would have said. Dad didn't keep any photos of her, so I didn't even know what she looked like. When I was six, I'd come home from school one day, a half-finished drawing clutched in my fist, crying because we'd been asked to draw our mum for Mother's Day and I didn't know which colour crayon to use for her hair. He'd sat me down and explained that she'd been an officer like him and had died from a bullet wound during a mission they'd been on. As with all his work, he couldn't elaborate, but I kept asking him questions. Finally he snatched the drawing out of my hand and tore it into pieces, screaming that I mustn't talk about it. I'd never seen him so angry before, or since, and I'd never asked about her again. I didn't exactly miss her but sometimes I would see Cecelia laughing or talking or bickering with her mum, Nancy. I guess I just missed that relationship. Nancy had always been more than kind to me, but it wasn't quite the same. Although it had come pretty close when she'd made me a litter-of-puppies cake for my seventh birthday. Literally, eight little cakes in different puppy shapes, iced in white and brown with chocolate buttons for spots. They'd been almost too cute to eat.

My phone buzzed again. Nancy would pick me up in an hour, after ballet. Cecelia and her two younger sisters all took lessons. I had tried hip hop for a while, but I didn't have an ounce of musicality or commitment to practise and the teacher eventually advised that perhaps I would prefer athletics, which had to have been a joke, except she said it with a straight face.

I pushed the TISC handbook away, dumped my bowl in the sink, changed into comfy jeans and an old hoodie and found my sneakers, thinking of going for a walk. I was mostly okay with my soft, size 12 physique. Well, 14 if I shopped at *those* stores, but I avoided their disproportionate mannequins and their smug, skinny sales staff. I knew I wasn't fat – I'd be a size 8 or 10 in America – and I wanted to be confident about my non-flat stomach, but damn it was hard, when media was full of rake-thin girls and airbrushed images. Even so, walking was more for reflecting on a book I was reading, or sometimes finding an idea for an essay. I needed more than an idea now though. I needed an intervention.

I peeked into Dad's room as I passed. He'd left his jacket slung across the end of the bed. I hesitated, then ducked into the room and slipped my hand into the fold of the jacket, careful not to disturb it. Dad had an uncanny eye for details like that. My fingers found paper and I drew the envelope out, my skin tingling even though I knew he wouldn't be back for an hour at least.

It was old-looking paper, thick and heavy in my hand, and had a roughened texture like parchment. The surface of it glinted in the light. Intrigued, with my ears straining for any sound of Dad returning early, I flipped the envelope over. It had been affixed with an old-fashioned wax seal in white, a lying-down figure eight with a line through it. He'd already opened it, so he wouldn't notice if I lifted the seal again. I peeled the flap back, careful not to tear it, and peered into the envelope. It was empty.

My first thought was that Dad must have removed the contents. My second was that it was an extraordinarily heavy envelope to have nothing in it. I was just about to put it back when it started to glow. The pit of my stomach fizzed with excitement as a white, translucent orb the size of a golf ball floated out of the envelope and hovered around eye height. Mesmerised, I extended my hand, wondering if it was ridiculously foolish to touch it, but before I could bring myself to move closer it exploded in a puff of glitter like tiny stars, a miniature elliptical galaxy bursting into life and fading from the room. Nothing remained except an empty, now suitably light, parchment envelope resting in my hand. I stared at the space where the orb had been, then inspected the envelope, but it contained no further clues. Was it a message? More importantly – the effervescence in my gut intensified – was it …

I couldn't let myself believe it. *Magic.* Maybe my mind was making up illusions to distract me from my career choices. I gave myself a shake, tucked the envelope back into Dad's jacket and retreated from the room.

CHAPTER 3

Impossible Blanks

As I locked the front door behind me, the strange orb still a fading after-image behind my eyes, I noticed something sticking out of the letterbox. It was a white card, like a postcard, but instead of an image it contained just my name, written in script: *Miss Gabrielle Whitehall.* I frowned. Dad's address wasn't public information. Only Alex, Cecelia and Zenna knew I lived here, and they were all well aware that I hated "Gabrielle". I turned it over.

Don't let them take you.

Look for May.

The buzz from finding the orb evaporated, and a chill settled in its place. Had the postcard come from the woman who'd stopped by? Some part of me didn't think so. I tucked the card into my jeans pocket and set off down the street with something else to ponder. Dad had always been concerned that I might get caught up in his work. He'd never said how or what might happen, but it was a large part of the reason I went and stayed with Alex when Dad was away. I supposed the card might be a threat, but I had a sense that whoever had sent the note – left it, actually, as there was no address or postmark – was trying to warn me, not threaten me. But of what? And "look for May"? Like, May the month? My brain had no other ideas. May was a long way off; TISC applications were due in September. Maybe the universities had their own police who came and interrogated students who were thinking of skipping out on the system.

A cat crossed the road in front of me, thick, steel-grey coat matching the colour of the sky. It sat with its tail tucked around its paws as I walked by, staring at me with wide amber eyes. I scowled. What was it with cats today? My skin prickled as I thought of the one I'd tried to draw. In my mind's eye it had been a grey cat.

I looked back, but it was gone.

At the top of a hill, I stopped at the entrance to a park. It was a large, open space that extended down the other side of the hill, mainly for dogs, and at the bottom was a fancy new kids' playground. It was always busy down there, but up here was an old swing set and a metal jungle gym that I often sat on to think or read. I climbed to the top of the jungle gym and watched the clouds rolling across the sky, forming towering shapes. Thunder rumbled like falling stones in the distance.

Despite the electric air, I struggled to lift my mind out of the fog I'd been swimming in for the past two years. I'd done, so far, what was necessary to pass, and sometimes I'd lucked out and achieved more – to the frustration of my teachers, who were torn between marking me down anyway because they knew I hadn't tried or berating me for letting my academic ability go to waste. Australia needs biologists like you, Flamebeard had said. And female media producers. And people with an instinct for communications. All my teachers had an opinion. Yet, I couldn't bring myself to apply for further study in any of those things. Perhaps there was something fundamentally wrong with me, some intrinsic thing I couldn't find. Or maybe it wasn't me. Maybe there was something missing from the world. The strange orb glimmered in my mind, but now the shock had worn off, I figured it had to have been a trick. A flashy effect to disguise a confidential message. More pressing was the postcard in my pocket.

Wind whipped my hair across my face and rushed through my ears, so I nearly missed the sound. The cat prowled around the bottom of the jungle gym, meowing and looking up at me. I had no idea what normal cat behaviour was, but this seemed odd. I gave it a withering look. The hairs rose on my arms, rubbing the wrong way against the fleece of my hoodie.

Closer to my ears than the distant thunder rumbling around or the weird cat racket, my phone beeped. Zenna.

Facetime in 30? Be good to go through portfolios.

I didn't care about my portfolio, and it finally clicked. I was bored. I had been bored for at least two years.

Soz Zenna, am out for a walk.

In this weather? Are you mad?

The wind intensified, tossing the treetops lining the park and buffeting me on my perch. It *was* getting a bit intense. I climbed down and almost stepped on the damn cat. Thinking it might be lost, I knelt and held out a hand to see if it had a name tag, but it turned and trotted away, still meowing. Whatever, cat.

The darkened sky lit up with a blaze of forked lightning. Seconds later, the air rumbled like a bass drum. A thrill shot through my body. The cat stopped on the footpath, amber eyes wide, staring at me.

Lightning flashed again, followed immediately by thunder. I hadn't realised the storm was so close. A loud buzzing emanated from the jungle gym, pushing into my head, and my thrill shifted to fear as Flamebeard's lesson on lightning strikes jumped to mind. I hurried down the path, off the top of the hill.

A prickling sensation spread over my scalp. I reached up to find my hair standing on end. Hair that normally fell past my shoulders, sticking straight up, a foot above my head. Thunder snapped across the sky. I started running. I knew it was too late. My phone slipped from my hand as I sprinted.

The air around me erupted in a white-hot blaze. I wasn't sure if I was seeing anything, or hearing anything. It might have been white fire or black flames, it might have been a stupendous roar or deafening silence, it might have seared across my skin and burned through my shoes and dropped me to the ground where my knees grazed the concrete path, but I don't know for sure that I was aware of anything. Perhaps my mind just filled in the impossible blanks.

I fell into nothingness.

CHAPTER 4

Unkillable Woman

Damp sandpaper rubbed my nose. I opened my eyes to find an amber pair staring back at me and the world came into focus around the grey cat, its coat blending with the steely clouds above it. I brushed the cat away, trying to work out what had happened. I was lying on the footpath, my knees stinging and my body feeling like it had been pummelled by a million soccer balls. My fingers met sticky blood as I touched my knees. Had I fallen off the jungle gym? But then how had I ended up so far away from it? My hoodie and the t-shirt underneath were sort of shredded, my jeans weren't much better and my sneakers were lying on the other side of the footpath.

Thunder crashed, close. Sirens screeched in the distance. I examined my hands, my arms, looking for some sign of what had happened, but my skin at least looked fine, and I could move all my fingers, even if it felt like pushing through melted ice cream. The cat kept rubbing my legs, looking at me, then trotting away, thick grey fur rippling, like it wanted me to follow it. Perhaps the stress of TISC decisions had finally rendered me insane. The sirens wailed closer now, cutting through the pealing thunder.

I climbed to my feet, teetered for a moment on wobbly legs and collected my shoes. I found my phone a few metres further up the hill, powered off. My head pounded. The sirens had stopped, replaced by tyres squealing on the road next to the park. I looked up as a black SUV mounted the kerb, drove up the grass towards me and swerved to a stop. Two men in dark suits jumped out.

Don't let them take you.

I froze, caught like peach slices trapped in jelly.

'Come with us, miss,' Suit One ordered. Suit Two backed the command up with an officious stare. When I made no move, they stepped forward, reaching for me. I stumbled back. Suit Two grabbed my upper arm while Suit One fished a phone out of his pocket. He nodded at us, and Suit Two began pushing me to the car. Panic snapped through my body like lightning, freeing me from my jellied state.

I dug my heels in and punched Suit Two in the throat. At least, I tried to. In the next second, my arm was twisted down behind my back and something small, hard and round pressed against my spine. I kicked at the man as he shoved me into the back seat, and shouted, but my voice was hoarse, ripped away by the howling wind. Suit One was already at the wheel. Fear spasmed across my mind. The door slammed shut behind me as I sprawled on the thick black leather, scrambling for the door handle, but it wouldn't open. Wire mesh separated me from the front seats. I clawed at it. 'Let me out!'

'Don't worry, miss, we're from the government,' Suit One said, eyes black in the rear-view mirror. His partner climbed in next to him and the car took off, bouncing over the kerb.

'Who are you? Did you leave the note?' I demanded, pushing against the mesh. The men exchanged a glance.

'They're close,' Suit Two said. Suit One looked grim. He swung around a corner, flinging me across the seat. I twisted towards the sound of more tyres screeching behind us. A small silver car swerved around and came after us, so close I could see a brown-haired man behind the wheel, face set.

The car followed us out of the suburbs, keeping up as the SUV careened around corners. I kicked at the window, wondering what my chances of survival were if I jumped out headfirst, but it didn't even crack, and I chickened out as we hit the freeway. The silver car got left behind, along with any ideas of escape. I hammered at the mesh again. 'Where are you taking me?'

No reply. Not even the turn of a head.

I dropped onto the back seat, helpless. If they were on my side, surely they wouldn't keep ignoring my questions. Maybe the man in the silver car had left the note. But who was he, and how did he know where I'd be?

We blazed down the freeway, dodging cars. Unbelted, I gripped an armrest as I slid across the back seat. I glanced through the windscreen: a wall of traffic, red tail lights snaking along all three lanes, bumper-to-bumper for as far as I could see. We were coming up fast. Cars around us slowed as they approached the jam, but we didn't break pace. The swerving through traffic became frantic. Horns blared around us. A police siren sounded, distant.

Too distant to help me.

I watched, unblinking, my eyes drying as we closed the final metres to the crawling traffic. We veered into the left emergency lane, to angry protests from other drivers, and flew past, inches from side mirrors on the right and the barrier on the left. At the last moment, we took an exit at full speed, flying towards a line of cars waiting to turn right. There was nowhere to go. We were going to crash.

I screamed. I wasn't the only one.

A second before we hit a delivery van, it jumped the kerb and got out of the way. Our SUV charged through, snapping off the van's side mirror. We barrelled left, where the road, narrowed to single lanes, was clear. I stopped screaming.

The other scream continued, but it wasn't human. It was the roar of an engine.

A motorcycle flew in from the left in a green blur, snaking through the jammed exit. In the rear-view mirror, Suit One's eyes widened as he swerved. He clipped a silver car passing in the right lane. More horns. The motorcycle swung in again from the right, pressuring us off the road. Suit One scrabbled at the steering wheel, but the car went off the shoulder, sliding on the gravel. The front airbags exploded as we crashed into a fence. My head smacked against a pillar, and my headache burst into a thousand more shards of pain.

Fighting against a wave of blackness, I tried to open my door again, but it was locked. One of the agents was beating back the airbags and reaching for something at his belt. I fumbled for my phone, praying it would turn on. I had to call Dad.

Someone wrenched my door open.

A tall, slim woman in black and grey leathers held the door with one hand, motorcycle helmet in the other. 'Huh. Dead ringer for Luce,' she remarked. She had straight, blonde hair cropped under her ears and the most perfect teeth I'd ever seen. Not that she was smiling – more like grimacing. Her hazel eyes were wild.

'Get out.' She jerked her head towards the monstrous green motorcycle posing in front of a massive tree.

My knees buckled under my weight, the grazes from falling on the pavement tugging painfully. The woman took a firm hold of my arm and shoved me towards the motorcycle before she turned back to the SUV. Two gunshots rattled my already ringing ears.

I whirled around. The woman ran towards me and shoved the helmet into my hands. Her other hand gripped a pistol.

'Did – did you kill them?' I asked, trying to keep the tremor out of my voice.

She arched an eyebrow. 'Will it make you feel better if I say no?'

As my trembling fingers struggled with the helmet straps, an engine revved. The SUV reversed out of the fence and gunned for us.

She huffed. 'Apparently not. Run!'

She spun back, drawing another gun. I stumbled a few steps out of the way, but I felt like I was stuck in a dream, unable to run. The car kept coming towards her, and she kept shooting, pulling another pistol from some imperceptible pocket in her leathers. The windscreen cracked through. Finally, the man slumped, but the SUV was too close. With a dull thud, it ran straight over the top of her, then into the motorcycle before it smashed into the tree with a metallic crunch, crushing the bike into its fender as leaves showered the wreckage.

I clapped my hands over my mouth in horror. The woman lay in a twisted heap on the ground. I started towards her when the little silver car that had been following us before the freeway – the same one, I realised, that had just run us off the road – pulled up next to me. The driver wound down the window.

'Quick, get in!'

I stared at him.

'Quickly!'

A fraction of my headache cleared and I remembered how to speak. 'You're joking, right? I'm not getting in another car against my will.'

The next voice came from behind me, impossibly familiar.

'It's not against your will if you climb in by yourself.' The woman. I turned around. She was walking towards me. Perfectly fine.

'How are you ...?' Alive? Walking? Maybe there really was something wrong with me. The woman stalked around the front of the car and folded her long frame into the passenger seat.

The man leaned out the window. He had deep, serious eyes, and his forehead creased with worry.

'Please. I'm Stephen May. Those agents would not have left you alive, and there are more coming. We didn't get you out of there just to hurt you.'

My mind whirled. I was stranded on a side road, probably in need of medical attention, and these two seemed genuine –

Look for May.

Not May, the month. I'd stuffed up the first part – not that there was much else I could have done. A note saying "Don't go for a walk. People will abduct you" might have been a bit more helpful. But I'd found May, or he'd found me. I took a deep breath and climbed in the back.

As I buckled my seatbelt, movement flickered at the corner of my eye and I nearly leapt back out of the car. The grey cat was curled up on the other end of the upholstery. As if it felt my gaze, it twitched an ear towards me. I stared at it, then turned my attention to Stephen May and the woman.

'I'm going to stop letting you come on these missions,' she remarked. 'What would you have done if I hadn't stepped in?'

Stephen's expression relaxed slightly as we pulled away. 'At least I didn't cause a crash on the freeway. Are you all right?'

'No,' she grumbled. 'I loved that bike.'

'Are you okay, Gabby?' He fixed his eyes on me in the rear-view mirror.

'That depends,' I remarked, unable to keep the surliness out. 'Who are you people? Have I actually lost it?'

The impossible woman laughed. I fought down an urge to hit her. To hell with her rescue.

'I'm Stephen,' the man offered again. 'A geneticist.' After a pause in which the woman inspected one of her many firearms, he added, 'this is Donovan. And you're not crazy.'

Well, it was an improvement on the "don't worry, miss, we're from the government" suits. I tested my luck. 'Where are we going?'

'Darkhaven.'

What kind of place was that? Before I could ask, Stephen continued.

'It's a sort of research facility, where we can make sure you're okay. You were struck by lightning.'

So that *had* happened. 'And those men?'

'Government agents from a classified operation that captures and eliminates people like you. We tried to get you out sooner, but they were quick. And cats are difficult to communicate through.' He said the last with a wry smile.

I glanced at the snoozing cat. 'So this cat ...'

'Followed you this afternoon. Savah is my closest connection. I asked her to keep an eye on you.'

The dreamlike feeling returned, my mind swimming in impossibilities. 'This is crazy.'

Stephen bit back a chuckle. Donovan let hers out. She turned to face me. 'Give me your phone.'

'Why?'

She held her hand out. 'Just do it.'

'If the sim is still viable, they will trace you,' Stephen said.

I pulled my phone out of what was left of my pocket. Donovan took it and tossed it out the window.

'Hey!'

'It was probably fried anyway,' she said, unapologetic. 'We should go –'

Something crashed into us from behind. I ducked instinctively.

'Shit!' Donovan whipped around. 'Who the hell is that?' she growled. 'Faster. Next left.'

Stephen accelerated, his knuckles white on the steering wheel as we careened around the corner.

I poked my head up to see another black SUV right on our tail. The driver pushed closer, recovering from the abrupt turn. Even through two panes of tinted glass, his stare jarred me, and as I gazed back, eyes wide, his look was one of recognition. I'd never seen him before in my life.

He slowed, letting us pull away, and by the next turn, we were cruising the suburbs as if nothing weird was happening at all, except for the ribbons of panic and confusion twisting in the pit of my stomach. Who were these people? Why had they backed off now? Stephen pulled over and paused, hands resting on the wheel, eyes closed. After a few minutes, he started the engine and merged back onto the road.

'We should go to the safe house,' Donovan said.

'We're okay. I've got eyes out now.' He flicked his gaze back to me in the rear-view mirror. 'There's a blanket somewhere back there.'

I had no idea what 'eyes' meant. More cats, maybe. I found the blanket, curled up under it and closed my eyes, hoping that

I would wake up slumped on Alex's breakfast bar, fallen asleep from a sugar overdose. Although if this was a dream, then apart from the kidnapping and car crashes and shooting people, it was a pretty cool one.

CHAPTER 5

Decision Eclipse

One too-short nap later, we pulled up at the end of a gravel driveway in front of a nondescript concrete building nestled in bushland. I dragged myself all the way out of my snooze and looked around. There were no signs anywhere.

'Welcome to Darkhaven,' Stephen said, relief melting the furrows in his forehead. I pushed open my door. Before I could move, Savah leapt across my lap, dashing around the side of the building.

The windowless, single storey structure stretched back into a forest of eucalypts, banksias and khaki-coloured native shrubs. Donovan led us up wide, concrete steps, slapped a key card against a panel next to the heavy door and strode through, vanishing into the cool gloom. Still wrapped in the blanket, I followed Stephen down a long corridor punctuated by unmarked doors, my footsteps muffled in the pervasive silence, questions loud in my head.

Stephen showed me into a room that was a study in stainless steel, from the bench lining two of the walls to the deep sink to the multitude of cupboards. A table and chairs broke up the tiles in the middle of the space and a blue sofa crouched beside the door. At Stephen's gesture, I sat on the rigid cushions.

Stephen pulled out a chair, clacking it across the tiles, and sat facing me. His gaze was intense – eyes the same grey as mine – but his voice was reassuring when he spoke. 'I'm sorry we had to bring you in like that. You must have many questions.'

Questions tangled like spaghetti. I didn't know where to start. I looked around and blurted the first thing that came to mind. 'Is the whole place like this? All steel and grey?'

Stephen chuckled. 'Not all of it. There are even some windows on the eastern side.' He sobered. 'How are you feeling, Gabby?'

My head ached. My eyelids felt like I'd spent the day on a windy beach, my body was heavy like I was still stuck in a nightmare and my brain felt like it was churning through thickened cream.

I shrugged. 'Fine.'

'I'm sorry,' Stephen said, sounding genuinely apologetic. 'But we don't have a lot of time and –'

An idea formed in the cream and I cut him off. 'Is this all about the lightning strike? Something happened, but I'm good. I mean, I feel crap, but I shouldn't even be walking around, right? Then I'm kidnapped, and now ...' I gestured around the room. 'Why am I here? How am I still alive?'

Stephen's forehead creased as he steepled his fingers, resting his elbows on his knees. 'You're here because you have a choice. And you're right. Lightning does more than people think it does, and humans have more potential than they know. So when lightning strikes, well, most people will be affected as you'd expect, but you are different.'

I raised my eyebrows at him. Before I could ask for more, the door banged open and Donovan charged in, a handful of papers in one hand and a soft bag in the other. She tossed the bag at me, then busied herself at the bench, extracting cups and a French press from various cupboards. I peered in the bag to find some clothes and a towel as the smell of coffee wafted through the room.

'Thanks,' I said, setting the bag aside. My eyes tracked Donovan's fluid movements before I turned back to Stephen, another question pushing to the front of my brain. Impossible things had happened. I had to ask. 'Um. So. Question.'

Stephen waited, expression open.

I swallowed. 'Donovan was run over by a car ... how is she walking around?'

'Perceptive,' Donovan remarked.

Stephen shot her a reproachful look. 'Yes. That will probably increase.' He turned back to me. 'Have you heard of *turritopsis dohrnii*? It's a biologically immortal jellyfish –'

Donovan interrupted. 'She hasn't heard of *turritopsis dohrnii*.' She slapped the papers on the table and pulled out a chair, scraping it across the floor. My eardrums throbbed. Some rubber feet on the furniture would not go amiss. And actually, I had heard of the regenerating jellyfish, and I was pretty sure it didn't just instantly repair itself if it got squashed by a truck. I opened my mouth to say so, but Donovan pulled her paperwork towards her, slurped at her coffee and stared me down. 'Humans have the potential to regenerate. Rapidly. And do a lot more. The Netica Project developed a virus that programs the right genes but doesn't switch them on, so to speak, until it's activated. The virus is called the Praegressus program. Lightning is the trigger.'

She opened a file and began reading; apparently that was all I was going to get. It sounded crazy, but somehow, it sounded true. Part of me was still waiting for reality to reassemble, the magic to fall apart at the wrong word or query. Like wanting something in a dream, only to wake as soon as I had it.

'So you were injured,' I said tentatively. 'And you recovered – regenerated – in a few minutes?'

Donovan didn't look up. 'Seconds, for gashes and scrapes. A minute for internal bleeding. Broken ribs . . . ' She rubbed her side. 'They still hurt. Bones take longer.'

I looked at Stephen. He regarded me warily, like I might self-combust. My curiosity bubbled. 'Rapid regeneration. Does that make you, like, unkillable?'

He nodded. 'Plus our telomeres don't shorten as quickly, so we don't age normally. We're not entirely sure how that will go over time.' A strange smile played over his face, like he was sharing a private joke.

I frowned. 'What does that mean? How old are you people?'

'I'm closer to fifty than forty.'

My mouth fell open. He looked about twenty-five. 'Donovan?' I pressed. I'd have guessed her to be mid-forties. But if Stephen was forty-something . . .

'Now,' she said, smirking, 'it's not polite to ask a lady her age.'

Stephen snorted. 'You are hardly a lady.'

Donovan turned over a page and slurped more coffee. 'You only say that because you have outdated ideas about what a lady is. I was born in 1896.'

Stephen turned back to me, carrying on despite the dumbfounded look I was sure was slathered on my face. 'We think we're among the first to get the program to trigger with any reliability. Donovan was the original Netica subject, so she's a bit different, but I had a lightning Event, and so did Liam and Catherine, the other two here at Darkhaven. There are other things too, like enhanced physical strength and speed, which makes some sense in the lab, but then there are abilities that seem more nuanced. Communicating with animals is something only I can do so far. Liam developed clairvoyance. Catherine would swear she's not special, but I think she's a medical medium – someone who can tell what is wrong with a biological system without diagnostics. It all starts with a genetic alteration program that we developed based on Donovan's altered DNA, and the effects are triggered by the lightning strike. This' – Stephen waved his hand around the room – 'is Darkhaven, our research facility. Donovan and I are the only ones left from the original team, but we've been studying the program together for years, trying to understand it.'

I attempted to sink back into the unyielding sofa. It was kind of how my brain felt about all this information. But it had happened in front of my eyes. The cat behaviour. Donovan's regeneration. My throat tickled and I coughed. 'It's like magic,' I whispered.

Stephen gazed at me levelly. 'Quite possibly. As I said, we don't fully understand it. We can't rule magic out.' He ran a hand through his hair. 'But we don't know how to test for it either.'

Quite possibly magic. The words settled over my racing heart like fairy dust. It sounded like a dream, a glimpse into an alternative reality where anything was possible. I hadn't asked the most pressing question because I was afraid it would break the spell, kill the dream, but I couldn't put it off any longer. I took a deep breath. 'What has all this got to do with me? Why was I abducted, twice?'

Without a word, Stephen stood and started gathering mugs and teabags from the cupboards.

Donovan huffed and laid her papers down. 'The Netica Project started in 1867 in Austria. The aim was to find a reliable way to activate what they call the "immortality" gene. It's a misnomer. The Austrian lab was discontinued, but about twenty years back, a man called Jan recruited three of us to set up a new research team: Stephen and I, and Luci Douglass, a gifted geneticist. Jan secured government funding to continue the Netica goal and create the perfect soldier.

'We almost did it. Luci developed the single-dose Praegressus and a way to trigger it with extreme voltage, and our job was to find the right candidates. It all fell apart when we couldn't fix the enhanced empathy. The subjects wouldn't step on a bug, let alone shoot another human. They shut us down and killed our active subjects. We escaped and started our own private lab, because we knew they were looking to eliminate us, but we each felt we needed to continue the research on our own terms.'

'Not for war.' Stephen's voice was quiet.

Donovan shrugged. 'You always were the romantic. Anyway, Jan snitched. Luci burned the lab to the ground, but they caught her before she got out.'

Stephen was staring somewhere past the sink, tea forgotten.

Donovan took a deep breath. 'They tortured Luci until they killed her, and then they came after us. No one knows about Darkhaven, but we're at risk when we pick up new Eventers – people who've just been triggered, like you. Liam's clairvoyance usually gives us some clues about upcoming Events, but we don't know how the Taskforce are getting to them.'

Stephen re-busied himself with the mugs. Something still didn't fit. I cleared my throat again. 'So I'm an Eventer.' Nervousness flickered across my body like tiny lightning. 'But how? What do you want with me?'

Donovan glanced at Stephen. 'Luci Douglass was your mother.'

The first thing I felt as the shock wave subsided was a flash of anger at Dad. He'd lied about my mother. What she did, who she worked for, how she died. 'Wow,' I said. 'So she had the program, and I ...' Inherited it? No. I knew there was more. The impossibly lithe, forty-something-looking 120-year-old stacked her papers and stood.

'Just before we shut down, we applied the Praegressus program to a number of children in a secret cohort. Including you.'

With what might have been an attempt at a sympathetic smile, Donovan drained her coffee and left. I stared at the space she had vacated, churning. It was unbelievable, but all my life I'd felt like something was wrong and I didn't know what. Maybe this was why. I thought I'd be excited, but instead of butterflies, my body felt hot and my hands were trembling. My head still pounded.

A steaming mug appeared beneath my nose. Stephen sat beside me on the sofa. I took the cup and wrapped my hands around it. 'There's something else, Gabby,' he said quietly.

My eyes flashed. 'Oh, so my mother was a genetic engineering scientist who applied her crazy program to unwitting babies, including her own daughter, and then went on the run from the government and got herself tortured to death. And there's more?' I was trying to be angry, but my voice cracked at the end. I wanted it to not be true. I'd pictured my mother as someone who must have loved me, in our short time to-gether, not . . . not this.

Stephen looked into his own mug. 'I'm sorry. It's a lot. And yes, it was completely unethical, but there's more to your mother than that. There is a government Taskforce pursuing us because they want to ensure no one ever finds out the military was funding the program. Our advanced evolution model created enhanced empathy and increased aversion to violence. They have no use for soldiers who won't kill, so they'll hide the research. It was never meant for civilians.'

'Just us test subjects,' I said bitterly, then recalled the shots from the SUV after Donovan had pulled me out. 'Donovan kills people.'

'She's different. You have a choice,' Stephen continued. 'Your DNA is undergoing the transformation process, but it takes a bit of time. We have an antiserum that can stop it if you don't want it. Because if you go through with it, you have to stay here.'

'What, like live here?' That in itself wasn't an appealing prospect, but the look on Stephen's face suggested there was more.

'As far as everyone else will know, you died in the lightning strike. We'll take care of the details.'

I could feel the blood drain from my face. 'Why?' I whispered. Stephen shifted. His forehead creased.

'The Taskforce will keep coming for you until they get you, or until they know you're not a threat to their cover-up. They won't kill you now if they don't have to, it's too messy. So either you go back with no memory of what happened, and you'll be like a regular lightning survivor. A lucky one with no serious after-effects. Or we file your death certificate, and you join Darkhaven. I'll tell you everything I can about Luci.'

'Don't they know you're sneaking people out of the system?'

Stephen sighed. 'It doesn't happen often. More Eventers were caught by the Taskforce than picked up by us before we found Liam. As far as the Taskforce knows, we're just the original team in an unknown location.' He paused, smiled and turned his palms up. 'You would be a welcome addition.'

My mental clot lifted, replaced by the stark clarity of the decision: leave my entire life behind and be literally superhuman, or go home and forget that such a thing was even possible. Assuming, of course, that all this wasn't some hideous and unfunny joke.

'How long?' I asked, knowing that a hundred years would not be enough for me to make this decision. I couldn't even decide what to study at uni.

Stephen looked at his watch. 'Timing on the antiserum is crucial. To be safe, you have an hour.'

CHAPTER 6

Petrichor

Stephen seemed to sense my internal panic rising and offered to let me finish my tea in private. When I asked if there was a room with a window, he gave me directions to get to a verandah on the other side of the building, then left me sitting on the couch, lost in a whirlpool of thought. I wanted to know more about my mother and why Dad had lied. And the Praegressus program sounded pretty cool. More than cool – quite possibly magic. But I couldn't leave Dad, Alex, Cecelia and Zenna believing I was dead, and definitely not without saying goodbye.

I stared into my mug, wondering if it would help if I could read tea-leaves. Dad would make tea in his favourite glass teapot when I was struggling with decisions. Everything is clearer, he'd say, with a good peppermint tea. All I saw in the mug now was the cold fluorescent light from the ceiling, reflected back at me.

I drained the tea and took the mug to the sink. With a watchful eye on the door, I changed out of my ruined clothes and into the ones Donovan had given me, folding the overlong leg hems up and pushing the sleeves to my elbows. Then, because I felt like these people definitely owed me, I rummaged through the cupboards, unsure what I was looking for until I found it: a jar of Nutella. Not quite roasted almonds, but it would do. I rinsed a teaspoon that was in the sink and followed Stephen's directions down the corridor, around a corner and through a door at the very end. I came out on a small patio with more flat-pack dining furniture. It overlooked bushland, and there was a treeless clearing in front of the patio that was trying to be a patch of grass. The whole compound seemed to be fenced with tall sheets of green Colorbond, topped with razor wire. Thankfully, the thick bush stretching before me blocked most of that from view.

The thunder had moved on and fat drops of rain started to fall, hitting the earth with loud splats. Fatigue seeped through my body. I leaned against the table and scooped out a spoonful of the choc-hazelnut spread, breathing in the smell of dust and rain.

'Petrichor,' said a voice behind me. I turned and almost dropped the jar. It was the boy from the school office, leaning against the door frame. He was still wearing the sunglasses – God only knew why, it was so overcast – and a bemused expression.

'From the Greek "petri", meaning stone, and "ichor", meaning blood of the gods. The CSIRO came up with the word to describe the smell of rain.'

'What are you doing here?' I demanded. It would have been more demanding without the thickness of Nutella on my tongue, but this day had been too damn long.

He pretended to look insulted. 'Why shouldn't I be here?'

My fingers twitched with an urge to rip the sunglasses off his stupid mocking face. 'Stephen didn't mention you.'

Stephen probably hadn't mentioned a lot of things, but I knew this guy was fibbing, even if I didn't know why. He laughed. The sound lanced through my headache.

'Okay, you got me. I snuck in.'

I raised my eyebrows. The fence was ten feet tall.

A coy smile brushed his lips. 'I have ways.'

'So you're stalking me,' I said. It took all my might not to slump over the table with despair and exhaustion. 'Why not? Everything else about today has been creepy.'

He straightened, his swagger melting like chocolate left in the sun. 'You can trust me.'

I took another spoonful of Nutella as I studied him, this strange boy standing before me, fidgeting with his hands like he didn't know where to put them – pockets, clasped in front, folded behind, dangling. For all my fumbling over the simplest decisions, I'd always had a good sense for people, and strange as he was, he seemed genuine.

'All right, I'll trust you. But answer a question for me,' I said.

He spread his hands, inviting me to continue. The sky beyond us was darkening without a sunset, the clouds too thick. The rain intensified.

'What would you do … sorry, what's your name?'

He stepped forward and offered his hand. 'Keraun.'

I took it. He had a firm handshake. 'Gabby,' I said. 'If you had the option to become superhuman and study crazy-cool science' – I wasn't quite game to say "magic" – 'but it meant you had to leave your family and friends forever, what would you do?'

For an instant, his face tightened, then he shrugged one shoulder and grinned. 'Easy. I'd choose the magic.'

My heart fluttered at the word, but he said it so casually he might have been joking. Then I thought "magic" could be a metaphor for either incredible science or the love of family and friendship, and I slouched over the table, Nutella in one hand, my head resting in the other. 'What should I do?'

'Well, you have no idea what to do with your future and here you are, being given a career and life package complete with human enhancement.' Keraun made it sound so simple.

'It's not a complete life package,' I protested. 'Life should involve friends, family, people you love. Not playing dead for the next however many centuries I'll live. Oh God,' I moaned, my despair deepening. 'Centuries. I don't even know what to do with the next sixty years.' I dug the spoon in for an epic amount of Nutella.

Keraun gave me an odd look. 'I think you've just made your case. Go back to your friends.' Then his face softened, and he tilted his head, like he was trying to see me from another angle. 'But there's something else.'

It wasn't a question, but it was nice to talk to someone who wasn't trying to steer me in any direction. I looked down at the jar in my hand, swirling the spoon in the sticky paste. 'Dad lied to me about my mum. I don't want to forget that, or that all this is possible, but if I choose the antiserum that's what will happen. It's like … I've always felt there was more to the world than I knew. And here it is.' I looked up. 'I can't make this decision in an hour.'

Keraun moved closer, standing opposite me. The wind gusted rain across the table between us. 'What if I said you didn't have to forget? What if I could buy you more time on this whole life-changing decision?'

My voice was unsteady. 'That'd be great. But how?'

He reached over, snatched the teaspoon out of my hand and stuck it in his mouth. 'Mmm, that stuff is good,' he said thickly. He swallowed with considerable effort. 'Stopping the memory mod should be easy. The antiserum . . . ' he frowned. 'I don't know. I might be able to fix it so it delays the process.'

'Then what?'

'You make your choice. If you don't want the transformation, come back in a week and get another dose.'

I nodded. 'And if you can't?'

He rubbed the back of his neck. 'I'll swap it for saline or something. You go through the transformation now, but you'll be back at home, memory intact.' A smile tugged his lips. 'Best of both worlds, right? It's up to you.'

Either outcome was better than what I had. I nodded. 'Yes. Please.'

'Give me half an hour, then tell them you want the anti-serum.' He sauntered back to the door, twirling the teaspoon in his fingers.

'Wait,' I called. 'Won't you let me know how you go?'

His fingers brushed the chain at his throat. 'I'll come back as soon as it's done.'

'And after . . . ' I still had too many questions, and Keraun might be the one to answer them, but shyness doused me like I'd stepped into the downpour. I swallowed. 'Will I see you again?'

He opened the door and flashed me a wicked grin. 'Oh, I think so. Good night, Gabrielle Adele Whitehall.'

He left me standing, speechless and spoonless, on the patio. I put the lid on the jar.

Keraun didn't return. By the time my hour was up, the rain had stopped, and I knew I couldn't put it off any longer. I'd have to take my chances that he'd managed what he needed to.

I found Stephen and Donovan back in the kitchen, bent over some notes at the table. They stopped talking when I tapped on the door.

I took a deep breath. 'I'd like the antiserum, please.' For a moment, it felt good to make a decision and declare it. Done. No taking it back. But then I remembered that it wasn't really a decision. Keraun was delaying the inevitable, and I would still have to figure this out. I set my jaw. The main thing was I wasn't going to have my memory modified, and I wasn't going to be abandoning my family and friends. The rest, including the lies Dad had told me about my mother, I could figure out later.

Stephen looked at Donovan, who shrugged, then turned his serious eyes to me. 'Are you sure?'

Definitely not. I nodded.

Donovan leaned back in her chair and flicked her boots up onto the table. 'It is fun, you know.'

'I can't. I have things at home.' I shifted on my feet. Standing still for too long hurt. Moving hurt. I longed to fall into bed.

She arched her eyebrows. 'Like what?'

'Family. Friends. School. A puppy.' And I meant it. I wasn't ready to give up my life. Not like this.

'A puppy?' Donovan scoffed. 'You'd give this up for a dog?'

'We could make arrangements for your schooling,' Stephen offered. A faint crease pulled at his brow. 'Do you even have a puppy?'

'She doesn't. There's no trace of fur or dog smell on her,' Donovan said. I glared at her. She shrugged. 'I have better senses than most Eventers.'

'Well, I'd like to get one,' I declared. 'And I'd like to go home, please.'

Stephen's frown faded, leaving a soft sadness on his features, but he stopped arguing.

The rest of the evening passed in a blur of tests. Catherine, the medical medium Stephen had mentioned, turned out to be a medical doctor as well, with a whole wing of the building dedicated to her research. She shone lights in my eyes, knocked every reflex in my body with a hammer, pricked me with needles, monitored my heart rate and finally administered the antiserum, which then required an hour of observation. I spent most of the time trying not to be bothered by her perfect features. It was as if someone had gone over her with a photo editor and fixed everything that was slightly off – teeth polished white, golden skin flawless, dark hair ends unsplit and shining against her white lab coat.

'Okay,' she said, voice cool and clinical as she unhooked me from whatever machine I was wired up to, 'now for the memory modification.' She donned a cap with a battery-powered LED torch attached to the front.

My skin prickled. I'd sort of been hoping that the amnesia was just built into the injection and Keraun had taken care of that. 'How does it work?'

'I give you a drug we've developed that essentially puts you into a semi-conscious state, a bit like a sleepwalker. You become open to suggestion. Then I recall your memories of the past twelve hours and give you new ones. You'll be hazy on specifics, but you won't have a gap. Before we start though, I will need contact information for your parents so they can pick you up from the hospital after.'

She paused, pen hovering over a notepad. I stared at her.

'Don't you just know all this stuff? Haven't you known about me all my life?' I asked, more aggressively than I'd intended. Unfazed, Catherine shook her head.

'All we had was Liam telling us roughly when and where your Event would be, and he can usually give us a name, but we didn't even know what you looked like until today.'

'Oh.' I gave the doctor Dad's mobile number, but I didn't volunteer our address. He'd made me swear to never give it out. Ever. I realised, with a pulse of regret, that I hadn't asked Stephen if he'd left the note. If Darkhaven didn't have my address, who did?

Catherine led me into a different room, a tiny cubicle of blank space. Somehow, they'd plastered the walls so it was hard to see where the wall ended and the ceiling or floor began. The whole room was a uniform white, including the two chairs and a small table holding a tablet. Catherine indicated for me to sit in the centre, leaned in close, and pricked my neck with a needle. She set a tiny blue syringe on the table, picked up the tablet and dimmed the lights. Another press on the tablet and her head torch turned on. It was too bright for this dark room, hard to look at. She sat down so the light was eye level.

'Look at the light, Gabby,' she said, voice sinking to a monotone.

'It's bright,' I complained. She didn't answer, just sat silently while I stared at the floor. Then I remembered that the drug was supposed to make me semi-conscious and compliant, and I looked up, trying not to squint. Keraun must have come through because I felt like a string pulled tight. I focussed on relaxing my face. My eyelid twitched and I willed it to stop.

'Good. I'm going to remind you what happened to you today, Gabby. Everything is okay. I want you to think about the ocean.'

'Darkhaven,' Catherine continued, before I had time to think about the ocean. Instead, I thought about Keraun. Catherine lifted her fingers to a point just in front of my eyes. I let my gaze lift to follow the gesture as she went on.

'Darkhaven is a place you have never heard of.'

Pause. I tried not to blink.

'The Netica Project,' Catherine said, moving her fingers again. 'You've never heard of the Netica Project.

'Regeneration. If you are mortally wounded in an accident, you will die.

'Donovan. You did not meet anyone called Donovan today.

'Stephen. You did not meet anyone called Stephen today.' And so it went. I sat as still as I could, blinking as little as possible and trying not to do anything un-trancelike such as swallow nervously. I ignored how scratchy my eyes were getting and paid attention to what the doctor said, in case someone spoke to me on the way out and I had to recite what they expected. My story was that lightning had struck a tree nearby in the park and I'd fallen and knocked myself out. A pedestrian found me and called an ambulance. I was treated for a mild concussion at the hospital and discharged after a few hours of observation.

Catherine finally turned off the headlamp, and I allowed myself to relax slightly. She showed me back to my bed, where there was a new pile of clothing that looked remarkably similar to the ones I'd had shredded by the lightning. My Event. A wave of vertigo swirled my head as I changed clumsily out of the oversized clothes. I stumbled against the bed, catching myself with tingling fingers.

The doctor looked around. 'Don't worry, it's normal to experience a lack of coordination. A side effect of the amnesia drug.'

Stephen stuck his head in the door as I finally pulled the hoodie on.

'Everything go okay?' he asked, voice low. I guessed I wasn't supposed to be computing much, and kept my face neutral.

'She seems a bit wired. Not as relaxed as I would expect,' Catherine replied.

'I guess everyone reacts differently. I'll test her when I drop her off.'

It was full dark by the time Stephen helped me into his car to take me home. The storm had passed and I stared out the window at the stars glimmering faintly way above the city lights. We drove past the West Beach exit. I nearly protested but remembered just in time that I was supposed to play along. Stephen parked at the hospital and ushered me into a large, bustling waiting room. No one looked at us twice. He sat me down on one of the hard, plastic waiting room chairs and knelt in front of me.

'How do you feel, Gabby?'

Nervous. Weird. My feet were tingling. 'Fine. A bit of a headache,' I mumbled, remembering to lie.

He nodded. 'Do you remember what happened?'

I swallowed. 'I ... I was out walking ... and there was lightning. I think I fell and hit my head.'

He searched my face. Relax. *Relax.* I blinked. Tried to drop my shoulders.

'You're okay. The doctor said it was just a mild concussion, and to take some ibuprofen if you need it,' he said, moving to sit next to me. 'Your dad is coming to get you.'

He reached out then, taking my chin and turning my face to his. My neck felt stiff. His grey eyes were deep and sad, and I didn't know why, but my heart softened around the edges.

'Goodbye, Gabby,' he whispered.

I blinked again, and he was gone.

Dad found me ten minutes later. He crossed the waiting room with long strides and crushed me in a bear hug. 'Gabby! Are you okay? Why are you out here?'

'Ouch,' I said.

He let me go. 'Sorry. What happened?'

'Nothing, it's just a headache. I lost my phone though.'

He scrutinised me. I sighed. We weren't going anywhere yet.

'I went walking in the storm and I slipped and fell. I hit my head and passed out. A passer-by found me and called an ambulance.'

'Where's your doctor? I'd like a word,' Dad said, rubbing my arm.

'Let's just go home, please?' I asked. 'She was very busy, she said I was fine. They kicked me out here as soon as they could. Probably need the beds,' I added, impressing myself with my improvisation.

He frowned. 'Wait here.' I hovered as he approached the counter and spoke to the tired-looking clerk. He watched over her shoulder as she searched on her computer, then spoke some more. But Stephen must have fixed something, because Dad came back, put an arm around my shoulders and took me home.

I turned down Dad's offer of hot Milo and went straight to my room, shutting the door. My bedrooms at Dad's and Alex's were pretty similar, although the one at Dad's was bigger and my desk fit in comfortably. Dad and Alex had decided early on that to minimise the stress of living in two places, I could dictate exactly how I wanted my rooms at any time, and they'd make it happen. As a kid, I'd had them both paint one wall and the ceiling dark blue so I could stick glow-in-the-dark stars everywhere and pretend to be gazing into the night sky. The stars had long since lost their glue and fallen off – some were probably still under my bed at Alex's, where it was pushed up against the wall. After a fairly inelegant movie poster phase in my first year of high school, I'd had an artsy burst and touched up the tack-damaged paint with metallic silver swirls. Not something I would do now, but I still liked it. The grey carpet in Alex's apartment supported my colour scheme better than the beige at Dad's, so Dad had bought a shaggy silver rug to go over the floor. Now I thought it might be nicer to have some contrast between the rooms, but it seemed silly to change the decor when everything was perfectly functional. I pushed aside the pinstriped curtain and opened the window, breathing in the cold night air.

And that was it. I was supposed to just go to bed, wake up, get on with my life and forget all about the possibility of humans having more potential than anyone ever guessed. Well, that was what Stephen thought. If Keraun had kept his end of the bargain, the memory modification drugs they had intended to give me had never made it into my bloodstream. I could think about this for longer. And if I wanted it, I could say goodbye properly. I had no idea where Darkhaven actually was, but Keraun did, and I knew I hadn't seen the last of him.

I flipped my laptop open to find a dozen notifications: Cecelia. Nancy. Nancy again. Three more from Cecelia. Those were just about missing study and dinner. Then the real panic set in. Dad. He must have talked to Nancy, because then there were another five from Cecelia and two from Zenna.

I sent a quick group message to my friends – *sorry, thanks, I'm fine, see you tomorrow* – and flopped onto my bed. How was I supposed to say goodbye properly? Because if I was honest, for the briefest moment before the ultimatum came down, I had been excited. Here was the thing I'd been looking for, that spark my teachers had been trying to fan all these years with Dickens and *Introduction to the Human Body* and flyers for student film festivals. Researching, or whatever it was these people were doing, the very fringe of human potential – *quite possibly magic* – was about the only thing I'd ever heard of that sounded real. I'd just never figured I'd have to give up the rest of my life for it.

I changed into my Hogwarts pyjamas and crawled under the quilt, wincing as the grazes on my knees pulled. Getting struck by lightning and falling onto the concrete footpath felt like years ago. I expected to lie awake for hours, but as soon as I thought about sleep, I drifted off dreamlessly.

CHAPTER 7

Not-Chocolate Overload

For three days, my body felt like it was floating in space and my head was fuzzy. I could barely remember anything I was doing and often found myself standing in a room with no idea why I'd gone in there, or forgetting what class I had next only to realise it was the end of the school day. I vaguely wondered if Keraun's messing with the antiserum had gone horribly wrong. When Flamebeard called on me in class, I had no idea what the question was until Cecelia pointed out that it was written on the whiteboard. She worried that my head injury was affecting my memory. I brushed off her concerns with excuses about a cold, which meant I had to stay home on Friday because I didn't actually have one and, observant as Cecelia was, she would definitely notice the absence of sniffling.

It was just as well. I slept all the way through Friday. Dad roused me before he left to find out why I wasn't getting up for school. Barely awake, I didn't have to pretend too hard to be out of it. He regarded me for a moment, probably to confirm that I really was sick, then left me to my snoozing.

I woke late Saturday morning feeling more energetic than I ever had in my life. The floating feeling was gone. My body still felt light, but it was back to being solid and real. My head was clear. I squinted as I walked into the bathroom – the light seemed brighter than usual, every detail sharper – and studied my reflection in the mirror. I looked the same, more or less. Except I was pretty sure my teeth were whiter. They'd always been fairly straight. My body was still soft and unfit, but it seemed to be less puffy. And my skin was clear. I put makeup on anyway, the brush bristles swishing audibly over my skin, and went to the kitchen, messaging Cecelia and Zenna. I couldn't see what Stephen's fuss had been about. If this was the transformation, no one was going to notice.

Dad, back from his morning windsurfing, stood at the stove, poaching eggs. A loaf of sourdough sat on the counter. He flashed his broad Saturday-morning smile, intended to goad me into a grumpy not-a-morning-person retort. I shrugged at him, declined the offer of eggs and went to the pantry, staring at the shelves until I saw the cornflakes. I poured a bowl with a generous spoonful of sugar scattered over the top.

Dad's forehead wrinkled. 'You shouldn't eat so much sugar. You'll get pimples.'

I shovelled cornflakes in as I sat down, before they got too soggy. 'That's what foundation is for,' I said through my mouthful. My crunching was too loud in my ears. I slowed my chewing. Maybe soggy would be less audible.

'Are you going to the Shack today?' Dad asked, sitting next to me at the table. West Beach Shack was where Cecelia,

Zenna and I met every weekend – they made the best milk-shakes. I nodded, still chewing slowly. I could hear Dad's teeth tearing at the sourdough crust, and his side of bacon still sizzled. It was hard to think of words, with all this going on.

He gave me an odd look. 'I'll drop you off if you like. I have a meeting.'

'Cool, thanks,' I said, getting up and dumping the rest of the cornflakes in the bin. The chewing was too loud, and the cereal was going stale.

Dad dropped me outside the Shack, a busy cafe that pretended to be all rustic and straight out of a beach town but was totally hipster. Being on the corner of a major intersection didn't help its chilled surfer vibe, and neither did being surrounded by other restaurants: Chinese, Indian, pizza, a bakery. Alex had better pizza near his place – a cosy Italian joint called Harrys – but the Indian here was particularly good.

Perth was doing its usual impersonation of winter, which meant a mild 19 degrees Celsius and sunny, so the beach, the road and the Shack were bustling. I walked into the cafe, squeezing past a pram that was parked across the doorway. Cecelia and Zenna, the latter today sporting purple tips in her hair, were already waiting.

I deliberated over the milkshake list. They'd added new flavours.

'Just pick the first thing that jumps out,' Cecelia advised. 'It's always the best choice.'

Salted banana toffee, then. Or quadruple chocolate overload. Or strawberry coconut swirl. In the end Zenna snatched my purse out of my hand and ordered for me.

She scrutinised me as we took our number to a table. 'Have you been working out, Gabby?'

Cecelia and I laughed.

'No, I mean it,' she said. 'What are you doing? You look slimmer, or something.'

'I'm really not,' I replied. I'd squeezed into my jeans this morning the same as every morning.

Cecelia leaned around to Zenna's side of the table, pursing her lips. 'Actually, her teeth look whiter.'

'They definitely do,' Zenna agreed. 'Oh! Maybe she's started flossing.'

Cecelia gave a mock gasp. 'And she's finally using the serum I gave her in her hair!'

'I'm right here,' I said. My head was starting to thud. A baby whimpered from the pram in the doorway, then burst into a cry. The coffee grinder whined and a toddler in a high chair hit her brother on the head with a toy dinosaur while he squealed.

Cecelia shook her head. 'It can't be our Gabby. This one is an impostor.'

Zenna nodded. They giggled until our milkshakes arrived.

I took a sip. 'Ugh. The milk is sour.'

'Surely not,' Cecelia said.

'There's nothing wrong with it, Gabby,' Zenna added, trying hers, then mine. I tried it again. It definitely tasted slightly off. I pushed it away and listened to my friends chattering about the weekend, trying to stay afloat in a sea of noise and bright light. A man smacked his lips at the table next to us and I clenched the sides of my chair to stop myself from upending our entire table in his direction. Zenna's phone beeped – loud and jangly – and she leapt up. My head throbbed.

'Gotta go, I've got my driving test. Wish me luck!' Her eyes danced. To a chorus of good lucks, she dashed out, taking her milkshake with her.

Cecelia ran me through her entire English essay plan, which I nodded along to, then pushed her empty glass aside and turned to me.

'So, what's up with you? And don't tell me it's TISC –'

She was cut off by a screeching of brakes and a crash. People screamed. I glanced through the windows – a car had turned across a red light and run into another vehicle. The cafe was filled with scraping chairs and raised voices as everyone rushed to help or watch. I put my head in my hands, trying to block out the excessive noise, but the pummelling in my skull just got worse. Then the sirens started, and I could hear every dissonant note and pitch variation like it was right in front of me. Cecelia, who of course had advanced first-aid training, had already raced out. I grabbed my bag and shoved through the people, emerging into the blinding sunlight. The street was overexposed. I couldn't make out any faces. I stumbled away, turning down the first alley I came to and huddling in a doorway, but it was no use. The sirens grew louder, and here the smell was overpowering: urine, rubbish bins and burnt oil from nearby kitchens.

I got to my feet and ran back to the main road, hurrying blindly away from the cacophony. The traffic was stopped in both directions, and I sprinted across the dual carriageway, car horns blaring around me, to the footpath that wound along the beach. I kept running until I reached a grassy park. My senses were a confused mess, and I could barely distinguish between sight or smell or sound. It was all just noise. I collapsed on the grass under a tree, hands pressed over my ears. It wasn't enough to block out the waves smashing onto the compacted sand a hundred metres away, or the cars passing on the main road, or the runners pounding the footpath. I closed my eyes, clenching every muscle, locked in panic.

I sensed movement nearby.

Holding my breath, I squinted up at a tall, slender figure: Keraun. He knelt, leaning over me so his body shielded me from the sun.

'What's wrong?' he asked, voice low and urgent.

I tried to think of words.

He placed a tentative hand on my shoulder. 'Gabby?'

His touch made it worse as my body registered the weight of each of his fingertips through my jacket. Wind rattled the palm trees overhead, the sunlight was blinding, I could still taste sour milk and smell iodine and salt and stuff and I couldn't sort one thing from the other. I felt like I might just disappear, lose myself forever in all the noise. But there might be someone who could help.

'Get Stephen,' I managed to choke out. Keraun moved, revealing the sun again. I raised my arms to block it, the jacket fabric rasping on my skin. Keraun pulled something out of his pocket, muttering to himself, but I didn't pay attention. I tried to keep a grip on my fraying mind.

Keraun returned in a few moments or minutes or maybe even hours – I couldn't keep hold of the time – and sat next to me, shielding me from the sun again. He didn't say anything. Slowly, very slowly, the sensory overload lessened. After a while I started to shiver in my light jacket as the sun faded. Peeking out from under my arm, I saw a blank grey sky. The wind had dropped. I let my eyes stay open, nervous that doing so would trigger all the noise again, but grateful for the lack of blinding sunlight. Then I saw another figure approaching. Stephen.

Gently, they pulled me to my feet. Guilt simmered in my chest when I saw the annoyed pinch between Stephen's eyes. Keraun would no doubt have filled him in on our deception to get him to come and rescue me. Ugh. Rescued.

'I'm sorry, Stephen.' It was a weak apology.

'I understand,' he replied. 'Let's get out of here.'

We made it to Stephen's silver Corolla without further incident. I huddled, miserable, in the front seat and didn't even protest when he asked for my phone, slipping it into a small black pouch and stowing it in the console.

'How do you do it?' I asked, after several minutes of travelling in tense silence.

Stephen looked grim. 'Years of training. There are specific practices that help to hone and filter the senses. It's part of the reason we don't let Eventers just fend for themselves. This happens.' He growled the last two words.

'It was my idea,' Keraun said. 'Don't blame her.'

Stephen flashed him a vicious look in the rear-view mirror. 'Oh, I don't.'

'I asked for it,' I said in a small voice.

'Doesn't matter. Your friend doesn't know anything about our work and shouldn't be meddling. I don't even know how he got into Darkhaven. It's not your fault,' Stephen said. His mouth set into a thin line of silence.

I stared out the window, brooding, but also thankful for the tint that dimmed the light and the relative quiet of the car. Just the muffled engine and three people breathing.

We pulled up in the Darkhaven driveway, and Stephen went to open his door, but I put out a hand to stop him.

'Wait,' I said. 'I know I called you for help, but I'm not ready to make this decision. I'm not going in there if you aren't going to let me out again.'

The edge in Stephen's grey eyes softened. 'You just experienced what happens, Gabby.'

'I can't leave my family thinking I've died,' I said. 'There has to be another way. I can get by until the end of the year. Then I can tell them I'm off to some interstate university or something. I'm not playing dead.'

Stephen gave me a long look, then nodded. 'Okay. At the end of the year, we'll work something out. But it will have nothing to do with the machinations of your friend.' He gave the last word a nasty emphasis. Keraun bowed his head and slipped out of the car. I hurried out after him, reaching for his hand. He turned before I could touch it.

'I'm sorry,' I whispered, 'and thank you.' He was still wearing his sunglasses, and I longed to take them off so I could see his eyes.

Keraun gave me a nod, then turned and walked back down the driveway. I wondered briefly how he was going to get home, wherever that was, but Stephen called from the doorway.

I turned and followed Stephen inside the concrete building. When I glanced back over my shoulder, Keraun had vanished.

We went to a different room this time, one that was more like a lounge, with slightly softer couches and a long window overlooking the enclosed bushland. I gratefully sank onto the couch that wasn't occupied by Savah, who hadn't moved upon our arrival. Stephen sat next to me.

'What is happening to me?' I asked.

'Your transformation. Your genes are all flipping over to the best possible version of yourself, so everything that is already expressed is enhanced. That's the issue you're having with your senses. And there are a few things not observed in humans currently that now will be. You'll live for much longer and heal rapidly from almost anything.'

He'd said all this last time, but somehow it hadn't sunk in the way it did now. I hadn't dared believe it. I ran my fingers over my knees, feeling the smooth skin through my jeans, no scabs or scars or twinges of pain despite their being shredded on the concrete path just a few days ago. The denim was coarse under my fingertips, each strand in the weave discernible. I could almost count the threads.

'The sense stuff…I can hear so much, and it's so loud. And bright. And the smells …'

Stephen smiled. 'It's overwhelming at first. But don't worry, you're a week in, it doesn't get any worse than it is now.'

I groaned, but even that was too loud. 'It's unbearable.'

'Like I said, there are techniques we can teach you. And the rest doesn't really affect you straight away, especially as you're so young. People will eventually notice that you don't age normally.'

'You said something about perception increasing last time I was here. What does that mean?'

'What do you think it means?' He gave me a pointed look, and I got the feeling it was a test.

'Not just normal senses. More like intuition.'

Stephen nodded. 'It's a subtle skill, and you will need to learn to use it so it works for you. But I think you might have a gift for it.'

I nodded. I had always had a sense for things, like when Alex wasn't telling the truth about his job, or if a teacher was going to be especially nasty that day and Zenna and I were better off skipping class.

Silence – which I was really learning to appreciate – stretched out.

'I have to apologise to you, Gabby,' Stephen finally said. 'I had no idea you struggled with decisions the way you do, or that you'd had a particularly stressful day already in that regard. It was unfair of me to put you in the position I did.'

I was taken aback. 'It wasn't your fault.'

'No, but I made it harder than it had to be.' He paused. 'Your friend complicated things though. You've undergone your transformation and we can't reverse it now. We really could use your help, you know.' A trace of hopeful excitement crept into his voice. 'I understand you are quite good with biology. An intuitive scientist would be something.'

To my utter embarrassment, tears formed, heating my eyes. Savah uncurled herself and jumped over to our couch, rubbing her face on my elbow.

'I don't know what I want to do,' I said.

Stephen scratched the cat's chin. 'You don't have to do anything yet. But it would be good if you didn't make any more deals with your friend. You can come to me, you know.'

I stared at my lap for a moment. 'He was only offering me another option.' Some small part of me prickled at Stephen's criticism of Keraun. Another part told me that was a risky thing to feel. I squashed both feelings.

Stephen sighed. 'I wish you'd told me how you felt.'

Annoyance welled. Maybe it was a bit about Keraun, but there was more. I'd just met Stephen and his crew. Admittedly, I'd just met Keraun too. But, the little prickly protective voice said, I had met Keraun first. I looked Stephen in the eyes, my jaw set. 'You wouldn't have done anything differently. You gave me my options. Firmly.'

Stephen's brow furrowed, eyes lost in some deep sadness. 'You're right.' The words were almost a whisper.

I sat back and folded my arms. 'Then I'm not sorry,' I said, with more toughness than I felt. I let that hang until the silence became awkward. I really did need his help, but the pissed-off feeling was still bubbling under my skin. 'So what happens next?'

Stephen ran a hand through his hair. 'You can't stay exposed in the public world. It's too dangerous. Like I said, we are hunted by a Taskforce who want to remove all evidence that this program ever existed.'

'I'm not disappearing. You promised I wouldn't have to do that.'

He nodded, thoughtful. 'If you come here for training and make sure you don't do anything to draw attention to yourself, we can probably give you until the end of the year, all going well. That gives you a chance to sort things out with your family and friends.'

Sort things out. Friendly code for "say goodbye to all the people you love forever, who will soon believe you dead". I bit back a huff. 'When you say don't draw attention to myself...'

Stephen smiled. 'Don't show off. Your memory is going to be a lot better. So don't let your grades go crazy. And don't go getting yourself injured in front of people.'

I nodded. I couldn't imagine my grades going crazy – I never did any study anyway. But there was one more problem. A big one. I took a deep breath. 'What about, you know, today? How do I stop that from happening again?'

'We'll coach you. I'll set it up so it looks like you have a regular appointment with a maths tutor or something. No one will think anything of it with your exams coming up.'

I tried not to be stung by the idea of pretending to get maths tutoring – aside from photography, it was my weakest subject, but Stephen couldn't know that – and sat back, feeling slightly more relaxed. The deal was as good as it was going to get. And saying goodbye at the end of the year ... well, I would deal with that later. A lot could happen in five months.

CHAPTER **8**

God of Lightning

Stephen didn't want me to go home yet, preferring to get started with my training immediately, but I insisted. I felt like all the energy I'd woken up with had drained away through the soles of my feet, and I wanted nothing more than to curl up in the comfort of my bed. I explained that Dad worked in national security, or something like that, and home was probably the safest place for me next to Darkhaven. Stephen relented, driving me back as the grey clouds pushed the afternoon into an early twilight.

My phone buzzed as I pulled it out of the black pouch: Zenna.

I failed.

I felt bad for her and knew she would probably appreciate company, but I didn't have the energy to visit. Her parents were okay, if a little odd. It was her grandmother. She lived with the family, and Zenna came to school in a sour mood at least once a week because of something the old harpy had said or done. I hadn't visited in nearly a year, since she told me I was overweight one Friday evening and actually threw away our entire weekend supply of ice cream. I sent Zenna a sympathetic reply and promised hugs on Monday.

There were no lights on at home, but Dad's car was in the driveway when we pulled up. Stephen advised me to stay home and indoors for the rest of the weekend, which sounded just fine to me, and to go to the eastern gate of the school grounds when my classes finished on Monday. I saved his number in my phone.

The house felt still when I stepped inside, missing the usual commotion that was Dad at home – making coffee, cooking something over-the-top for dinner, playing Mozart while he worked in his office. The hairs on my arms prickled and my still-raw nerves set themselves on edge. Red fear bloomed in the bottom of my stomach as I closed the front door. Then I shook myself. Dad must be home, maybe on a confidential call or something, and I was just overreacting after a stressful day. That was all. I strolled down the hallway, trying to trick myself into feeling casual.

The lights were off in the open-plan kitchen/living room. Dad sat at the dining table in the semi-dark, turning a pen in his fingers, with the air of someone who'd waited while the afternoon wore away and the light faded. Of course: the accident outside the Shack. He would have been worried. And he had been expecting me home hours ago. I rushed towards the table. 'Oh my god, Dad, I'm so sorry, there was an accident at the Shack, I'm fine, just Ceel and I went for a walk on the beach. I should have called, I didn't think.'

Dad didn't respond. His face was grave. I stopped and took in the rest of the shadowy room. Two hefty men in suits stood in the kitchen. Another man, also in a suit but looking less like a security guard, stepped forward from my left. Some bizarre, detached part of my brain wondered if he'd actually been hiding behind the bookcase for dramatic effect.

'Miss Whitehall,' he said. His voice was soft and warm, and it hit my nervous system like a trip-switch pinging.

I backed up a few steps. 'Who are you?'

He smiled. I'd never really understood the term "crocodile grin" until now, but this guy with his slicked-back hair had it. All teeth and wiles. 'My name is Sean. I am here to help you. I understand you've recently had an unusual experience.'

I bristled and turned away from the man. 'Dad, what's happening?'

Dad said nothing, just stared past me while he flipped the pen over and under, over and under.

Sean came closer. 'Tell me about Darkhaven.'

My muscles turned cold and my skin went clammy. How could he possibly know about Darkhaven, unless … I shook my head and pressed my lips together, fighting off the urge to turn and sprint from the room. The suits behind me looked too much like the men who had nabbed me in the park. It had to be the Taskforce. I shot Dad a quizzical glance.

Dad lifted his deep brown eyes to my face. 'Those people are terrorists. Whatever they've told you is a lie.'

I hated the twinge of fear that shivered through me at the word. Stephen had tried to help me. He was the only one who'd told me the truth, or had at least tried. I gazed at Dad, trying to divine what he knew, whether Sean and his goons had pretended to be legit, above-board government agents and got Dad on side, or whether Dad actually worked for these people and knew more about Netica than I'd thought. My intuition leaned on the latter, but it didn't help much.

Sean drew a dining chair out and gestured me towards it. 'Please, Gabby. We want to protect you.'

The need to run pressed into my skin. 'Cool. You do that. I'm going to bed now.' I turned back to the hallway. I'd grab my bag and go, via the window, to Cecelia's. Or maybe Zenna's; they were less likely to look for me there.

I made it about three steps. With a starchy rustle of clothing, the two security guards grabbed me.

I thrashed. 'Let go of me!'

One pinned my arms behind my back with hands like man-acles while the other reached into his pocket and pulled out a syringe. I eyed the needle as he uncapped it, straining and kicking against my captor. All I managed was to twist around enough that I was facing Sean and my dad at the table again.

Sean nodded at the suits. 'Bring her in.'

The suit with the needle stepped closer.

'Dad!' I yelled.

The suit paused. Dad met my eyes for a moment, face hard in the gathering darkness, then fixed his gaze on Sean. 'It doesn't have to be like this,' he said.

A look passed between them that I couldn't read, Sean's eyes sparking with defiance. He sauntered up to me, stopping a few inches from my face. 'It's up to you, Miss Whitehall. Are you going to cooperate?'

Some small voice of logical self-preservation bleated that I should at least play along, but I couldn't help it. My blood squirmed in my veins when I looked at him. 'Not with you,' I muttered.

I felt the jab of a needle in my neck and everything went black.

I woke, shivering, with my face stuck to a cold, hard surface. I sat up and looked around, but there wasn't much to see. I was sitting at a bare desk in a tiny room with no windows and one door. It was locked, for sure, but it would be silly to sit here having not even tried it, so I dragged my heavy body over and rattled the handle. Locked.

I dropped back onto the chair and rubbed my arms to warm my skin. Keys jingled outside and with another rattle of the handle, the door opened. A tall, slim woman with vibrant red hair and green eyes that matched her crisp business shirt dropped a bundle of keys on the table, right next to my hand.

She stood opposite me and leaned against the wall, the pewter of her suit like a shadow on the tiled background. 'You dye your hair,' she observed.

I stared at her. I had no idea how interrogations normally went, but that seemed like an odd start.

'I find red hair gives me power,' she continued, 'but maybe some people just can't handle it.'

I'd touched up my roots just over a week ago. How did she even know my natural colour was red?

'What do you want?' My throat felt like one of Perth's beaches and the words rasped over the sandpaper tissue like a hot wind.

'You don't beat around the bush though. I'd say you get that from your mother.'

I didn't respond. Where was I? What was so important and secret that Dad would just sit and watch while I was knocked out and brought in by some jerkhead and his muscle? My veins bristled with angry fire despite the chill of the room. Not even an explanation. Just a needle in the neck. I couldn't imagine that this was legal, but I'd come across so many things that were outside the law lately nothing was surprising to me. Except Dad.

The woman leaned over the table to peer at my face. Her nails were short but manicured and painted light green, matching the shirt under her jacket. She had a straight nose, a mole on her right cheek and perfect teeth. My fingers tapped the edge of my chair. I willed them to stillness.

'I want you to tell me about Darkhaven,' she said.

'I don't know what you're talking about.'

The woman stood and paced in front of the desk, heels clicking on the floor. 'What do you know about Stephen May?'

'I don't know anything about him.' Which was true. I could pick him out of a line-up, but I had a hunch that a physical description was not what she was really after. I could tell her he was gentle and serious and had an air of lingering sadness about him, but I couldn't imagine why she'd care about any of that either.

'We know you were struck by lightning. We know you met May, and Esmerelda Donovan. You know about the Praegressus program, and you know *where they are*.'

I shrugged, keeping my arms crossed tightly in front of me. She sighed, stopped pacing and leaned in again, even closer, her breath hot on my face. Her hard voice was so low that even with my newly enhanced hearing, it was barely audible. 'You probably think I'm government. But I am way more than the government. I am not bound by their rules. Now' – her knuckles whitened as she flattened her long, elegant fingers on the desk – 'tell me what you know about Darkhaven.'

I remembered the intended amnesia, designed for my protection. Or the Darkhaven's, more like. It made more sense now. I shook my head and changed tack. With such a dry throat, a husky sincerity wasn't too difficult to muster.

'I'm sorry, I wish I could help you. But I don't know what happened. I went for a walk. I remember climbing up the jungle gym, and the next thing I woke up in hospital. My dad picked me up.' I blinked at her.

Her left eyebrow twitched. She turned away, her shoulders dropping in defeat. I relaxed by about point-one per cent. Then she whirled back, grabbed my hair and wrenched my face up to an inch from hers. My eyes watered and I yelped as my scalp pulled.

'Liar! Tell me what you know!'

Without even thinking, I shouted back. 'I don't know anything! Something happened, and I don't remember what!' Spittle flew at her face and landed on her nose. Her nostrils flared. I didn't back down. Instead, on a raging autopilot, I swung my left arm back, folded my fingers into a fist and snapped my arm forward. I was surprised by the speed. I was even more surprised by the crunch of bones as her nose crumbled under my punch, then I reeled with the stabbing pain as my own bones cracked. Blood from her nose splattered onto my face, and I pulled my hand to my body, curling it protectively into my chest. It throbbed. I'd only ever punched someone once before – a skinny boy called Dylan Rickshaw, when he asked me if I wanted to go out with him for the fifth time in a fortnight. My movements then had been way slower, and all I'd gotten for my trouble was bruised knuckles.

The woman let go of my hair, muttering under her breath. My hair tangled in her fingers, and as she shook her hand free, I noticed little sparks of red-gold light flashing between her fingertips. It was subtle; if I hadn't been looking directly at her hand, I might have missed it. She caught me staring and folded her arms behind her back.

'What was that?' I asked.

She turned away and opened the door. A security guard was waiting on the other side, hat pulled low over his face. I thought I saw the corners of his mouth twitch into a smile.

'Take her to the holding cells. Tell Sean this one is his to sort out.' The woman's voice was like an iceberg in still water. She strode away, boot heels clacking. The man ducked into the room, peered back down the hall, then closed the door.

'You can do whatever you like, I have nothing more to say to you people,' I said stubbornly. Perhaps not the best move, but I was pissed. The man perched on the edge of the desk and pulled his cap off a familiar shock of jet-black hair. Sunglasses gone, his light brown eyes met mine for the first time.

I opened my mouth, but Keraun pressed a finger over his own lips, motioning for silence. He pulled me to my feet, jammed his cap back on, pinned my arms behind my back with strong hands and pushed me out the door. My mind must have still been fuzzy from the drug, because time passed in strange jumps: one moment he was marching us down the wide hallway; the next we were staggering up endless concrete stairs.

We went up one flight, then another. By the fifth, my legs became about as useful as strawberry mousse, at which point he scooped me into his arms and, with surprising ease for such a slight figure, carried me up the rest of the stairs and out – had there been another door? I missed it – into a sweeping, white-tiled foyer, glancing about as he raced us across the floor. In a blinding flash, a panel of glass next to the door shattered. Alarms squealed, piercing my brain through my overactive eardrums. Still carrying me, he leapt through the glass, bundled me into a car and then, with a fairly pathetic screech of tyres, we disappeared into the night.

After about four blocks, my ears recovered from the shock and my heart rate dropped down to the realm of merely rapid.

'Who are you?' My voice was dry.

Keraun reached onto the backseat and retrieved a bottle of water. I took a grateful sip.

'I told you,' he replied. Way too innocently.

'You gave me a name. But you show up at my school. Then at Darkhaven, and you know my full name and about the antiserum. You just appeared at the beach on Saturday. And now you break me out of a secret government facility. Don't play dumb. I saw all the security cameras. How did you get in? Who are you working for? Did you leave the note?'

Keraun kept his eyes on the road. 'I didn't leave any notes.'

'And the rest?'

'You wouldn't believe me.'

I scoffed. 'Maybe not last week. Try me.'

He gave me a curious glance. His hand tightened on the steering wheel. 'God.'

Just that, deadpan.

'Yeah right. Thanks for uh, well, are you rescuing me? Or was I better off with the other guys?'

He gave a short laugh. 'You're better off with me. I'm God.'

I was not in the mood. 'God. Right. Pull over.'

He didn't slow down. We closed in on the car in front. 'What?'

'You're delusional. I'm getting out.' I put my hand on the door handle and checked the speedometer. Sixty-five kilometres an hour. I'd probably survive, if I rolled properly. Check that – I would definitely survive, and this was one of those moments where I shouldn't draw attention to myself. But Stephen's warnings hadn't included possible abductions. I cracked the door open. Alarmed, Keraun reached across and pulled it shut.

'Okay, I'm not *God*. I'm the God of Lightning.'

'That's worse! Let me out.'

'Well, I did say you wouldn't buy it,' he said. We were tailgating the car now, which was doing all of fifty. I'd have been annoyed about it if I were in one of my driving lessons and not stuck in a moving vehicle with a complete maniac. There was a grassy shoulder coming up. Now might be my only chance to escape, while he was consumed with road rage.

'I'm Keraun, God of Lightning. Actually, all weather, but – for Husa's sake, get out of the way!' The car had indicated then not taken the turning lane, slowing to forty-five. Next thing, there was a thunderous crash and a white bolt shot down on the car, sending it off the road onto the soft shoulder.

I looked across at Keraun and completely forgot about escape. His eyes. They were yellow. Not just a little bit, not just the irises, but the whole eyeballs were yellow, and glowing, so it was hard to see the edges of his eyelids. I took a moment to process what I'd just witnessed.

'Did you just . . . ?'

Keraun tried, and failed, to hide his smugness. His lips pressed together in concentration and another bolt, this time just across the sky, lit up the street ahead, while his eyes flashed brighter. He winked at me, the glow in his eyes fading, returning them to a mostly normal human brown. That explained the sunglasses in the rain, then. I wondered if there would be a point where my head would actually explode.

'Don't worry, they're fine. Although their car might have some electrical problems now.'

I had so many questions, I couldn't pick one out from the jumble. I was miffed that he had been so familiar, so casual, when he was literally some sort of god. Like he should have disclosed who and what he was at the start. 'A God of Lightning would drive a better car.'

Keraun surveyed the interior. 'What, is this not any good?'

I poked at the gear knob. The cap flew off and disappeared into the foot well.

'Oh.' He frowned. 'Eftychi said it was good. I suppose she owed me one, I made it rain on her birthday party.'

I didn't want to know who Eftychi was. I went to wind down the window and realised that my left hand – the one I'd just punched my interrogator with – didn't hurt any more. I flexed and stretched the fingers. It was perfectly healed.

Keraun glanced across. 'I didn't have time,' he said cautiously, 'to fix the antiserum.'

I folded my arms against my welling rage – surely he could have let me know, if he was a god – and stared straight ahead. 'I figured.'

'I did try. It's not really how my power works. So I went to get help, but I ran out of time.'

It was such an inadequate explanation, I considered punching the stupid god's face with my newfound strength. I knew it wasn't his fault. He'd explained what might happen, and I'd made my choice. But I was angry at Dad and bristling about the woman's rough interrogation. My senses were turning me inside out, and I still wasn't clear of Stephen's ultimatum. I didn't want to say goodbye to everyone at the end of the year. I wanted something, anything, to make sense. I wanted to move. The cabin of the car closed in on me, too small and too loud, and the low volume of chatter on the radio wormed into my ears as I clenched every muscle in my body. I couldn't hold it in.

'Argh!' I punched the dashboard instead, instantly regretting it as my hand smarted.

Keraun stared resolutely at the road. To my ongoing rage, his lips twitched, like this was all some big joke. Maybe it was. I must be a pawn to the likes of him.

'Shut up,' I growled, turning off the radio.

His mouth gave in to a grin.

I wanted to squash him. He turned to look at me, but I avoided his gaze. I didn't bother asking how he could drive without watching where he was going.

'I'm sorry I didn't come back. If it's any consolation, I spent the next four days after I tried in bed. Lightning god power isn't meant to mess with biology stuff.'

'Good.' I glared out the window, although my rage started to fade. 'Why are you following me?'

He hesitated for a heartbeat too long. 'Just making sure you're okay. After I stuffed up the antiserum.'

Okay. It was such a tiny word. Despite my ebbing anger, I was glad he'd been around. 'Thanks for helping me out back there.'

'Anything I can do.' His tone had lost all its levity.

I looked over. We stared into each other's eyes for a long moment, vying for something. Trying to figure out who the other really was. I didn't want to believe he existed, in case it still all turned out to be a joke. I wanted to know the real reason he was following me around. He looked at me like I was a puzzle to solve, his eyes still tinged with fire.

Keraun broke away.

We were on the freeway now, approaching the West Beach exit. 'Can you take me to my uncle's, please?' I asked. 'In the city.'

He nodded. I told him the address, in case his god-brain didn't already know.

We pulled up outside Alex's apartment building. I told Keraun to wait for me and raced up the stairs, calling Cecelia as I went. I must have been out of it in that woman's cell for hours. It was two in the morning, but Cecelia was a light sleeper. After three rings, she answered.

'What's wrong?'

'Can I come over?'

'It's two a.m. Can it wait until morning?'

I hesitated. 'It's a Sunday incident.' The "Sunday incident" referred to two previous occasions. The first one had been mine. It had been Sunday evening, the night before Dad was going on his first long stint away. I was seven and he was leaving me to live with Alex for three months. I loved Alex, and I'd stayed with him plenty of times before for a week or so, but I stamped my foot, yelled that I hated Uncle Alex and took off into the night. I pedalled my bicycle all the way to Cecelia's house, where I ran crying to my best friend's room. Nancy had called Dad and he'd come over and slept on the couch so he could see me in the morning before he left.

A few years later, on another Sunday night, Cecelia had gone through a pre-teen rebellious patch and run away from home. She'd shown up at Dad's and tapped on my bedroom window. Her parents read her note in the morning and, naturally, rang Dad first. He found us curled up in my bed, chuckled and assured them Cecelia would always have somewhere safe to run to. A Sunday incident was important, no questions asked.

Cecelia's voice sharpened. 'Do you need Mum to come and get you?'

'No. I'll be there soon.'

I raced into the apartment, thanked God – well, whichever god might be responsible, certainly not the one waiting for me downstairs – that I had toothbrushes, makeup and clothes at both houses and stuffed things into a bag. I rushed back downstairs and came outside to find the God of Lightning gone.

'Keraun!' I roared because I couldn't keep any more in. As I reached for my phone again, a car came flying around the corner. It was a tiny, boxy, bright orange convertible, top down, and it whined as Keraun thrashed it up to the kerb.

'Better?' he asked, grinning. I walked around it, shaking my head, and chucked my bag in the back before climbing into the cramped passenger seat.

'Worse.'

'But it's a convertible. That's cool, right?'

Somehow, despite everything that had happened tonight, I laughed. 'Maybe if it's a Porsche. Did you steal it?'

'No!' He looked offended, but his mesmerising eyes were mocking. 'Maybe.'

'You've probably done some poor person a favour, saving them from this car. It's just as well you didn't pay for it.'

Keraun rolled his eyes. 'It's a car, and it goes. Where to?'

I gave him Cecelia's address. He dropped me off, taking my phone number and promising he'd let me know if any Task-force suits came looking for me.

Cecelia let me in without a question, just a worried look. She'd already made up the roll-out bed in her room for me and went straight back to sleep. I fell into vague, fragmented dreams of needle pricks and red hair and unlikely lightning flashes.

CHAPTER 9

Superhuman Jeans

I woke a few hours later to the Sunday morning commotion of the Wilson house. Robert (Cecelia's dad, the inspirational Doctor Wilson) was being all suburban-family-man-like and mowing the lawn. Nancy's blender whirred in the kitchen. Alyce and Fiona, Cecelia's sisters – fifteen and eleven respectively – ran around getting ready for ballet, Alyce frantic over a missing hairband, Fiona prattling about wanting a horse. Or a ferret. Robert was allergic, so although Cecelia had campaigned for a cat at a similar age, the Wilsons' had remained a pet-fur-free zone.

The crazy unreality of the previous day faded, and I was left with a heavy realisation: my life had changed. I mean, I'd never had a normal family, except by being an add-on in the Wilson household, but now not even Italian dinners with Alex trying not to give away any work secrets was normal. I had secrets of my own.

Despite the drugging, punching and escaping of last night, I felt good. Maybe a bit tired, and worried that I would succumb to another sensory overload panic attack, but physically good. I took my time in the bathroom putting my usual makeup on, even though my face was clearer than it had ever been, and waited until the commotion subsided before venturing out. Nancy and the younger girls were gone, and the lawnmower racket was replaced with the snick of secateurs as Robert pruned the roses outside the kitchen window.

True to the Sunday incident rules, Cecelia didn't ask any questions, but that didn't make it easier. Cecelia and I shared everything. Words burned on my tongue, pushing to be spilled. *Cecelia, you won't believe what happened. I was struck by lightning. Now I'm some kind of superhuman. I don't know what to do.*

We unpacked our books and sat in the Wilson's dedicated study room. It was large and sunny with a massive skylight and a square table in the middle, room for eight people to sit with books all around them, complete with power points for laptop chargers along the underside of the desk. At the window, which overlooked the backyard, were several pots of thriving peace lilies. A comfortable two-seater sofa sat in the corner next to the plants. It was a pleasant room, but it was bright. I could feel the light pushing through my eyes and into the back of my brain. Although my memory seemed to be sharp – I could remember everything I'd seen on the menu at the Shack yesterday, including almond milk being an extra $1.50 and malt sixty cents – I couldn't even read the human biology book Cecelia had thrust at me. Words swam on the page and my skin felt hot. Cecelia was buried in her chemistry notes. I mumbled something about going to get a glass of water and slipped out of the room.

The house was calm, with Nancy and the girls gone and Robert pottering in a flowerbed. I leaned against the kitchen bench, sipping water.

My phone buzzed in my pocket. It was a message from Alex, confirming that he was flying in tonight. Apparently Dad had been called away on an urgent mission. I hesitated. I hadn't heard from him at all. The timing was suspicious. The Taskforce was a government operation, albeit unsanctioned, and Dad worked high up in government intelligence. It wasn't an unreasonable leap to imagine that Dad was involved, and that this urgent mission was dealing with whatever fallout my escape had caused last night. I had no idea if I could trust Alex. But I couldn't avoid both of them forever.

My phone buzzed again, this time with a message from an unknown number.

Call if you need anything. K.

Then, about ten seconds later:

God of Lightning.

Maybe he could be useful and help me out if Alex tried anything. I saved Keraun's number and messaged Alex back to say I'd be there for dinner. Then I rejoined Cecelia and tried to study. Enhanced memory or not, I wouldn't be raising suspicion by acing exams if I never looked at a textbook, despite Stephen's admonitions about keeping my grades in check.

I made an honest effort. But, I thought as I found myself staring out the window at Robert's perfectly trimmed hedge for the fifteenth time in as many minutes, Stephen probably didn't have to worry on that count.

My uncle and I had a custom for the first night of my stays in the city: he'd forego his healthy regime and we'd eat out at Harrys. We jagged our favourite table, outside on the street front, screened by lush potted plants. I watched him carefully, but Alex didn't say anything about Dad, or anything else that seemed odd. Then our meals arrived, and I stopped thinking altogether.

I didn't have words to describe the tastes I was experiencing. The food at Harrys was always delicious, full of oregano and fresh tomatoes and handmade pasta, but tonight it was incredible. I was too distracted by flavours dancing on my tongue to hear Alex talking.

'…worried about you.'

'What?' I asked with a mouthful. I swallowed. 'Sorry. Why are you worried?'

Alex put his fork down, frowning. His expression pulled on the scar that ran down the left side of his face. When I was eight, he'd picked me up from school one day with an angry red gash, stitched up and made even more grisly by a purpled eye. I was terrified. He'd told me, with what must have been a painful laugh, that he'd clashed swords with a pirate for the release of an innocent man. I had believed him at the time.

'Nancy is worried about you. And you've been unusually quiet this evening.'

I had to know if he knew. I wondered if I could slip a question in without sounding obvious.

'Has Dad said anything?' So obvious. I cringed internally.

Alex's fork hovered in mid-air. 'Only that he had to fly out urgently.'

Somehow, I knew he was being truthful. He didn't know. I breathed a sigh of relief.

'Are you okay, Gabby?' Concern warmed his voice.

I toyed with the straw in my lemonade. 'Yeah. Just worried about my university applications.'

'I know,' he said, sipping his wine. 'Nancy told me.'

I frowned. 'I haven't talked to Nancy about it.'

Alex nodded. 'That's what she said. You usually talk to her about things like this.'

My throat felt hot and I could feel my eyes watering, something that happened annoyingly often these days. But the thing was, I hadn't planned to talk to Nancy, even before my Event. I knew it was stupid, but I felt it was my fault. Like somehow, in my nearly seventeen years, I'd taken so many wrong turns that I now had no other options. Or I was just fundamentally flawed, and that was why I felt no calling. If someone had told me a week ago that I'd be getting a genetic upgrade, I'd have thought it would fix these feelings. But it hadn't, and they were closer to the surface than ever, stinging my being.

I blinked back the tears, taking a sip of my lemonade to hide my face. When I looked up, Alex was busy with his tagliatelle. We ate in gentle silence for a while. Alex had always been good at giving me space when I needed it.

While we waited for dessert, Alex reached into his laptop case, which went everywhere with him, and pulled out a long, thin box with a ribbon around it. 'I got you something. I know you're probably moving out next year, to a uni college or your own place.'

I felt squirm of guilt. 'I don't know what I'm doing yet, Alex,' I said. Great. That would have been a good opportunity to start sowing seeds, preparing him for my eventual disappearance. *I have my eye on a course in Brisbane,* perhaps, or *I was thinking of backpacking for a while.* My mind was a mess.

'Well, you know you have my support in whatever you pursue.'

'Thanks.' His concern was moving, and it made me uncomfortable, knowing I was supposed to say goodbye sometime soon.

I opened the box. Inside was a silver bracelet, with an intricate chain that almost looked like tiny pieces of silver ravioli linked together. I smiled. Opposite the clasp was a flat plate with *Gabby* engraved on it.

'Turn it over,' Alex said. On the other side of the plate were the words *Superhuman Jeans*. My breath stuck in my throat. It had been our little joke for years, since my high school did some stupid superhero dress-up day. I had, at thirteen, sworn off skirts, leggings and tight jeans because I thought they made my developing thighs look chunky. It ruled out all of the cool costumes. Alex had said I could be my own superhero, and he'd helped me come up with a costume that included my favourite slouchy jeans. I'd ignored the derisive looks from the other girls because at least they weren't laughing at my legs and told Mrs Johnsen I'd read a webcomic about a superhero in comfy clothes. I had eventually come to terms with my thighs and discovered that I could pull off skirts and skinnier jeans, and now I lived in them.

'Just so you know,' Alex said, voice slightly lower than before, 'that it doesn't matter if you don't fit the mould. You can do anything.' When he smiled, his scar almost disappeared. I struggled with the clasp. He took the bracelet and secured it around my wrist. I met his eyes, blinking furiously.

'Thank you,' I whispered. A pang of remorse shot through me: unless I found a way out, I'd be going to Darkhaven and leaving him forever. And I kind of wanted to go to Darkhaven. But he'd believe Superhuman Jeans was dead.

CHAPTER 10

A Bad Plan and a Deal

Monday was my first day back at school with a clear head. I started to understand why Stephen was worried about my grades drawing attention. Even though I was distracted all day by my pending training and a persistent fear that Dad might have me abducted again, I found it easy to follow what was happening in classes. I was terrified that I would have another sensory overload attack, so I avoided anything stimulating and holed myself up in the library at lunchtime. Cecelia was all too happy to sit and study and Zenna wasn't at school anyway. I messaged her, but she didn't reply.

At the end of the day, I told Alex I was staying late for tutoring, chucked my books in my locker and headed for the eastern gate. There was no one around; main roads ran past the north and south of the school, so most students came and went from the gates on those sides. The eastern gate was mainly for service access. Keraun had promised he would keep watch, but my skin still prickled as I recalled Dad's men appearing out of nowhere in the living room. I stood next to a peppy tree, glancing around for signs of movement and wondering if I would see them coming anyway.

Tyres crunched on the gravel driveway. My muscles tightened, but I saw the silver Toyota and relaxed a few degrees. Stephen passed me the black pouch again as I got in. 'It blocks your phone signal. Make sure you use it when you come to Darkhaven, or leave your phone behind.'

I stuffed my phone in the bag, trying to look calm, but my hands trembled.

'Are you okay?'

'Sure.' I didn't meet his eyes, taking my time stowing the phone in the glovebox.

'What happened?'

'Nothing.'

'Gabby,' Stephen said, voice stern, 'I can tell. You're nervous.'

I shot him a glare. 'Shouldn't I be? This whole experience is nerve-wracking.'

'Have you had another breakdown?'

I pressed my lips together and looked away. I could let him think that. But it irked me. I'd been careful, since Saturday, to monitor my senses and stay away from anything potentially overwhelming.

Stephen's brows drew together. 'Is it that Keraun guy? Is he bothering you?'

I almost laughed. If only he knew. I trusted Keraun when he said he didn't know what Darkhaven was up to, although I suspected he still knew more than he was letting on. Hell, he was a god. He definitely knew more than he was letting on.

Stephen let it go, at least until we arrived at Darkhaven. Back in the stainless steel kitchen, he directed me to the table, placed a glass of water in front of me and sat opposite, waiting for me to speak. I'd been telling myself to keep quiet about Dad and my visit to the Taskforce because I didn't want Stephen to lock me in a stainless steel room for my own safety, yet that wasn't entirely true. I didn't want to admit that my own father had betrayed my trust. And I hadn't seen it coming. It was like he'd ripped out the rug I'd been standing on, and now I was scrabbling for a foothold.

But by being so stubborn about not talking, I'd given away the gravity of the situation. Stephen might only have guessed before, but now he knew something was wrong. I mentally kicked myself. Savah leapt onto the table and sniffed my water glass.

'Okay,' I said, shooing the cat and wrapping my hands around the glass, just to have somewhere to put them. 'The Taskforce got me. At least, I think it was them.'

Alarm flashed across Stephen's face for half a second, then he resumed his normal calm. 'When?'

'After you dropped me back at home.' I couldn't bring myself to say "Dad" out loud. It was too much like a sound that I was supposed to associate with love and safety.

Stephen sighed. 'I should have stayed.'

I shrugged. 'You couldn't have known. How do they even know?'

Stephen looked thoughtful, but he didn't reply. He pulled a phone out of his pocket, sent a message, then turned back to me. 'Tell me what happened.' His voice was gentle, encouraging.

I swallowed. 'Dad was waiting for me inside with a guy called Sean, who got all in my face. I refused to talk, so Sean had his men jab me and I passed out. I woke up in some kind of interrogation room.' I gripped the glass a little tighter to stop my hands from trembling. In all my pre-superhuman years, I had never felt so powerless. 'Dad has pretty high security clearance. He must know about the Netica Project.'

Stephen nodded, waiting for me to go on. I bit my lip. My story ended with Keraun's rescue, and I suspected Stephen would not be hugely excited about that. While I stalled, the door to the kitchen swung open and Donovan appeared. She lounged against the wall just inside the door, arms folded, her gaze a strange mix of intense and distant.

'They asked me about you, and this place,' I continued.

'What did they say?' Stephen's voice was sharp. 'Tell me exactly.'

'I didn't tell them anything!' I said quickly. 'There was a woman. She knew both your names, and she knew about Darkhaven, but she didn't know where it was. She seemed to know I'd had the Praegressus program applied, and she called me a liar. That was about it.'

'That was it?' Stephen asked.

I looked at the table. 'I, uh, punched her in the face,' I said. From the doorway, Donovan let out a bark of laughter.

Stephen stared at me. 'The woman. What else do you remember?'

I was surprised to find I could recall her face perfectly, despite the trauma of the situation. 'She had green eyes. Wavy, red hair. And she was tall. Aggressive. She wore a grey suit. And she had a mole on her right cheek.'

I stopped. Stephen's face was ghost-white. He exchanged a long, pointed glance with Donovan.

'It's not possible,' Stephen whispered. Donovan shook her head.

'What is it?' I asked.

'She always did like her suits.' Stephen's voice was hoarse with shock. He fished around in a pocket and pulled out a piece of paper. He unfolded it and held it out to me. It was an old photograph, crisscrossed with white fold lines.

'Yeah, that's her. Who is she?'

Stephen sagged back on his chair. 'Luci Douglass. Your mother.'

After I'd stared at Stephen for about five minutes, he stood up, busied himself at the bench and returned with two cups of tea, setting one down for me. Savah curled into his lap. Donovan poured herself a glass of vodka and joined us at the table. I wondered if it would be better than the tea. I'd stolen some of Dad's fancy gin once and drunk it neat. It hadn't been worth the effort of acquiring it, or the explanation after. I blew on the hot tea.

'Fuck me,' said Donovan.

Stephen massaged his temples. 'Yep.'

'But you said my mother was dead.' I was numb. I'd never even seen a picture of her before. Dad didn't keep photos around the house. It was one of his weird security things, and I'd never known if it really was part of his job or some quirk specific to him. Maybe now there was another explanation.

'What are we going to do?' Donovan asked.

'We have to go and get her. They've had her hostage for sixteen years.' Stephen's voice cracked.

'How do we know she wants rescuing?'

Stephen stared at Donovan. 'Wouldn't you? If she's working for the Taskforce, it would only be to keep herself alive. She wouldn't have a choice. We have to help her.'

Donovan took a sip of her vodka and gave me a calculating look. 'Do you think she recognised you? She hasn't seen you since you were a baby.'

I recalled the woman's – Luci's – comments about my hair colour. They'd made no sense at the time, but now I realised: I got my red hair from her. 'She knows.'

Donovan nodded, then turned back to Stephen. 'I don't like this. Why has she not reached out? Rather, why haven't the Taskforce used her as leverage to get to us?'

Stephen shrugged. 'She was the only one of us who understood how Praegressus worked, so she's probably more use to them if they keep her. But it's not about hostage politics, Es, it's about Luci. She's one of us. We have to help her.'

Donovan raised an eyebrow at "Es", then drained her drink and poured another one. 'So what's your mad plan, May-boy? I assume you have one.'

Stephen's plan was more or less to get someone – and by someone, he meant me – back inside to get access to Luci. I was doubtful that the woman even wanted rescuing and privately thought Donovan made some good points, but Stephen insisted.

'Luci always could be a bit hard-edged,' he said. I rolled my eyes at that description, but he ignored me. 'She has to cope in there however she can. She's your mother, Gabby.' He gave me his most intense stare. 'You have to give her a chance.'

Presumably the Taskforce hadn't forgotten about me, but Donovan's network confirmed that Dad had flown to Canberra, and since we didn't want to raise suspicion by eagerly knocking on their door, we had to wait until he was back. In the meantime, I'd learn to handle my senses and develop whatever skills I could to be effective at my infiltration. When Dad returned, I'd make a show of trying to avoid going home but otherwise be an easy target. Then I'd be in the building, with a tracking device, leading Stephen straight to Luci. After that, the plan largely hinged on my mother being willing to come with us, but if she couldn't – or wouldn't, Donovan added – cooperate, Donovan would be ready to break us out.

A sly idea slipped into my head. I cleared my throat over Stephen and Donovan's discussion of extraction tactics. They stared at me, mid-argument.

'This sounds like a lot of risk,' I said.

'It is,' Donovan said. 'It's a shit plan.'

Stephen implored me with his eyes. 'It's not much of a plan, I know, but you're the first chance we've had to get right into the Taskforce, Gabby.'

'I understand,' I said. 'And I'm willing to do it.'

Stephen's face relaxed. Donovan looked suspicious.

'But I want something in return.'

Stephen opened his hands. 'Anything.'

Donovan's jaw clenched.

'If I do this, and I train and I get control of my senses and all that, you let me go. I might still work for you, but I'm not going to be legally dead.'

Stephen's face tightened. 'It's not a good idea, Gabby.'

Desperation edged his voice. I used it. 'Putting me up as bait isn't a good idea. How about if I succeed – I get us in, and we get Luci out – then you let me go. If I stuff it up, then I'll follow your terms.'

Stephen looked at me intently. I met his eyes, resolute. Finally, he shrugged. 'It's a deal.'

'I stand corrected,' Donovan grumbled. 'It's a fucking stupid plan.'

'It's not hopeless,' Stephen said. 'Liam can help us.'

The room was quiet for a moment, except for Savah's purring.

'How many Eventers are there?' I asked.

'Just the four of us, currently,' Stephen replied.

'You, Donovan, the doctor and whoever Liam is.' I couldn't remember what else Stephen had said about Liam or Catherine.

'Liam is a clairvoyant. He doesn't see everything, but it's still useful.'

'And you were all part of the original research team?'

'No, Donovan and I are the only ones from that far back,' Stephen said. 'We had Luci, of course, and Jan. He was the one who turned us in.'

'What happened to Jan?'

'He died in the lab fire. He never had the program applied to him. Maybe he had a problem with that, but he was the one who said there should be someone who didn't violate absolutely every ethics rule in research.'

'Pious hypocritical git,' Donovan added. 'All that ethics talk and he turns out to be a rat.' She downed the rest of her drink, pushed her chair back with a clatter and stalked out of the room. I stared after her, wondering what made her so prickly.

'Don't mind her,' Stephen said, as if he had read my mind. 'She hasn't got a shoulder left to have a chip on.'

I smiled. So he did have a sense of humour. 'Okay, there's you and Donovan from the original team. How did Catherine and Liam find you?'

He stroked Savah's fur, rubbing her ears when she tilted her head. 'Whenever there was storm activity, Donovan and I would be out, searching. We knew there were fourteen kids on the list. The Taskforce knew who they were and where they all lived. When an Event happened, they got in quick and made it look like the lightning strike was lethal. Three died before we even got there.'

I shivered. My name would be on that list, wherever it was. I could have been one of the three.

Stephen continued. 'Liam was one of the toddlers in the group, and he had just turned twelve when his Event happened.'

'Twelve?' I cut in. 'You took a twelve-year-old away from his family and told them he was dead?'

'Relax, Gabby. He was an orphan. I'll let him tell you the story. We got lucky and found him first, and he developed remarkable clairvoyance. He could predict lightning Events weeks ahead, within a kilometre or so of where they were going to happen, and usually tell us who it was. We could stop our endless vigil. We could be there for people when it happened.

'Catherine only joined us last year. She was the oldest, nine when she had the program, and she'd already completed her internship by the time her Event happened. She was on the roof of the hospital in a storm, waiting for a helicopter transfer. We weren't able to get in past security, and the Taskforce got there first. I used birds and a well-placed pair of rats to scare her away from them, and that gave Donovan time to get her out. It took some convincing, but she came on board.'

'What made her stay?'

'I'll tell you some other time. Don't worry, you'll get full disclosure.' He glanced at his watch. 'Right now, we have other things to discuss. I want a security detail on you.'

I shifted in my chair. I didn't want the Taskforce to sneak up on me, but I also didn't like the idea of bodyguards following me around at school.

'Don't worry,' Stephen said. 'Donovan's people are discreet. You won't even know they're there. Now, training.'

Thank goodness for the enhanced memory because my routine was about to get intense. Over the next few weeks, I was to come to Darkhaven every weekday to practice filtering my sensory input and to hone my intuition. Stephen would pick me up after school at the dodgy east gate and drop me back for Alex to collect me in time for dinner. I'd tell him that, worried about my university options, I was staying back to study, which many kids were doing now that we were less than four months away from exams. I didn't like having to lie, but it was better than the fake-death alternative. For now.

CHAPTER **11**

Stereos and Sun Orchids

It was remarkable how life just ground on as if nothing crazy had happened. I still had to get up, get myself out the door with some sort of sugary sustenance and make it to class more or less on time every morning. Unfortunately, it seemed that having supergenes didn't mean I'd become thin while still eating chocolate for breakfast, or that it was easier to crawl out of bed before nine.

Despite Stephen's assurance that Donovan's people were keeping an eye on me, I was still worried about Dad coming back. And I was terrified of the breakdown that happened when I became overwhelmed. I skipped lunch on Tuesday because a quick peek into the school canteen was enough to know that the cacophony of noise and smells and jostling of hungry teenagers on Burger Tuesday would be enough to set me off. I hurried into the relative quiet of the next corridor, leaned against the lockers to gather myself and resolved to bring food with me tomorrow.

Zenna had promised she'd be at school, but she was still distraught over not getting her licence. The documentary company she wanted to do a summer internship with wouldn't take someone who couldn't drive. When she didn't meet us for lunch, I went and found her in the media lab surrounded by notes and storyboards.

'I'm useless.' She sniffed, not taking her eyes off the monitor where she was editing film footage.

I squeezed her shoulder. 'You are not useless. And you still have plenty of time. Take it with me in November.' My birthday was in September, and I already had the test booked for a few weeks later. I was tired of relying on people to shuttle me between school and two homes.

Looking slightly less surly, Zenna nodded. 'Sure.'

I logged in to the next computer and booked the test for her, then sat and wasted half an hour on the internet.

'Maybe I should file your TISC form for you,' she said as she opened her email confirmation from Driver Services.

I groaned. 'Don't talk to me about TISC.'

'You could always run off and join a circus.'

'That sounds more like something you'd do.'

'Probably.' Zenna smiled.

I grinned back at her.

'Are you free after school?' she asked as the bell rang for the end of lunch.

'Nope.' I pulled a face. 'Tutoring.'

'Look who's turning into a pre-exam control freak.'

'Oh no, I'm not taking Cecelia's title away.'

Zenna giggled, reaching into her bag. 'How many highlighters do you have in your pencil case?'

'None.' I elbowed her, and she swiped at my hand with a marker, leaving a streak of green ink on my skin.

'Hey!' I snatched her bag, dodging green as I dug out another marker. We laughed as we left the lab, painting each other in bright colours.

I had assumed that I would be working with Stephen, but for my first training session he delivered me to a sparsely furnished office with a tidy desk and a couple of armchairs in the corner. The little table between them was taken up entirely by an expensive-looking stereo amplifier, and tall speakers stood in opposite corners of the room.

Donovan banged through the door. 'Don't you know it's rude to enter someone's office when they're not there?'

Stephen replied with a playful punch. 'You're never here.'

Donovan kicked him out with a growl and pointed me to an armchair. I took the seat, suppressing a strong urge to run from the building. I had no idea what to say around her. She plonked down in the other chair.

'Sensory control,' she began, 'is something you've been doing all your life. Your eyes take in a lot more information than the brain ever recognises. Now your senses are enhanced, and your brain is going to have to learn to filter your perceptions again so you can consciously manage the data. Have you ever meditated?'

I shook my head.

'The control required is like meditation. You have to know the input is there but not let it into your conscious awareness. Sit up straight.'

I lifted my back away from the chair. Donovan huffed and came to stand next to me.

'Sit forward.' She pushed and pulled my shoulders and prodded my spine until she was happy. I was using muscles I hadn't known existed. Oh, I knew now.

'Maintaining focus is easier when you can sit properly. You need to work on your posture. Lift your sternum. Relax your neck.'

I had no idea what she wanted, but I had the sense that asking questions wouldn't help much. I shuffled around a bit, mostly to ease the ache in my back.

'Close your eyes.'

I complied, uneasiness swirling in my stomach.

'Now focus on your breath. No matter what you hear, keep your attention only on your breathing.'

My breathing was rushed and shallow. I tried to slow it down but that just made it erratic. I couldn't get it under control, and my shoulders burned from the posture I was unaccustomed to.

BANG! A cannon blast shattered the silence, followed by an alarm, horns blaring and people yelling. My eyes flew open and I leapt to my feet, but a strong hand pushed me back into the chair.

'Focus on your breath!' Donovan's voice was hot in my ear. Her hand gripped my shoulder like a vice, shoving me down. 'Nothing but your breath! And sit up straight.'

Hard to sit up while being pushed down, and I struggled to breathe at all. 'I can't,' I gasped. She let go and the sounds faded away as I sagged, my face in my hands.

After a few seconds of relative quiet, I glanced up to see her sitting in her chair, toying with the stereo remote. The cacophony hadn't been outside, but in the room. She'd controlled the whole thing.

I glared at her. 'That wasn't fair.'

Her eyes flashed at my defiance, but she didn't rise. Instead, she gave a careless shrug. 'That's how it is in the real world. If you want to break all the rules and live out there, you have to be able to handle it. Sit up. We'll try again.'

'Can you wait until I'm ready this time?' I asked, trying to keep the tremor out of my voice.

Donovan laughed coldly. 'Nothing ever waits until you're ready.'

I was no more prepared for the noise the second time: a plane taking off, truck reverse signals beeping and men shouting commands. The sounds rose like a wave in my head, blotting out any ability to think or focus or breathe. I pressed my hands over my ears.

On the third round – people screaming and sirens wailing and babies crying – I slid out of my chair and curled into a ball on the floor. Donovan pulled me up, her fingers digging into my arm.

'I shouldn't let you go home,' she observed.

I stared at her, taking in her muscled physique, light hazel eyes and sharp chin. Her jaw was tight.

'I'm going home,' I said, trying to inject some strength into my voice. 'That's the deal.'

'The deal is you have to be better at this than just about anyone else.'

I slumped in my chair. Screw posture. 'Are we doing it again?'

Donovan turned off the stereo. 'I don't think you can take it.'

I wanted to argue. I wanted to get it right, prove that I could do this. I looked at her ice-firm face and instead swallowed my anger and embarrassment. Donovan opened one of her desk drawers and riffled through the neatly filed CD collection inside. She handed me a disk in a blank cover.

'Guided meditation and mindfulness techniques. Do it every day.'

'Thanks.' I tried to sound grateful, but I couldn't keep the surliness out of my voice.

Donovan opened the door. 'Stephen will meet you out the front.'

Her office door closed with a snap behind me, leaving me trembling and alone in the hallway.

Thankfully, Stephen thought my intuitive sense would be important for his rescue plan, which meant I didn't have to see Donovan every afternoon. Tuesdays and Thursdays would be spent in her office, a place I quickly came to loathe. Mondays were mine because Alex insisted on one evening a week with me, and he threatened to take care of my tutor if I wasn't allowed a night off. That left Wednesdays and Fridays with Liam, working on intuition.

The first Wednesday, the day after my disastrous session with Donovan, I was apprehensive. Stephen cast worried glances at me as we arrived at Darkhaven, but I kept my mouth shut. I didn't want him to renege on our arrangement and lock me up here or file a death certificate.

Liam was almost the total opposite of Donovan. He wasn't as fit, tanned or muscular as Donovan or Stephen, but he still had an almost unexpected beauty to his softer features, and the same perfect teeth and unblemished skin. It was like that rare photograph that caught your best angle in a flattering light and made you think, wow, I look good. That was Praegressus. No matter how you were built, what shape your nose or chin or cheekbones were, you were beautiful. I wondered if that was how I would look to other people soon. Then I remembered Cecelia and Zenna's teasing at the cafe – a day I had tried to block out of my memory – and figured I was probably starting to look different already. It was unsettling.

To my surprise, Liam didn't usher me into his office, but led me down the corridor and out the door to the patio. We continued across the clearing and down a little dirt path through the bush until we came to a small pergola draped in climbing white and purple blooms. Inside was a little wrought-iron table with four matching chairs, and on the table sat a small pot containing a plant showing an exquisite purple flower. A birdbath stood next to one of the pergola pillars.

Liam pulled up one of the ornate chairs, gesturing for me to sit. He still hadn't said a word. He breathed deeply, and without intending to, I found myself doing the same. The scent was heavenly. I didn't normally care much for nature or gardens, but this was an oasis in the concrete-and-stainless-steel world that was Darkhaven. If anything, the rest of the olive-grey Australian bush surrounding it added to the austerity of the place.

'Do you know any of the flowers here?' Liam's voice was quiet, with an almost melodic inflection.

'Jasmine,' I said. 'My friend wears a jasmine perfume. It's the white one, right?' I pointed at a vine twining up the pergola.

Liam nodded. 'The other one is false sarsaparilla, or purple coral pea. This,' he indicated the pot, 'is a sun orchid. They come in a lot of varieties. I won't trouble you with the botanical names.' He gave me an enquiring look. 'Am I telling the truth?'

'Of course,' I answered, confused. He kept peering at me, macchiato eyes under a creased brow. I paused, feeling into the situation, into my gut. He was being honest, but there was more. It was a bit like talking to Flamebeard, just before he launched into a passionate monologue about the inner workings of the nervous system or something. 'But you want to tell me the botanical names, even though you know I, uh, am not really into botany.'

'Aha! Very good.'

'So that was a test?'

He chuckled. 'No, just a curiosity. I think you have a good sense for whether someone is being truthful with you.'

I shrugged. 'I guess so. I think I always have.'

'That's usually how these things go. Ever known something was going to happen, just before it did?'

I considered. 'I don't remember anything specific. But I usually have a feeling if something is, like, a good idea or not, like some nights it's not safe to walk home in the evening. And sometimes I know things in Human Biology or English, without really knowing how I know. It's just right. Dad' – I felt another pang of betrayal – 'said once that I was highly intuitive, but I can't be. I can't make a decision to save myself. And if I was ... I would have known he'd turn me in.' I bit my lip. 'I'm not sure why I'm telling you this.'

Liam opened his hands, palms up. 'Why are you telling me then?'

I thought about it. 'Because I know I can trust you.'

He smiled warmly. 'Sometimes, our intuition works against us. We get so used to relying on it for little things – how much milk to add to a batter, whether a plant is suited to a particular spot, how a friend will react to some news – that we take those nudges for granted. When the time comes to make a major decision, we expect it to do something it doesn't do. If we have all these small, accurate feelings for small situations, we think the bigger problem warrants a bigger feeling. We want a symbol, an unmistakable sign that what we are about to do is right. We stop paying attention to the little signals our body and spirit are sending us.' He rested his elbows on the table, interlacing his fingers. 'There are two things that can mask your intuition. Any idea what they are?'

'Fear,' I answered, automatically, then stopped myself, wondering why I'd said that.

Liam laughed, the sound gentle like a tinkling water fountain. 'You see! The other?'

My brain went blank. I shook my head.

Liam smiled. 'The very idea of fear is enough to stop the process. The other one is love. Again, counter-intuitive. Intuition comes from a place of calm, which you would think is love. It is not. Intuition is value-neutral. It doesn't care one way or the other what you think of the situation. Humans place judgements like "good" or "bad" on things. Intuition, at its core, is simply knowing what is. Love is the least value-neutral thing of all. And fear is really just the risk of losing love.'

He paused, looking thoughtful, then continued, voice a little softer. 'Don't blame yourself about your father. You love him. You wouldn't have wanted to have seen that coming, and if you had, you couldn't have believed it. We can't easily sense things that are very close to us, like family. It's the same for my clairvoyance.'

My eyes prickled, but to my surprise, I wasn't embarrassed. I traced my finger around the edge of the ceramic flowerpot and blinked slowly, letting the tears trickle down my cheeks. We sat in silence for a few moments. Water splashed nearby and I looked up to see a tiny, bright blue bird playing in the birdbath.

'A splendid fairy-wren,' Liam said. 'Stephen's favourite.'

'What's yours?'

He smiled. 'Black cockatoos.'

We watched the fairy-wren splash in the shallow water, then perch on the edge of the bath and fluff its electric-blue feathers out. After a minute of preening, it hopped down and flitted over to a banksia tree.

For the next hour, Liam spoke at length about managing and controlling emotions. It sounded similar to what Donovan wanted me to do, but it was a lot easier to imagine being in control out here, in the peaceful surrounds of the pergola. Liam also set me homework, asking me to start a journal of times when I automatically answered questions, or sensed something I had no conscious knowledge of. I left that afternoon feeling a lot more hopeful about my chances of surviving in the outside world.

CHAPTER 12

Secret Wafer Stash

Donovan crushed those hopes the next day. I might have quit, but I had alternating sessions with Liam to balance out the trauma of being in her office, and I was determined to succeed at infiltrating the Taskforce and finding Luci.

'I understand you've been practising mindfulness.'

Liam and I sat under the pergola on Friday afternoon. I'd bailed on my regular TV binge night with Cecelia and Zenna, promising to make it up to them soon without any real idea as to when. I shifted on my chair, not meeting Liam's gaze.

'No?'

I looked at him, disappointment welling in my gut. 'Donovan gave me a CD. My laptop doesn't even have a CD drive.'

'And you didn't ask her for a different format?'

I shook my head, kicking myself for being so stubborn. I could have said I wanted something else. I could have looked it up online, found a download or something. But it was Donovan. I hadn't been about to make her job easier.

'I didn't realise it was for your lessons. I'm sorry.'

Liam frowned, his brow crinkling. Then he sighed and leaned back. 'You have many questions.' He said it simply, without the judgement I felt from Donovan. I mentally reached for my list of questions I'd been too embarrassed to ask anyone else.

'Is that okay? I can't concentrate, and I'm kind of sucking at everything.'

Liam laughed. 'It is your first week. Ask away.' He waved his hand in invitation.

'So am I invincible? Immortal? Undying? What is this?'

'None of those things. But there's not a lot left on this world that could kill you. Total decapitation would do it. The Task-force have a specialised bullet that will kill us if we're hit in the heart or the brain. We now know, thanks to you, that they also have a tranquilliser that works. As for old age, we don't know, it hasn't been long enough. Donovan is the oldest. She seems to age, but far more slowly than a normal person, and there's no sign of degenerative disease. Catherine thinks our lifespans now will be in the high hundreds.'

'And I have superhuman stuff, like strength and speed? How does that work? I don't feel faster or stronger.'

Liam reached into his pocket, pulled out a pen and threw it at my face.

'Hey!' I caught it.

'Would you have caught that before?'

Probably not. I wasn't exactly made for ball sports. 'Maybe.'

'Your reflexes are faster. You'll be a bit stronger than you were. You won't develop illness from poor lifestyle choices. But you still have to train if you want a big improvement. Same goes for your other abilities. You have a knack for intu-ition, but you have to practice it.'

'How do you know?'

He tilted his head. 'I can see it. The way you move. The questions you ask.'

Pity, I thought, I hadn't had this on-tap intuition before I came to Darkhaven. I supposed it was something since I didn't think any amount of magical enhancement or gym workouts would improve my athletic abilities much.

'Okay. What does Darkhaven do?'

Liam leaned back in his chair, which puzzled me, since the chairs were straight-backed, wrought-iron things that dug into my butt no matter how I arranged myself.

'Research, mostly. I think Stephen is the best person to ask.'

I huffed. 'Will he tell me?'

A little gleam came into Liam's eyes. 'Pay attention, and you'll know which questions to ask and when. Now, I'd like you to try a mindfulness exercise. Ignore the pain in your buttocks and focus on this flower.' He indicated the purple orchid in the centre of the table. I bit back the comment I'd been about to make on how the chair dug into my butt.

'Notice everything about the orchid. Think of nothing else. What does it look like? What would it feel like if you touched it? Touch its leaf and notice the sensation. Does it have a sound?'

We spent the rest of the afternoon on similar focus exercises. I tried to keep my mind on task, but it was boring work. Keraun kept invading my thoughts. And how to keep this secret from my best friends. Even the English essay popped up at one point. I cheated a bit and started focusing on Liam's voice instead, finding it a bit easier to pay attention to the words as he instructed me on things I should be noticing. What did I feel in my body? In my muscles? What emotions was I experiencing? Just notice. Don't react.

Boredom. Don't react.

Dad drifted to the forefront of my mind. Anxiety. Don't react.

A kookaburra burst into raucous laughter. I pounded the table with my fist, almost sending the orchid flying. Liam steadied the pot, decided that was enough for one day and set me more homework.

Two weeks later – three weeks since my Event – I couldn't put my friends off any longer. They were already suspicious, and after their comments about me at the Shack, I didn't want to have to fend off any more awkward questions. Fortunately, just being a Year 12 and taking ATAR classes excused most behaviour. It was kind of appalling how much I could brush off as exam stress.

Dad was still away, which wasn't unusual in itself, and I relaxed slightly about the Taskforce hiding around every corner. I convinced Cecelia that a TV-and-pizza night at Alex's on Sunday would be beneficial for her mental state and might even help her studying ability, then called Zenna.

'So we are still friends?' she asked, pretending to be joking. I could hear the hidden hurt in her voice.

'Zenna, I'm not spending my free evenings with a tutor for fun. I'm really sorry. But it's just until exams. And I want you to come.'

'You won't even spend a lunch break with me.' Her voice took on a less-veiled edge, part threat, part anguish. I'd been spending most lunchtimes in the library. I snuck Iced VoVos and Life Savers in and tried to study to keep Cecelia company. She no longer seemed to need food and instead found nourishment in textbooks and pencil dust.

'I'm sorry. But exams only happen once. I have to do this. There's no way I have a future as a filmmaker.'

Zenna laughed. 'Okay.'

'Okay, you're coming over?'

'Okay, I'm coming over. But you're providing the Maltesers. And if Cecelia even mentions a chemical element or anything about trigonometry, I'm going to eat all of her pizza.'

Alex ordered pizzas from Harrys and left us in the cinema room with copious Maltesers, M&Ms and Snickers Pods. We munched through the bags and watched four episodes of *Stranger Things* before Cecelia seized the remote and turned off the screen.

'It's a school night,' she said. Zenna and I moaned.

'Just one more,' I pleaded. 'Sunday doesn't count.'

Cecelia shrugged. 'You can watch it without me,' she said, gathering her phone and jumper and clambering out of her bean bag.

'Come on, we wouldn't do that,' Zenna said.

'Are you sure you don't want to sleep over?' I asked. 'Alex can take us all to school in the morning.' Zenna had already arranged to stay the night.

'Thanks, but I have to study.' Cecelia started stuffing her things into her bag.

Zenna looked up from hunting in the empty Pod bag for a stray. 'What, now? It's, like, nine p.m.'

'I can get a few hours in.'

'You're crazy,' Zenna said, tossing the Pod bag aside. She drained her cola and gave me a conspiratorial glance. 'How about Monopoly?'

I grinned. Trump card.

'Not without me!' Cecelia flung her bag back down. Monopoly was her favourite game. She usually won. All thoughts of leaving abandoned, she jumped on the couch.

'Just one hour,' she said, sending a text to Nancy.

Zenna smirked. 'Two.'

I went to fetch the board game. On my way back, I found Zenna in the kitchen. Alex was holed up in his office, giving us the run of the apartment. Zenna emerged from the pantry, holding a bottle of port. Alex didn't drink; the port was a gift that had been sitting in the pantry for the past two years.

'Do you think he'll mind?' she asked, a cheeky gleam in her eye.

I felt into the calm, intuitive place Liam had taught me to reach, ignoring his admonishments about using my intuition for good. I didn't think Alex would mind. Much.

I grinned back at Zenna and grabbed three glasses from the cupboard. 'Let's do it,' I said, making a show of tiptoeing back to the cinema room.

Cecelia's look of horror was priceless. 'It's a school night!' she hissed, as if the mere presence of the bottle would magically enable Alex to hear us. He couldn't. The door was shut and his office was at the other end of the apartment. I could hear him, though, typing on his laptop.

'Exactly,' Zenna said. 'It's Monday tomorrow, so we should take pre-emptive action against the worst day of the week.'

'You two go ahead,' Cecelia said. 'I still have homework to do. There are a bunch of carbon chemistry equations I still haven't got my head around.'

Zenna gave me a dark look. 'She's lucky she's already eaten her pizza. I'll have her wine instead.'

I poured two glasses and bagsed the car token as we set up the board. My experience playing Monopoly in the past was agonising: every roll of the dice presented me with a decision – should I buy Pall Mall? Wait until I got to Piccadilly? Risk it all for Mayfair? And that was just the start of my problems. After I'd botched all of my purchasing decisions came the bargaining round, when everyone made deals to trade properties for cash. I would inevitably second-guess my way into every possible bad deal and be the first bankrupt player, usually out long before anyone else. Maybe with wine it would be better.

And it seemed to be. Or, a little voice – sounding suspiciously like Liam – said in my mind, maybe it wasn't just the port. I made decisions instinctively. Sure, it was just Monopoly, but I found it fun, matching Cecelia and Zenna on their deals, knowing when they were making dodgy offers and turning them down, or bargaining back. After an hour, I owned all the railways, had hotels on Bond Street and was decidedly in the lead. Cecelia jumped up.

'You win, Gabs, and I have to go. Carbon chemistry awaits.'

'I can come back from this,' Zenna said. 'You're not winning so easy, Gabby.' She rolled high, skipped over my house on Coventry Street and landed her cat token in jail. 'Aha! Missed your Bond Street hotel. Another?' She indicated my empty glass.

'No thanks,' I replied, jumping up to walk Cecelia to the door and leaving Zenna to bail herself out of jail.

Cecelia hugged me while she waited for Nancy. 'Tonight was fun. I've been worried about you. You've been really quiet lately.'

'Aren't I always quiet?' I smiled to cover what I was feeling: sadness that I couldn't tell my best friend what was happening, amplified by the alcohol I was unaccustomed to. And an edge of fear – if Dad thought my friends knew something, would he hesitate to take them in? He'd as good as abducted his own daughter without apology, so I had to assume not. Secrecy was the only option.

'Sure, but you seem kind of wired. Are you sure you're coping with the extra study?'

I suppressed a laugh at the irony. 'Are you sure *you're* coping?'

A horn beeped outside.

'I'll see you tomorrow,' Cecelia said. She picked up her bag and disappeared out the door.

Zenna wasn't in the cinema room when I returned. I took the port bottle back to the kitchen and washed the glasses, removing the obvious evidence. By the time I'd dried them and returned them to the cupboard, she still hadn't appeared. My gut twisted. Something was off. I tried to brush it away – there was no reason to think anything was wrong.

She wasn't in my bedroom, where her bag sat on her makeshift bed. I went to the bathroom. The door was closed. I knocked on it. Alex's office door opened at the other end of the hallway.

'Zenna?'

I could hear the sounds of something being put away in a hurry, and then a tissue being pulled out of the box.

'Are you okay?' I asked, leaning close to the door. Alex wandered down the hallway, eyes on his phone, hovering without intruding. He was always careful to give my friends and I space when we appeared to be dealing with something tricky.

'Fine.' Zenna's voice was shaky.

I didn't need my intuition to disagree with that. I opened the door. Zenna stood at the bench, a tissue pressed against her forearm. She pulled her jumper sleeve down as I came in and slipped something off the bench into her jeans pocket. Alex stepped in behind me. Zenna's face drained of what little colour it had left.

'Please don't tell my parents,' she said, addressing Alex. He slipped past me, holding out his hand.

'Give it to me,' he said, voice low and gentle. Zenna shrank back against the bathroom bench, but he just stood there, hand out, waiting. Finally, she dug her hand into her pocket and handed something to him. In the mirror, I saw the silver glint of a blade.

'Please,' she whispered.

'We'll talk in the morning,' he said. Then he turned around, squeezed my shoulder and left.

We stared at each other for a long moment. I tried to figure out what to say, but my intuition gave me nothing. Zenna sank down onto the floor. I sat next to her. After a while, I gave in to the silence. 'What's going on, Zenna?'

Zenna pulled at a loose thread on her sleeve. Finally, she spoke. 'It's like how listening to sad music when you're sad helps. Or more like when you know you're sad, but you can't quite feel it, the music helps. You know?'

I kind of got that. I didn't get how it led to self-harm.

'I think I probably learned to block all that stuff out somewhere around Year 10 exams,' I said.

Zenna kept toying with the thread. 'Sometimes I feel most okay when I'm cutting.'

'I get it,' I said, mostly to be agreeable. 'But if this is like listening to music, you need to find a better song.'

Zenna gave a stuttered laugh. After a second, I chuckled too. It had a bitter timbre, but there was a feeling of relief too. The sound petered out.

'Thanks,' Zenna said, looking up.

I met her eyes. 'Promise me you won't do it again.'

She broke away. 'I can't do that.'

'Okay,' I replied. 'Promise me you'll tell me if you have. Don't show me, for God's sake, but call.'

'Then I probably won't do it.'

'That's the general idea.'

Zenna shook her head, red-and-gold hair falling over her face. I placed my hand on her trembling shoulder.

She whispered. 'But … what if … '

'Spit it out, Zenna.'

She choked, tears sliding down her cheeks. 'I don't know what else to do sometimes. I think it stops me doing something worse.'

I put my arm around her shoulders and pulled her into a hug. 'Call me first, then.'

Zenna sniffed.

'You know what we need?' I asked, listening to the sounds around the apartment. Alex padded around in his en suite. The shower started.

'More port?'

'No, we've had enough of that.' I gave Zenna my wickedest grin. 'We need chocolate wafers.'

It was Alex's one guilty pleasure, which he maintained was an important part of a healthy diet. He kept a tin of them in his desk drawer, and while everything in the pantry was fair game – an argument I intended to present when he discovered the missing port – the wafers were strictly off-limits. But this was the kind of situation that broke limits. I snuck into his office, took the tin and stole back to my room. Zenna was curled up on the bed in her pyjamas. I handed her the tin while I changed, then we polished off the wafers as we chatted until midnight about everything other than what had just happened.

'GABRIELLE!'

I rolled over. My phone hadn't gone off, so I wasn't late. Well, no later than usual – my alarm gave me about fifteen minutes to get out the door, which wasn't really enough. Alex never called me Gabrielle. He knew I hated the name. I didn't like Gabby a whole lot more, but at least I'd chosen it.

'Gabrielle Adele Whitehall!'

Louder this time. He was advancing down the hallway. I sat up, worrying that I'd been wrong about the port, and he really was mad. Zenna grumbled incoherently from her mattress on the floor and burrowed deeper under her quilt. I flopped back down in bed and pulled a pillow over my ears. Missing port wouldn't make him that mad.

The door flew open. I peeked out with one eye. Alex stood in the doorway, empty wafer tin in hand, dressing gown lopsided, with thick Explorer socks on his feet – one a mustard yellow and the other burgundy. He regarded me with mock-wild wide eyes, then softened his face into a grin. Of course he'd found the wafers. Or rather, lack of wafers.

'Have you,' he asked sweetly, 'been into my wafer tin?'

I rolled my eyes. 'You know I hate it when you use my full name.'

'I have it on reserve, for when it's something extremely important.'

'Life and death situations,' I reminded him. We'd discussed this when I was younger. I'd been about nine when I'd spilled red creaming soda on a white rug and tried to hide it. Alex had told me off, doing the exert-the-power-of-the-name thing, and I'd gotten so upset over his not taking my name preference seriously that he'd promised from that day on to only call me by my full name if it was a dire emergency. Then of course I'd cleaned out his wafer reserves a year later and, professing it an emergency of epic proportions, he'd called me by full name and dragged me out on a midnight snack run to replenish the stores with my pocket money (he gave it back in ice cream the next day). It had been a running joke ever since.

'Yes. And wafer theft.' He waved the tin at me.

I grunted. With a swish of terry towelling, he disappeared. His voice drifted back down the hall. 'Get up. You'll be late.'

'I like being late,' I muttered, but I rolled out of bed onto the floor and started looking for my jeans while Zenna pretended to snore under the quilt.

We weren't late. We were absurdly early. It was seven a.m. when we sat at the dining table. A stack of buckwheat toast cooled in the middle of the table. Alex had dropped his jovial attitude of wafer-theft accusations and somehow looked awkward and stern at the same time, a frown creasing his forehead. 'Zenna, I am obliged to talk to your parents.'

Zenna stared at her place mat. 'I wish you wouldn't.'

'I need to know you're okay,' he said gently. 'They will look after you.'

'Is there anything I can do?' she asked. I squirmed, feeling like I was eavesdropping but also that it would be rude to leave. I slipped a piece of toast onto my plate and buttered it as quietly as possible. The knife scraping on the toast was like metal grinding to my ears.

Alex cocked his head to one side, face thoughtful. 'There might be. Gabby, can you please give us a minute?'

Thank God. Or whoever it was. I slapped some strawberry jam on my toast and hurried back to my bedroom.

Zenna appeared ten minutes later, looking decidedly happier than she had at the table.

'Everything okay?' I asked.

'Yeah.' She folded her clothes and stowed them in her bag.

'Alex isn't going to tell your parents? How did you get him to agree?'

'Remember how he used to teach me cryptology, back when we first started hanging out here?'

'Sure,' I said. Zenna had often come over, supposedly to hang with me, but had spent hours with Alex at the dining table, poring over books and papers, learning all about writing and breaking codes, something I'd never had any interest in. He'd told her many times that if the film career didn't pan out, he could get her a job any time.

'We have an arrangement,' she said, smiling. She refused to divulge any more, saying it was all strictly classified. I flopped back on my bed and gazed at the silver swirl pattern on the ceiling. Everyone had their secrets.

Alex drove us to school, turning off my Top 40 radio station so he could play his favourite Beatles playlist. By the time we arrived, we'd sung *Hey Jude* about five times, voices growing hoarse from top-volume "nanananas". Zenna skipped off to her first class and I slouched away to meet Cecelia and the wrath of Mrs Johnsen – essay outlines were due today, and I hadn't even looked at it.

CHAPTER 13

Poker Face

Zenna was on her own in her Monday misery. For me, the miserable days were Tuesdays and Thursdays. After a particularly nasty session that Donovan cut short, raging at my incompetence, Stephen dropped me back at school early.

'How are you going?' he asked as we pulled up. He always enquired, but I got the feeling he wanted more detail this time. I liked travelling in silence; it was half an hour each way of blissful quiet, of not having to consciously suppress my senses, and Stephen gave me space.

'Okay, I guess. Except for sensory control.' Understatement of the year. I spent most of Donovan's sessions huddled in the chair, trying to remember to breathe through the barrage of experiences she presented. Between her projector, migraine-inducing bright lights and the endless library of sounds created just to assault my ears, I was a quivering mess. I forgot to breathe when she produced the first example from her morbid collection of strong smells. I passed out and woke up in the care of Catherine, who told me I could refer to her as Doctor Whittaker and sent me straight back to Donovan's office.

Stephen nodded. 'Donovan is tough. But, believe it or not, she's the best person for the job. No one has control down to an art like she does.'

'Huh. I wish she'd develop teaching down to half an art.'

'Be patient. Sensory control is a hard thing to learn.'

I bit back a snarky retort. I had a sense that now might be the time to ask more of the questions I wanted answers to. I took a breath. 'What makes you think it's magic?'

Stephen clasped his hands in his lap. 'Luci used to keep rabbits. I left my jacket behind one day and went back to the lab. She didn't know I was there, and she had a pair of rabbits in her lap. One of them had a broken leg. She moved her hands over the other one' – Stephen moved his own hands in a complicated circle – 'and red light sparked between her palms. The rabbit fell asleep. She kept working her hands, and the other one's leg straightened and healed. The next day, both rabbits were perfectly fine.' He looked at me. 'Tell me that doesn't sound like magic.'

I nodded. 'Did you ever ask her?'

Stephen shifted in his seat. 'Not directly. Jan was always there, and whenever I tried to broach it, he'd change the subject or call one of us away. I think he was jealous of not being an Eventer. And Luci and I weren't on the best terms by then.'

'What happened?' I asked, without thinking.

Stephen looked away. 'Some other time, perhaps.'

I centred myself and reached back into my intuition. 'Has Darkhaven found out anything about the magic?'

'Not yet. Liam and I work on it when we have time. Catherine is more interested in the science, and that's good too. We'll keep looking.' He gave me a sly smile. 'I think you could help.'

I ducked my head to hide my own grin. I didn't want Stephen to think I wanted this too badly, lest I lose some of my bargaining power. Researching magic sounded like a dream. Giving up Alex and my friends was a nightmare.

'Have you heard from Keraun again?'

'No.' Between the Darkhaven sessions, keeping up with school and trying to spend enough time with Alex and my friends to stop them being suspicious, I barely had time to think about Keraun, although I couldn't deny that he was there, in a corner of my mind. I'd thought about calling him last weekend, but Cecelia had demanded a study session and I'd run out of excuses to brush her off.

'Good,' Stephen said. 'I think you should stay away from him. He's trouble.'

I guessed Stephen didn't know who he really was, or he would phrase that a little more forcefully. As if a god of lightning wouldn't be trouble. My phone buzzed in my pocket.

'Okay,' I said. 'I'd better go. Alex will be here soon.'

I climbed out of the car, grabbed my bag, and waited until the Corolla had disappeared before pulling out my phone. It was Zenna, hassling me to join her for a movie tomorrow after school. I offered Saturday instead. I was excited about tomorrow's session – it wasn't with Donovan, for a start, and Liam had promised something different for Friday afternoon. He'd told me to bring my makeup bag, wear dressy sandals and tell Alex I would be out late.

With Liam's encouragement, I was making progress. He helped me pinpoint different feelings in my body that were clues about what I knew subconsciously. I still guessed a lot, but I was getting better at the process: taking my awareness out of my mind and all its mental clatter, past my heart with its lurching and longings and into what Liam called a "calm place", somewhere around my navel. It wasn't calm a lot of the time, but when it was, I found I knew things. I could answer questions from that place without even thinking. We'd been playing card games, poker mostly, and although Liam was formidable with his clairvoyance, I was starting to get closer to matching him. He might know what the cards were, but he couldn't change them, and I was starting to know when he was bluffing, as well as having pretty good hunches about a hand. I'd also borrowed Alex's laptop to copy Donovan's CD. I hadn't had any more overwhelm attacks, but I wasn't confident that a big enough sensory shock wouldn't send me flying out of control.

Like the one coming tonight, when Stephen announced the plan. 'The casino?' I asked, wings of excitement and anxiety fluttering through my belly. 'How can we go to the casino?'

Stephen didn't answer. He took up one of the chairs under the pergola, poured himself a cup of tea and sat back, watching the birds play as if he did this every afternoon. Maybe he did.

Liam gave me a cheeky, playful look. 'Well, Stephen has offered to drive, and we walk up the stairs and ta-da! We are at the casino. Fair warning though, it's a test. If it goes well, we know you're on track for the Taskforce mission. But don't worry, it'll be fun. We all need to get out of Darkhaven sometimes.'

I had to agree with him on that point. I flopped down in one of the chairs, regretting the abrupt movement as my buttocks hit the unyielding iron. 'But I'm underage, and do you even exist in the real world?'

Liam laughed. 'After a fashion.'

He fished a slim wallet out of his pocket and showed me a driver's licence. It looked legit, with the WA crest, a photo of Liam and a birth date. If the date was correct, he was only four years older than me. But the name offered on the licence was James Hall.

'Is it real?'

He grinned. 'The birthdate happens to be accurate.' He handed me another piece of plastic, this one with my photograph on it. My birthdate was definitely wrong, making fake-me eighteen years old, and apparently my name was Ellen Hall.

'If anyone asks, you're my sister, and we're out for your birthday.'

'Do we have to dress up?' Liam knew the story: the last time I'd worn a dress was to a school dance three years ago. Nancy had picked it out for me, assuring me the knee-length, pink-and-black thing with mesh panels was striking and feminine. I'd frowned at myself in the mirror, tugging at the seams that dug into my upper arms and sucking in my stomach. Then Dylan Rickshaw followed me around all night, complimenting how the magenta went with my pale skin – which it obviously didn't – and I hadn't been to any school dances since. Staying home in my pyjamas with a book was much more appealing.

Liam tucked his wallet away. 'It's not Casino Royale. But if you like, I did pick out a couple of outfits for you.' His brow wrinkled. 'I hope it's not too presumptuous, but I didn't think your dad would support this expedition.'

Dad gave me an allowance for my phone and coffee dates, but I usually had to borrow his credit card for clothes. It would have been impossible to hide or explain a dress purchase. If someone like Keraun had shown up with hand-picked outfits, I might have squirmed, but this was more like my older brother busting me out for the night. Excitement started to outweigh my fear. 'I can't wear my school clothes, right?' I said, grinning. 'Thanks.'

Liam's expression relaxed. 'They're hanging in the wardrobe in the bathroom.'

After three weeks of training here, I'd figured out which unidentified doors led to the important rooms, like the kitchen and bathroom. I set my makeup bag next to the basin and opened the wardrobe, apprehensive. In it hung a drapey cardigan and behind it, a long, black dress. Well, it was long on one side; on the other, it was slit up above the knee. The top half looked like it would be tight-fitting, although with a high neckline and full sleeves. I left the dress in the wardrobe and showered, taking my time. I'd told Alex I was having a girls' night with Zenna and Cecelia – at Zenna's, because her parents were less likely to talk to Alex and reveal that I wasn't there at all.

I took my time with my makeup, using a green eyeshadow that I didn't usually wear because it felt too fancy, glimmering above my grey irises. There wasn't much I could do about the roots beginning to show in my hair. Zenna liked the look – of course she did, my roots were red, and she loved bright and contrasting hair colours – but I preferred to keep dying them. It wasn't going to happen today.

Finally, I turned to face the slinky dress. I pulled it off its hanger, noticing another outfit behind it: a killer black skirt and a satin top. I hesitated.

Stop it, a morbidly curious part of me said. *Just try the dress.* Well, I could always take it off if I didn't like it.

I turned away from the mirror and pulled the dress over my head, trying not to smudge makeup on it as I shimmied into the stretchy fabric and smoothed down the skirt. The slit was high, almost to my hip, but my upper thigh was covered by a sort of ruffle that went around my waist on an angle. I shifted towards the mirror, so I could see the back of it, and stared.

The ruffle complemented my hips as it slinked up and around the snug dress. Long, fitted sleeves smoothed over my arms, finishing in subtle ruffles at the wrists. The whole piece glittered as I twisted and turned, like a sheet of midnight cloud veiling the stars. Nothing dug in or was uncomfortably tight. I drew in a deep breath. For the first time in my life, I didn't want to rush away from the mirror.

I'd worn my usual boots to school, but I had packed a pair of block heels with black straps, shoes I hadn't worn since the school dance horror story. They worked much better with this dress than they had with the magenta one. Ready to go, I placed my hand on the doorknob, then paused, nerves fluttering in my stomach – not because I felt silly or unattractive, but because I felt too attractive. Sexy, even.

A knock sounded on the other side. I jumped about a foot in the air as the rap of knuckles banged through my ears. Trying to shut out my hearing, I mentally lowered the volume the way Donovan had taught me. It sort of worked.

'Gabby?' Liam called. 'Are you ready? Stephen is waiting for us.'

Another fear hit me: the casino would be busy. Loud. Full of the scents of perfume and drinks and bodies. Bright lights and people brushing shoulders. This wasn't a test for my poker face.

'Are you okay, Gabby?' Liam called again.

'Yeah.' I grabbed the cardigan, stuffed my makeup back into its bag, scooped up my jeans and school shirt and opened the door. Liam was dashing in deep navy slacks and a jacket.

He smiled. 'Feeling good?'

Not trusting myself to speak, I nodded and followed him down the hallway, dumping my stuff in his office on the way out.

To my relief, Donovan had chosen not to join us, and I spent the drive gathering my thoughts and nerves while Stephen and Liam chatted quietly in the front. It had rained while I was getting dressed, and the casino loomed over the slick car park, dwarfing the twisted gum tree Stephen parked next to in the enormous lot. Row upon row of cars glimmered under the amber lighting.

Liam led the way inside and up the escalator. A kaleidoscope of colours, sounds and smells pressed in from every angle, pushing on my brain. The venue itself was assault enough – gaudy carpet, brightly lit walls, abstract paintings and posters everywhere and music coming from all directions, including wailing from a karaoke bar. I struggled to keep up with Liam and Stephen as people swirled around us. The air was thick with cologne and the rich aromas of food wafting from the surrounding restaurants. Talk and laughter babbled like lemonade bubbles, and I could hear three different bands playing at distant locations. I stopped walking, struggling to breathe.

Within a moment, Liam and Stephen appeared on either side of me. Liam took my arm. 'It's all right,' he said, his voice low. 'We're not going to lose you.'

I focussed on his voice and the pressure of his hand on my elbow to keep everything else at bay. We passed through security – my Ellen alias worked – and entered the main gaming room. Rows of poker machines lined one side, all noise and flashing lights, coins and chips clattering on plastic trays. I was shocked at the range of people sitting at them: young girls in heels and slinky dresses, giggling and sipping green cocktails; men donning dark jeans and blazers laughing and jeering at each other; older folk, some wearing scruffy jumpers and track pants, hunched over their screens as if they were part of the installation. I turned away from the poker machines and surveyed the rest of the room, careful to control the sensory input, keeping my awareness on Liam and Stephen.

Liam stopped at the door to the poker room, his eyes alight. 'I'll get us some drinks,' he said. 'Ellen' – he had to jab me with his elbow before I remembered he was talking to me – 'I want you to watch a game. See what you can pick up about each player. What do you know about them and their hands? I'll be back.'

He ducked away, disappearing into the crowd. Stephen stood stiffly at my side. I watched the tables, sinking my awareness down to my calm place. Now that I was standing still and had a single thing to focus on, the rest of the room was not so overwhelming. Of course, if it had been Donovan issuing the challenge, I would be a crying heap on the floor right now.

There were others watching the game in front of us, but I felt like I stood in a spotlight as I judged their plays and discerned their intentions, as if someone would see what I was doing. I quickly sensed who was bluffing and had a pretty sure idea which player was going to win.

Liam returned, bearing three pink, icy drinks. Stephen raised his eyebrows, questioning.

'They're non-alcoholic. Let's play,' Liam said, passing out the drinks and leading us away. 'Who was going to win?'

'The woman in the white shirt,' I answered. 'She was bluffing. So was the man with the goatee, except he's more nervous, she'll outlast him. The man in blue probably had the best hand, but he was about to fold.'

Liam nodded. 'Good.'

'You knew all that?' I asked.

He nodded again. 'I could see the outcome of the game, after I tuned in to it. I usually have to focus on an event to see what is going to happen.'

'And you can see the outcome of any event? Does it have to be close? Does it work on any scale?'

Liam smiled. We hadn't really had a chance to discuss his abilities; our sessions were always packed with exercises for me. I hadn't even dared ask Donovan what she could do.

'It's a difficult thing to test the limits of, but it seems distance is no barrier. Neither is time. But there are some limitations.'

'Like?'

'It's harder to see things around people I'm close to. And I can't connect with the dead.' A frown creased his face. 'I also can't see our upcoming mission,' he began, but Stephen cut him off.

'Not here.'

Worry edged into my mind. I assumed he was talking about my getting us into the Taskforce, but I didn't have the mental space to stress over something else right now. I gripped my drink, fingers chilled around the icy glass, still taking care to keep the sensory input at a manageable level. This was why Darkhaven was so quiet and out of the way. It was mentally exhausting being anywhere else.

We stopped at another poker table with two empty seats. Liam took one and gestured for me to take the other. My pulse quickened. I hadn't realised I would actually be playing.

'Um, Li—James,' I whispered. 'I'm not ready for this.'

'Of course you are.' With a wicked grin, he passed me a pile of coloured chips.

'I don't know what I'm doing,' I hissed.

'You know how the game works. You'll figure the rest out.'

Since stalking off was my only other option and that would put me alone in an overwhelming place with a fake ID, I took my seat at the table. Stephen stood behind me.

'Won't you play?' I asked him.

He shook his head. 'It's not really my game.'

The dealer welcomed us to Texas Hold 'Em and announced the big blind of one hundred dollars. I swallowed. My throat felt thick. A big blind of one hundred meant an early raise of three or four hundred. It was a lot of money. Real money. Not mine, which actually made it worse – if I lost spectacularly, I was losing Darkhaven's funds. Most likely I would whittle it away with low bets on crappy hands that I'd bail out of because I wouldn't be able to decide what to do.

With deft strikes, the dealer sent cards flying to land in front of each player. I peeked at mine.

Maybe having a fixed thing to focus on was the trick. As soon as I saw the cards – a two of spades and nine of hearts – my body relaxed. They were bad cards, but I didn't just know that intellectually, I knew it in my gut. The dealer came to me.

'Fold.' I dropped the cards in front of me. The dealer swept them away.

The player next to me, a slight woman with straight, dark hair falling over her high cheekbones, raised to $300. Liam called it. He didn't look at his cards when we played at Darkhaven – he just knew what they were – but he made a point of doing it here. The next three players folded. A man in a red shirt raised to $500. The flop came down: king of hearts, ace and four of diamonds. The woman raised again. Liam called. The man in red toyed with his collar, then folded. The turn was a queen of clubs. The woman beside me folded and – no surprise – Liam took the pot.

My next hand was better, but not by much. I folded on the following four rounds. Finally, my intuition shifted as my cards were dealt. This was it. A shiver ran down my back and I lifted the corner of my cards: jack and ten of hearts. I was in.

I raised the bet to $2400.

The woman next to me flicked her hair and called. Liam called too. Sometimes when we played, we'd deal and instantly declare a winner – Liam knew what the cards were, and I knew whether or not I could win. But poker wasn't just about the cards, and I could also sense if I stood a chance. If I did bet on a hand, suddenly the game became about the players and who could bluff, out-bluff or unnerve their opponent. Liam couldn't predict that because I didn't make any decisions in advance. I just stayed still, and when the time came, I did whatever felt right. It was a liberating experience.

A blonde woman, a bearded man and the guy in the red shirt continued betting. The flop supported my hunch: queen of hearts and two threes. The air around the table thickened. I raised again to $4800. The woman next to me called. Liam, I realised, was playing to push the pot up. The turn was an eight of hearts. My heart raced. The blonde and the red shirt were out. By the end of the round, the pot was nearly $60,000. And it would be mine. Well, Darkhaven's. My fingers tingled. The final card was turned up: nine of hearts. I had a straight flush. The hardest part was keeping a straight face. I tried to look ponderous and deliberate as I placed my bet, resisting the temptation to go all in. I sensed that if I did that, everyone else would fold.

Liam folded. The woman called my bet. So did the bearded man. The dealer called for the showdown: queens full of threes. Four threes. And my straight flush. I took the pot. Liam smiled to himself as he stacked.

My next hand was a pair of kings. Anyone would probably keep it, but I knew it wasn't a winner. Yet . . . play the players. I had a sense I could bluff this one. As the flop showed up three completely useless cards, I saw the guy in red touch his collar. He'd bet high and he didn't have the cards. I raised. Satisfaction rippled through my body. For the first time, I felt I really stood a chance to fulfil my end of the deal with Stephen – if I was successful on the rescue-Luci mission, I would get to keep my friends and my memories and have the option to stay with Darkhaven. On my own terms. It wasn't that I was indecisive. It was just a matter of whether the hand was worth keeping.

The turn was another king. It was just me and the guy in red, who looked a bit more confident now. He raised the bet. We waited for the river. I could still feel that I could bluff him, if I just kept cool and –

A firm hand landed on my shoulder.

'Excuse me, miss,' a gruff voice said, 'can we see your ID?'

My lifted mood splattered like a tossed water balloon. I turned to find myself looking up at a tall security guard with a hard face. Behind him stood a woman, shorter, stouter and even harder. Was it my winning streak? Did they suspect I was cheating? I kind of was. Or had they figured out I was under-age? I felt panic start to rise, and with it, the volume and intensity of the sounds and sights and smells increased.

I took a breath. Pushing the fear down, I sank into my calm place, allowing the answers to come to me, as I had been doing in the poker game. Perhaps because I had so recently been in that zone, it was easier to slip back into. I weighed the options: cooperate or try to escape. The thought of handing over my fake ID sent an unpleasant shiver through my body.

I smiled at the guards, overly sweetly. 'Sure. It's in my purse, let me get it.' I stood. Liam jumped up to take my hand, expression neutral. Stephen was on the other side of the table with a white-knuckled grip on his drink. I made a show of looking around, under my chair.

'Oh, I must have left it in the toilets,' I gushed, playing it up. 'The ones just behind the pokies. I hope it's still there!'

The male guard stood back and said something to the woman. She left, heading in the direction of the bathrooms. I hadn't known she would leave, but I knew this was our best opportunity to escape. I shot Liam a look.

'Run!' I said, just loud enough for Stephen to hear too, but still too low for normal human ears. I picked up the chair and shoved it at the guard, then, on impulse, grabbed two handfuls of my chips as Liam, Stephen and I ran. The chair didn't slow the guard much, and he was close behind us as we skirted tables and pushed past onlookers, creating angry shouts and more than one spilled drink. I ran towards the rows of poker machines, bounding like a giraffe in my heels.

'He's after me. Split!' I said. Liam and Stephen melted away as I rushed down the rows of people sitting at the machines. The players barely noticed me until I got to the end. I turned. The guard was halfway down the row. I lifted my hands and tossed the chips back down the rows.

'Free chips!' I called. People turned from their chairs, scrambling to collect the chips, holding the guard up as he tried to get out of the melee.

I hitched my dress up a little and kept moving, no plan, just calm instinct, until I approached a wall. Stephen and Liam were nowhere to be seen. But my instinct paid off – a few metres down was a fire exit. I took it, glancing back. The guard was still tangled in the press of people, but he saw me. I leapt through the heavy door, letting it close behind me as I raced down the stairs, two at a time, praying I wouldn't roll an ankle in my sandals. I didn't count the flights, but halfway to the bottom I realised I should have. I'd been on the third floor of the building, and I wanted to come out on ground level. Now I wasn't sure, and I didn't have time to stop and count them.

I paused on the last landing before the bottom. I could hear heavy boots banging on the flight above me. I felt like this was the right level. But there were two crash doors, one on each side, and the signs that should have hung above them had been taken down. If my bearings were correct, one led to the basement and further pursuit, the other outside to freedom. The boots were getting closer. I didn't have time to think. I took another deep breath, dropped into my calm place and went left.

I burst out into the night. I was on the outside of the building, looking across a road to a car park. There was the twisted tree. Gasping in the cold, damp air, and also enjoying the rush of successful escape, I slipped off my shoes and pelted across the wet road. I could hide in the car park if I got there before the guard came through the door.

'Gabby!'

Liam and Stephen were walking down the road towards me. Stephen had his phone at his ear. I stopped. The guard didn't show; perhaps he had taken the other door. Liam pulled me into a hug. 'So, how much was guesswork, and how much did you do on intuition?' he asked as we headed for the car.

I wasn't done with my intuition. He didn't sound relieved, but rather smug. Something clicked. No signs on the doors indeed. 'Wait,' I said. 'You set all this up?'

Stephen gave a rueful smile. Liam looked triumphant, but there was a guilty flash in his eyes. 'It was my idea. I wanted to see how you could use your intuitive skills in different situations, and under varying pressure.' He climbed into the back-seat with me.

Stephen glanced at me in the rear-view mirror as he drove us out. 'Are you okay?'

'I'm fine,' I replied. 'Why the casino, though?'

Liam shrugged. 'Donovan has a contact in the security department. We knew we could call it all off at any time. Good idea not giving them your licence, though. It's best if people don't have documents with your picture on them floating around.'

'It felt like the right thing to do. I didn't plan anything. I knew, without knowing I knew, where the exit was and which door to take. If that makes any sense.' I rambled, elated at having passed the test.

Liam squeezed my shoulder. 'You've done well, given the short time we've been working together.'

'But you knew how this would all pan out, anyway,' I said, sitting back, feeling the adrenaline start to seep away.

'Your snap decisions do sometimes mess with my clairvoyance. But it was a safe test, and I hoped you would have some fun.' He flashed me a playful smile.

'I did,' I replied, realising it was true – set up or not, I had enjoyed being in my intuitive zone. Blocking out all the background sensory noise had been easier when I thought the stakes were real and didn't have Donovan's aggressive expectations to deal with. I could imagine having a fun night out with Cecelia and Zenna when we were officially old enough, and enjoying it, not having to worry about the safety of three girls out in the city. I wondered if Liam's excitement had been about the casino outing, or more about seeing how I handled his test. He was so at home in his garden at Darkhaven.

I voiced my thought. 'Why the casino for the test? It doesn't seem like your scene.'

'It was convenient.' Then he looked aside. 'I've lived at Darkhaven most of my life. I don't really know what my scene is.'

It was the first time I'd noticed his wistfulness, but now I realised it had been there all along. We sank into silence for the rest of the drive back to Darkhaven, each of us deep in thought.

Zenna bailed on my offer to catch a movie, so I slept through all of Saturday morning and spent most of the weekend hanging out with Alex, practising using my intuition in the real world. I was cautious though, and it was hard to keep my mind focussed on managing sensory input and still get into my calm place. It didn't work on everything. My mess of homemade pizza dough on Saturday night proved that my cooking was not enhanced. It seemed like my strongest points were sensing people's intentions and knowing where to go, or when.

After the pizza disaster, Alex suggested Harrys. They were always busy on Saturdays, but I followed my intuition to wait fifteen minutes, and we arrived just as a couple left and our favourite table became available. Maybe it was coincidence. Or maybe I actually stood a chance of succeeding at the Taskforce and winning my deal.

Chapter 14

——

Apologies

Cecelia became more and more insistent about a study date. I'd stalled her so far with my maths tutor excuse, mortifying as it was, although it was not as humiliating as the fact that she wasn't surprised.

'Well, good. I'm glad you're taking this seriously now,' she said as we spent a Monday lunchtime in the library. I had to make it up to her for skipping our old after-school routine, but despite being behind on homework and English reading, I wasn't really studying. It was nice to just have half an hour to chill out.

'What are you, my mother?' I teased, lowering the library's copy of *A Tale of Two Cities* and flicking the pages of her human biology book over to annoy her. She snapped a ruler in between the pages, too late to save her place. Zenna pored listlessly over some maths. Even in a non-ATAR program, there was no escape from maths. But she seemed to be doing better now, and Alex had not expressed any further concerns.

'Can we go outside?' she asked, staring out the window. 'The sun's out.'

'It is nice,' I agreed, following her gaze to a free bench gleaming in the wintry sunlight. I'd spent most of the last week indoors, even for Liam's sessions, because of the rain.

'For July, at least,' Zenna said, with a soft sigh.

Cecelia slammed her pencil onto the desk to pick up an eraser. 'It's not July, it's August!' she snapped.

Zenna cringed. 'All right, keep your freckles on. It's only the first of August.'

Cecelia scribbled furiously in the margin of her notes page. 'First of August! It's six weeks until mock exams, and some of us need to study! I guess it's okay for those who don't have to work because they aren't even doing exams.' She got all of this out without even looking up, pen still scratching over her page. The minuscule sound wasn't enough to fill the silence that expanded over the table.

Zenna stuffed her working-out pages into her book and slammed it shut. 'Fine. I guess it's okay for those who think they're better than everyone else just because they're going for an ATAR of a hundred-and-fucking-one.' She stood up stiffly, pushed her chair in and turned to leave. I stared at the first page of *A Tale of Two Cities*. Age of foolishness indeed.

'You can't get a hundred and one, it's 99.95,' Cecelia said. I wilted inside. I knew she hadn't meant to sound condescending, but it was like she couldn't help herself. Zenna turned around and swiped Cecelia's pencil case onto the floor, its contents spilling across the carpet.

'I hope you fucking fail,' Zenna snarled. She started out tough, but her voice cracked at the end. She spun around and ran out of the library, shouldering past the elderly librarian, who called pointlessly after her.

I bent down and collected Cecelia's pencil case, stuffing the stationery back in. I straightened to find her still writing, but with tears running down her face. A fat drop fell onto the paper and smudged the ink.

'Dammit!'

'Let's pack up, Ceel.' I placed a hand on her arm.

She jerked away. 'No! I need to get this chapter revision finished.'

'We can do it later. I'll come over . . .' I began, unsure how I could possibly finish that sentence. Alex had claimed me for this afternoon; we were going to look at cars.

Cecelia did it for me. 'When, Gabby? When was the last time you were free to come over?'

'I'm sorry! It's just Dad has me doing these tutoring sessions, and –'

'And what? It would be inappropriate for me to sit at the same table? Something is going on, because you're not at the library most days! And you don't even care about university.' She was crying openly now, cheeks shining with tears. But she kept writing.

I sat back. 'I'll make it up to you, I promise.' My voice was small. 'What can I do?'

Cecelia swiped at her face with her jumper sleeve and picked up a different coloured pen.

'Just go. I'm going to keep working.'

'Cecelia, I –'

'I don't want to hear it. Please go.'

I wandered out of the library, completely forgetting to check out Dickens until the machine blared at me and the librarian tottered out, roast-irresponsible-students mode engaged. I apologised vaguely and handed the book back to her, definitely not in the mood to read it now. It wasn't until I was sitting in my last class – a double period of Economics, a subject I'd long ago lost interest in – that I realised what had happened. I'd walked right through an alarm ringing in my ears and not freaked out. I grinned to myself and was caught completely unawares when Mr Digby-Williscroft asked me a question, then requested that I share my personal joke when I couldn't tell him what the day's class was even about.

So much for intuition.

I was still feeling buoyed by my success over the alarm the next afternoon. Donovan was less thrilled about my breakthrough.

'So whenever you've had a fight with a friend, you'll be good for the next hour?' She seemed, if possible, even crabbier than usual.

I was undaunted, even having the audacity to shrug. 'Maybe two,' I joked. Donovan glared at me. I'd always thought I had a pretty strong glare, but I was no match for her.

She picked up her jacket. 'We're going out today.'

Better than staying in her office all afternoon. 'Where?'

'You'll see.'

Donovan drove the same way she walked around: maniacally, and with no consideration for the things or people around her. I clung to the armrest, wishing I could take more time to appreciate her Nissan GT-R, and grateful I'd never had to ride on the back of her motorcycle.

We pulled up in a lonely little car park next to a tall mesh fence. At the end of the car park was a steel gate and a little gatehouse. A truck rumbled towards it. I got out of the car and jumped as a loud crash echoed around my ears.

'What is this place?'

'A quarry.' Donovan rummaged around in the boot and pulled out a shoebox. 'You'll be a seven, right?' She ripped open the box and tossed a pair of sneakers to me. They still had scrunched paper packing in the toes. I had never replaced the pair that got destroyed in the lightning strike. I gave her a disgruntled look.

'You can't run in those.' She flapped a hand at my heeled boots.

'We're running?'

'Yes.'

'Do I have to?'

'"Do I have to?"' she mimicked.

I grimaced at the childish tone – and more so at the fact that it was accurate.

'Yes,' she said. 'Genetic advancement isn't free licence to be a sloth. If you want the perks, you have to work at it. Put them on.' She started stretching while I fiddled with the laces.

'And hurry up. We haven't got all day.'

I'd barely got my feet in them when she took off, loping effortlessly on her long legs. Within seconds, I was puffing and panting as I shuffled along behind her. We ran around the perimeter of the quarry, which would have been bad enough without heavy machinery roaring and clattering. The bare stone faces were perfect surfaces for sound to echo and amplify, bouncing around in my skull like it too was a stone quarry. I might have tried to strangle the blonde woman striding along in front of me, if I could have caught up.

At what I hoped was past the halfway mark – the GT-R was well out of sight, and it felt like we'd been running for hours, even the machinery sounds had faded to nothing – Donovan looked at her watch and stopped. I pulled up several metres away and leaned against the wire fence, trying to not fall over in the dirt.

BOOM.

I gasped out the tiny breath of air I'd caught as I crumpled to the ground. It was like the Shack on the first day. I couldn't breathe, I couldn't think, and within moments, I couldn't see either as everything around me dissolved into crushing blackness. More explosions fired from the quarry. I curled into a ball, unsure if I was screaming or if that was just more noise in my head.

Something slapped me across the face. The stinging broke through the blackness, and I opened my eyes to find Donovan standing over me, barely breaking a sweat, with a vicious gleam in her eyes.

'How's that breakthrough going now?' Her voice was laced with malice. I wondered if it would be better or worse for me if I slapped her back. I couldn't have summoned the strength anyway. She stepped away.

'What was that?' I asked. I hated the weakness in my voice. I hated that Donovan had put it there.

'Drilling and blasting.'

'Nobody would be ready for that.'

Donovan's face was hard. 'Get up.'

'Why do you want me to fail?' I'd meant the question to be rhetoric and under my breath, but it came out somewhat louder than that, and whiny. Donovan heard. I cringed inwardly.

She didn't even look at me. 'I don't.' Without any further elaboration, she took off again, jogging easily along the fence line. Since the alternative was lying out in the bush until someone or something found me, probably shattered into a million mental pieces by more blasting, I clambered to my wobbly feet and stumbled after her.

I spent three-quarters of the drive back to West Beach imagining all the sharp, witty things I might say to Donovan's face if I could somehow turn my wrath into actual courage. Stephen cast me worried glances but said nothing. I sighed and pushed the thoughts out of my head. It would all be so much easier to handle if I could talk about it with Cecelia. Or, at this point, if we were talking at all. I needed time to patch things up with her. I twisted to face Stephen. 'Can I have tomorrow off?'

He frowned.

'Please? She's getting suspicious and she knows I haven't been at the library.' I gave him a pleading look, sensing that it would work on him.

'Okay, one afternoon. Only because Liam says you're doing well.' Stephen finished with a hint of pride in his voice.

I grinned. 'I knew you'd say yes.'

'I see. Do you know what my condition is?'

Oh no. 'Not Saturday.'

'Yes, Saturday. But it's not with Liam. It's with me. If you want to make it through the Taskforce expedition, we still have more to do.'

I was curious, but Alex was waiting on the other side of the school. I'd find out on Saturday.

After school on Wednesday, I sent Cecelia a message suggesting that she meet me in the library. We hadn't spoken since the fight on Monday. She came to class right as the bell rang, sat at the front of the room without a glance in my direction and left as soon as we were dismissed. Bereft, I dragged myself through lessons in a miserable haze and spent lunchtimes sulking in the media lab with Zenna, who didn't want to hear about Cecelia and was barely talking to me herself.

Cecelia replied. *Don't you have a tutoring session?*

I sighed and messaged back. *I cancelled it. You're more important.*

Nothing.

I went to the library anyway, figuring she might be there and if not I could actually use the time to catch up on school work. With my improved memory, I was having no trouble maintaining pass grades in my homework without studying, but I knew I should lift my game if I wanted a shot at university.

Apparently every Year 12 had the same idea, because there were no free tables in the common area. Nor was there any sign of Cecelia. I circled around, surreptitiously checking to see if anyone had started packing up their books, and saw a familiar head of scruffy, black hair. He sat alone at a corner table, reading, tapping his fingers on the table to some imagined beat. I dumped my backpack into the chair next to him.

'Hello, Gabby,' he said, flashing a dazzling smile. He was wearing his sunglasses again. My twin reflections scowled back at me.

'Keraun,' I said, sitting opposite him and pulling books out of my bag. 'What are you doing here?'

His cheeky grin didn't slip. 'What are *you* doing here?'

'This is my school. I study here.' I maintained a dignified poise and flipped my Mathematics Applications book open to my homework bookmark – Chapter 7. The class was up to 22. Whoops.

He gazed at me intently. 'I hoped I might run into you. Your friend was here earlier.'

'How do you know my friends? Actually, don't bother, I don't want to know about spooky god things.' Not true, but I was in a churlish mood.

'It's not spooky. This was the only table not full, so I asked to share it. I glanced at the person's phone and saw the messages with your name at the top.'

He sounded earnest. I stopped myself from rolling my eyes. 'How is that not spooky?'

'Anybody could have read them. The phone was just sitting there.'

'Fine, not spooky. Creepy.'

He cast his hidden gaze down. 'Yeah, I guess. Sorry.'

'Don't apologise to me. It's Cecelia's privacy you've invaded.' I went back to my homework, trying to find a fresh piece of paper.

'She typed a reply before deleting it. Do you want to know what it said?'

I looked up. He was being serious. 'She'll tell me when she's ready.'

'You are an admirably patient person. She's lucky to have you for a friend.'

I shrugged. 'I'm lucky to have her. She's under a lot of pressure at the moment, but we'll be okay.'

'It's nice. Your friendship.'

I closed my maths book with a snap. Clearly, I wasn't going to get any work done.

He grinned, victorious. 'Shall we get out of here?'

I smiled in spite of my annoyance. Maths could wait. 'Sure.'

We wandered out of the library and into the mild winter sun. I fell into step beside Keraun as he headed for the car park. Once we were away from people, he took off his sunglasses. It was nice to feel the sun on my face; as much as I hated the relentless heat of summer, I still enjoyed the warmth. Spring was my favourite season. It suddenly occurred to me that the weather today may not have been an accident. I eyed Keraun suspiciously. He met my gaze and arched an eyebrow. 'What?'

I looked away, feeling silly. 'Nothing.'

'Tell me.'

'What, you can't just pluck it straight out of my head? Some god you are.'

He chuckled. 'I'm the god of weather. I'm not an all-seeing, all-hearing, omnipresent being.'

'I thought it was god of lightning.'

'Lightning sounds cooler, right?' He gave me a cocky grin. 'Technically, god of weather. But I'm pretty new to the team, and most of it was set up before I got here. I tweaked the systems a bit so it pretty much does its own thing. I kept the lightning though, 'cause that's the fun part.'

He made some corny shooting motions with his hands, and I half-expected sparks to emanate from his fingers. Before he could request another admission of my foolish thoughts, I asked my own question. 'These systems, do they create lightning themselves?'

'Yeah. I just add my own when I feel like it.'

We arrived at his car, today a bulbous, two-door thing that had to be from at least the 1970s.

I smirked. 'So you're basically the horse and cart of meteorology. As in, totally obsolete. Like this car.'

He slid into the driver's seat, pouting. 'I thought old cars were cool.'

'Outdated,' I continued as I climbed into the passenger's side and fiddled with the analogue radio. It didn't work. 'Defunct.'

'Okay, okay, I got it the first time.'

Something occurred to me. I stopped playing with the radio.

He sensed my tension. 'What is it?'

I stared at the air vents – just a fan, no chance of climate control – wondering how to ask.

He tapped his fingers on the steering wheel as he navigated out of the busy car park, shooting me an imploring glance. 'Please?'

'How often does lightning happen without your direct control?'

'I have taken the blame for a few errant bolts. In a thunderstorm, it's usually a bit of both. Why?'

'Did . . . did you . . . when I was . . .'

A laugh burst out of him. My face burned.

'Did I deliberately strike you? It's okay to ask.'

Instead of turning onto the road that wound along the beach, he pulled over onto a grassy verge next to a park, his face suddenly serious.

'No, I didn't strike you. Well, not directly. But I was being foolish, and what was supposed to be some innocent intra-cloud activity high in the storm cloud met with a negative streamer coming from you. I didn't mean for it to happen, but it was my fault. So I followed you, after. I wasn't sure what any of the people pursuing you were going to do, but I was ready to get you out if it became apparent that you were in danger. Although that's difficult with moving vehicles, even for me, so I wasn't much help.' He paused to take a breath. 'Since then, I've been trying to find an excuse to talk to you. To apologise.'

My stomach did a strange sort of sliding down into my boots, landing in a puddle of disappointment. I had kind of hoped – without even realising – that he just wanted to hang out, for no reason. I mentally slapped myself and straightened my shoulders. That line of thinking was only going to lead to trouble. I watched a couple of kids playing on the swings in the park.

'Well ...' I began, looking across to him, but I was stopped by his eyes. They were a bright, burning yellow, the colour pervading his entire eyeball and blurring out his eyelashes with the glow.

'Gabrielle Adele Whitehall, I'm deeply sorry for hurting you, and causing you all this trouble.'

I couldn't remember how to think. His eyes slowly faded back to their light brown, human form.

'That's a very formal apology,' I whispered. His face was just a foot away from mine.

'A god can only do it one way, and only when we mean it.' His voice was soft. I straightened and stared out the window again. The kids had disappeared.

'Thank you. Your eyes ... how do they do that?'

'Do what?'

'*Glow.*'

He shrugged. 'Just a god thing, I guess. Subtle magic.'

I wanted to turn him upside down and shake him until all the answers to everything fell out, but I tamped down the urge to pelt him with questions. 'Can we do something?'

'What do you have in mind?'

'Well, I can't go home yet, Alex thinks I'm studying.'

'Oh, right.' There was a hint of disappointment in his voice. Perhaps I imagined it. He pulled back onto the road and drove us to the coast, parking at a quiet stretch of beach. Although the sun was out, a biting wind was coming off the ocean and hitting me through Keraun's open window. The sea was a deep, bluish grey with little white caps dotted over it. Keraun reached for his door handle. 'Coming?'

'Out there? You must be joking. There will be sand blowing about everywhere.'

His eyes flashed yellow again. 'Come and see.'

The wind had stopped. It was still cold, but I had my school jacket on and without the breeze, I was quite cosy.

'How does anyone predict the weather with you doing things like that?' I asked as I hopped onto the raised footpath. He jumped up next to me, his cheeky grin lighting up his face even more than his gilded eyes. I tore my gaze away, breathing in the familiar salty air as we walked.

'I don't do it very often. But there are some disappointed windsurfers further up the beach.'

'Dad would be mad,' I said without thinking. A disconcerting mixture of anger and pity curled around my heart. I hadn't forgiven him, but I missed him. 'How does it work?' I asked. 'Your weather control thing?'

'What do you mean?'

'Well, if you pretty much let it do its own thing, how do you know? If there's a thunderstorm or something?'

'I'm aware.'

'You might need to explain that.'

He huffed, but his eyes danced. 'It's difficult, explaining to someone without it. I'm aware of all the world's weather, all the time. I can tune in and out for more specific details. And I can still make it do what I want, like an override, although I can't do much without upsetting all the programs. A slight wind change is easy enough. Stopping a flood or reversing years of drought – things like that don't work.' A hint of regret crept into his voice.

'So you just go around striking things with lightning.'

He grinned. 'Yeah. It's really the only thing I can go nuts with, without ruining the weather systems. I have to keep my hand in it somehow.'

'By smiting people.' I meant it as a joke, but his face crumpled in horror. 'Sorry!' I said quickly. 'I didn't mean it like that.'

He chuckled darkly. 'I don't kill people. You humans have more control than you know. You decided way back that a lightning strike could be deadly. I don't control that. Although, neither do you now, because it's been happening like that for so long that it's sort of what happens.'

'"Sort of what happens?" An all-powerful god and all you can come up with is "sort of what happens"?'

He laughed again. 'I never said I was all powerful. It's like part of the fabric now. The fabric of humanness.'

I scoffed. 'That's actually worse. But what you're saying is . . . humans subconsciously decide how they work with the world, and how things affect them, and then reinforce those ideas into patterns that become belief, and then independent truth?'

He frowned. 'That's a way better way to say it. Why couldn't I say that?'

I elbowed him playfully. 'Well, you can't help it if you're not a genetically enhanced human with advancing intuition.'

He elbowed me back. 'That's where it all starts.'

'Where what starts?' I felt like I'd never run out of questions.

'Magic. Intuition is key to subtle magic. That's the magic that creates worlds. We can interact with it, but there's a greater force than us at work. Energetic magic is different, that's a memory thing that you can study, more tangible. It's a bit strange that you don't have it, actually.'

A breeze lifted my hair, but Keraun's eyes hadn't changed. Maybe it was just his weather systems reasserting themselves.

He gazed out over the horizon. 'We should turn back. I can't keep the wind down all afternoon.'

We turned around and walked in companionable silence while I let the idea of different types of magic sink into my brain. There wasn't much traffic, and I enjoyed the relative quiet, listening to the complex tumbling of sea water onto the sand below.

'You should call your friend tonight.' Keraun broke into my peaceful zone as we climbed into the godawful car.

'Cecelia?'

He nodded.

I stared across the tumultuous, wind-tossed water as we drove away. 'What did she think of you?'

'She hasn't met me.'

'But you said you were reading her text – oh. You were invisible, or whatever it is gods do.'

He chuckled. 'I asked if I could sit with her, and she moved a stack of books aside without taking her eyes off her reading. She didn't look at me once.'

'That sounds like Cecelia. So you're not an apparition?'

'We're all apparitions, in a way.'

'But are you, like, real?' I playfully punched his arm.

'Hey.' He punched me back lightly. 'I'm not a total fabrication. This is sort of my default form. It would take a lot of effort to change it.'

'But do you have an actual body?' My skin fizzed under my jacket where his fingers had brushed it.

'Yes and no. Not as you'd understand it, I suppose. But then, neither do you. Our bodies are just constructs that allow us to interact with the world. Which is also a construct.'

'Now you're talking about spirituality.'

'Isn't that all there is?' He flashed a smug grin. I gave up. My brain couldn't process any more otherworldly ideas today. Keraun pulled up outside Alex's apartment block.

'Well, thanks for the lift.'

'You're welcome.'

The silence stretched out. I was about to ask if I we could meet again, but somehow I suspected it was up to me. Probably a choice better made with a level head, after a good night's sleep. I got out of the car.

A hint of a smile played over his lips. Sometimes it seemed like he could read minds, despite what he said. Yet if he could do that, he would have plucked out the big question that I wanted to ask but felt too stupid to. 'See you then,' I said.

'See you.' He drove away in a cloud of black smoke.

'Hello!' I called as I chucked my school bag down next to the kitchen counter.

Alex appeared from the hallway. 'Gabby. I was just about to come and pick you up.'

'Sorry, I meant to send you a text. Nancy dropped me home.' I found a fresh carton of milk in the fridge and went hunting in the pantry for Milo. It was easy to find among the neatly stacked boxes of raw nuts and goji berries. I snuck a teaspoonful of it before I emerged from the pantry.

'Good study session?'

'Mmhmm,' I replied through the dry Milo. I swallowed. 'Yeah, pretty good.'

'You must be getting on top of things, with all this extra work.' Alex padded over to the fridge in his socks and pulled out a kombucha.

I nodded, trying to conceal the guilt bubbling up. 'I think so.' Even with an enhanced memory, I wasn't going to pass if I didn't read my textbooks in the first place, and I wasn't sure how to explain the very average results I was going to get after all this supposed study. Exam nerves, perhaps. Or I could see if Keraun would bribe somebody. If I saw him again. 'I still feel like it won't be enough.'

Alex pulled me into a hug. 'You'll be great.'

I hugged him back. 'Thanks, Alex.'

'I was thinking pumpkin soup for dinner.'

'Sounds good.'

After dinner, complemented by a pretty good organic spelt sourdough, I stole away to my room, shut the door and called Cecelia. She answered after several rings.

'Hey, Gabby. What's up?'

'Just ringing to see how you're going. And to say I'm sorry.'

'Oh my god, I'm sorry too. I should never have snapped at you like that. It wasn't fair.'

Waves of relief washed over me. 'Yeah, well, you're under a lot of pressure. I shouldn't have pressed the point. I mean, I don't really remember what it was, but I'm sorry just the same.' It was always like this. We'd fight, but we always made up.

Cecelia giggled on the other end of the phone. 'Yeah, I'm not sure either. Something about . . . oh, I don't even know.' She was quiet for a moment. Years of companionship had taught me when to give Cecelia room to find the words she wanted; I was the one who blurted out whatever was on my mind.

'Have you spoken to Zenna?' she asked.

'No. I've been kinda busy.'

'Don't think I've forgotten that you're hiding something from me. Wait. Is it a boy?'

My jaw dropped in indignation. 'Definitely not!'

'Well, something has gotten to you. I'll give you until after exams, and then you're coming clean, okay?'

'I don't know, Ceel. That sounds like I have to make a major admission.' I tried to keep my tone light.

'Best friends since forever, remember? We're better when we share our secrets.'

'I know.' I sighed. 'I wish I could tell you.'

Her intake of breath hissed though the phone. 'So there is something! You have to tell me, Gabby.'

'Not now. After exams,' I said, gritting my teeth as I promised something I couldn't give.

'I'll hold you to that, you know.'

Oh, I knew. I pleaded exhaustion and got off the phone before I could make any more impossible promises. I brushed my teeth, changed into my pineapple-print pyjamas and crawled into bed, but I couldn't sleep. Something was nagging at me. After an hour of fruitless puzzling, I drifted off.

I jolted awake at two a.m. The nagging thought was Keraun. He'd made it sound like striking me had been an accident, like I'd just been in the wrong place at the wrong time, and his interest in me had arisen from that. But I'd met him before my Event. He'd been in Mr Cantwell's office earlier in the day.

It was a long time before I could get back to sleep.

CHAPTER **15**

—

Rally

I didn't have to worry about Cecelia hassling me any more. Exams loomed like a thunderhead on the horizon, and she became frantic. She spent every lunchtime in the library, leaving me in an awkward position: go and study with her, which I sorely needed to do, or hang out with Zenna, which, while less daunting than Cecelia chanting muscle attachments or reciting laws of physics at my side, was tense for different reasons. Neither option felt right while I was neglecting the other. Most of the time I opted for the study-in-the-library approach, since if I didn't start catching up it wouldn't so much be a matter of explaining to everyone why I'd not been brilliant despite all my apparent work, but rather of explaining how I'd managed to fail Year 12, period. I begged Zenna to come and study with us, but she was not as quick to forgive as Cecelia.

She can stew in her own bitchiness. And you haven't said sorry either.

I didn't answer. She hadn't pressed me for an apology before Cecelia and I made up.

'Really, I don't mind,' Cecelia said as she copied chemistry notes onto flashcards, 'go and hang out with Zenna. I've got plenty to do.'

'I need to study too,' I replied, doodling on my notebook.

Cecelia eyed my progress darkly. 'I think you'll be better off getting some fresh air. And not distracting me.'

I flipped my Human Biology book open. There wasn't anywhere else to go. I enjoyed my own company just fine, but the barbed glances that sitting on the lawn or in the cafeteria alone attracted did ruin the solitude.

'Can we do something this weekend?' I asked, knowing the answer, but wanting to make a point. Cecelia didn't even pause. She just shook her head and carried on working.

'I just think we're putting a lot of work in, we deserve a bit of a break. Need one, even.'

She didn't answer. I stared, unseeing, at a diagram of muscle cells, then turned to my phone. I typed a text to Keraun – *Want to hang on Saturday?* – and paused, tapping my pencil on the desk.

Cecelia's bony hand clamped down over mine.

'Gabby, I love you, but if you're not going to work, please find somewhere else to be.'

I sighed and packed up my stuff.

Stephen called while I was still in bed on Saturday morning. I'd forgotten all about the make-up session. I sent Keraun a profuse apology and raced to Lartte, a busy cafe a block from Alex's. I hadn't been to a cafe like this since the car accident at the Shack. The venue bustled with chatter and clinking cutlery. My nerves felt like they had petrol poured over them and a match might be thrown at any moment. I jumped as someone scraped a chair across the floor.

'What,' Stephen asked, 'are the chances of your uncle spotting us here?'

I shrugged, trying to look relaxed. 'I don't know, I'm not clairvoyant.'

'I'm not asking for a prediction, just your hunch.'

I considered. 'Not high, but possible. He sometimes comes here for lunch.'

Stephen shook his head. 'No reasoning. Just the feeling.'

I got out of my head and rummaged around in my gut. 'Dodgy. The feeling is dodgy. But you already know that.'

Stephen chuckled. I wondered why he was in such a good mood. A waitress came up and handed him two takeaway cups. He passed me a hot chocolate as we headed out the door. It was sunny, but with a chilly breeze, and I was grateful for the solid warmth between my hands, calming me. 'Thanks. What are we doing?'

'Going for a drive.'

I felt my muscles ease slightly. The car was safe.

'How is your driver training going?' he asked as we buckled seatbelts.

'Not as well as I'd like. I don't have a lot of time.' I didn't mean it as a complaint. It was just true. I didn't want to reschedule my test, but Darkhaven took priority. School was a distant second. I rarely got to a third item. Alex and I had not settled on a car – I wanted an orange 86, but Alex thought a Golf was an excellent, reliable choice. Of course he held the trump card: access to Dad's bank account.

Stephen smiled broadly. 'I figured as much. I thought today we might do something about it.'

My nerves switched from worried agitation to excited delight. I hadn't had a driving lesson since before the invasion of the TISC handbooks.

Stephen drove us out to an old gravel pit where a white W-RX was parked, and he tossed me the keys. Too late, I reached out to catch them and missed. With a prolonged rattle, they slipped down between my seat and the console. Stephen snickered as I wound my hand down to fish them out. 'We have some work to do on your reflexes. Which is partly why we're here.'

I straightened up, keys in hand. We switched to the Rex, and Stephen started me with simple things: changing gears, braking, reversing. When he was convinced that I wasn't a total beginner, he had me demonstrate a hill start and reverse park into a space that he marked out with some rocks. Both manoeuvres were flawless.

Not convinced that I hadn't fluked it, or maybe because I celebrated with an outburst of 'Nailed it!', he had me do it all again, and I stuffed up the hill start the second time. We spent the rest of the morning daring each other to execute perfect hill starts on increasingly steep inclines until I tried to drive up a hill that even the all-wheel-drive rally car simply couldn't manage.

'I think you'll pass,' Stephen said, laughing as we rolled down the slope to a halt. 'But we're not done yet.'

He unbuckled his seatbelt, got out, and leaned back in the window. 'Drive out of the pit and follow the road south-east.' He pointed.

My gaze followed his hand across the gravel to a dirt track disappearing into the bush. 'Where am I going?'

'You'll know when you get to the end, there's a flag. Drive as fast as you can, and don't stop until you get there. No matter what happens. Got it?'

'Drive to the flag.'

'No matter what happens. As fast as you can.'

He turned and climbed back into the Corolla, driving off the way we'd come in. I grumbled to myself as I put the Rex into gear and steered towards the track at the end of the pit. Whatever this was, I would have preferred to have known something about it. If it was some vague test of intuition, I had nothing.

I crawled onto the road in first gear, trundling along cautiously, nerves bristling. Nothing happened. Maybe it was just a driving exercise. I shifted up to second, about to accelerate, when a thud on the roof startled me. I slammed on the brakes. The car stopped almost instantly and my body whipped forward as a large black-and-white shape rolled over the bonnet and onto the ground. Keraun sprang to his feet, grinning, and hurried around to the passenger seat.

Irritation battled with an eager flutter in my chest. 'What are you doing here?'

'You wanted to hang out.'

'Until I said I was busy.'

He pulled the door closed and wound down the window. He wasn't wearing his sunglasses today, and his eyes were, for now, a normal human brown. 'You want me here for this. I've seen the course, I can be your navigator.'

I folded my arms. 'What if I was meeting a boyfriend?'

Horror flashed over his face, followed by a faint yellow glow about his eyes. 'Oh. Um. Sorry.' Without looking at me, he leapt out of the car and shut the door. 'Sorry,' he said again through the window. His face creased in puzzlement as I cracked up laughing. 'What's so funny?'

'You're in luck.' I tried – and failed – to straighten my face. 'The guy didn't show.'

He stood awkwardly, fidgeting with the chain at his neck, then shoving his hands in his pockets and staring at the ground.

'Get in,' I said. I revved the engine a little.

'But what about ...'

'I was messing with you. Are you going to be my navigator, or what?'

He shuffled for a moment, then opened the door and climbed back in.

'How did you get here?' I asked as he adjusted his seat, sliding it back. His eyes still burned with what I suspected was embarrassment. Serve his presumptuous arse right. 'We're in the middle of nowhere.'

'Magic,' he muttered. My stomach gave a little leap –

BANG. I jumped so high I actually hit my head on the roof of the car. Without another thought, I rammed the car into a random gear and floored it. The car jerked along until the revs were high enough for second, then sped off with an increasing whine. In the rear-view mirror, a cloud of dust rose from what must have been some kind of explosion.

'Change gear!' Keraun called over the keening engine, breaking through the mask of panic filling my brain. Donovan had given me a complex about explosive noises.

'What?' I glanced at the tacho. 'Oh!' I quickly changed up to third, then fourth and fifth as I kept accelerating. Another explosion shattered the dirt behind us. I found a groove though, and even a moment to be a bit pleased with myself as I deftly swung around a corner, then another one. It didn't last. The next bend kept curving around, until the back end of the car flicked out to the side. Without thinking, I went to brake, lifting off the accelerator.

'No brakes!' Keraun reached across to put a firm hand on my leg, stopping my movement. I clutched at the steering wheel, trying desperately to hold the car straight. The car slowed enough for me to get it under control just as another explosion fired. I took a deep, shuddering breath, speeding along the now straight road. I also became aware of Keraun's hand, a warm pressure on my thigh. 'Uh,' I began.

'Oh.' He snatched it back to rest casually on his own leg. 'Sorry.'

I came around another corner, slightly slower and in better shape than last time, to see a billow of smoke obscuring the road. It was too late to stop, and besides, I had a sense that the explosions behind us weren't finished. Smoke filled the air. My eyes adjusted rapidly to the diminished light, but I felt trapped by the lack of visibility, somehow even more acutely now that my vision was supposed to be sharper. The explosion earlier had left me feeling unsettled and out of touch with my intuition. I still struggled to push down the rising panic.

'On your left,' Keraun whispered. He seemed to know that if he yelled, I would lose my grip on self-control.

I glanced to my left just in time, swerving to avoid an object looming out of the smoke. Then another on the right. I wasn't quick enough. I clipped it with the corner of the car, flinging it away with a solid thud. I just missed a third on the left, but this one I could see in the smoke, and I reeled with horror. It was the shape of a person, standing on the edge of the road.

'Breathe,' Keraun said.

'They're people! I hit one!' Another explosion crashed behind us. I should go back. I couldn't go back.

'Think about it,' Keraun said. I took another deep breath, finding the calm intuitive place that Liam had taught me to cultivate. It was tiny, almost impossible to reach, but things came into focus. Stephen had set this up. It wasn't real.

'This is an exercise,' I said. 'They're mannequins. But what are the explosions?'

'Mostly smoke and noise. Stephen's not really tearing up the forest.'

I gritted my teeth and kept going. I didn't want to admit it, but Keraun's presence was calming, and I kept my hold on my intuition.

'Don't think so much. Just drive,' Keraun suggested. I relaxed my vice grip on the wheel and let my chest soften so I could breathe without forcing it through an iron cage. Driving and dodging the mannequins became a little easier. The smoke cleared, and I was only half-surprised when Stephen's Corolla flew into view on my left. It crept up on me, threatening to push me off the road. I accelerated and gave in to my reflexes. I still had some dodgy moments on the corners, but it was better. After I nailed a particularly gruelling bend, I found myself beaming.

'Yes!' Keraun whooped. I laughed with him, but it was short-lived. I ran over a branch on the road, shooting sideways as I jerked – too late – at the steering wheel. I wasn't prepared for the immediate sharp left. I went in too fast and too close, and I knew before it happened that I couldn't recover it. The car spun around, narrowly missing a tree, and stalled to a halt facing the way I had come. Stephen pulled up in a cloud of dust in the Corolla and waved at me to continue. I started the engine, did an awkward three-and-a-half-point-turn, and drove on, picking up speed as Stephen harried me, tailgating and zipping from side to side behind me. He blared his horn.

'I think that's an indication that you're failing the time trial,' Keraun said.

I grunted, putting my foot down. The road was starting to get all twisty again. I scrabbled at the steering wheel, trying to balance intuitive reflex and careful driving. There was a roar of an engine, and a motocross bike flew out of the trees. The figure on it was clad entirely in tight black leathers and a black, dark-tinted helmet, but I could guess who it was.

I lost my calm place.

Donovan rode right up beside me, so close she could have reached out and touched me. She was riding with one hand. In the other hand was a gun. She fired. I ducked, swerving across the road. Cracks splintered through the driver side window, but it stayed in place.

'Faster!' Keraun yelled. For the first time, I heard a hint of fear in his voice.

I flattened the pedal. Donovan dropped back, still shooting at me. I hit a deep pothole in the road. The window shattered out of the door, bits of glass falling into my lap. My mind fogged over, sinking into panic, and I flailed at the steering wheel as it slipped under my sweating palms. Keraun reached across and grasped the wheel, but I couldn't drive any faster. A chequered racing flag up fluttered up ahead – the finish line! I knew if I could get there, my pursuers would stop. Keraun held the wheel and I gunned it for the flag. Donovan drew alongside me and fired again.

The shot punched me in the side, throwing me against my seat belt as the burning metal lanced my chest. Blood soaked my shirt and I gasped, trying to find air somewhere in the blooming pain. I couldn't. I sagged in the seat, blackness creeping into my vision, my hearing muffled. We swerved across the track. Keraun was almost in my lap now, pressing on my

side, muttering about getting the bullet out. Pain fired through
my body. The last thing I heard before I passed out was Keraun's voice, saying something pointless about everything being okay.

CHAPTER 16

Wattle Blossoms

'You weren't supposed to actually shoot her! What happened to blanks?' Stephen's furious voice jolted me back to consciousness.

'What happened to preparing her for the real world?' Donovan, cavalier. A wave of loathing surged through me, washing out the pain that suffused my chest. I opened my eyes to find myself lying on a blanket on the ground, Keraun hovering in the distance, a crease between his brown eyes. I took a tentative breath. Both lungs worked. The pain receded moment by moment as bone, muscle, fascia and skin realigned and knitted together. My jumper was wet with blood, and I shivered. Nearby, the finish-line flag flapped in the breeze, slapping against the pole with irregular clangs. I squinted into the blue sky, tried to talk and croaked like a frog.

Stephen appeared at my side, muttering about guns being the most unnecessary invention on the planet and peering at me, grey eyes full of concern. 'Are you okay? How do you feel?'

'Okay,' I said, pushing myself up to sit. Physically, at least, I was okay, except for a pounding ache in my ribs like a bruise to the bones. I took another breath, appreciating how good it felt to have both lungs back, even with pain lancing my side. I rose to my feet, swaying but managing to stay upright.

'She's fine. We needed to test her heal speed.' Donovan shoved my shoulder, pretending to be playful, but I could feel the aggression underneath.

'Leave me alone,' I growled. Well, it sounded growly in my head.

Donovan laughed as she buckled her helmet. 'See you Tuesday.' She mounted the monstrous motorbike, gunned the engine and vanished in a flagrant spray of dirt. I groaned and sagged against the side of the Rex. My adrenaline drained away, taking the last of my body heat and most of my anger with it, although I still seethed over Donovan and her awful test.

'How was it then?' I asked through chattering teeth. 'My heal speed.'

Stephen perched on the passenger seat with a laptop balanced on his knee. He looked up, then set the computer aside, shucked off his hoodie and handed it to me, goosebumps dimpling his forearms. 'You'll get faster.'

I took the jumper, but my shirt was still covered in blood, so I didn't put it on. 'I thought I was supposed to be, like, superhuman,' I grumped. 'All this is so hard.'

Stephen ran his fingers through his hair. 'Do you have any idea what we're asking you to do with these challenges? They're well beyond what I'd expect a new Eventer to manage, but we need to know where you're at for the Taskforce mission.'

'And I failed.' I glared at the flag, still twenty metres away from where I'd pulled up. My gaze caught Keraun's. He leaned against the Rex's bonnet, his posture stiff.

'It was a benchmark test. Your stats on here' – Stephen indicated software that had, unbeknown to me, been analysing my driving – 'are quite good. I'm sorry about your getting shot, that wasn't part of the plan.'

'Not your plan,' I muttered.

'Donovan has her own way. She means well. You,' he said, climbing out of the Rex and turning to Keraun, 'were also not part of the plan. What are you doing here?'

I bristled. Keraun showing up uninvited was my concern – if I wanted to be concerned. 'He's with me.'

Stephen eyed Keraun with suspicion, then flashed me a questioning glance. 'I thought we talked about this.'

I shrugged, stifling a gasp as my ribs screeched, but I wasn't about to explain my choice of friends. If that's what Keraun and I were.

'I'll go,' Keraun said, breaking the silence.

'Do you need a lift somewhere?' Stephen asked. My intuition flared – Stephen was partly genuine in his offer, because he was Stephen, but he was also fishing to find out how Keraun had got here in the first place.

A thin smile twisted Keraun's lips. 'Nah, I'm good, thanks. See you, Gabby.' Without waiting for a reply, or another loaded question from Stephen, he turned around and loped away, back down the gravel road. It looked like walking, but he covered ground awfully quickly.

Stephen turned his back so I could strip out of my cold, bloody clothes and don the hoodie. I simmered over Donovan and her rubbish training and now Stephen's open dislike of the one person who had helped me out. Stephen squeezed my arm as we climbed back into the Corolla. 'I'm just looking out for you,' he said. 'I don't know who Keraun is, but he's not your average teenager.'

I grunted. There was no arguing with that.

I expected to be driven home, but apparently we had one more thing to do today. Stephen took an unusual route, refusing to answer my questions until we pulled up on the side of the road in a leafy suburb. The building we were in front of looked like a house, except for a sign out the front: *Wattle View Hospice*. A wattle tree in full yellow bloom took up most of the front yard, and I could smell its perfume even with the car windows up.

'Don't worry, we're not going in.' Stephen reached into the back seat, produced three manila folders and handed them to me. They had little labels on the tabs: #1.1, #1.6 and #1.14.

'What are these?'

Stephen's eyes were filled with regret. 'The files that convinced Catherine to stay.'

'And now you think I'll be convinced too.' The paper was heavier in my hands than it should be. I didn't want to look.

Stephen sighed. 'No, it's just for your information. Full disclosure, remember?'

I opened the top one, #1.1. A photograph was paperclipped to the inside of the file. It was one of those horrendous school photographs, but this kid actually looked cute instead of awkward, which was all I'd ever managed. He was about eight years old, with brown hair gelled into spikes, a freckled nose and a broad, dimpled smile. The sky-blue school polo shirt complemented his light blue eyes.

'I bet he had to beat the girls away,' I commented to fill the silence. Stephen didn't reply. I felt silly for saying it.

The next page was some kind of transcript, but most of it was blacked out. At the top were handwritten initials: T.J. The rest of his name was redacted. So was his date of birth, parental details, address . . . the only other readable information was an army enlistment number. At the bottom of the page was an authorisation for 'Subject 1.1' and a signature dated for November 1999 – the year I was born. I turned the page over. The next was a memo, stating that Subject 1.1 was commencing with the application of the Praegressus program. More redaction. A series of reports followed, all dated between November 1999 and January 2000, noting things like "no adverse effects", "program retention successful", and other words that didn't make sense without the surrounding context. There wasn't a single name on any of these. The final page had no black lines. I read it, feeling even more the callousness of my comment.

FILE CLOSURE REPORT

Date: 20 July 2002

Reference: Subject #1.1 – T. Johnston, age 9

Subject Status: Deceased

Comments: T. J. experienced his Event on the morning of 19 July 2002. Donovan and May pursued unsuccessfully. He was not recovered.

The report was signed by Stephen May. I closed the file and toyed with the edges of it. Eventually, Stephen spoke.

'We'd lost three Eventers already, without even knowing their names. It was just too hard, trying to be everywhere whenever there was storm activity, so Donovan snuck into the Taskforce and managed to retrieve some files. As you can see, there's not much in them. We pieced together the data, and we found the boy. We were so close.' He paused, twisting his hands in his lap. 'The Taskforce got to him first. They killed him and made it look like a lightning-induced cardiac arrest.'

Sensing that the worst wasn't over, I opened the #1.6 file: Charlotte Sulley. Her Event report was dated 2010, age 19. There was no redacted Taskforce information, just pages of medical or psychological words I didn't understand. Donovan had signed this one.

'We found her first, but she was nineteen and she didn't want to leave her fiancé to stay with us. So we let her go.'

'What, no memory loss, or deactivation or whatever?'

Stephen shook his head. 'She was the first who had a choice, and, like you, we felt that was important. But Donovan and I, and Liam by then, we were supported through our transitions. We didn't have the pressures of the outside world to the same degree, and we didn't realise.'

I nodded as I understood. 'She couldn't cope with the sensory overload. So why didn't she come back?'

'She didn't want to. She said she could get by, and by then she was pretty angry – rightfully so, I know – and she didn't want anything to do with us. But it got worse. She had a genetic disorder prior to her Event that affected her hearing and vision, so when that corrected and everything enhanced, the transformation was too much. After that, we set the policy that we gave you. Stay and transform, or deactivate and forget. Peter's Event was a couple of years later. He chose to forget. We keep an eye on him. He's doing fine.'

Peter was Subject #1.14. His file didn't have a closure report, just a cursory log of his Event, and some basic medical information – where he worked, who his GP was, details of a stint in hospital for an allergic reaction to seafood.

I closed Peter's file. 'What happened to Charlotte?'

Stephen waved at the building we were parked next to. 'We tried the antiserum, but it was too late. The memory adjustment worked, so she has no memory of what happened to her, but we couldn't reverse the Praegressus. She lives in a home now.'

I gazed past the wattle tree. The hospice building had no windows, the better to keep sound and light out, I supposed. Charlotte would be sitting inside, her enhanced senses driving her mad, with no idea why.

Stephen's voice was pained. 'She spends most of her days under varying levels of sedation to cope with the overload and anxiety she doesn't understand.'

'For the rest of her life,' I said softly.

'The rest of her greatly extended life.'

The suburb was silent except for the warbling of a magpie outside, singing happily in the winter sunshine.

'How does the lightning strike so many of us? It seems unlikely.'

Stephen nodded. 'The lightning provides the energy for the genetic changes to happen all at once; without it, the program takes weeks of painful electrotherapy to fully activate. We thought the lightning trigger would be more efficient, and we developed a way to make all Praegressus subjects susceptible to lightning strikes. Luci was the wizard behind it, I'm still not entirely sure how it's possible, but a Praegressus candidate generates larger negative streamers around them in a charged field.'

I nodded, even though I wasn't entirely sure how that worked. 'Why? Why do all this?'

Stephen implored me with his eyes. 'I didn't use myself as a test subject because I wanted to be superhuman and live forever. I did it because there was no way I was risking it on other people without knowing the effects. Only after we developed a successful program did we even consider expanding, and Donovan and I thought we were using military personnel. Consenting adults. Jan set up the test group. By the time we found out who was in it, it was already done.'

'So my mother didn't volunteer me for the program?'

Stephen's eyes muddled with tears. 'I don't believe so.'

'But why do it at all? Genetic experimentation?'

'To save the human race. The brief we were given by the military initially was that they had intelligence of a new type of biowarfare, a virus that could genetically modify entire populations and make them infertile, or deformed, or worse. We needed a defence, one where human DNA could be made to express perfectly despite external influences. Of course all that turned out to be a lie and what they really wanted was a superior soldier. But I still believe it's important. This is our evolution. Humans that can survive on low-nutrient food or thrive in wider environmental conditions? Humans that aren't subject to genetic or degenerative diseases? And if it turns out we have magic ...' He took a deep breath and expelled it, fogging the windscreen in front of him. 'It's still how we're going to save the human race.'

I was silent all the way home.

CHAPTER 17

—

All the Secrets

Cecelia agreed to let me into her sacred study space on Sunday. By the time I rolled out of bed and got around to her house, it was after lunch. She greeted me with a cursory hug and hurried back to the enormous study table. It was meticulously laid out with towers of texts, five-subject notebooks with colour-coded labels and folders containing loose notes and class handouts all carefully sorted and filed. She had about a square foot of space in the middle for working. Her laptop had been evicted and was charging on an extra table, an addition since the last time I'd been here. Even by Cecelia's standards of organisation, this was a new level.

I sat, pulled a box of barbeque Shapes out of my bag and waved them in between her nose and her maths workbook. She shook her head. The silence stretched, filled only with my munching and her pencil scratching.

'Should we work on English?' I hadn't bothered bringing maths stuff; we took different classes.

Cecelia held up a hand, eyes still on the maths problem, working steadily until the end of the page when she finally arrived at her answer. 'Uh, sure.' She placed her pencil back in its neatly labelled caddy, glanced back down at the page and stiffened. 'Oh no.'

'What is it?'

'I've made a mistake.' She picked up an eraser and began working back through the lines of numbers. I put the Shapes away and dug out *A Tale of Two Cities* (I'd checked it out this time), along with a bag of crispy M&Ms. I propped the bag against a stack of books and began to read.

'Can you stop that?' Cecelia's voice was clipped.

I crushed and swallowed the M&M I'd just popped in my mouth. 'Stop what?'

'The noise. The crunching.'

'Oh. Sorry. Do you want some?'

'I wasn't asking for any, just for you to let me concentrate.'

I thought about slapping *Two Cities* down on the table, but I placed it gently.

'Cecelia, are you okay?'

She paused in the middle of erasing the offending line of numbers. For a moment it seemed like she was going to brush me off and continue, but she grappled with herself for a fraction of a second too long. We'd been best friends for years. I put my hand over hers, stopping the eraser that seemed to be possessed of a fault-correction will all its own.

'Are you okay?' I asked again. I knew it would push her over. Her eyes glistened with tears that she fought to contain.

'Not really,' she whispered. 'I'm so afraid that I'm going to fail.'

'You aren't going to fail. Look at this desk.'

She laughed wryly. 'Being organised isn't enough to get you over the line. And I have to get into medicine, Gabby.'

'There are other pathways than a perfect score, you know.'

'Yeah, but Dad did it. And Bryce.'

I sighed. Cecelia's older brother Bryce had been a model student, Dux of the school, had his name on all the UWA honour boards and was now the best intern at his hospital. 'Your dad will love you regardless.'

She laughed half-heartedly. 'Are you sure?'

I put on a thoughtful face and pretended to weigh the situation. 'Actually, it's not certain. He might decide you are unfit to be a doctor and make you renounce the family name.'

Cecelia giggled. 'He'll send me to study librarianology, or whatever it is. Something he knows I'll suck at.' Nancy had been a librarian before leaving work to raise her four children. She had tried to instil a love of books in all her family, but Robert said fiction was for dreamers and only Fiona, the youngest, was an avid reader. And me, of course. After Dad realised I had no interest in windsurfing or spending too long in the summer sun, he left me at Cecelia's where Nancy had delighted in having another bookworm in the house.

I laughed too. 'Maybe. But don't worry, he'll still pay for your tuition and expenses. Nancy will make sure of it.'

She sobered. 'I don't think I've laughed for weeks.'

I looked at her face, her pale skin gone sallow. Her eyes were dark and worried, with bags under them.

'Please look after yourself, Ceel. Eat an M&M.'

Cecelia rolled her eyes at my choice of sustenance, but she took one.

'I'm sorry I got snappy. I just feel like my nerves are on the brink all the time, and the slightest little thing just sends them over the edge, you know? I can't really explain it.'

She didn't need to. I knew exactly what she meant, even if it was for different reasons. I shivered at the thought of what, or who, waited for me at Darkhaven on Tuesday. Donovan.

Cecelia pushed her maths away and picked up her English file. 'Come on. Let's go over essay structure, and then I have to kick you out so I can work on chemistry.'

By the time Cecelia moved on to chemistry, I'd well and truly had enough of studying, but I wasn't ready to go home just yet. I declined Nancy's offer of a lift and wandered towards the bus stop, mindlessly flicking through socials on my phone. There was nothing interesting. I opened messages, went to Keraun's conversation and typed *Up for a walk?* Then I paused, finger hovering over the send button. I was way too young for a relationship, or so Dad said, and although I argued with him about it, that was just to be disagreeable. He wanted me to have a crush, a date for the ball, but nothing serious. And he was right. I did feel too young. What if it was like, the real thing, and I screwed it up with my stupid inability to make rational decisions? Stephen had warned me away from Keraun, despite not knowing what he was, but it was probably still good sense. Keraun was a who-knew-how-old god so accustomed to magic he barely noticed when he used it, and I was a teenage human girl who couldn't pick a university or decide what flavour milkshake she wanted and fell into a quivering heap whenever there was an unexpected loud noise nearby. But the more reasons I thought of to avoid him, the more I just wanted to press the stupid button.

So I did.

He was waiting for me at the end of the street, in his usual casually-coolly-untidy black-and-white outfit, an enormous dorky grin stretching from one ear to the other. He had his sunglasses on. I figured he had to wear them in public where people might see his eyes if they changed.

'That was quick. Almost like you knew I was going to message,' I remarked, not breaking my stride as I turned the corner. He fell into step beside me.

'I didn't know,' he replied with earnest honesty. 'But I was hoping.'

So whatever this was, it was mutual. Maybe. Or maybe he was just toying with me. I reminded myself that he was, literally, a god.

'Do you always wear the same thing?'

Concern creased his face as he looked down at his white t-shirt and black jeans. 'Is there something wrong with it?'

I laughed. He was genuinely puzzled. 'No, but us humans usually have a more varied wardrobe. And we get cold in winter.' I indicated my black bomber jacket that I'd zipped up against the nippy wind coming off the ocean.

Keraun didn't answer. I glanced across. He was now sporting a deep blue, woollen jumper. I pursed my lips. 'If I was cold, and asked to borrow that, would it work?'

'You are full of questions today.'

'Everyone has questions for God.'

He huffed. 'I'm not God. Just a god, kind of. Ask me about weather.'

I rolled my eyes. 'All of creation to talk about and you want to discuss the weather?'

'Sure. It's, like, my thing. See, I'm even picking up the lingo.'

I laughed. 'Until you said "lingo".' We reached the end of the road and came out at a beach car park.

'Which way?' Keraun asked.

I shrugged. 'Doesn't matter.'

We wandered south for a while before I couldn't wait any more. 'So would it work?'

'Would what work?'

'Your jumper.'

'Sure. It's real. I just didn't have to shear a sheep, spin the wool and knit it together to make it.'

'So you just conjured it out of thin air?'

'I conjured it out of wool. I'm best at meteorological effects, obviously, but my status in the Sol Group means I can manipulate the matter of this world with subtle magic. To a small extent, anyway. A jumper is simple enough. A car or something more complex is another matter. Stealing is much easier.'

'How does it work? Creating a world and humans and all this.' I waved my hand to encompass the ocean and horizon.

'Well, we were like you, once. Human beings with the same sort of thought processes you have. And we evolved. Once you get to a certain stage, you become aware of … truths.' He paused.

'Truths?' I prompted, skipping around a seagull that wouldn't give up its chip and get off the footpath.

He fidgeted under his jumper. 'I shouldn't be telling you really. Some things you aren't meant to know, yet.'

'Come on. I'll add it to the list of things I can't tell anyone. Please.'

'Okay. This is already in your writings, I suppose, just not that many read it, and fewer still understand. I'll see if I can explain it. Remember what I told you, that you so elegantly rephrased, about humans shaping their own interactions with the world?'

I nodded.

'Well, once a race of advanced beings gets to a certain stage, they become capable of creating a new world. A planet, basi-

cally, with the requirements for evolution and spiritual awareness. They can leave their own planet, travel –'

'Wait, you have a planet?'

'Sure. One of several in the Cyrea system. We can travel to
other star systems –'

'You're an alien then?' I burst out, then ducked my head.

He frowned. 'I suppose so. Can I finish?'

'Yeah,' I said, mollified.

'We find a suitable place in the universe for a new world.
We sort of create the star, but it's already there too. In a way.
Husa, this is hard. We shape it. Like painters, we create all the
little details of the natural world, its planetary systems, and we
manifest life. We design the framework that allows for growth
and evolution. Plants and animals thrive, sometimes on multiple planets, sometimes on one, sometimes it goes to plan, or
better, and sometimes it fails. If it works, we add human DNA
like ours. And then we watch. We're like caretakers. Initially,
we have a lot of control, but slowly things start to look after
themselves. I only joined the Sol Group recently though.'

'The Sol Group?' I glanced at him, my mind awhirl, and
nearly tripped on a crack in the footpath.

'The people who look after Earth,' Keraun said. A frown
marred his face for a moment, then smoothed away. 'Anyway,
the new humans grow and evolve. Not physically, much, that's
pretty set, we're fundamentally the same all over the universe,
but spiritually. Again, you can fail, and there are points where
that is more likely. If you succeed, you will eventually be able
to travel the universe and start your own world.'

'What happens if we fail?'

'You become extinct. We start again.'

'What about our souls, if the human race becomes extinct?'

He shrugged. 'Your guess is as good as mine. We believe all souls come from a single source, a place both outside and encompassing the universe. Multiverse, whatever it is. I still have a lot to learn.'

'So you're not really a god at all,' I mused. I regretted saying it aloud, worried he might take it the wrong way, but he smiled.

'Alien is technically more accurate. God is just a word humans made up to explain the notion that someone created you, which is essentially true. What we do is not dissimilar to you creating a baby. You did the work to start the physical growth, but the soul? It's still a mystery. Another kind of magic.'

I thought of his impossible lightning strikes, whipping cars off the road with the passengers unharmed. 'Tell me more about magic.'

'I'm what they call a Vi magician, able to manipulate space with energetic magic.' He gave me a sly smile. 'That's how I get around so quick. And it makes me good at the weather stuff, although that's more subtle magic.'

So cavalier. 'And it is, like, proper magic? Or is it all just advanced science?'

'We use both. Most civilisations do, although some lean more into technology, and others more into magic, especially Pamavianda, the energetic magic. It's kind of odd that Earth doesn't have Pamavianda.' He frowned. 'I'm disclosing all the secrets. Markarios is going to be so mad at me.'

'Markarios?'

'Boss of the Sol Group. Keeps the rest of us aware of the big picture and sorts out any conflicts.'

'How many of you are there?'

He mocked offence. 'Only one of me!'

I elbowed him. 'You know what I mean.'

'Twelve in the Sol Group, who are mainly focussed on monitoring Earth. But as a race, our population is in the trillions. We span several star systems.'

I let my mind boggle as I gazed out across the horizon. Fat, puffy clouds were building up in the distance, just visible against the sky as the sun began to sink behind them. Somewhere, way beyond the blue atmosphere that I was familiar with, there was another sun, lighting up a planet that Keraun had grown up on. 'How old are you? What was it like, growing up?'

He didn't answer straight away. I thought he was avoiding my question, but when I looked across, his face was thoughtful.

'It's hard to say. Cyrean time moves a little bit faster than Earth's, and I'm nineteen there, so maybe eighteen Earth years. I spent six years in Abell, which only counts for one Cyrean year, but then the past three years here, and that's slowed me down slightly. It gets complicated. I'm way too young for this job.' His face darkened at that, although I had no idea why. 'But time doesn't really have the same meaning for us. Most Cyreans now live into their thousands. Once you have that sort of lifespan, you stop counting the years so much.'

Okay, this friendship, or whatever it was, was definitely a bad idea. Although I was going to be around for a while too, presumably. But a thousand years? I hadn't thought about it like that. The wind tugged at my hair.

'We are still a young race, in the scheme of things. This is only the second life system we've created, and the first that I've been involved with. I grew up like any kid, I guess, playing on the hillside of my parents' home. My family has been involved in the Sol Group for generations, so my sister and I were groomed for the job from a very young age. I never really got a choice.'

'Is that why you tried so hard to give me a choice?'

He shrugged. 'Maybe. Who knows how much choice we really have? Even immortality isn't really forever, it's just a nice way of saying you can't die by accident. At some point, a Cyrean becomes aware that it is time to die, and they do. There's some fancy name for it, but we call it the Change. It's peaceful.'

We wandered on for a while as my mind swam. My phone rang – Alex. I felt a flicker of intuition that I should respond, but I was learning about aliens and magic. I messaged Alex to say I'd be home later, then turned the phone off. 'So do you know what's happening to me? With the genetic thing, and my body regenerating?'

'Not really. Most civilisations advance through natural evolution, although Earth is running a bit behind. If this works, it might catch you up. The ability to survive just about anything should mean you can achieve interstellar travel faster, but there are some other things you don't have, like Pamavianda magic. Accelerating evolution artificially is tricky.'

'Could I maybe visit your star system one day?'

Keraun peered at me. 'Would you want to?'

I shrugged, but my mind swirled at the possibility. I wondered if his home planet had beaches to walk along. 'Sure.'

'Maybe,' he said. 'We have a long time to figure that out.'

I tried to ignore the fluttering in my chest when he used "we" and "a long time" in the same sentence, and changed the subject.

We walked and talked for hours. He told me about other star systems he'd visited with his parents and how the thing he most wanted to do was travel the universe for a while, but his parents were strict about him following the family legacy and working on Earth. His sister Eftychi was older than him – by several centuries – and also worked in the Sol Group alongside their parents.

Just after sunset, we left the beach footpath to venture into a burger bar, where Keraun opted for a chicken and brie burger and, after I oscillated for five minutes between beef and chilli, beef and bacon or lamb with mint sauce, ordered me the beef and bacon with lamb, jalapeños and mint sauce added. It was monstrous. And amazing.

'See. If you can't decide, just mash your options together until you have what you want,' he advised. Melted cheese and cranberry sauce dripped between his fingers.

'Do you even need to eat?' I asked when I finished my mouthful. I was starving, but I was also mindful of not looking like a dog that had just been given a meaty bone.

'Not for nutrition. But I can still experience things. That's really the whole point of manifesting a physical appearance.'

I continued the questioning as we walked back. He was from a race called Cyreans. Yes, he could actually die, but very few things in the known universe could kill him – mostly highly evolved life forms who probably wouldn't kill a sentient being anyway. When his Change came, he would know, and he would choose to lie down and die. He had been involved with Earth and the Sol Group for the past three years – a short time compared to his sister's two hundred, and she was still considered new – but he hadn't done much with the weather lately other than strike down the occasional offensive driver. The earliest human civilisation was the Abellites, now approaching ten billion years old. "Husa", long since departed from the known universe, had been the first to discover how to use subtle magic and create new worlds. A god of gods.

We arrived at the car he was claiming today – a sleek, silver sedan. He caught my doubtful glance at the badge on the rear bumper.

'It's fine. I know about the bad ones. This is a later model.'

'Why don't you have something cool?' I asked as we climbed in to the plasticky interior. He took off his sunglasses, which he'd been wearing all evening.

'What would be cool?'

'A Maserati. Or a Lamborghini. You're a lightning-wielding alien god. You can have any car in the world, and you get hold of stuff that's boring, broken down or both.'

'They're practical.'

'A Maserati would get you through the traffic faster.'

'It doesn't. People hold you up just so they can ogle the car. Where to?' he asked.

I saw the time on the dashboard – eleven-thirty p.m. Oops. I turned my phone back on to several missed calls. 'You'd better take me back to Alex's before I get into some epic trouble.' Hopefully Alex hadn't called Nancy. I thought of asking Cecelia to cover for me, but I didn't really want to tell her where I'd been all evening either.

'Keraun,' I said as he parked on Alex's street, 'I wanted to say thanks. For helping me with the rally driving thing. You were right. It was better with you there.' I remembered his statement, but I wasn't about to say anything with the words "I wanted you" in it. I didn't need intuition to know that would be awkward.

It was awkward anyway. Keraun met my gaze, eyes just beginning to smoulder. 'You're welcome.'

I picked up my bag and was halfway out of the car when he spoke.

'Is that why you called me? Just to say thanks?'

Sheesh. What did that mean? 'Uh, maybe,' I replied, without meeting his gaze. I could feel those strange eyes burning into my back. 'Bye, Keraun,' I said as I shut the door.

After Keraun drove boringly away in his sedan, I unlocked the front door, taking care to be quiet. The scents of fresh tomato sauce and parmesan cheese wafted from the dark kitchen. I found the source in the fridge: takeaway from Harrys, ravioli and lasagne, stacked on the top shelf. A foil package revealed garlic bread. I was a bit puzzled – Italian was our special meal, not something we did on any old weekend. Craving something sweet, I opened the freezer for a frozen fruit yoghurt thing that I remembered seeing a box of yesterday, but before I dug one out, I came across pistachio gelato. I grabbed a spoon and took the tub to the table. There was a note from Alex sitting on my place mat.

Gabby

I got dinner for us but you didn't make it home. Leftovers in the fridge.

I rolled my eyes. Where else would they be? Then I saw the next line.

Something's come up and I have to fly out first thing. You can stay here while I'm away if you want. Good luck with exams.

Alex.

A wave of guilt swept in, quelling my appetite for gelato. This had been his goodbye dinner. I should have known when I saw the Italian in the fridge. Actually, I should have known when he called me. I was supposed to be all intuitive.

And then I remembered. I had known. I had realised his call was important – he'd obviously wanted to talk to me about not going back to Dad's, which was curious – and I'd chosen to ignore it to spend time with some stupid alien god-boy. I sighed and slumped on the table. My chest ached. My brain hurt. I was probably still going to flunk exams – and whatever Donovan was planning for me – and now that I actually had to face Dad and go back to the Taskforce, I was more nervous about it. So much for being superhuman. To top it off, I'd just skipped out on Alex for our last meal together for the next however-many weeks and I wouldn't see him to fix it. I pulled my phone out of my pocket and was about to press call on Cecelia's number when I recalled that it was nearly midnight. And she was just as likely to bite my head off these days. Zenna was online. She answered on the second ring.

'Hey Gabs, what's up?'

'Not much.' Now that I had someone on the other end of the phone, the despair that had threatened to engulf me moments ago ebbed away, replaced by a wave of fatigue. The silence stretched while I toyed with my bracelet and searched for an excuse for the call.

'Are you okay?'

'Yeah, fine. Tired,' I said.

'You can talk to me, you know.' Zenna's voice was concerned.

'I'm okay, Zenna, I promise. Just feeling a bit stressed about exams and stuff.' More the stuff part. Stuff I couldn't tell my friends about.

'Okay.' I could hear mouse clicking in the background; she was working on something.

'How're your things going?' I asked.

I heard a chair move. 'I'm getting there. Maybe.' She sighed. 'I don't know. Do you have time to chat?'

I could hear a touch of something deeper in Zenna's voice. It was an edge that I hadn't heard since her cousin died two years ago. 'Sure.'

'I …'

Silence. I waited, but she didn't continue. 'Zenna?'

'I'm here.'

'What's going on?'

Her breath hitched.

'Zenna, talk to me.'

'I can't.'

'Are you ...' I tried to think of how to say it. 'Hurting yourself?'

Nothing.

I bit back my frustration. 'Please tell me what's going on.'

She sniffed, tried to cover it with a cough. 'I don't know how to explain.'

'Try.' I didn't know what else to say. I didn't want to presume, or make her feel worse, but a sob scratched down the phone and my chest squeezed. 'Please,' I said.

The phone grew hot against my face. 'Is it school?' It was a stupid question, but I wanted her to say something. Anything.

'I'm fine,' she whispered.

Except that. 'You have to let me help, Zen.'

'You can't. No one can.'

A sigh slipped through my lips. I hadn't meant it to. But I wanted to help her, and she was pushing me away, through a door I didn't have the key to.

'I'd better go. Night,' she said, all in a rush.

'Night,' I replied. 'I'll see you tomo—'

She'd already hung up. I put my phone down, folded my arms on my place mat and buried my head in them.

A firm, gentle hand rested on my shoulder. I jerked awake.

'Wha—oh.' I looked around. It was still dark, but the gelato had melted into a green pool in the tub. I must have fallen asleep at the table.

'Imshorryalx,' I mumbled, too groggy for separate words. I squinted as a light fell across the table. Alex was pulling his pre-prepared breakfast shake out of the fridge. He packed it into his backpack and filled a water bottle.

I took a breath and tried again. 'Sorry I missed dinner.'

Alex smiled, but it didn't quite fill the distance in his eyes. 'It's okay. Go to bed, Gabby.'

He leaned down to kiss my forehead, and then he was gone.

CHAPTER 18

Tim Tams and Lemonade

I regretted sleeping at the table in the morning. I'd always needed at least eight – preferably nine – hours of sleep a night, and it seemed that enhanced physical strength and tissue repair didn't mean I could suddenly get away with less. With negative-ten minutes to get ready, I waved a toothbrush in front of my teeth, nearly poked myself in the eye with mascara and raced out the door, still applying lip gloss, hoping I wouldn't have to wait half an hour for the next bus. That was the worst thing about Alex's – Cecelia's, Dad's and my school were all within a few kilometres of each other in West Beach. If Dad had an early meeting, Nancy was always happy to drop me at school. From here, if Alex was busy, I had to bus it, which always made me late. Nothing to do, of course, with me pushing it and catching the last possible option.

I shut the security gate behind me, turned to the footpath and froze. Parallel parked next to the apartment building was a sleek, black, dark-tinted Mercedes: Dad's chauffeured car. I ducked back behind the gate pillar. I hadn't had a chance to tell Stephen that Dad was back; in all my guilt and self-pity last night, I had forgotten about the threat hovering over me. Across the street, a dark-clad figure shifted in the shadows of an alcove, and I recognised my security detail. I could signal them to intervene. Or I could go back inside – Dad probably hadn't seen me yet. I reached into my pocket for my phone, but shuffling sounded behind me, and a man laden with a suitcase and bags shunted through the gate. I had no choice but to step onto the path.

Dad's driver came forward. I teetered for a moment longer, then waved my security detail off. This was my best chance of getting to the Taskforce, and the security people would update Donovan. The driver to usher me into the back seat, where Dad sat in the tinted gloom.

'Hello Gabby.'

'Hi.'

Dad made small talk as we drove north on the freeway. I answered with vague grunts and mumbles and tried not to fidget, but sweat was soaking through the underarms of my polo shirt despite the cool temperature. I wished I could take off my jacket, but I didn't want to move. I had the strange dreamlike sensation that if I did, I would be caught, like a mouse hiding from a cat that was waiting for it to run.

After twenty-five minutes, we pulled up at the front of the school. Before I could catch myself, I shot Dad a look of surprise.

'I thought you might need a lift to school.' He reached across and squeezed my hand. I wrenched it out of his grasp and jumped out of the car. Perhaps he was just keeping an eye on me.

'See you this afternoon,' he said, waving. The car pulled away with a quiet purr.

Well, I wasn't late now. I messaged Stephen.

Dad's home.
He replied in seconds.
Usual gate, ten minutes before your last class ends.

Last period Monday was a study period, so I escaped early and waited for Stephen under a scented lemon gum, leaning against its smooth white trunk. I stared up at the long, slender leaves being tossed around by the wind, carving invisible shapes out of the overcast sky. My hands trembled. I folded my arms, tucking my fists behind my elbows. I jumped when something tapped me on the shoulder, then spun me around, put me a headlock and tackled me almost to the ground.

'Ge-off-ee!' My voice was muffled in my assailant's arm. I twisted and found myself staring at Donovan's flat expression. She dropped me into the dirt.

'Ouch.' I rubbed my hip as I pulled myself to my feet. 'What was that for?'

'You have to be vigilant. What if I'd been one of the Task-force?' She fished into her pocket for something.

I tried to keep the tremor out of my voice. 'Isn't that why I have security? Where's Stephen? I'm not ready for this.'

'He said to tell you "you'll be fine". But no, you're not ready.'

The trembling was threatening to take over my entire body now.

'Take off your bracelet,' she commanded.

'What? No.'

'You'll get it back,' Donovan said, with the tone of someone speaking to an idiot. I suppressed an urge to punch her in the face.

'My people can't follow you into the Taskforce undetected. You're getting a GPS tracker. It also picks up and transmits nearby sounds, but you have to keep it on, it gets muffled if it's in a pocket or a bag.' She held up a replica of Alex's bracelet. It looked identical, except the engraved plate was thicker. I tried to take the original off my wrist, but my fingers were shaking and I couldn't manage the clasp. Despite my deal to go free after the mission, I suddenly didn't want to do it. I didn't want to be locked in an interrogation room again, I didn't want to face my mother and find out if she'd left me by choice and, right now, I didn't want anything to do with Donovan or Darkhaven or even Stephen. He could have at least shown up for this. The plan was hardly a plan, and I was barely in control of my senses.

'Oh for fuck's sake.' Donovan shoved my hand away and grabbed my wrist, unfastening my bracelet and slipping it into her pocket.

'I can't do this,' I mumbled.

Donovan paused, her face inches from mine. 'I didn't catch that.'

'I can't do this,' I said, slightly louder, but still wavering. 'I've had enough.'

'So you're quitting,' she spat, still holding the tracking replica. 'After all the time everyone has put into you, you're going to give up.'

I gave her a disgusted look. 'I'm not giving up! But this, your bullying, it doesn't work. It's insane!' My voice rose to a yell and the dam crumbled. 'I won't be another one of your guinea pigs to mess around with and leave broken in an asylum somewhere! You can't do this to people. I will do the work. And' – I summoned some internal courage – 'I'll help with the mission. But not for you. I'll do it to keep my word with

Stephen. I'll do it to give Luci a chance to escape. Not because you tell me to. You can go screw yourself. And tell him that next time, he can come and see me himself.'

I reached out and snatched the replica from her hand. She was staring at me with an odd mix of surprise and fury. I tried to fasten the copy around my wrist, but I fumbled and it fell to the ground.

Donovan laughed coldly. 'You're more stupid than I realised. Stephen is using you,' she said as she turned away. My hearing seemed even more acute than usual, and for the first time, I could feel it working with my intuition, so I understood the nuance. Her voice was loaded with repugnance and malice as she added, 'Your mother probably doesn't even care.'

My vision coloured, clouding over, but it wasn't the usual crushing blackness. It was a red haze. I took two strides towards the woman, grabbed her shoulder and, winding back my right arm, spun her around and slammed my fist into her face. Blood sprayed from her nose and a split on her cheek. Without even waiting for her to respond, I swept the tracking bracelet out of the fallen leaves, tucked it into my pocket – no sense ruining my moment by trying to put it on – and stalked back onto the school grounds.

Once I was out of sight, I doubled over and cradled my surely broken hand to my stomach, thinking I really should learn to punch properly if I was going to keep hitting people. I stayed where I was until the throbbing subsided and I could feel my hand starting to heal. I was almost sorry; by the time my hand was back to normal, Donovan's nose would be too. But at least I'd ruined her shirt with the blood.

I felt oddly empowered, although I suspected it was more to do with adrenaline than any kind of sensible reaction. I fastened the tracker onto my wrist and approached the black

Merc at the front of the school at with a facade of confidence. The driver ushered me into the car. Dad wasn't there. I slid into the backseat and tried to sit calmly, wondering if this was better or worse than a session with Donovan.

Ten minutes later, I stood in Dad's driveway, my backpack heavy on my shoulder, fingers trembling as I shuffled through my tangled keys, looking for the metallic orange one to unlock the front door. Before I could lift it to the keyhole, the door opened.

'Gabby,' Dad said warmly. He looked like he was about to give me a hug, but he stopped. Thankfully.

'Dad.' I tried to make my voice as cold as possible. He let his face drop slightly, saddened.

This was not going the way I had expected. I'd been prepared to be strong-armed after school, and to try and make a run for it. Now, I wasn't quite sure where I stood. Was Sean waiting inside?

What the hell. I was wearing a tracker. Someone – hopefully not Donovan – would be watching and listening. I ventured into the living room, dumped my bag in its usual spot at the end of the hallway and made for the fridge.

'Allow me.' Dad cut me off and waved me to the dining table. He brought over two cans of lemonade and a packet of double coat Tim Tam biscuits. I bit into one, raising an eyebrow at him as he cracked open his can. I had a penchant for Tim Tams, but it was unlike him to look at any dessert on the supermarket side of a Dutch chocolate brownie with vanilla seed ice cream. Generic soft drink was unthinkable.

He gave me a tentative smile. 'I want to apologise. It was unforgivable of me to let Sean take you in.'

I nibbled at the chocolate biscuit. It was starting to melt between my fingertips. I had no idea how to play this.

Dad took a sip of his lemonade. 'I'm very sorry,' he said softly.

I knew he was being genuine. Apart from sensing it intuitively, his partaking of junk food was his way of meeting me entirely in my corner. He wasn't asking me to come halfway with this. And I sensed he didn't expect me to forgive him, not yet. I wanted to explode at him. Now that I knew he wasn't about to hand me over to some guards in suits, I wanted to rant and yell and carry on about how he mustn't ever have loved me at all, to betray me like that. But none of it was true. And now I had the problem of getting to his facility, wherever it was, and taking Stephen to Luci. My confidence waned, my anger sagged like a lettuce leaf left out of the fridge too long and I had nothing to say.

'I usually stay back at school most days, studying until seven,' I said eventually. 'Didn't Alex tell you?' The brothers didn't talk unless they had to, but they usually put aside their differences when it came to my education.

Dad toyed with the ring-pull on his can. 'I haven't spoken to him. Nancy told him about your latest Sunday incident. He thinks I upset you with university pressure.'

That explained Alex's offer to stay at his place. I kept my face neutral.

'I wanted to give you some space, after what happened at the Taskforce,' Dad said.

I knew he wanted a talk, a serious one, where he could explain himself and get everything off his chest. He was waiting for me to open the conversation.

He wasn't patient. 'Please know, Gabby, I thought I was doing the right thing.'

I chucked the rest of the Tim Tam into my mouth, plucked another one out of the packet and pushed my chair back. 'I have to go study.'

I left him sitting at the dining table. As I picked up my bag, the biscuit packet rustled, followed by the soft crunch of a Tim Tam. I almost smiled. I knew I would forgive him, and let him have his D-and-M. But not yet. I wasn't that kind.

I sat at my desk in my room with my scant notes on Dickens, but I couldn't concentrate. I thought back to my last experience at the Taskforce, wracking my brain for some clues as to where it was, how to find it again. I remembered the interrogation room and Keraun pressing a finger to his lip – Keraun. His name crashed into my mind like a tonne of bricks. How had I not thought of this before? It had been a chaotic day. But Keraun knew where the Taskforce building was. He could take me there.

I reached for my phone. Stephen might not like the idea, but his plan had largely hinged on Dad still insisting on handing me over to the Taskforce, something he was now clearly not planning to do. I made the call.

'Absolutely not.' Keraun was adamant. After a short phone conversation, he had instructed me to wait, hung up and, two minutes later, texted from the front door. I'd snuck him past Dad's office, and now he lounged across my bed while I perched on my desk chair and pleaded.

'Come on Keraun, we knew this was going to happen.'

'Actually, I didn't know. Stephen' – he said the name with unfriendly emphasis – 'practically kicked me out of Darkhaven after your panic thing. He barely spoke to me at the rally drive.

And you' – this time with accusatory emphasis – 'never filled me in on this plan of yours.'

'It's not my plan,' I mumbled, mollified.

'It's not anybody's plan, because there is no plan. Just for you to sacrifice yourself to a cause that you don't have anything to do with. Why do you want to do it?' Anger edged his voice like faint thunder.

'I said I'd help,' I protested. 'It's the least I could do since I lied to them.' Okay, that was an excuse. Although I was reluctant to say it, or even think it, in case something went wrong, there was a chance I could confront my mother and find out if she'd abandoned me, or if she really was, as Stephen insisted, a captive there. But Keraun didn't know that.

'You don't owe them anything, Gabby.'

'If this works, they'll let me go. No fake death. No conditions.'

'I can help you with that.'

'Exactly! You can help. You got me out easily enough last time.'

Keraun threw his hands up in exasperation. 'That was not easy. I can't guarantee I can do it again.'

'But you're a god!'

'Magic has limits. And it's you I'm worried about. I could get myself in and out, but with you? Like I said, no guarantee we wouldn't get caught.'

I shrugged. 'But I can regenerate. What could they do? I'll heal, if they, like, shoot me or something.' I suppressed a shudder. Rapid healing or not, being shot was not something I ever wanted to repeat, no matter how long I lived.

'If you get out.' Keraun's slender face darkened. 'They know what you are, remember? In human terms, you're pretty tough, but you're not indestructible. No one is.'

His vehemence surprised me. 'Could they harm you?'

'It doesn't matter. I'm not taking you there. I can't stop you trying to talk your father into something stupid, but I won't be responsible for this.'

I slouched in my chair, arms folded. 'If I'm going to do it anyway, it would be safer if you came.'

Keraun looked away, defeat clouding his eyes. 'I'll follow behind, hoping you come to your senses and call it all off. But your dad seems to be repentant. If he's with you, maybe you'll be afforded some protection. Hopefully he won't agree to take you in at all.' He looked back, eyes yellowing as they bored into mine. 'Did you really think asking me was going to work?'

I bit back my indignant auto-reply and sank into my calm place. No, I wouldn't have, if I'd stopped to think and feel out the situation. I'd been too eager to avoid a difficult conversation with Dad. I sighed.

'Fine. I'll talk to Dad.'

'Talk to Stephen first. Your dad's change of heart is something they should know about.'

I nodded. 'Tomorrow then.'

'I'll leave you to your study,' Keraun said, making for the window. I wanted him to stay, but I knew he was still mad, and I didn't want to ask. I closed the window behind him.

The conversation with Stephen lifted my hopes slightly.

'This is good, Gabby. It gives you some protection. But you do need to find out if your dad believes the amnesia story you gave them. Without tipping him off.'

'I know.' After a pause, I asked the question that had been bothering me since Donovan's parting remark. Since before then, if I was honest with myself. 'Do you think Luci – my mother – will be interested?'

I could feel Stephen weighing the question in the silence. 'She cares. She has to stay distant, as long as she's under their control. That's why we have to help her.'

I nodded, even though he couldn't see me. I hoped with all my being that he was right, not just so I might have a chance to get to know her, but also so the risk would be worth it. I couldn't get a handle on it intuitively and wondered if this was family closeness getting in the way of my developing sense. Keraun seemed genuinely concerned. With all his lightning-god-power, what could make him so upset? In the scrap of calm place that I could find, doubt was waiting, like a seed that needed a drop of water.

Stephen suggested taking a day or two to get through to Dad. I felt self-conscious of someone having overheard my conversation with Keraun, even though it had been perfectly innocent. Well, innocent as far as any feelings of friendship – or otherwise – went. Stephen didn't mention it, which could have been good, if that meant he wasn't bothered, or worse, if he hadn't heard and it had been Donovan monitoring me. I shuddered. My training was cancelled for the week in case Dad was keeping tabs on me, so at least I didn't have to face up to her yet, and the security detail was called off. I was sorry that I wouldn't get another session in with Liam though. I could have used his calming presence right about now.

CHAPTER 19

Tie Off

I sulked at Dad for another two days. Rather, I pretended to sulk so he wouldn't realise I was nervous. When I finally sat down to dinner with him, my mouth felt like sandpaper. He thought I was quiet because I still hadn't forgiven him, but I found that I wasn't entirely sure about that. I was definitely still mad, and he had a lot of making up to do, but the feeling of betrayal seemed to fade as we chatted about menial stuff over his special parmigiana with bechamel sauce. He hadn't put up much of a fight for me, but his hands probably had been tied by his job. If the government believed me to be caught up with terrorists, as Sean had suggested, his own loyalty would have been questioned if he had actively defended me. And if he'd believed it, well. Maybe he'd wanted answers too.

'So is there a boy in your life?' Dad speared a cherry tomato with his fork, fixing me with a beady eye. He had an odd way of knowing things.

I shrugged. 'Not really.'

'Aha! That's a yes.'

Damn it. I scowled.

He laughed. 'It's all right, I don't need gory details. But I hope he's good enough for you.'

'He might be too good.'

'Not a chance.'

I stabbed at a tomato with my fork. It slipped out from under the prongs and slid to the other side of the plate.

'I don't think anything will come of it,' I said dismissively as I pinned the tomato down with the flat edge of my knife and pierced it. The tomato exploded, splattering me with juice and seeds.

'Ah well, you should focus on finishing school first.' He passed me the serviette holder. I took one and dabbed at my shirt.

After a moment, I decided to jump in. 'I ...' My resolve was shaky. I couldn't find the words.

Dad's face softened to concern. 'Are you okay, Gabby?'

I dropped into my calm place. Don't think. Just talk.

'I've been having a rough time,' I admitted. I tried to not crumble into tears. I hadn't realised it was so true until I said it. Dad reached across the table to offer a comforting hand. I kept both of mine clasped under the table.

'I remember things,' I said softly. 'Things I was meant to forget.'

He nodded with understanding. 'It's okay,' he pitched his voice to match mine. 'You don't have to do anything. You're my daughter. I thought I was doing the right thing.' He sighed. 'I see now I was wrong, and I'm sorrier than I can say. I want you to know that. You can do whatever you want with this. I'll protect you.'

I nodded and gritted my teeth. No backing out. 'I know. I want to help. The woman, she asked me questions. I think I can answer her, now.' I raised my eyes to meet his. 'Can you take me in to give her my statement?'

'You don't have to go in. You can just tell me,' he offered.

I shook my head. 'I was very rude to her. It was a strange night. I'd like to do it properly,' I said, trying to sound like I was being polite. He set down his knife and fork and leaned back in his chair, steepling his fingers as he considered.

'It might not be safe, and I'm not sure how far I can intervene in there.' He chose his words carefully, but I understood the meaning. He might be on my side, but the Taskforce definitely wasn't.

'But I'm going to cooperate. It'll be fine.'

'It's a risk.'

I shook my head. 'This isn't just about me telling them what I know. This is also about me trying to find some answers. What's happened to me is going to change the course of my life and have an impact on what I do after school. The woman I spoke to knew something about me, I could tell. I feel like I can make some sense of my life if I do this. It's my only shot at figuring things out. Please, Dad.'

He looked slightly taken aback at my address. 'You feel like your life doesn't make sense?'

It never had. I stood in the doorway with a pair of woolly slippers while everyone else fastened their heels and went dancing. I didn't mind – slippers were comfy – as long as I had some other purpose. And now, with the truth about my mother within reach, I felt like the jigsaw might come together. Of course, Dad didn't know that I knew about Luci. I wondered if, somewhere behind his concern for my safety, he was also worried that he'd be unmasked, that I'd figure out he'd lied to me about her.

I held his gaze, and after a long moment of internal deliberation, he relented. 'Fine. We'll go in the morning. I'll write you a note for school in case we're late. If you're okay with missing classes this close to exams,' he added hopefully.

I rolled my eyes. 'Nice try.'

I felt smug right up until my head hit the pillow. Dad's concerned face swam behind my eyelids as his veiled warning echoed in my ears. Keraun's *they could do a lot worse than shoot you* rolled around in my head, and pretty soon I was imagining being locked in a musty cell with no windows or doors that even Keraun couldn't weasel his way into, slowly desiccating for lack of food or water but unable to die.

I lay awake for what felt like hours, twitching at every tiny sound, trying to follow Donovan's meditation techniques. Keraun's dark voice in my head only grew louder. I pressed my pillow up around my ears. An ambulance wailed somewhere in the distance, but I jumped as if it had careened straight around the foot of my bed.

Breathe. Just breathe. Liam's words for when I was too wired to feel intuitive. I focussed on my heart rate as the siren faded away, slowing the alarmed beating down. I sank into my calm place. Here, there was no sense of dread. Uncertainty, yes. Perhaps an unsatisfying outcome. But I didn't feel afraid for my life, or anyone else's. It was good enough. I drifted off to sleep.

Early in the morning, after I managed to choke down some toast, Dad ushered me into the car. I tried to pay attention to where we were going, but my mind kept wandering to what I planned to say to Luci, and after we left the freeway, I became lost in the maze of traffic lights and constant turns. I figured it didn't much matter. Darkhaven was tracking me.

Dad slowed the car as we approached a multi-storey building in a half-developed industrial area. The building was an ugly collection of glass and steel, with pieces of red sheeting stuck all over it at abstract angles. Everything on the block was like that, all with high-security gates and cameras on the building corners like little antennae, although none of the surrounding buildings had the height of the one we approached. I started typing a message to Keraun as we drove through the metal gates, but my phone had no signal.

I climbed out of the car, squared my shoulders and followed Dad through tinted glass sliding doors. Our footsteps echoed around the vast space. The floors were a white tile that I recognised from my last visit, sparkling under the skylights. The only piece of furniture was a sweeping, stone-topped reception desk, also white, with a single black telephone on it and nothing else. Mirrored glass filled the wall behind the desk. The only other features were a door marked with an emergency exit sign and an elevator. No people to be seen.

'The ground level is mostly vacant space. Only the security staff are down here. The offices and storage are on the upper levels,' Dad explained as we took the lift to the second floor. He used a swipe card to press the button.

'How many levels are there?'

'Four, plus the podium.'

I thought of the long climb up the stairs when Keraun had busted me out the first time. 'But that's just what you can see above ground, right?'

He gave me a sidelong glance, but the doors slid open and he didn't answer. The corridor before us was still wide, but it felt claustrophobic after the bright expanse of the podium, even with the glass walls all the way along it. We walked past another reception desk, this one cheap black laminate. Behind it stood a man in a black suit, appearing to casually read a file, but there was nothing casual about him. He gave Dad a barely perceptible nod. I kept my eyes forward, but the man's watchful eyes tickled my neck as I followed Dad to an office at the end of the corridor. The floor was unfamiliar, and I guessed I must have been on a different level last time, where the internal walls were not panes of glass. All the offices were empty. The silence weighed on my ears.

Dad ushered me into an office, and I realised why it felt so claustrophobic: the internal walls were the only glass. There were no outside windows. Where I would have expected a view of the city, the street or at least a car park, there was a panoramic photograph of a long, white-sand beach, turquoise waters shimmering under sunlight the room had never seen.

Dad went to let the Taskforce higher-ups know I was here, saying he'd see me when I was finished giving my statement. I sat on the surprisingly comfortable sofa under the photo print and stared around the room. There was a desk, but it had nothing on it either, just another telephone. After a quick glance through the glass wall to be sure I was out of the sightlines of the suit, I snuck around to the other side of the desk and perched on the chair behind it.

I slid open the top drawer. It contained a cursory stationery collection: pens, a ruler, a pocket calculator. The second drawer was devoted to a lined paper pad and blank envelopes. If someone worked in here, they made a point of being tidy, but my gut said this was all for show. The third drawer didn't even open. Nerves tingling, I got up, tucked the chair back under the desk and returned to the sofa, not a second too soon. Another black-suited figure came around the corner, pushed the glass door open and sauntered in. Unlike the guard, this man's jacket was unbuttoned, and his tie was removed for a casual look. Probably just for the purposes of meeting me – I could see the tie poking out of his jacket pocket.

Sean extended his hand to me.

'Miss Whitehall.' His voice was friendly. 'I am glad you finally came in.'

I didn't shake his hand.

'Can I see Luci?' I asked, crossing my arms. Where had Dad gone?

Sean wheeled the desk chair around and sat opposite me. He held a clipboard stuffed with pages. 'Ms Douglass is unavailable. But I can take your statement,' he offered, smiling. 'She will contact you, if she needs more information. Can you start by telling me about the afternoon at the park?'

His light blue eyes watched me, the colour of the ocean on the wall, but without the sunlit sparkle. His face was encouraging, yet wary. He wanted me to trust him. He didn't trust me. Well, then. I sat back on the sofa. 'I'm only speaking to Luci. That's why I'm here.'

He kept his patience. 'She is sorry she can't meet you today. But it was short notice.'

'I'll wait.' Patience and stubbornness were the same thing, most of the time.

'She won't see you, Gabby.' He shifted, crossing his legs, and knocked the clipboard with his knee. It slipped out of his grasp and onto the floor between us. Papers swept across the carpet to my feet. I almost didn't move – he could pick it up himself – but then I realised I might be able to glimpse what was on it. I reached down and collected a few pages, but Sean grasped my wrist and took the papers out of my hand before I could read what was on them. He smiled coolly, holding my gaze. I shivered and pulled away.

'Let's start over. I'm Sean Richards. We can shake hands later.' He chuckled as if he'd just made a joke. To stop myself from actually doing it, I imagined rolling my eyes as he continued.

'I know you are in your final year of high school. Your mother died when you were a baby, and your dad took a year off work to care for you. When he had to go back, your uncle stepped in and offered to care for you while he was away.'

I folded my arms again. 'So you have a file on me. None of that stuff is exactly state secret.'

'Sure. But I'm not trying to uncover secrets. I just want to get to know you better. So, ask me something. We can trade questions, if you like.' He leaned forward, resting his arms on his knees, the clipboard safely tucked away.

'What, do you think I'm five?' I cringed as I said it. It sounded childish.

'I'm trying to be nice, Gabby.'

My nerves jangled as my intuition called out his lie. I tried to keep myself anchored in my calm place, but Keraun's words kept floating back into my head. *If you get out.* I had to find Luci and get out of here. Panic rose in my brain and words fell out. 'Well, that's too bad, 'cause I'm not. Here's a question for you. Did you know my mother didn't die when I was a baby?'

Something flickered across his face. I realised, too late, that I'd just given away my position. Now he knew why I was here, and he hadn't known that before. He'd probably thought I was just another Eventer – he'd had no idea that I was Luci's daughter. I tried not to let my mistake flash across my face.

'I'm waiting for an answer, *Sean*,' I over-emphasised his name, pretending that I'd meant to tip my hand, and it didn't matter. Sean didn't buy it. He stood.

'We know a lot of things, Gabby.' He pulled his tie out of his pocket, buttoned his collar and started tying the strip of black fabric around his neck. 'We know Cecelia Wilson needs top marks in her final English exam to get into medicine. It would be such a shame if one of the examiners marked her down. We also know Zenna Robinson is struggling with depression. Her family doctor is taking care of her for now, but I am friends with a very talented psychiatrist. He's always keen for a referral. Obviously we know you're not at the library until seven o'clock every day, and we know that your uncle doesn't know you're not there. Alex's bosses aren't aware that his niece is part of an illegal genetic mutation experiment with government fugitives. He might not have told you that he's up for a big promotion next year. So, I hope you'll reconsider my offer of a quiet chat. It could all work nicely. We need someone with your … abilities.'

Panic bubbled in my gut. I kept my lips pressed together and shook my head. Sean leaned down closer to me. His tie swung in my face.

'All right, you don't have to join me. I'll make you a deal. All you have to do is tell me where Darkhaven is, and I'll leave you alone. I'll ensure no one bothers you – or your loved ones – about this again.'

His insincerity prickled against my intuition, even as he offered me exactly what I'd wanted since all this started: to remain an Eventer, to keep my friends and for everyone to be safe. No more torture with Donovan. She could deal with Sean herself. But then Stephen's gentle gaze brushed my memory, accompanied by Liam's tinkling chuckle as they sat and

watched fairy-wrens play in the fountain while black cockatoos squawked from the treetops. I stood to glare evenly at
Sean. He stood too, pinning his tie in place. We were almost
the same height.

'Screw you,' I said.

Tie straight, he picked up his clipboard and pulled open the
door.

'You will help me, Gabrielle. Soon,' he added, giving me a
final look. His eyes were flat. The door swung shut behind
him. I watched him disappear down the glass corridor and into
the elevator.

CHAPTER 20

Cohort 3

I stood where I was until the trembling became too severe and I sank back into the couch, trying to push out the feelings of shame and embarrassment – state secrets indeed – and terror. Not for myself. Now, any fear I'd harboured for myself last night and this morning had vanished. But Alex. Zenna. Cecelia. How did the Taskforce even know? What if they ruined Alex's career that he'd worked so hard at all his life? Or Cecelia's, before it even started. And Zenna. I knew she was having a rough time, but I had no idea she'd seen her doctor about it. Some friend I was.

I realised, then, alone in the windowless office that only looked inwards, that I was the one jeopardising the lives of the people I loved, and I'd made that choice when I refused Stephen's offer to go home and forget. Or transform and leave them to live their lives, happy and fulfilled. I'd decided for them. I'd decided they wouldn't cope if I "died". That would have been a tragedy, a sad occurrence, but ultimately, something that had happened to someone else. In that moment, I'd traded one tragedy for three, three events that wouldn't pass and fade into the background, but things that would hobble them forever. If I'd loved them, I'd have let them go. Let them lose me, grieve me, and move on while I chased another dream. And if I'd really loved them, I'd have given it up, forgotten, stayed with the people I supposedly loved. Maybe I could have been happy too. I let that fill me with hopeful regret for a moment.

But the most crushing thing was knowing that even now, I still couldn't have chosen to forget. I wouldn't do it differently. I rushed out of the room, back to the elevators, past the now-vacant reception desk. I had no idea where Dad had gone, or how long before Sean came back. I hammered the elevator button and stood in front of the sliding metal doors, fighting back the waves of despair. *No,* a small part of my mind said. The least I could do was try to fix something. Luci had to be here somewhere. Stephen would be listening, waiting for me to find her. If I left now, the mission failed and my deal was off.

I stilled my emotions and sank into my calm place. I knew, somehow, that the floor was largely deserted. Sean had left me to sweat. I also sensed that there was something to be learned around here. The plaque on the wall above the elevators said I was on level two. I slipped back down the hall. I didn't bother with the glass offices I could see from the corridor. I knew they'd be more of the same – empty notebooks and false drawers. Instead, I followed the corridor around until the glass stopped and came to a small room, brick instead of glass, with a solid door. I ducked back around the corner as the door opened, pressing myself into the wall. My intuition told me to stay, still and silent. I pulled my phone out – still no signal – opened the camera app and poked the phone just far enough around the corner to see the back of a dark-haired woman disappear into another room.

I ran on tiptoes down the corridor and ducked into the room she'd just left, rolling my ankle on a pile of cables inside, my heart thumping at the noise. I shut the door, forcing it over the wrinkled mat, and kicked off the cable I'd trailed along the floor. The space was dark and narrow – some sort of server room. Tiny LEDs flashed and fans whirred from a stack of computers on the right, and a workbench ran along the left, scattered with cables, tools and equipment I didn't recognise. A filing cabinet stood at the far end of the room, hidden in shadow.

A monitor on the bench had some server management software open and a swipe card rested next to the mouse. Even with the computer already logged in, I didn't have the skills to know what I was looking at. I stared at it for several seconds, hoping for some intuitive nudge, but intuition didn't fill gaping holes in knowledge.

I turned to the racks of computers behind the bench. At chest height was a machine with several slots, a disk sticking out of one of them. I gave it a tiny experimental tug. It slid out of the slot without a sound. I paused, waiting for some kind of computer alarm to go off, but there was nothing. I looked at the disk, but there were no markings of any kind, except one side had a sort of holographic print on it. I tucked it into my back pocket and turned to the filing cabinet just as the door at the other end of the room cracked open.

I froze. The door caught on the mat. I ducked into the shadows beside the cabinet, but if the woman came down to the monitor, there was no way she'd miss me. She stepped into the room, kicked the mat flat and shut the door, the aroma of instant coffee swirling in the air.

Trip. Spill the coffee. Never had I wished so hard for anything. Even if I could fight my way past her – and it was unlikely she would be worse than me in a fight – I wasn't sure if I could escape the building without Dad's swipe card, at least not without triggering door alarms. And I didn't really want to tip anyone off that I was snooping. Maybe she was just cleaning up the cables. Perhaps she'd pick them up and leave.

But she wouldn't have brought coffee back if she wasn't planning to work in here. She was heading for the monitor. *Please trip.*

I almost felt bad when her toe caught on the cable I'd trailed down the room and she stumbled, splashing coffee down her shirt and over the floor. She cursed, set the cup down and left, the door swinging behind her.

I snatched up the swipe card and peeked out the door. No one in sight. Skin tingling, I dashed down the hall, resisted the urge to glance over my shoulder, reached the elevator and pressed the button, praying that it wouldn't make me wait forever. I heard cables whizzing over pulleys before the doors silently slid open. I leapt in, slapped the security card against the panel and jabbed a random button as I heard footsteps down the corridor. The doors slid shut.

I took a deep breath and examined the space in more detail than when I'd come up with Dad.

Labelled buttons showed the upper levels and the podium. Below those were three unlabelled buttons. I'd managed to mash the first unlabelled one and it glowed orange. Anxiety jittered over my skin like ants, but curiosity drove me on.

The elevator moved down, the doors sliding open when it stopped. I peered out at an underground car park. There was nothing down here, just a few of the black SUVs parked up. I ducked back into the elevator, debating.

Just looking at the lower buttons filled me with terror. In my gut, in the place where I'd felt that my poker bluff was going to fail, I knew it was risky. But I'd come all the way here. I might not get another chance. And Stephen and Donovan were waiting, listening in for word about Luci, ready to move. I hoped the tracker worked this far underground.

I pressed the bottom button. Pressure squeezed across my chest.

The elevator dropped, flying further down. I took a deep breath as the doors opened and I peeked out. The corridor was deserted, but fear gripped my stomach.

It was the floor from my interrogation with Luci.

I clenched my jaw. No use going back now. I made my way along the corridor, pausing at each door, wondering if I should open it, but I couldn't feel into my calm place. All I could feel from there was an urge to turn around and go back. *Get out*, it said. *Get out while you still can.*

One of these doors led to my interrogation cell, and I had a feeling, deep beneath the rising panic, that they were all much the same. I kept going down the corridor and crept around the corner.

I stifled a gasp. The corridor opened into a room full of cages. Not the miserable kind of cages I'd have expected, but spacious, stuffed with hay and green leaves and plush beds. A man in a lab coat sat next to one of the cages, cuddling a large black-and-white rabbit. Two more people in lab coats stood at a long workstation with their backs to the room, busy at computers. I ducked down below the cages, tried not to think about what the animals might be for and crept to the door at the other end. It opened noiselessly into another, larger room. My insides were screaming at me to go back, get out. But I had to find Luci.

I tiptoed in. This time I had no squeal. I stared in shock. The room contained rows of beds, and in each bed, a child – some infants, others maybe ten or twelve – all asleep. Or comatose, I couldn't tell. In the middle of the room, a woman in a white coat, mask and cap waved her hands in a spiralling pattern over the kid's body. Sparks of static electricity jolted from her fingers while the man opposite her – also head-to-toe in white – observed and made notes on his clipboard.

That was strange enough, but then I noticed the pair of rabbits sitting on the end of the bed, alert, sniffing around. As I watched, their ears dropped and they lowered their heads, hunching up into balls. Weird.

I glanced at the chart hanging at the foot of the bed closest to me: *Subject #3.8*. The kid was strapped down.

The combination of words and numbers triggered a memory, one of files labelled "Subject #1.1" and "Subject #1.6" and I realised, with a sinking feeling, that the Taskforce wasn't eliminating the Praegressus program. They were continuing it. I had been part of the first group. This was the third cohort of children who had been subjected to the virus, and whatever crazy things these people were doing with clipboards and hands full of static sparks.

My stomach dropped. Sean didn't want to kill me. He was trying to collect me, make me part of his laboratory, study my transformation. My legs turned to liquid under my body, held together only by my jeans and a thin thread of nerve. I clung to it and cast about for somewhere to hide before the people in coats spotted me.

At the far end of the room was a cluster of filing cabinets and beyond them, another door. If I ducked below the middle row of beds, I could crawl to the cabinets and get to the door unseen, but before I could move, another white-coated figure stood up from behind them, eyes on his handful of files. My pulse tripled until I recognised the familiar shock of scruffy hair. Keraun looked up and met my gaze, a tight smile flashing across his lips. I let out a quiet breath of relief.

The boy in the bed next to me groaned.

Keraun dropped the files, alarm striking his face. The two workers with the rabbits glanced over. Too late to hide now. But before I could run, the woman lowered her mask. Her cold green gaze was unmistakeable.

Luci. My hand went to my wrist to touch my tracking bracelet, to reassure myself that Stephen and Don—

It was gone. The bracelet was gone, and the feeling of Sean clasping my wrist while he looked me in the eyes shivered over my skin. He'd dropped the clipboard on purpose, a ruse to touch my arm. I had no phone contact. Stephen and Donovan weren't coming.

Time froze as Luci looked at me and I stared back, locked in moment of uncertain disbelief. I could see my lips on her face, my nose, the jut of my chin. I had her hair underneath the dye. She'd known who I was before, but now I knew her. And I could see in the twitch of her jaw and certainty of her gaze that she knew I knew. The years hung between us, heavy in the disinfected air.

'Mum,' I whispered, barely audible even to myself. I stood up straighter. 'Luci. We've come for you.'

She gave a minuscule shake of her head, but whether in warning or denial, I couldn't tell. The man next to her recovered from his initial shock and pulled a radio off his belt, muttering something into it about a code two.

Then he dropped his chart, scattering the rabbits, and charged towards me.

'Run!' Keraun yelled. He vaulted over the filing cabinet and rushed the man, tackling him to the ground. Buying me time. But I had to be sure.

I glanced back to Luci, who was gathering up the rabbits. 'Come with me,' I said. 'Stephen said –'

She tipped her head back and laughed, a closed, hard sound. 'That was always Stephen's problem. Thinking I needed to be rescued.' She settled the rabbits back on the end of the bed and picked up the fallen clipboard, reviewing the notes and peering at the supine figure on the bed while I stared in disbelief.

She spoke without even looking up. 'Get out of here while you still can, Gabrielle.'

I didn't know her, had never known her. She hadn't died when I was a baby. She'd given me up. It shouldn't have mattered, but shame and loss and abandonment welled like a mountain in my chest anyway, pushing reason aside. I bolted through the rabbit room, so fast the workers there didn't have time to react before I was gone, tearing down the corridor. Crashes and yells rang behind me.

I reached the elevator and pummelled the button. There was a door next to the lift – the same one Keraun had taken me through last time I was here. The lift pinged and the doors opened, but I hesitated. The stairs must lead me to the podium door he'd used, although it was probably all unlabelled, and I didn't know where I was going. On the other hand, I knew where the elevator went, and how to get out – but the lifts relied on electronic access, and they could easily shut those down. I wrestled for an agonising moment before I remembered to gather my nerves and let my intuition guide me. I took a deep breath, shut everything out and found my calm place.

Stairs it was.

I staggered up, making sure to count the flights. Two flights for a level. But there were too many. The sub-basement lab was deeper underground than I'd realised. I stopped at the second door I came to and peeked through it. The car park was bustling with cars moving and suits running and shouting. I ducked back into the stairs and kept running up. My fingers slipped on the handrail as I neared the podium level landing – I hoped it was the podium – and I scrambled up the last few steps, stubbing my toes on the concrete.

There were two solid doors, one to each side of the landing. I didn't know which to take. Fear and fourteen flights of stairs had stripped me of any sense of direction. My memories of Keraun's rescue were too fuzzy to be useful. I hoped he was okay. I sank into my calm place again, waiting for my intuition to show me the way. Panic rose like a tide, and I struggled to shove it down.

The door on the left.

I stumbled through. For a moment I was weightless, lifted off my tangled legs, then I melted in horror. Two men in suits held me still. A third man stepped up to regard me with a cold sneer. Sean.

I frowned, confused. There was an elevator door next to the stairway door, and a plaque marked "P", so I had to be correct ... then angry tears filled my eyes as I looked up and down the white-tiled corridor. Opposite me was a room full of computer monitors: the security offices on the podium level. The stairwell must open on both sides. Right floor. Wrong door.

'I might have been more impressed if you'd known which door to take.' Sean's voice was smug.

I lifted my head to glare at him, forcing a sob down with gritted teeth. 'People know where I am,' I said, more defiantly than I felt, struggling against the two pairs of arms holding me.

Sean smiled. 'This?' He asked, holding up my fake bracelet. Or what remained of it – part of the plate was gone. 'I've sent the GPS on a mission of its own. Your friends are heading in the wrong direction across the city. It still records sound' – he tapped the link in the chain that concealed the microphone – 'but we've jammed the signal for this whole block. So go on. Shout.'

'Leave them alone,' I growled, imagining Stephen running into an ambush.

Sean smirked. 'I will catch them anyway.' He dangled the bracelet. 'Last chance. Join me and help your real friends.'

'Fuck you.' I didn't usually swear out loud; Alex didn't like it. The word tasted metallic on my tongue.

Sean sighed. 'You only have yourself to blame, then.'

He flicked a nod to one of my captors. I followed his glance and saw the suit preparing a needle and syringe. I struggled, fighting with all my remaining might against the relentless arms, but I wasn't strong enough. Apparently Donovan was right, and even for a superhuman, strength had to be gained through training.

'Stop!' A commanding voice ricocheted along the hard-tiled hallway. The suits froze. I looked up. Dad strode across the tiles, shoes slapping the floor with percussive purpose.

Sean recovered first. 'Stick her!'

I struggled and felt the prick of the needle against the skin of my neck. The next second, something shoved past me as Dad, with one neat elbow strike to the head, knocked the syringe-bearing suit away from me, sending him crashing to the floor. The needle fell out of my neck and clattered on the tiles. Dad took my shoulders and held me up straight. The other suit stepped back, apologetic. Once I was steady, Dad stepped around me to glare at Sean.

'I have authority for this,' Sean muttered, unable to keep the whine out of his voice.

'Not if I say otherwise.'

I'd never heard that tone before. It was unquestionable authority, belonging to someone you obeyed without question.

Sean flung the broken bracelet at Dad. It jangled onto the tiled floor. While Dad bent to pick up the silver chain, Sean stepped up close to me. 'I'll get you,' he whispered, voice burning in my ear. 'I will make it so you have nowhere else to go.'

Dad clamped a hand on Sean's shoulder and wrenched the man back, flinging him to the floor like a wooden puppet. Sean scrabbled up against the wall, pressing his lips together so firmly they turned white as he pummelled the elevator button. His eyes glittered. 'I'll make you pay!' he spluttered, still half-slumped on the floor. 'You might be untouchable, but your brother isn't!'

Dad regarded him with his sternest warning expression. It sent shudders over my skin.

Sean stood, brushed off his jacket and limped into the waiting elevator. There was an awkward silence while he waited for the doors to close, and I allowed myself to relax slightly, taking a deep breath. Sean looked over, directly at me. I sank back into my calm place, thinking of the jasmine-draped pergola at Darkhaven, Liam's sun orchid catching the light. In a sudden rush, from the pit of my stomach, I was hit with an overwhelming feeling of doom. Before I could place it, it was gone.

Dad didn't take his eyes off Sean until the latter was firmly sealed away behind the elevator doors. Then he knelt by the suit who was still on the floor, examined the man's head and beckoned to the other suit, still standing to the side.

'Help Tim to the infirmary,' he ordered, but his voice was kinder now.

'I'm fine,' Tim mumbled. The other suit nodded and began to drag his colleague to his feet. Dad ushered me through a door into the main foyer, out through the wide glass front doors and into the waiting car.

CHAPTER 21

Hearts Beat

'Are you okay?' Dad asked as we walked into a swanky cafe. I nodded vaguely. He watched me like he was waiting for me to faint or something. My neck stung where the needle had jabbed it, but I figured whatever Sean had wanted me injected with, presumably some drug to knock me out, had mostly stayed in the syringe when Dad had intervened. The restaurant was almost full, although thankfully not loud, and most of the customers were sitting at tiny tables set for one or two with their laptops or notebooks. The hushed room was dim, every dark wood table lit by its own lamp hanging just above it, giving each area a sense of enclosed privacy. It seemed like a peaceful place to read a book and enjoy a hot chocolate.

Dad led me to a table in the corner with high-backed, cushioned chairs. I sighed as I sank into mine. A waiter appeared, and Dad ordered a chocolate milkshake, a latte and two eggs Benedict. The waiter disappeared with barely a word, leaving a jug of chilled water on the table.

'All-day breakfast,' Dad said, smiling serenely.

'Don't you want to know what happened? Why I was being attacked?' I asked.

He gave me a sympathetic smile. 'It's a top-secret facility for a black-ops Taskforce commissioned by a security office that I direct. I know what happened, Gabby. I'm sorry I didn't get back sooner.' He put his hand on mine.

I swallowed. He hadn't gone to see the higher-ups. He *was* the higher-ups. I let his admission sit for a moment, and then pulled my hand back. 'So is that where you work when you're in town?'

'It's part of where I work.'

'What you just did, getting me out – will that be a problem for you?'

'How about,' he said, pouring water and pushing a glass towards me, 'you leave that for me to worry about.' He smiled warmly, but there was still a shadow in his eyes. I held his gaze for a moment, then looked away. I couldn't get an intuitive sense of him, but he was obviously troubled.

'I'll always look out for you,' he said.

'Thanks,' I mumbled, wondering if I should be grateful or wary. My intuition was giving me nothing. For now, I knew it was safe enough to trust Dad. But something about him still nagged at me. He knew more than he was letting on.

Our drinks arrived. I took a sip, still struggling to control the trembling that came in various waves. Shock, I supposed. But even through my mental haze, I realised the milkshake was delicious. No sour milk detected by my super-taste buds this time, but I did get a hint of carob. Unlike Alex's health chocolates, this was ...

'Amazing.' I hadn't meant to say it out loud.

Dad flashed a grin. 'Right?'

'How come you've kept this place secret? Or is it like, a special government restaurant or something?'

'Let's go with "or something".'

'If it's exclusive, how come I can be here now?'

'Well, I am one of their best customers.' The waiter brought our meals. Perfectly poached eggs sat atop piles of house-smoked salmon, fresh spinach and lightly buttered English muffins, all drizzled with a deliciously lemon-scented hollandaise. Two glasses of sparkling wine were placed on the table.

'Compliments of the house, Mr Whitehall.' The waiter gave a reverent smile and vanished. I stared at the bubbles streaming to the top of the glass, then at the space where the waiter had been.

'You're like royalty,' I remarked.

Unperturbed, Dad picked up his glass and took a sip. I was cautious. The first and last time I'd tried wine, I'd been twelve years old. It had been a stinking-hot summer afternoon. Dad had poured us drinks – apple juice for me and Chardonnay for him, both in wine glasses since I insisted on having a grown-up beverage. Dad looked so refreshed, sitting back on the patio, sweating wine glass in one hand, frozen strawberry in the other, that I begged for a sip. Of course, it was disgusting, all sour and mouldy-tasting, and I impetuously declared that wine would never be for me. Since then, I'd stuck to light apple cider when Dad permitted a quiet drink on special occasions, and a four-pack of bright green, zesty-lime premixed vodkas when Zenna and I had been feeling bold enough to sneak into a dodgy-looking bottle shop on her seventeenth birthday. Stealing Alex's port had been a rare break. It was a tame life.

After a surreptitious sniff of the sparkling wine, I took a tiny sip. Bubbles burst across my tongue, then it was gone, before I even had a chance to taste it. I tried again with a bigger mouthful. The fizz was delightful, the flavour subtle and fruity. Sipping away, I found myself two-thirds down the glass.

'You should eat while you drink that,' Dad suggested.

I set the glass down and turned my attention to the salmon and eggs, but it was too late. I felt as if the bubbles had escaped up to my brain and were jiggling it around so that every time I tried to catch a thought, it slipped out of reach like a butterfly evading a net. On the other hand, the sensory overload dulled a bit, and I felt my muscles relaxing for the first time in weeks. Even my mind started to drop its guard.

I smothered some salmon in sauce and relished the complexity of the tastes and textures. The fish was so tender it melted into my tongue, and I savoured the smoky flavour. Since my advanced taste was easier to control – *just don't eat anchovies* was the extent of Donovan's advice – I'd simply avoided strong flavours and focussed on getting my other senses in order. Now I wondered if I'd been missing out, not exploring more taste options, or if I'd just been too stressed to notice what I was eating lately. Maybe both.

I washed down a mouthful of spinach and runny egg yolk with more wine. I wanted answers, and Dad seemed to be in a good mood. Besides, he owed me.

'So you know about Luci,' I began. It wasn't a question, but I wanted him to acknowledge it. He nodded as he took a mouthful.

'Do you know…' I tried to think of a way to tease it out of him without telling him about Netica, in case he didn't know. Then I thought of Sean. Dad was obviously even higher up in this system than I'd realised. Whatever Sean knew, Dad had known for ages.

He lowered his fork. 'That she's still working for the Netica Project?'

'How long have you known?'

A sombre look came into his eyes. 'Nearly eighteen years.' His voice was barely more than a whisper, but I had no trouble hearing it.

'Does Alex know that she's still alive?'

Dad shook his head. 'He doesn't know about any of this. The Netica Project is well above his clearance level. What was done to you, he never would have allowed. He's always tried to protect you, far better than I ever did.'

What was that supposed to mean? His eyes tightened, creases deepening around his features as his expression closed. Now I had to be cagey, careful, and ask questions that would garner answers instead of shutting him down. It was tricky, what with my brain floating around in a champagne bubble bath. 'Why do you hunt the people who found me?'

'We don't hunt them. They're not animals.' He smiled, but it looked forced.

'But you have them on a hit list.' I wondered if that was the real term. Funny, how you could be so close to someone and have no real idea what they did, and then find that they had entire eating establishments pulling out all the stops for them just for a late brunch. As if on cue, our empty champagne glasses and plates were cleared, and within seconds two glasses of red wine appeared out of thin air, although I noticed that Dad's was a few shades darker than mine. I was amazed again at how pleasant it was to drink. Dad toyed with the stem of his glass.

'They are a Taskforce set up specifically to eliminate all un-controlled traces of the Praegressus program. Obviously, we don't want to kill innocent people, so we don't target the test subjects until they become active. As for the people you mentioned, well, they had the choice to come over quietly. They still do.'

'What would happen to them?' I asked, voice small. I hadn't missed the terminology: uncontrolled traces. Obviously the Taskforce wasn't eliminating all traces. Just the ones that weren't in their laboratories.

Dad shrugged. 'That's for me to decide, if it ever arises.' His shoulders were strained, in a way I'd never seen, as if he were carrying a heavy weight.

The waiter took advantage of our silence to return and clear our empty glasses. 'Excuse me sir, but Chef Antioni has requested that you try their new dessert.'

Dad looked up, smiling, all melancholy slipping away as if it had been a mask of smoke. 'Please tell them we'd be delighted.'

The waiter returned minutes later, placing two plates with a chocolatey square in the centre on the table. The dish looked simple, presented with a swirl of sauce and an intricate chocolate lace thing jutting out on top. I picked up the cake fork and took a bite.

I had to stop myself from sliding off my chair and face-planting into the plate to inhale the whole thing. If heaven had a taste, it would be this. It was smooth and textured, like fine layers of wafer between moussey fudge, a decadent chocolate that melted into every crevice of my mouth and lingered with a subtle orange flavour right at the end. I could have cried.

We didn't talk for a while, enjoying the dessert and yet another wine – this one a deep amber that danced in its glass, felt like syrup on my tongue and tasted like nostalgia and raisins sitting in the sun. I was surprised to find that my glass was empty.

I tried to stand and my head, rather than tittering about on its bubbles, swam in circles instead. I paused, hand on the chair to steady myself.

Dad chuckled. 'Come on,' he said, taking my arm with a firm, gentle hand. 'Let's go home.'

Initially, I insisted on returning to school, but Dad wouldn't hear of it. He settled me on the couch, supplied me with a glass of water and a juice that looked suspiciously green, then snapped open his briefcase and lifted something out of it. It was the remains of my tracking bracelet.

'I imagine you'll be wanting this back,' he said, passing it to me. I clasped it around my wrist so I wouldn't lose it in case Donovan wanted it back. The damaged plate scratched my skin.

Dad disappeared into his office, leaving me on the couch pretending to read Dickens. I was still only halfway through. The words swam around the page dizzyingly, making even less sense to me than usual. I longed to read, to lose myself in someone else's story for a while, but all I could think about, now that both the shock of the events and the buzz of the wine were wearing off, was how I'd failed. I hadn't got Luci out. The deal was off. After the next thunderstorm, while my friends were preparing for uni and internships, a body that looked like mine would be found lying on a footpath or something, apparently killed by a lightning strike. I'd never see them again. I wondered if Keraun could stop all thunderstorms in Perth for the next decade or two.

A phone beeped, startling me out of my musings, but it wasn't mine. Dad hurried past, briefcase in hand, and after admonishing me to rest and drink water, took off. I was left alone. I shivered as I looked around the open living room, where Sean had first met me.

I hadn't really wanted to go to school. I'd just wanted to get away from any prying ears and speak to someone from Darkhaven, but now that I had the opportunity, I found that I was reluctant to call Stephen. What would I say? I'd failed. I tossed the book aside and plodded down the hall to my room. I still felt light-headed, unable to make sense of things properly. Perhaps reading some *Discworld* would make me feel better. Granny Weatherwax always left me in a good mood.

I opened my bedroom door, glimpsed a dark shape on my bed and started, staggering against the door frame. Keraun was sprawled over the unmade mess, reading my economics textbook. He was trying to look casual, but I could feel the tension rolling off him.

'Hey,' he greeted me, his voice taut.

'What?' I asked bluntly, caught off-guard and grumpy about my mission failure.

He looked up, angry brown eyes grazing my face before returning to the book. He closed it and set it on my bedside table, interrogating me with his gaze. 'Why didn't you tell me?'

'Tell you what?'

'That it was your mother you were after. That she put you into the Praegressus program.'

I stared at him. If I was awkward admitting it before, it was nothing to the humiliation that flooded me now. Now that I knew she'd left me.

'I don't know.' I flopped down on the bed next to him and lay back. My head was still spinning from the wine, and words like *Praegressus* were slippery in my mind.

'I found your file at the Taskforce, and more on the Prae-gressus. Luci's signature is all over it.'

I didn't answer. It was hard to form a complete idea as I swayed between righteous anger and tipsy indifference. She'd been dead to me all these years. She could just go back to being dead. Why did it matter?

After a moment, Keraun lay back too, staring at the ceiling with its galactic swirls and one lonely glow-in-the-dark star that had survived all these years. 'I know what it's like.'

I gazed at the star. 'What's that?'

'Having a mother who doesn't see you.'

Except my mother had seen me. Stared right at me, and told me to leave like I was just one more irritation in the ointment of her day. What she hadn't seen was the little red-haired girl clutching an unfinished crayon drawing while her father yelled at her. 'What happened?' I asked.

He clasped his hands on his chest, twisting his thumbs. 'I dropped out of school. She hasn't spoken to me since, except for Sol meetings.'

'Sounds harsh.'

He sighed. 'It wasn't just her. But she took it personally.'

'Screw them both, then.'

Keraun flipped onto an elbow, his face just inches away from mine. His eyes burned at the edges.

'Is she the reason you wanted to get into the Taskforce?' He watched me, face intense. I tried to keep my expression re-laxed, which actually wasn't that difficult. The alcohol re-asserted itself, making things seem trivial, and suddenly his vexation was amusing. He frowned, inhaling deeply. 'Are you drunk?'

'Maybe a little.' I giggled. 'And yeah. Well, that was some of it. So what?'

He moved his arm, lifting it past his hip towards me, but then stopped, letting it fall onto the bed. 'What was the rest of it?'

No point holding back now. 'Stephen promised me that I could live on my own terms if we were successful. No fake death and leaving my family and friends.' Except all that was bust. Unless . . . Keraun had mentioned there were files. Files that might help Darkhaven's research. If I could go back and get them, convince Dad to help . . . I toyed with the bedspread, ruffling it, then smoothing out the creases, not meeting Keraun's gaze. After a moment, he placed his fingers under my chin and lifted my face to look at him. I pulled my chin away but held his gaze.

'I understand why you did it,' he said. 'But I need you to promise me something.'

His eyes drilled through mine, straight through my brain and into the place I called my "guilt centre", a special part of my mind that Cecelia was particularly good at appealing to when she wanted me to study with her instead of going to the Shack.

Reflexively, I nodded. 'Sure.'

About a millisecond later, I regretted it.

'Please don't go back. To the Taskforce.' It was like he'd pulled the idea out of my head with his stare.

'Why not? Luci could have captured me today. She didn't.' I had to admit that the small part of my brain that seemed impervious to wine agreed with him.

'She also didn't call off security. When that agent caught you in the hallway, there was nothing I could do. Not without risking everything. And Gabby, I don't want . . .' he trailed off, eyes glowing yellow. I met his gaze questioningly, waiting for him to finish. He looked away. 'Just be safe, okay?'

'Okay.' For an alien god, he was rubbish at explaining things. I figured I could be safe on my own terms. I didn't want or expect him to swoop in and save me from anything. He stared at me again. It was mind-scrambling, with the yellow eyes.

'Sure? You did just promise. You can't get out of it because you had a glass of wine.'

'I promise to be safe.' I had no idea how exactly to keep that promise, so I tried changing the subject again, just to ease the gaze he had skewered me with. 'How do you know it was wine?'

He laughed and rolled away, his eyes returning to brown. The pressure that had been building between us simmered down. 'I can smell it.'

I giggled again, almost swallowing a burp. Half of it escaped. We lay in comfortable silence for a few minutes.

'Can I ask you something?' I said, speaking up to the swirly ceiling.

'Sure.'

'What else did you find in the Taskforce files?'

'Praegressus is a retrovirus that rewrites human DNA with subtle magic. You wouldn't be the first race to genetically modify yourselves to accelerate your evolution, but very few actually make it work.'

'There have been others?'

'It's happening all over the universe as we speak. Our history books cover major events. Usually, modification goes horribly wrong without the magic to back it up.' A cloud drifted over his face.

An unsettling sensation crawled through my stomach. I rolled over to look at him. 'Am I, like, healthy?'

He grinned. 'More than healthy. Whoever started this used Ma, the healing magic, so it's stable. We all have basically the same DNA, humans all over the universe. Other civilisations have wiped themselves out with accelerated modification, but you now have genetic expression that just about matches mine. Of course, you need to train it. You can't cheat that part.'

So we were magically modified humans. I recalled an earlier conversation. 'Could you help me train so I can travel to other star systems?'

This time he laughed outright. 'Talk about pick the hardest thing.'

'Why is it the hardest?'

Before he could reply, my phone rang. I bent down to pick it up from the floor where it must have fallen and saw Stephen's name flashing. I silenced the phone and clambered back onto the bed.

'Shouldn't you answer that?'

I shrugged. 'It can wait. He didn't exactly drop everything to see me off before sending me into the Taskforce.'

Keraun pretended to look hurt. 'And here I was, thinking you were just enjoying my company too much to leave.'

Rolling my eyes, I turned to give him a sarcastic smirk, but I stopped – he had slid closer, and his face was inches away from mine. I swallowed, uncomfortable looking into his eyes this closely, but unable to look away. In my peripheral vision, his hand hovered in mid-air, indecisive, inching towards me as his eyes began to glow with their surreal yellow. I was acutely aware of the doona rustling with every micro-movement and the feel of my shirt on my back as I let my eyes drift down to his lips. They were closed, but I knew that if I leaned a fraction closer, they would part, and so would mine, and I hadn't re-freshed my lipstick when I got home, although maybe lipstick was actually kinda gross for kissing, or perhaps he wouldn't want Siren Red on his face, and I could hear both our hearts beating, this close; mine was racing, and his barely above a slow thud so it could be that I had read this whole thing wrong and how was a person ever supposed to –

My phone rang again, puncturing the moment like an overinflated balloon and leaving it in tatters on the floor. I fumbled for the phone. It slipped down between the front of the bed and the wall and continued ringing on the floor.

'You're a woman in demand. I'll go,' Keraun said, already standing and stretching one side, his lanky arm reaching up to the ceiling.

'Stay,' I urged. Belly down on the bed, I thrust my arm after the phone. It stopped ringing.

'It's okay. Call me.' Keraun flashed a grin and, in a movement so fast he might have just vanished, disappeared out the door.

I crawled under the bed to rescue my phone from the dust bunnies and saw it was Zenna calling this time. Head still spinning from either Keraun's recent proximity or perhaps the three glasses of wine and sudden standing up, I flopped back on the bed and sent Zenna a text.

What's up?

Meet outside the surf club, ten minutes?

Sure. Aren't you at school?

I didn't really expect her to answer that, since I was obviously absent too. It was about ten minutes into lunchtime. I booked a rideshare and waited in the driveway, thinking of what Sean had said and hoping she hadn't done anything reckless.

CHAPTER 22

More Like Mutants

I found Zenna sitting at a picnic bench next to the West Beach Surf Club, listlessly picking at chips and gravy with a plastic fork. I climbed onto the bench next to her, plopping down as I lost my balance. My butt cheek landed on something hard – the disk from the Taskforce was still in my back pocket. I took it out and put it on the table so I could sit comfortably. 'Hey, girl.'

'Hey.' Zenna's voice was bleak, like all the life had been sucked out of it.

'What's wrong?'

She heaved a sigh and flicked a fallen chip off the bench onto the grass. An opportunistic seagull pecked it up.

'Zenna?' I asked softly.

Her face scrunched like she was about to cry. 'I'm not going to graduate.'

'What?'

'I flunked my English test. Now I'm going to fail the unit and I won't get the internship if I don't pass high school this year.'

'What, like, literally failed?'

'Forty per cent.'

'Well, the marks still count. That's only a small difference to make up in the final exam, right?'

'I'll be lucky if I even get fifty on the exam, and I'll never scrape sixty.' She tossed another morsel out to the gathering seagulls. They squabbled and consumed it before it even hit the ground.

'The exam has more weighting, you wouldn't need sixty. I thought you were going okay with English this year.' Last year, after Zenna had nearly failed first semester, her parents had arranged a tutor for her. She had pulled things together by the end of the year.

Now she shrugged. 'I just can't do it.'

'You can,' I urged, stealing a chip before the whole lot went to the birds.

'That's easy for you to say. You've always been smart.' The words stung a little, until she continued, voice lowered to a miserable whisper. 'I think I'm a mistake. God, or whatever it is, made a mistake with me.'

My hand was halfway back to the chips. I redirected it to her shoulder. 'You are not a mistake. You have amazing talent. Besides, God or whatever has nothing to do with it.'

'So I'm an evolutionary failure.'

I went for the chips. 'More like an adaptation that will go on to be something totally new and brilliant.'

Her lips almost twitched into a smile. 'So a mutation, then.'

I giggled. 'If you like. Maybe you're at the wrong school.'

'Mutant school.' She smiled wanly. 'Sounds about right. What's been going on with you lately? I've been trying to find you to talk for ages, and you're never around.'

It was my turn to shrug, although the accusation felt unfair. She'd bailed on me often enough, and for every message she answered there were three she didn't. 'Just study. I'm worried about passing too.'

'Yeah right. When have you ever been worried about studying? You can't lie to me, Gabs. I know you're hiding something.'

She was right. Although Cecelia was my oldest and closest friend, Zenna had a knack for seeing straight through me. I was so tired of lying. I yearned to tell someone about what I was going through, someone who wasn't involved in all this crap, someone who just cared for me and not what I could offer the organisation. I closed my eyes for a moment, sinking into my quiet place, testing the feeling. Was it safe to tell her? And then the question hit, the question so obvious and stupid that it had never occurred to me to ask in all my training with Liam. How would I know? What if I didn't? Fear shot through me as I recalled being in the stairwell a few hours earlier. I'd used my intuition. I'd made the wrong call. Because I didn't know.

And just like that, it turned off. The calm place that helped me know what to do, what people around me were feeling, how to react, was gone. My intuition vanished, leaving me adrift. I scrambled internally after it, but I couldn't find it. There was no calm place, just a tumultuous sea of ragged thoughts and jumbled emotions.

'Gabs? Are you okay?'

I turned blindly towards the sound before registering that I could still physically see, even if I could no longer sense anything intuitively. I stared at Zenna. 'I'm not the same,' I whispered.

'I know that much. What's happened, Gabby?'

Her voice was soft, gentle, yet firm, like it could handle what was happening. I didn't need intuition to know that even if I could tell Cecelia, she was too busy and under too much stress to take it right now. I couldn't implicate Alex in something that his brother had been hiding for years. I couldn't trust Dad, not completely. I wasn't ready to be vulnerable with Keraun. And everyone at Darkhaven was on the wrong side of the looking-glass. They hadn't tried to live in the real world with this. Zenna's voice, concern cracking around the edges, broke through my front. 'I was struck by lightning. About a month ago, I guess.'

Zenna gasped. 'What? How are you, you know . . .'

'Alive?'

She nodded. 'Isn't that supposed to kill you?'

Flamebeard's lesson popped into my head. 'Apparently not, but that's not the point. Something happened. When I was a baby, my mum put me in an experiment that means when I get struck by lightning, I get all this enhancement. Long life, super-fast healing, stuff like that.'

Zenna's eyes widened. 'So you're, like, superhuman?'

I shifted. 'I guess so.'

'Wow.'

'I've been working with a team who find people like me – the other kids who were in the experiment – and train us. Sort of. Stephen can talk to animals telepathically. Liam is clairvoyant. I saw Donovan get run over by a car and just get up and walk away. And she's crazy strong.'

Zenna's eyes kindled. 'Strong like . . . super strong? Like, lift-up-a-car strong?'

'Fish it out of a dam and throw it over her head like it's a handbag.' I'd seen her do it. I'd have been amazed if I hadn't been in the car.

'That would be awesome.' I could see Zenna's mind working at about a million miles an hour, melancholy forgotten.

'You can't use Donovan for your film project. Actually, yes, yes you can. Take her away. If I never see her again, that would be great.'

'What else can you do?'

I told her everything. I told her about the casino, the rally drive and my advancing intuition. My chest lightened tenfold just talking about Donovan's torture sessions. I choked up as I explained how I'd screwed up at the Taskforce, taking the wrong door and getting caught and not noticing that I'd lost the tracking bracelet. To cover my emotion, I told her about playing poker with Liam.

'That sounds fun,' she remarked.

'You'd be rubbish at poker,' I said. Zenna's face was a picture book of her feelings.

She pouted. 'I might not be.'

'Anyway, it doesn't matter because it's gone. My intuition. I screwed up. I'm basically a human with a keen sense of smell who has no idea what to do with her much-extended life.'

'Well, look on the bright side,' she said. 'At least you have a lot longer to figure it out.' Then she stabbed me, hard, with her plastic fork.

'Ow! What are you doing?' I pulled my arm away, rubbing at the red marks on my skin. The fork was bent in half.

'Testing your healing thing. Apparently you have iron skin now.'

'It's a plastic fork. It folds up at the sight of a cooked potato. Are you some kind of sadist?'

'No, more a masochist,' she replied, shadows deepening in her eyes. 'Sorry.'

'Yeah.' The marks were gone, but I was still miffed. 'Do you really need proof?'

'Would it bother you if I said yes?'

I considered, then stuck with candid honesty. 'A bit, but I understand.'

'I believe that you're telling the truth.'

'But you think I'm a crazy person?'

A frown darkened her face. 'If anyone is crazy around here, it's me. But I guess I just can't reconcile it in my mind.'

'That makes sense. Really. I would struggle to believe this if I hadn't experienced it first hand.' And also met a lightning god in the same month. But I'd left Keraun out of my narrative. I was too churned up about him, and besides, an alien god was a level of unreality that no one could be expected to believe.

'What are you going to do?' Zenna asked, interrupting my personal Keraun tangent.

'About what?'

'Donovan. She's abusing you, Gabby. You don't need that.'

'I don't know.'

We were quiet for a while. Absentmindedly, I picked up the disk and toyed with it, turning it over in my hands. Zenna reached out to take it.

'What's that?'

'I don't know. Some sort of backup disk, I think. I stole it from the Taskforce.'

Zenna lifted it out of my fingers and examined the holographic side. 'It's a holofoil,' she said, peering at it from different angles.

'A holo-what?'

'Holofoil. Difficult to copy.' She kept inspecting it. 'But it's unusual. The pattern almost looks familiar. Like a cipher,' she said, handing it back.

My phone rang. I sighed, contemplating throwing it in the ocean. But I couldn't put this off forever. I answered it. 'Hey Stephen.'

'Where are you? Are you safe?'

'I'm fine, I'm at the surf club.'

'The West Beach Surf Club?'

'Yeah. I'm okay. I'm with a friend.'

'I'm five minutes away. Wait there.'

Stephen hung up. I'd forgotten, what with the wine, Keraun's confusing yellow stare and Zenna's latest crisis, that Stephen must have tracked me to the Taskforce dead zone, then been redirected when Sean took my bracelet. He had no idea if I had found Luci, or made it out, or been captured. I shuddered as I thought of how close I'd come to being locked back in an interrogation cell.

Then I had another awful thought. I was still wearing the bracelet. Darkhaven had heard everything. Including my confession to Zenna. I gripped her arm.

'Go back to school.' My voice was urgent. I tried to keep the panic out of it. Zenna looked offended.

'What? Bugger that.'

'Just get out of here. They're coming.'

'Who's coming?'

'Stephen and Donovan. I'm not supposed to tell anyone.'

She scowled. 'Don't you trust me?'

'Of course I do, it's just...' I hadn't told her about the memory modification. I hadn't wanted to scare her.

'Never mind,' she said, collecting her bag and scooping up the chip box. 'I'm not good enough to be part of your superhuman life.'

I huffed. I was trying to protect her, not shut her out. 'That's not fair, Z.'

'Well, not much is.' She stalked off.

I watched her go, every muscle tightening as I fought the urge to run after her. But it was safer for her to leave. I unclasped the bracelet and shoved it deep into my back pocket, picked up the disk and walked in the opposite direction, hoping that Stephen would spot me first and Zenna would get away. The last thing I wanted was for her to be more caught up in this than she already was. Guilt stabbed at my heart. I'd been selfish to tell her so much.

I stomped down the street, waiting for Stephen to find me. The crash of waves on the beach became louder, the briny scent of seaweed overpowering, the sunlight reflecting off the footpath too bright as it lanced my pupils. And I had no calm place, no intuition. I couldn't sense what was going to happen. I had to find a way to make another deal with Stephen. I wasn't going to abandon my friends and family. I would go back to the Taskforce, find Luci and bring her back, whether she wanted it or not. And take Sean and his stupid threats out of the equation.

Keraun's face swam into my mind, and my stomach twisted at the thought of breaking my promise to him. But I had no choice.

The pounding walk helped. My muscles loosened as my stamps were replaced by firm footfalls, my stride lengthened and my legs swung through for each step. I found a tiny grip of control over my senses and felt into my calm place, seeking some feeling. But where before I had been a still pond, into which I could drop a single stone and feel the ripples fan out, indicating what I wanted to know, now I was a roiling ocean, a swirling mass of black doubt. Maybe I'd never had intuition, and it had always been a self-delusion. I shied away, coming back to my external senses. A car was approaching from a block away, and it sounded like the silver Corolla. I heard it slow as it pulled up behind me, but I didn't stop.

'Gabby!' Stephen called over the sound of the engine, still running.

I kept walking.

'Gabby!' There was an edge to his voice, but it wasn't anger. At least, it wasn't all anger. Worried frustration, perhaps. I slowed to a shuffle, but didn't turn around. The car pulled up alongside me. 'Please get in the car,' Stephen begged.

'Do I have a choice?' When there was no answer, I looked across. My heart dropped a few inches when I saw that Stephen's eyes were slick with tears. Unabashed, he met my gaze.

'Always,' he said softly. 'Is that what you'd like? For me to leave you alone?'

My eyes went hot too. I looked away. 'I don't know what I want.' My stuffy voice betrayed me.

'How about we go somewhere else? Not Darkhaven.'

Still staring at the silver buckles on my boots, I nodded. My fingers fumbled on the door handle. Stephen leaned over and pushed it open for me. I climbed in.

'What happened?' he asked as we drove. It took me a minute to realise he was asking about my expedition into the Taskforce. I gave him a full report, including Sean's request for me to join them, Luci's refusal to see me, my bracelet being tampered with and my discoveries on the lower floors. I told him about the children and my theory that they were up to at least a third iteration of the program. Stephen's lips pressed into a firmer line.

He and Donovan had followed my tracking data up to the block where Sean's jammer cut the signal, then they'd begun painstakingly surveying every building in the area for signs of the Taskforce. Before they'd found anything, the tracker had reappeared on the map, moving, and they figured I was being taken somewhere else. They'd followed the little dot across the city for over an hour before Liam caught a vision of Sean's trap for them. Then they heard Dad giving the bracelet back to me on the mic transmitter. By the time they drove all the way back to West Beach, I'd already gone to meet Zenna.

'I'm sorry about Luci,' I said, after we'd been driving in silence for a while.

Stephen looked over, eyes pained. 'No, I'm sorry. I should never have involved you in this.'

'It was my choice,' I said stubbornly, fiddling with the hem of my shirt. I wasn't entirely sure I agreed with my assertion, but stubbornness was all the defence I had against crying.

'I don't know if it was. We don't always take the right path in the work we do. With you – and not just you – we may not have done the right things.'

My stubbornness faded, leaving a wash of confusion and disappointment.

'I don't think there was a right thing,' I whispered. It was more to myself. There wasn't a right choice to be made. Not about uni, not about whether to become some sort of superhuman outcast, not about confronting my mother, not about Keraun. The pile expanded in my mind, flooding out until my chest went tight and the tears erupted. It started as a flow, then escalated into mortifying sobs. I gasped for breath.

Stephen pulled over, passed me a tissue from the glovebox and rubbed my shoulder. I just managed to get it under control and take a breath when I thought of Cecelia and how crushed she would be if Sean stopped her becoming a doctor. A whole new wave of sobs tumbled over me as I mentally writhed in helplessness. How I'd parted with Alex. Zenna getting dragged into this mess because I wasn't strong enough to keep it to myself. I stopped trying to fight it. I closed my eyes and curled up in the front seat, letting the storm wash over me.

CHAPTER 23

Option B

We wound up at a dingy lunch bar. The man sweeping the floor informed us that they closed in half an hour. Stephen ordered drinks while I huddled at a table in the corner. Liam appeared out of nowhere and pulled up a chair next to me. I supposed he'd been out looking for me too, and I wondered how he hadn't simply found me. But he'd said his visions were often unpredictable and not always what he was hoping to see. Maybe he'd just seen me coming here.

'Are you okay?' he asked.

'Sure.' I slumped onto the table.

'Breathe, Gabby.'

I took a quick gulp of air into the top of my ribs.

'You remind me of Donovan sometimes,' he observed, a cheeky glint in his eyes. 'Ferociously stubborn.'

The comment hit me in the belly, knocking any breath I did have out like a physical blow. I spluttered wordlessly.

'Breathe,' he said again.

I took a deep, shuddering breath, trying to hold it together. Bad enough to cry in front of Stephen like that, in the privacy of a car. No way was anyone else going to be privy to the embarrassing sobs. Especially someone who'd just insulted me.

'I've lost it, Liam,' I said. He didn't need to ask what "it" was. I wondered vaguely if he'd ever lost his clairvoyant ability. 'But there was something before I left the Taskforce, before I lost it. I don't know what it meant.'

Liam gazed at me like he could read the thoughts straight out of my head. As if it would make sense if he could. 'Tell me,' he said softly. 'It doesn't matter what it is. Any information is good.'

'It was a feeling of dread, like something bad is coming. But I don't know what it means. What if I'm just overreacting, and it's nothing?'

Liam pursed his lips, considering, reaching into his own place of intuition. 'Do you know what it was about?' he asked.

I opened my hands in my lap in a gesture of helplessness. 'Darkhaven, I think. But, Liam, it's gone. I can't use my intuition at all. And what if I got it wrong? It was a split second. It could just as easily have been exams or something stupid.'

His hands covered mine and closed them back together. Warmth spread up my wrists and I realised I was shivering.

'It's all right.' Liam spoke in the comforting, hypnotic tones he used when teaching me relaxation techniques. He shrugged out of his jacket and pulled it around my shoulders. I lifted my chin, still refusing to give in to being cold or on the verge of epic, gasping sobs again, but I couldn't deny that the jacket felt like sinking into a warm bath.

Stephen appeared with three takeaway cups. I smelled coffee and the earthy tang of green tea, but mine contained chocolate. I took a sip and felt some semblance of humanity return.

'I was joking, you know,' Liam said, lifting a corner of his mouth into a smile. 'About Donovan.'

'No you weren't,' I replied. I hated the bitch, but even I couldn't deny that I dealt with frustration about as well as she did. I flashed Liam a grin. 'You don't get forgiven that easily.'

Stephen glanced at his watch. 'It's time to go, your dad will be worrying.'

I wondered what I was meant to do now. All the training had been working towards getting to Luci. Maybe it was the lack of intuition, but now that the mission was over, I was directionless.

'I have a question for you,' Stephen ventured as we pulled onto the freeway back towards West Beach. Liam had insisted I keep his jacket, but as the heater warmed up the car, I shrugged out of it. I folded it and placed it on the back seat, mumbling in acknowledgement of Stephen's comment. Every muscle was resistant to moving, and my neck still ached from the needle jab.

'Why were you running away from me this afternoon?'

'Because I wanted you to follow me, instead of Zenna.'

'Why would I follow her?'

'Because I was wearing the bracelet when I –' I stopped, kicking my exhausted brain for dishing out answers without thinking. 'You didn't know I told her everything.'

Stephen smiled. 'The bracelet was just for your protection at the Taskforce. Not so we could pry into your private conversations.'

'But all this is supposed to be secret, right?' Stupid, slow brain.

'Yes, but all the genetic engineering in the world won't change the fact that you're human. Sometimes these things happen. You've been through a lot today. It's natural that you would need to debrief, and she was there. Obviously I would have preferred if I'd found you sooner and we could have avoided complicating the situation.'

I hmphed.

'So who is Zenna?' Stephen asked lightly. Even though I'd banked on them not knowing who I'd been talking to, I was surprised again by how little information Darkhaven actually had on my life. Especially compared to the Taskforce. I supposed it was just as much for their protection as to preserve my privacy – the fewer people in the real world who could recognise them, the better. It felt weird that I could be so involved with these people, and yet if someone from Darkhaven met my dad or uncle or friends on the street, neither would know the other. Well, Dad might know everyone.

I decided a little vagueness wouldn't hurt. 'A friend.'

'And she knows about your Event, and what's been happening since.'

'Yeah, kind of.' All of.

'You trust her?'

'Sure, she's one of my best friends. What are you going to do to her?'

Stephen smiled, but his eyes were sad. 'To her? We're not an evil institution. One person knowing about this isn't going to change the world. If you trust her, so do I. You could probably use some best friend advice. But please don't tell anyone else. I don't want to scare you, but the less people who know, the safer it is for everyone.'

I nodded, staring out the window at the scrubby trees blurring by. Sean's threats stuck in my head like thorny burrs. 'What do I do, Stephen? About losing my intuition?'

He shifted in his seat. 'You've been under a lot of pressure. I think you should probably take some time off. It might come back by itself.'

Time off sounded amazing. But I didn't think time off would help with much of the stuff that was starting to pile up. I'd been hoping that my mission at the Taskforce would take care of the Darkhaven issue, but having failed at rescuing Luci, that deal was obviously off. I was back to being declared dead. And if I did find a way to make another deal, it was now nearly the middle of August. TISC applications closed at the end of September. I still had zero ideas about uni. On top of that, exams were looming and I could no longer rely on my intuition to get me through without studying. I felt like I'd forgotten how to study; it had been so many weeks since I'd actually read a chapter in a textbook. Maybe time off would help with that particular problem.

'How long?' I asked. I expected him to say "take a week" or "until Monday".

'How about we pick things up after your exams? If you feel comfortable with your sensory control. Of course you're welcome to continue your training with Donovan if you want to.'

Ha. Donovan's harsh approach was the number one thing I wanted respite from. But I was prepared to keep enduring that if it meant something. If it meant I could choose to keep my friends and family.

'I was thinking . . .' I began, unsure how to phrase my idea. I swallowed. 'I could try to get into the Taskforce again. Sean would take me in. Then I can report back to you.'

Stephen shook his head. 'It's too dangerous. We need to find out more about what they're up to, and if they're abducting children to do it, we need to stop them, but I won't send you in again. Not like that.'

I had no plan to make a case with. I sat in silence. Mental silence, even. I wasn't thinking anything. The day had caught up with me, and I was about to crash. Stephen pulled up in Dad's driveway.

'Focus on your exams. Spend some time with your friends. At the end of the school year, we'll make a plan,' he said.

By which he meant a plan to say goodbye forever. Ugh. But I couldn't argue. Without my intuition, exam study was at the top of my list. Except that now I was back to being conscripted to Darkhaven, and by January I would be dead to the world of TISC and ATAR exams and it wouldn't matter anyway.

As if Stephen knew what I was thinking, he added, 'You can still study from Darkhaven. Get your ATAR, Gabby.'

'Okay,' I grumbled, opening the car door and climbing out. Something flashed in the corner of my eye, and I glanced down to find the disk had fallen beside the seat. The holofoil glinted in the sunlight. I gave it to Stephen.

'Gabby,' Stephen called, leaning across the seat. I peered back in through the window.

He looked on the verge of saying something important. I could see doubt stacking up in his eyes. But after a moment he blinked, and then all he said was, 'Stay safe.'

Opening my diary for the first time in ages delivered a rude shock: mock exams were four weeks away. After an afternoon of fuzzy studying, dinner and more studying, I stumbled into my bedroom and flopped on my bed, soaking in the softness of my feather quilt, wondering if I could be bothered having a shower. Something scratched my face. I rolled over and picked up a folded piece of paper. It was a note, in spiky handwriting.

Call me as soon as you can. K.

Odd. Why wouldn't Keraun just ring? Then I sighed. Probably because he knew that right now, I wouldn't answer my phone. I dialled his number.

'Hey, you got my note,' he said.

'Yeah, what's up? I'm about to fall asleep.' I wanted to talk to him. I even wanted to see him. But the day had been too long already, and I mostly just wanted to fall into bed.

Keraun's voice was hesitant. 'If you could take it back, would you?'

'Take what back, Keraun?'

'The transformation. You said you have to leave your family. If you could go back to being normal instead, would you?'

'I don't know. Maybe.'

'I stole a file from the Taskforce, one I didn't get a chance to read before you appeared.'

I waited.

'There's a cure for the Praegressus program,' he said. 'You can reverse it.'

I was silent for so long, he must have thought I'd fallen asleep because he said something about calling soon and hung up, his voice a velvet susurrus against my eardrums.

I stared at the silver swirls on my ceiling, suddenly less tired. I was back to my original choice, with no better ideas now than I'd had at the start. With a cure on the table, Stephen would force me to choose between Darkhaven and my life here, with or without my memories of the last five-and-a-half weeks, respectively. And there was more now than just the Netica Project that I didn't want to forget, although I wouldn't admit to myself that I was at all interested in a boy.

CHAPTER 24

More Than a Boyfriend

I called Stephen the next morning to tell him about the cure, something called Viciretro. Keraun had messaged me the technical details. Stephen stuck to his word and agreed to let me take the rest of the school year to decide what I wanted to do, encouraging me to put it out of my mind until after exams.

In the two weeks following the Taskforce debacle, I caught up on all the study I'd been pretending to do since my Event. Sort of. A lot of time disappeared as I sat thinking about Dark-haven and worrying about TISC. If I did actually do some work, I ended up doing the wrong stuff. When I was supposed to be reading Hawthorne, I found Atwood compelling and lost a week of lunchtimes to *The Handmaid's Tale*, leaving *The Scarlet Letter* lonely in my bag. I still hadn't finished *A Tale of Two Cities*. I had a complex about that book now; trying to read it seemed to jinx things. Cecelia's pencil would snap, prompting a frustrated outburst, Zenna would come over all moody and sullen or Alex – Dad was away again – would make green bowls for dinner. He called them "healthful gardens of Eden".

I called them glorified salad posing as real food, which should at a minimum contain two kinds of cheese.

Human Biology posed a similar problem. If I was meant to be reading a chapter on the nervous system, I suddenly found metabolism fascinating and would spend all evening on the Krebs cycle. I told myself it would be helpful to know all this stuff in the exam, but it did set me back in class exercises. Economics was all boring, and I was starting to think I really did need a tutor for maths. Having a better memory helped, but it wasn't that useful if I didn't understand the concepts. I missed my intuition.

Then of course there was another distraction, in the form of a human-looking alien god. Keraun seemed to know when Alex was going out and would appear on the doorstep five minutes later, casually suggesting a walk along the Swan River. Just as often, I messaged him when my brain was too full for more information and needed ice cream or some other sugar source. I hadn't forgotten my realisation that he had met me before my lightning Event, but I wasn't sure how to broach the subject. And I enjoyed hanging out with him. He was the one person from whom I didn't have to hide anything about my life. I laughed when he rocked up one day in a purple t-shirt with a lightning bolt on it.

'What?'

I kept giggling. To be fair, Cecelia and Zenna had started it, when we skipped out on Thursday afternoon's Phys Ed class and spent the hour in a vacant classroom overdosing on lollies and throwing Skittles at one another's faces. Five points for a hit, ten for a nose shot, but if the other person caught the Skittle in their mouth, it was twenty points to them. Due to my general lack of focus, I had lost. Significantly.

'What?' Keraun demanded.

I snickered. 'Cute shirt.'

'You were the one who suggested I should change my clothes sometimes. What's wrong with it?'

'Nothing. Just ...' I lapsed back into giggles. 'Nothing.'

'What is it?'

I tried to sober myself. 'I think I have a bit of Skittle shell in my eye.'

'Would you like me to have a look?' He was genuinely concerned.

I suppressed another laugh. 'No thanks. I'll be fine.'

'Are you sure?' he asked. It was innocent, a playful question, poking back at my amusement over his shirt. But I lost all desire to laugh. I still didn't have my intuition back. I didn't *know* things any more. The sense was gone. Even the sense of the roiling sea had vanished. I'd hoped that once my feelings had settled, I'd have my calm place back, but the turmoil had drifted away and left me floating in a void, far away from any sense of intuition. I didn't know how to get back. I didn't know where I was to get back from.

We took our gelato – I told Keraun to pick a flavour for me – and wandered to our favourite park bench. There had been no more charged encounters like the one in my room after Dad got me out of the Taskforce. I was grateful for the lack of complications but more than a little sorry as well. I kept reminding myself that study was priority, and besides, he was a super-evolved alien human with god powers and probably not even interested in me that way.

'Can I ask you something?' I said, between mouthfuls of strawberry ripple.

'Sure.'

'When we were talking, after the Taskforce thing, you said something about risking everything. What did you mean?'

Keraun was quiet for a while. 'I was afraid I would kill them. To save you. And then I would have to leave.'

I wasn't sure what I had been expecting, but that wasn't it. 'Why would you kill them? You're a god. Can't you just make them fall over or something?'

He gave a grim smile. 'I'm not an overlord. Markarios doesn't like it if we use Pamavianda in front of people, and my control of subtle magic is pretty much just weather and my personal appearance.'

'So you'd have to interact like a normal person. That still doesn't answer my question. Why would you kill them?'

'You were up against multiple armed men. Trained agents. I wouldn't be able to fight my way through before they hurt you. I was afraid that I'd be forced into a situation where I'd have killed them to get to you. I would've used lightning.'

I tried to picture that. 'Inside?'

Keraun gave me a sly look. 'Lightning is the one thing on this earth that I really can manipulate to my will. I can make it smash windows or strike down a hallway. I could make it work, but it would've been deadly to anyone standing in the way.'

I thought about that. Sean's smug face floated into my mind. 'If you'd killed Sean, I would have been grateful.'

Keraun's face darkened. 'You don't understand.' His voice was low. 'Cyreans are stage five humans. If we kill someone, even in self-defence, it's murder. No excuses. The Uzrun handle it, they're like an agency for intergalactic stuff. Either way, I wouldn't be staying here.'

We finished our ice creams in quiet thought. I wouldn't say it aloud, but if he left now, I would miss him. More than I probably should. Sean was a small matter to deal with in comparison.

Cecelia stared at me, arms folded, pen down for the first time in weeks. September had begun with a flurry of icy rain and even hail. It was Sunday morning, and we'd holed up in the Wilson study room.

'You have been hiding something from me,' she said. It wasn't a question.

Well, damn. I shrugged.

'I know, Gabby. Did you think I wouldn't notice?'

I met her unrelenting gaze. 'I wanted to tell you . . . ' I faltered. But someone told me not to? It seemed safer for you not to know? I didn't know where to start? This was my best friend across the desk. All my reasons crumbled away.

'Spill, Gabs. You have to tell me about him!'

'Him?'

'Unless it's a her. Either way, I don't have time for a boyfriend, or a girlfriend, and if you're not going to study for exams, you can at least let me live vicariously through you. So tell me, have you kissed yet?' All her hardness melted as she leaned forward, eyes glowing, elbow on her physics book and chin resting in her hand.

'I, ah, no.' I still hadn't caught up.

'It's okay if you're gay, but that better not be the reason you've been hiding it.'

'I'm not gay. Not that it would matter, I'd tell you. Ceel, what is this about?'

'Your secret relationship! You've been sneaking off all semester, and I can't think what else would be more important than exams!' She sat back, frowning. 'Actually, it isn't more important than exams. You should prioritise your study.'

Oh. Now I wasn't sure what to do. Ham this up, so she stopped obsessing over my activities, or pretend it wasn't serious, which, well, I wasn't sure I should be serious about Keraun, no matter how many times he intruded on my brain while I was studying.

I wanted to tell her the truth. About everything. Just thinking about that made my whole body sag with relief. But no. Stephen had said not to. I would be putting her in danger, more than she already was. I still kicked myself every time I thought about how I'd put Zenna at risk just to have someone to talk to. I had to tell Cecelia something to throw her off, but I didn't know where to start. This was my best friend. Where was my intuition when I needed it?

I brooded for too long.

'Oh, have you had a fight?' Cecelia's voice was tender. She put a hand on my arm. That was all it took. I fell to pieces, again. This embarrassing tendency had to stop. Cecelia came around the table, dragged me up from my chair and dropped me on the couch in the corner. She sat next to me and pulled me into her lap, and I gave in to the despair and the sobs and let every bit of tension I hadn't known I'd been holding run out with the tears. Cecelia stroked my hair.

'This is more than a boyfriend,' she said when the worst of the crying had stopped. I swallowed and traced the pattern on a cushion with my pinky-tip.

'What would you do if you were offered the perfect job, and guaranteed success as a doctor, but it was on Mars and meant you could never see your family and friends again?'

Cecelia was quiet for a moment, still playing with my hair. 'I'd say my family is my guarantee.'

I sighed. Somehow the world was clear-cut for her. 'But what if that was my choice? You know how rubbish I am with decisions.'

'Have you been offered your perfect job?'

I had no idea what I'd been offered. 'It's complicated.'

'Well, just do what feels right, I guess. But unless you are piloting a manned mission to Mars, I don't see what would be worth losing our friendship.' She squeezed my shoulders, then slid out from under my head. I sat up. She was looking at me with resignation. 'You can't tell me what this is, can you?'

If she'd said that two minutes ago, I probably would have told her everything, but my resolve crept back. I shook my head. 'I'm sorry,' I whispered.

'It's okay. But don't forget that I'm still here for you, even if I don't know what – or who – is making you so upset. Anything I can do to help.'

I smiled. 'Thanks.' My voice was stuffy.

'And so you know, I don't see you liking Mars. It's a dusty desert. We can find something more suitable for you than that.'

I laughed weakly. 'I'm not going to Mars.'

'Good.'

I pulled myself up to a sitting position. 'There is a boy, though.' I could give her something, at least.

Her eyes sparked. 'I knew it! Tell me. Do I know him?'

'I doubt it. His name is Keraun. He's tall, a bit skinny, dark hair, pretty terrible taste in cars' – Cecelia rolled her eyes, she'd never remotely cared about cars – 'and he's older.'

She pursed her lips. 'How much older?'

Keraun's words echoed in my mind. *You stop counting the years.* What did age matter when it came to an alien god? 'He's eighteen. Nearly nineteen.' Maybe. Give or take half a dozen years spent on the other side of the universe.

'Well, as long as he's still a teenager.'

I elbowed her. 'He's nice. I like him.'

'And he likes you.'

My chest went all tingly. 'Yeah, I think so.'

'Keraun,' Cecelia repeated. 'Unusual name.'

I raided the kitchen for Milo as Cecelia, declining my offer to make one for her, returned to her study. I heaped a glass with four generous teaspoons, ate another spoonful straight out of the tin and poured milk into the glass. It bubbled for a moment, then a chunk of Milo burst to the top and spread out across the surface. I stirred it in.

'How about I make a birthday cake out of Milo for you?' a warm voice said behind me.

'Nancy!' I spun around and gave her an awkward one-armed hug, still holding my glass. I hadn't seen much of her since my Event, and I hadn't realised how much I'd missed her.

'What are your plans?' she asked, setting her grocery bag on the bench and pulling out vegetables.

'Nothing, really.' My birthday was on Friday, but with everything that had been going on, I'd been happy just to let it slide. Cecelia was busy with study, and Zenna hadn't answered my last two messages. Birthdays were always awkward because I wanted to celebrate equally with Dad and Alex, but after one stiff, uncomfortable gathering ended with Dad being rude and Alex storming out, I'd stopped bothering. That said, Nancy's cakes always made suffering through a birthday party worthwhile.

'You can't do nothing, you're turning seventeen!' Nancy fussed. 'Tell you what, we'll do something here. If it's still raining, we'll clear out the study.'

'Cecelia won't be happy with that,' I said, laughing.

Nancy's eyes took on a wicked gleam. 'That girl needs to take a night off anyway. What do you say, we hide her books together, and I'll cook? Jon and Alex are both welcome.'

She always said that, even though she knew I'd only invite one of them – I'd long ago given up on unravelling their drama. I smiled. 'Sounds good.'

She gave me a motherly appraisal. 'Your skin has cleared,' she observed. 'Stressed, though, I can see it in your face. I hope you're getting more sleep than Cecelia. It's not worth it, you know.'

'I know, Nancy. I'm not going overboard. It's just a busy time.'

Nancy nodded and continued washing carrots. 'How are you going with your TISC applications?'

I hopped onto one of the stools behind the breakfast bar. 'Hopelessly.'

'Well, you can just do a general degree, and specialise later. You're good with science.'

'I'd fail the maths though.' Which was the main thing putting me off science, I realised. I liked human biology, but I wasn't good at maths. Or chemistry.

'What about English? I did English and History majors. You learn a lot of transferable skills in Arts.'

I gave her a cheeky grin. 'Isn't that, like, code for a degree that leaves you unemployable?'

She pouted in mock outrage. 'I was never unemployable! Four children probably did more to reduce my job prospects than an Arts degree.'

We laughed together. She kept putting up suggestions, and I kept coming up with excuses. The bottom line was nothing appealed. I could overcome my difficulties with maths if I really wanted to. But I didn't care enough. When I'd been at

Darkhaven almost every day, I'd missed my friends and chatting to Nancy while she cooked Sunday dinner (she'd let me help in the kitchen once, then banished me to on the other side of the breakfast bar). Now that I wasn't at Darkhaven, I realised that I also missed my sessions with Liam and conversations with Stephen. Darkhaven – and by extension, magic – was enticing. But soaking in the warmth of Nancy's kitchen and thinking about Cecelia and her unconditional acceptance of me, I wondered if being intrigued about a career, even a magical one, was a good enough reason to leave everyone I loved.

CHAPTER 25

Poetry

The last week of any term in school had always felt pointless, with assessments done and teachers grumbling about being babysitters. The final weeks of Year 12 were pretty much the same, except for a charged current of tension about the impending exams. Those who didn't care how their ATAR went could taste the freedom after twelve years of formal education and their brains had already checked out. The students who were deeply invested in exam scores were frustrated with pointless lessons that took up valuable revision time. And then there were a few like me, too distracted by other things to be in either camp.

Regardless, no one wanted to be in fifth-period English on our final Friday afternoon. I absently scratched my fingernail at a chip in the desk surface as I re-read *Witches Abroad*. Cecelia and I had finished the classwork – in pairs, analyse and discuss one of the poems that might come up in mock exams – and she'd moved on to her chemistry notes. In front of us, Michaela had a stack of books from her philosophy class. Mrs Johnsen was in her usual position, reading a novel at her desk. I had the distinct impression that the teacher had set a talkative group activity so she wouldn't have to worry about keeping the class quiet. Todd and Martin were engaged in a lively discussion about a photo of a nude woman that one of them had stuffed into their poetry book. Two girls sitting behind them, Leila and Samantha, had seen it too, and noticed that the woman was touching herself. Samantha's obnoxious cackle burst across the room, and I scowled in her direction.

'She's quite hot,' Todd was saying. 'I'd do her.'

Leila scoffed. 'She'd want a man with experience. She can probably show herself a better time in five minutes than you could in a night.'

Martin sniggered. 'I bet she'd take it up the –'

At that moment, Samantha caught my scowl. 'Hey Gabby!' she called, cutting Martin off. 'Do you masturbate?'

The whole class fell silent. I stared at her, my face burning, wishing that one of the powers granted to Eventers was the ability to turn back time, or at least skip past the mortifying parts. Even Cecelia had looked up to see what had happened. I didn't know how to answer. If I said no, they'd assume I was lying and taunt me, and if I said yes, they'd tease me for the rest of the lesson, which still had a good forty minutes left. I teetered in the lose-lose scenario. 'I don't know,' I said, sinking lower in my chair as if it could hide me.

Samantha hooted.

'What, you don't know if you're doing it right?' Leila asked, voice dripping with sweet sarcasm.

The whole class burst out laughing. Mrs Johnsen finally looked up. While my face burned hotter than a lightning bolt, she set her book aside and stood, placing her hands on her desk.

'Does someone have a question for me?' she asked. She didn't need an obnoxious voice for it to command the whole room. Her eyes darted around, seeking a guilty student to pin with their power.

Todd, fool that he was, rose to the challenge. 'Yeah, miss. Do you masturbate?'

Mrs Johnsen stared at him, unflinching. 'Yes.'

The class was shocked for just a moment, either unable to decide if she meant it, or not wanting to picture their teacher pleasuring herself. But Martin wouldn't be outdone for idiot of the year. 'Miss, I've got one too,' he said. 'Why don't you wear a bra?'

Mrs Johnsen released Todd and fixed her gaze on Martin. Then she shrugged. 'Because they restrict lymphatic flow.'

The class tittered. Mrs Johnsen straightened up. 'You must all be done with your poetry discussions if you have moved on to other topics. Leila, please share what you and Samantha talked about.'

'Ah, I, umm ...' Leila's smirk faded.

'Perhaps Samantha can remember more of your conversation.' The teacher's voice was ice-sharp.

Samantha shifted in her chair. 'We were discussing something else, miss.' She couldn't contain her snicker as she flashed a glance at me.

'I see.' Mrs Johnsen peered around at everyone, taking in Cecelia's chemistry notes, Michaela's philosophy essay, Todd's pornography, my lack of schoolwork altogether and every other offence to her final class with us. An evil gleam suffused her face. 'There is a new assignment for you all. You have half an hour to write a five-hundred-word essay analysing a poem of your choice from the reading list. It is worth ten per cent of your mark. You will hand your essays to me at the end of class. Make sure your handwriting is legible.'

The class erupted in groans and complaints.

'Your time starts now.' Mrs Johnsen said, as if that would prompt everyone to work. The indignation only grew louder.

'But miss, you can't do that.'

'I can't write that many words!'

'You can't change the marks now! Can you?'

'You can't DO that!'

'Do I have to count them?'

Mrs Johnsen's eyes glittered and the outbursts trailed off. 'Now,' she said, sitting back at her desk and picking up her book, 'there will be *silence*.'

Except for the furious shuffling of pages and scratching of pens, there was.

Nancy did create a Milo cake, throwing a dinner party for me that evening. Alex even broke his health nut regime to sample the cake before he had to leave for the airport. Cecelia stopped studying for a solid three hours, Zenna made a chirpy appearance and Fiona recited her entire book report on the collected works of Elyne Mitchell to me.

Apart from not having heard from Keraun for almost two weeks – I'd wanted to invite him, just to see how he responded – the party was great until Dad arrived. He'd planned to pick me up, and it should have been fine, but Alex was late leaving, and they ran into each other at the door. I hadn't noticed until my sharpened hearing picked up angry voices. I ventured down the hall, not really wanting to get involved, but also not wanting them to spoil the night for everyone else.

' ...back off.' Alex's voice was a low growl.

I paused, hidden in the shadows.

'She's fine, Alex,' Dad said. 'Perhaps you're the one who needs to back off.'

'She's my niece! Too many kids break in this system, and I won't let it happen to her.'

'I know you have issues, Alex.'

'This isn't about me.'

A pause. 'Is it about Toby?'

I'd never heard of any Toby. I crept close enough to see them, shadowed silhouettes squared off against each other on the porch.

Alex sagged. 'He was too young.'

Dad reached out and squeezed Alex's shoulder. After a moment, Alex leaned against his brother. Dad patted his back.

'We shouldn't have done it,' Alex muttered, his voice rough.

Dad stiffened and pulled away, holding Alex by the shoulders in front of him. 'Done what?'

'The program.'

Dad reached for his briefcase. My ears prickled. "Program" couldn't be the Praegressus, surely – Dad had said Alex wasn't involved...

'The curriculum they put these kids through is too much,' Alex continued. 'Children need time to play and' – he heaved a breath – 'be kids.'

Dad's posture relaxed. 'Don't worry, Alex. I'm looking out for her.'

'Are you sure? Because –'

'Stop questioning me!' Dad snarled. Alex shrank back. Even I started at his tone.

'You'll be late for your flight,' Dad added, turning to the door.

I scurried back to help clean up the kitchen before he spotted me, wondering what had him so on edge.

With school over, exams pressed with increasing weight, building on the horizon like tomorrow's thunderstorm. I had no time to think about the strange argument between Dad and Alex. It was Saturday morning, one week before mocks and less than eight weeks until ATAR. Cecelia was studying and Zenna had a driving lesson, so we'd postponed our milkshakes at the Shack. I resigned myself to the fact that the only way I had any hope of passing Economics was if I put in some serious reading and just tried to commit as much to memory as possible. I settled onto my bed at Dad's with my textbook open in front of me.

My phone rang. I glanced over, thinking maybe Cecelia had an English question. It was Keraun. My stomach fluttered, although that could have been the leftover Milo cake I'd had for breakfast.

'Hey,' I said.

'Hey.'

I broke the silence. 'What's up?'

'I, ah, have to go out of town for a bit.'

'Okay.'

'I thought I should tell you.'

That was odd. We didn't owe each other anything. But somehow, I was glad he had called. God, or rather Husa, forbid I should miss him randomly showing up in the library or at my house. 'Thanks,' I replied.

'Sure.'

I broke the silence again. 'Where are you going?'

'There's a weather anomaly happening in Europe that I have to sort out. My system seems to have broken down there. All that carbon dioxide.'

'I don't recall you driving a hybrid.'

I could hear his grin over the phone. 'Maybe I'll get one of those next.'

'When . . . ' I began, then stopped. Was it presumptuous to think he was coming back? For me? He must have things happening all over the world. Or the universe.

He pulled the words from my head anyway. 'I'll be back soon. Good luck with the exams.'

'Ugh.'

'Well, buckle down, or whatever it is you say, and I'll be back to help you celebrate when you're done. Assuming you pass,' he added. I could almost hear the cheeky grin.

'I will definitely pass,' I replied, with more confidence than I felt. 'Well, probably.'

There was a more comfortable pause.

'Gabby, how are you going with your decision? About Darkhaven?'

Terrible. Anguished. No idea what I was going to do. Steal his spaceship or whatever it was and fly away. 'Fine.'

'Liar.'

I sighed. No point arguing.

'You'll figure it out,' he said.

'Helpful,' I replied, with only a hint of sarcasm.

'Sorry, I have to go,' he said suddenly. 'I'll see you later, Gabby.'

'Yeah. See you,' I said, feeling a pang of something I'd only ever experienced reading books. The phone beeped, and he was gone. The sensible part of me suggested I get on with my studying, forget all about Keraun and assume he wasn't likely to land in Perth again, since he'd probably forget about me. The less sensible part started imagining what kind of weather anomaly I could create to bring him back and how I could perhaps answer all my life questions by dedicating a career to such an experiment.

I ended up in the pantry looking for chocolate.

CHAPTER 26

—

The Shoemaker Clue

Exams were never going to be good, but I'd imagined that I'd skate by with my intuition. Having an accurate instinct for the answers had been helpful in class, and I'd maintained fairly good grades just with that and my minimal attempts at homework. But I sat down to my first ATAR exam – Mathematics Applications – feeling hollow. The sure feeling I used to get when solving a problem that let me know I was on the right track was gone. Any sense of how to approach something I couldn't remember seeing before was also gone. Since it all felt like a lost cause anyway, I spent most of my remaining study time writing in my journal, trying to figure out what had happened to my intuition. And what to do about Darkhaven. Was it worth the cost? My mind ran in circles.

With exams came the onset of Perth's relentless summer heat. The gymnasium warmed up like a greenhouse and my thighs, only half covered by my skirt, stuck to the plastic chair while the 37 degree day pressed on the nerves of three hundred anxious students like a soporific. I stumbled through the maths questions, skipping every second or third and only finishing half of the problems I did tackle. I ran out of things I could do just as the invigilator marked the thirty-minutes-remaining mark off the whiteboard, meaning no one could leave until the end. I flicked through the pages again, hoping some answers would jump out at me, until I finally gave up and rested my cheek on the cool desk. My neck twinged – the needle jab from the Taskforce still hadn't quite healed. Maybe it was infected. I shouldn't be able to get infections, but it was the Taskforce. Who knew what crazy stuff they had.

Geography was better, in part because I wore longer shorts that prevented my legs from assimilating themselves into the furniture. Economics may as well have been in German. English was easily my best, since half of it was comprehension, so I just had to read the material provided and answer some questions about it on the spot. I'd never actually finished *A Tale of Two Cities* – I'd left my library copy at Alex's and couldn't be bothered going all the way back to get it – so I breathed a sigh of relief when I saw there were two options for the long-answer question. I wrote an acceptable essay linking Harwood, Hawthorne and the feminist movement, resisting the urge to include a quote from Todd or Martin as proof of my point, and finished week one of exams feeling drained. At least I only had Human Biology left. I hadn't heard from Cecelia all week. Even with my recent distractions, this was the longest we'd ever gone without seeing each other.

For some insane reason that I'm sure was clear before the reality of Year 12 – not even mentioning my Event and Darkhaven – set in, I'd thought it would be a good idea to do my driving test on the Saturday in the middle of the exam period. I'd almost forgotten I'd booked Zenna in for the same day. Cecelia sent me a cursory good luck message.

'She didn't send me one,' Zenna remarked, mock-insulted, as we waited in the Driver Services seating area. Dad had dropped me off for my final driving lesson and gone to pick up the car we'd finally agreed on. If everything went well, I'd be driving my new – well, new to me – Mazda 3 home and he'd call his driver.

'It doesn't actually say my name,' I said, showing Zenna my phone. 'Just "good luck". I think we can count that for both of us.'

Two officious examiners carrying clipboards came towards us. 'Good luck, Z,' I said as we parted.

Zenna nodded back, looking faintly green. 'Yeah, you too,' she croaked.

The air was hot and heavy with an overcast sheen as I followed my examiner outside to where my driving school car was waiting. Hopefully it wouldn't rain until after the test. I started out doing everything right, checking seatbelts and the handbrake and that the car was in neutral before I turned it on. Then I stalled it as I pulled out of the car park.

'It's all right,' my examiner, a woman named Sally, said. 'Just start the car and carry on.'

The second attempt was better. I made up for it – in my mind, at least – by nailing the hill start, but then in my smugness I nearly forgot to indicate to go around a parked car on the road and only just remembered in time. I snuck up behind someone doing ten kilometres under the speed limit. Keraun flashed into my mind, blasting cars off the road with his lightning tricks. Unhelpful. I banished him from my thoughts and maintained a respectful distance behind other cars for the rest of the trip, being over-careful to indicate for the correct lengths of time everywhere.

'Well, you need to work on consistency,' Sally said as she made marks on a complicated-looking matrix. 'Your indicating in particular could be better. But you passed.' She tore off the top page and handed it to me. 'Take this and go back inside to arrange your licence. Congratulations.'

She got out of the car and that was it. I sat still for a minute, breathing deeply, before going back to the service counters. I could barely wipe the stupid grin off my face for the photo and started signing the form with an excited flourish until I realised I was supposed to keep the signature within the white box. I collected my permit papers and turned to see Zenna walk in, ashen-faced. I felt bad for her but couldn't quite squash my own excitement.

'No luck, huh?'

'You could be less smug.' She glowered as she walked up to the counter and handed her form over. I stood in the middle of the room staring at her back, torn between pity and anger at her unfairness. It was hardly my fault she couldn't get it together. She turned and marched out of the building.

Dad leaned against my little red car. 'So, who's driving?'

I shrugged, hoping he'd drop the upbeat attitude.

'Gabby,' Zenna muttered, looking at her feet. Dad threw me an apologetic look, but I could see pride mixed in there as well.

'I'll leave you girls to it, if you like,' he said, fishing his phone out of his pocket and turning to me. 'I have to fly out tonight. Alex is on his way home.'

I nodded, my mouth watering for a celebratory dinner at Harrys. Dad gave me a hug, whispered "well done" in my ear and slipped across the road to wait for his driver away from the stream of people flowing in and out of Driver Services. Moments later, the Mercedes pulled up, paused, then sailed away.

I turned to Zenna. 'Milkshakes?'

'Nah.'

'Walk on the beach?' Storm clouds smudged the horizon. The beach would be wild and enthralling. From the footpath, of course.

'I just want to go home.' Zenna's voice was flat.

'Did you book another test?' I asked as we settled into the Mazda and I connected my phone to the Bluetooth. It felt weird, sitting in the driver's seat without a supervising adult next to me. I was more nervous now than I had been during the test.

'No.'

'Don't you need it before the summer internship?'

She didn't reply. I navigated out onto the busy road. After a few sets of traffic lights, my fingers started to relax their grip on the steering wheel. That made using the indicator a bit easier.

We didn't talk again as I drove to Zenna's house. Except for the occasional lurching clutch release and one missed turn-off, the drive was uneventful.

'You'll get it next time,' I said as she was about to get out. She turned and looked at me for the longest time. Her eyes were flat and hollow.

'What would be the point?' Her voice was almost too soft for even me to hear, and it took my brain a moment to register what she'd said.

'What do you mean?' I asked, but it was too late. She'd already got out of the car. The door swung shut.

I sat in Zenna's driveway for a while, typing out a text message, then deleting it, typing it again, deleting it. I tried to think of a way to reach out to her. No matter how I worded it, it sounded presumptuous or silly. *Hey, if you want to talk, I'm here.* Obviously. *Don't worry about your licence.* But she was worried, and fair enough. *I hope you're okay.* Dismissive. The whole time I was just hoping she'd come back outside and we could talk and joke about it. She didn't.

A text from Alex interrupted my next attempt to type a message, asking me to pick up some coconut milk on the way home. Sighing, I tossed my phone onto the passenger seat and drove away.

I managed to find Alex's favourite brand, a local raw food mob called Triple L that made a lot of cold press juices and the kind of carob treat I didn't care for. Coconut milk in one hand, I juggled my keys in the other, but the key wouldn't fit into Alex's front door. Sean's face sprang to mind and my skin chilled. He'd said I'd have nowhere to go. Had he made good on his threat by locking me out of my homes? I wished I had my intuition back so I wouldn't walk straight into a trap.

The key caught the light as I jiggled it, glinting metallic oran—orange. Alex's keys were silver. I was using the key to Dad's house. I laughed in relief, my grip loosening, and the keys fell to the doorstep. I bent to pick them up.

The corner of something sticking out from under the door-mat caught my eye. It was a postcard, one of the free promo-tional ones from Lartte. This one was a cappuccino with foam art that reminded me of the Cheshire cat. I turned the card over.

Gabrielle

My blood stopped moving around. It was Alex's handwrit-ing, and this time it wasn't about chocolate wafers.

With numb fingers, I scooped up my keys. When the cor-rect key still didn't go into the lock, I stooped and peered at the keyhole. A key was snapped off in it. I turned back to the street, searching within myself for some clue. It had to be Alex's key in there – he and I were the only ones with keys – so he'd snapped it off himself accidentally, or deliberately to stop me from going in. Or, a nastier warning whispered in my mind, someone had stolen his keys and used them. If I'd had my intuition, I would have had a pretty good idea what had happened, but all I could do was guess. At least I didn't need intuition to follow the first clue.

I slipped back down the steps and out the side gate, glancing about for signs of trouble. I took a roundabout route and a back alley to get to Lartte, sneaking in the back door that they kept open for toilet access.

I hovered in the narrow walkway, earning a glare from a waitress as she brushed past with arms full of cups and plates. I wondered if it was safe to stick my head out and debated whether it was better to sneak through or just stroll across like I was a customer with nothing to worry about. I compromised, walking straight across the floor but somehow unable to stop myself doing a totally idiotic tiptoe like I was in a B-grade horror movie, ducking behind absolutely nothing as I turned to check the front door. Since it was evident that no one was waiting to assail me, I pulled myself together and looked around properly.

No Alex.

So either he'd meant to meet me here and been held up, or he was directing me here for some other reason. My eyes caught on the postcard stand.

I set the coconut milk on the edge of the cake display and flicked through the Cheshire cat stack first, but there were no markings on any of them. Then I stared at the long row of postcards. Not all of them were from the cafe: the rack extended the length of the wall, and it seemed like a lot of businesses printed cards and left them here. My skin prickled. I had no idea how long I was safe to browse, but I had to assume it wasn't long.

I started flicking through. After five different stacks, my feet were tingling with the desire to run and I was starting to wish I had another clue, even without intuition.

'Excuse me, miss?' a voice said behind me.

I jumped and dropped a handful of unhelpful postcards promoting jet ski adventures on the Swan River.

It was just the waitress. 'I think this is yours,' she said, holding up the coconut milk.

I quickly gathered up the jet ski cards and turned to take it. 'Thanks.'

Stuffing the jet ski cards back, I went through another three stacks before I saw it: a postcard featuring a decadent display of raw chocolates decorated with tiny flowers and coconut flakes, made by Triple L. I should have known. Halfway through the pile, I found it.

I am learning to make shoes in the Bastille
100 2 11 – 107 2 2 – 26 22 8 – 121 2 1 – 184 2 4 – 216 2 2 – 246 2 7

It made zero sense to me. I assumed that Alex was not coming back, since he'd directed me to the coconut milk presumably with the intention that I find this note without him. My next best option was to try and catch Dad at home before he left. If Sean was behind this, Dad would know, or at least be able to find out. I ditched the coconut milk on the nearest table, stuffed the postcard in my shorts pocket and, forgetting to take the back exit, hurried out the front door and into the gathering-storm humidity.

There was a black-suited agent across the road.

This time my body behaved itself, and I turned away and walked down the street, quickly, but like a normal person in an everyday sort of hurry, pressing through the carefree crowd. I hoped he hadn't seen. I wasn't sure if glancing back to check was the right thing to do or if it would give me away, so I walked faster instead. And faster. My breath caught in my throat. My toe caught on a crooked paving stone and I lurched forward, breaking into a run just to get away from the tingling sensation sprawling like cold jelly all over my back.

I was nearly at my car. I stuffed my hand in my pocket, grasped my keys and was just about to step off the footpath when something hard brushed my shoulder.

I whirled, fists ready to fly, although even with somewhat enhanced strength I had no better idea about combat now than I'd had back in the park after my Event.

'Sorry!' The man who had run into me wore gym shorts and an orange singlet and was already loping away from me, trailing a cloud of musky cologne.

I jumped in the car and, shaking all over, and started driving to West Beach. Just as I hit the freeway, my phone rang – Zenna. I pushed the answer button on the steering wheel.

'Hey,' I answered.

Silence.

'Zenna?'

More silence.

'Zenna, what's wrong?'

'Oh. Nothing really. I just wanted to talk.'

Of all times, but I wanted to help. 'What about?'

She was quiet, except for intermittent sniffling.

'This is where you say something, Z.'

'I don't know what to say.'

Me either. I fumbled these conversations anyway, without the added mental load of driving around the city on my first day with my licence and something being up with Alex. I kept checking intersections and street signs and my speed. 'Are you okay?'

'I don't know.'

I pulled up at a set of traffic lights, squeezing the steering wheel like a stress ball. I wanted her to be honest with me. Maybe I should try the same. 'I don't know what to do, Zenna.'

'I just need you to listen.'

I sighed. 'That kind of requires you to talk.'

She sniffed harder. 'Just be here to help, then.'

I needed to invest in a heavy-duty steering wheel cover. 'I'm trying, Zenna. But I feel like you keep shutting me out.'

She was silent.

I pulled up in Dad's driveway, suppressed a frustrated grunt and tried to be sympathetic. 'Look, I'm sorry, can we talk tomorrow? I'm a bit busy now.'

More silence. Then a sigh. 'Sure, Gabby. Bye.'

CHAPTER 26

Breaking All the Rules

Dad wasn't home. I let my breath out in an exasperated huff and called him. He didn't answer his phone either, so I left a message telling him that Sean was after me.

I didn't want to add Zenna to the list of things I was currently worried about, but she was there. We'd always been upfront with each other. If one of us needed something, we just came out and asked, no games or codes. Well, I was – it was a code, I realised. Alex's note was a code. I was useless at lateral thinking, especially without any intuition, but maybe Zenna's call had been timely. If anyone could break a code of Alex's, she could. I called her back.

No answer.

Fine. How hard could it be to crack a code? Surely he wouldn't leave me a note I couldn't understand.

I sat at Dad's kitchen table with a pen and paper. I thought there might be a phone number hidden in it, somewhere I could call Alex, but if there was I couldn't find a way to extract it. I went through every pattern analysis tool I could think of. I reversed the numbers, rearranged them into numerical order, reverse numerical order, found the median and, after what felt like much longer than twelve minutes, concluded that even if I found some pattern or logic I would have no idea what it meant.

I tried Zenna again. Still no answer. I called her home number too, but no one answered there either. Her parents must be out. My gut plummeted as I thought of how I'd dismissed her. Fine. I'd go to her house. And I should probably call Stephen.

Unlike Zenna, Stephen answered on the first ring, but I pressed the wrong button while trying to turn up the volume without taking my eyes off the road and the Bluetooth dropped out. I picked up my phone and held it to my ear. Day one of having my licence. Whoops.

'Gabby, are you okay?' Stephen asked, breathless.

'Um,' I said, taken aback by his obvious stress. A traffic light changed to orange – I was tempted, but it was cutting it fine. I pulled up at the lights. A police car stopped opposite. I threw the phone down into the footwell.

'Gabby?' Stephen called, voice tiny from the floor. 'Gabby!'

'Hang on!' I yelled, hoping the phone would pick up my voice. It must have worked because he stopped talking. The lights went green and I drew away slowly, waiting until the police car was well past before retrieving my phone. I glanced down to put it on speaker. 'Honestly, it would just be safer if we didn't have to try not to look like we were on the phone.'

'You're not supposed to be on the phone at all, not just look like you aren't,' Stephen said. 'What's going on? We got a message about your uncle.'

'You did? Thank god, I don't need to worry about the code.'

'What code?'

'Wait, what do you know?'

'The Taskforce have him,' Stephen said, voice strained. 'I was hoping they didn't have you too. Don't tell me anything else, this line might not be clean. Come quickly. You know where.'

Did I?

'I can't, remember?' I was reluctant to reveal my weakness, my lost intuition, in case Sean was listening in. Could he do that? I had no idea.

'You'll find me,' he said. 'And keep worrying about it.'

'Worrying about what?' I asked, but the line went dead. Angry frustration welled up, saturating my bones. 'Crap!' I yelled, whacking the steering wheel. More cryptic clues.

I took a deep breath and replayed the conversation in my head. Worry about it. We'd been talking about the code. Okay. That must be what I was meant to worry about. As for where to meet, Darkhaven was the only place I knew.

I pulled up in Zenna's driveway. Storm clouds obscured half the sky, eerily reminiscent of the day this whole business had started, although since it was now closer to summer, the air was oppressively warm instead of cold and sharp, like the slow and inevitable press of Alex's auger juicer.

The front door was locked and no one answered, so I went around to the side gate, climbed on the air conditioning unit to unhitch it and went down the side of the house to Zenna's bedroom window. I banged on the glass. She appeared, headphones covering her ears, saw me, then disappeared. I went to wait by the back door.

Cecelia rang.

'How'd you go?' she demanded.

'Um, what?'

'Your test!' Her voice was excited. Then it changed. 'What's wrong?'

There was no hiding anything from Cecelia. Zenna was unlocking the glass sliding door, and I had Alex's card clutched in my other hand.

'Gabby?' Cecelia pressed.

I took a deep breath. 'The thing I told you about. That I couldn't tell you about. Alex is missing.'

Zenna ushered me in, although she looked sullen.

'Where are you? I'm coming over.'

'I'm at Zenna's. Look, Ceel, thanks, but don't stress, you have study to do.'

The line was already dead. I looked at Zenna. Her eyes were red and her face puffy. Her headphones hung around her neck now, her hair all frizzed up from where they'd been sitting. She was wearing a jumper, even though it was thirty degrees outside and the air was becoming a swimming pool in water content.

'I'm sorry, Zenna. I shouldn't have brushed you away.'

She shrugged. 'What's up?'

'It's Alex. Sean – the guy from the Taskforce – I think he's taken him.' Unlike Cecelia, Zenna didn't shock easily. I handed her the card. 'Alex left this. I think the number is a code. I thought you might know what it means. Please,' I added.

Zenna sat down at the table with the card. She pulled out her laptop and started tapping away while I sat opposite, fidgeting, staring at the numbers and trying in vain to reach into my absent quiet place.

The doorbell rang. I jumped up and met Cecelia at the door. She dragged me into a hug, her shoulder-bag full of books bumping into my hip. 'What can I do?'

'We're trying to crack this code that Alex left.' My voice was thin.

Cecelia took the card. 'Are you sure he's not just out some-where?' She looked at it for about three seconds, then her eyes widened in surprise. 'Oh! It's a book cipher.'

Zenna and I stared at her.

'Fiona made me watch Sherlock with her last night, there was a book cipher in it. Gabby, Alex isn't missing. This implies he's imprisoned.' She frowned. 'Sort of.'

'How do you get that?' I asked.

Cecelia gave me a questioning look. 'Didn't you read A Tale of Two Cities?'

I shrugged. 'I didn't finish it.'

She pulled the novel out of her bag and started referencing pages. Zenna got up and disappeared down the hallway. After a minute, Cecelia had the message written out: House not safe. Get friends to father's.

'What does that mean?' I asked. House not safe was obvious enough. I hardly needed a secret message about that now. But get friends to father's? Did that mean Cecelia and Zenna? Or my Darkhaven friends? Presumably Alex didn't know about Darkhaven, so he must have meant my school friends. But Dad was gone, so how was he going to help?

'Gabby?' Cecelia asked softly. 'If this refers to me, I'd like to know what's going on.'

It was a fair request. Undecided, I looked down at a steak knife that had been left on the table. I could show her, cut my hand to demonstrate the healing, explain everything. Have my best friend back as the one who knew all my secrets. It seemed so simple.

But it wasn't simple. There was danger. And Stephen may have been lenient with Zenna so far, but I didn't fool myself into thinking that was going to last once I had made my deci-sion, one way or the other. If I chose to return and forget, someone would be slipping into Zenna's room with a little blue syringe, and she would be forgetting too. If I stayed at Darkhaven, well, they'd have to modify her memory so she'd believe I was dead along with everyone else.

I pushed those thoughts out of my head. Now was not the time to think about that decision. Cecelia sat in front of me, expectant.

'I, ah . . .' I wracked my brain for a plausible lie.

'What is going on, Gabby?'

Half-truths, maybe. The knife glinted in the light and I thought of the disk, the glittering holofoil. 'I stole something.'

She frowned. 'What, like from a shop?'

'No.' I twisted the knife in my fingers. 'No. From some bad people.'

'Drugs?' Her voice was barely a whisper.

I shook my head. A door slammed down the hall, and I jumped, my hands slipping, and the knife sliced across my palm. I hissed in a breath. The knife clattered to the table with a speckling of blood.

Before I could stop her, Cecelia reached out and took my hand, uncurling my fingers. She watched the blood clot, the skin close and the wound heal over, leaving my palm unblemished. Her face blanched as she lifted her eyes to mine. 'What was that?'

I took a deep breath. 'I'm going to tell you only what you need to know, okay?'

She nodded, biting her lip.

'It's a genetic experiment. Enhanced healing, strength, senses. I'm supposed to be super intuitive too, but I've lost that, so I should have some hunch about what's going on at the moment, but I don't.' My gut twisted painfully. I continued with a basics-only information dump, trying not to think about how much like Donovan I sounded, and hoping that without specifics Cecelia might be left with her memories intact.

'Right now, I need to go and meet the people who have been helping me develop my skills. The people who took Alex are trying to take over the experiment and they are ruthless. It's dangerous, the less you know the better. But you're my best friend. I should have told you ages ago.'

Cecelia eyed the knife lying on the table. 'Okay.'

'Okay, what?'

'I'll come with you.'

'I'm not asking you to.'

'But I want to.' She met my eyes, determined.

'You can't, Ceel, it's too dangerous.'

'More dangerous if you go by yourself. They might not do anything if there's a witness.'

'Or they'll kill the witness.'

Cecelia was silent. Until now, we'd talked of danger and trouble, but not death. Nothing that real. I wished I had my intuition, but I didn't need it to know I wouldn't be talking Cecelia out of this easily. I needed her and Zenna to go to Dad's house. Stephen was waiting. I was running out of time.

The silence was broken by a sharp cry. Cecelia and I jumped out of our chairs and raced down the hall to Zenna's room, but she wasn't there. Panicking that somehow the Task-force was here too, I pounded on the bathroom door while Cecelia went to check the study. I'd drive them to Dad's, I decided, then think of a way to trick them into staying there. I knocked again. 'Zenna? We have to go.'

I heard a sob.

'Zenna?'

The door flew open. Zenna stood in front of me, arm held up to my face, blood dripping from shallow cuts striping her forearm in vivid, angry lines. I glanced past her to the bathroom vanity, where a razor blade rested next to the sink.

My own blood drained from my face.

'This is how I feel,' she said, voice glittering with icy hatred. 'How would you like to be the second-best friend of a superhuman girl who can do everything better than you anyway and only calls you when they're waiting for their other friends to call them back?'

'Zenna, that's not how it is. I need your help.'

'Well, I needed yours. And now it's too late. Tell Alex I'm sorry.' She turned back to the bench and picked up the razor.

'Zenna, no!' I cried, reaching towards her. She turned, eyes lifeless, pushed me out of the room and slammed the door in my face. The lock clicked in the door just as Cecelia appeared behind me.

'What's wrong?' she asked.

'She's hurting herself.' I raced down the hallway to grab my phone off the table. As I picked it up, Stephen rang.

'Can you call an ambulance?' I begged Cecelia. She nodded. I answered Stephen's call. I couldn't shake the image of Zenna's arm and barely heard Stephen's voice. Something about hurrying up.

'Go.' Cecelia was firm.

'Are you sure?' I asked, already gathering my keys.

'We'll be fine. Go save Alex.'

I gave her a quick hug and turned to leave.

'Wait,' Cecelia called. 'What did she do?'

Somewhere deep down I had some empathy, a flash of guilt for leaving, but it was a long way down. I had tried, and she kept throwing it away. Rage and shock swelled over the top. 'Shoved her sliced-up arm in my face and basically told me it was my fault,' I spat. Then I realised Cecelia was just trying to figure out if she needed to break into the bathroom to stop a suicide. I bit my lip. 'Sorry,' I whispered. 'I don't know. They weren't deep. But maybe she's going over the edge.'

Cecelia's arms were back around me. 'She's going to survive this. We'll figure it all out.'

Fighting back tears, I jumped in my car and tried not to speed too much on my way to Darkhaven. Sirens howled further down the freeway and fitful rain splattered the windscreen. I turned on the wipers and gripped the steering wheel until my knuckles turned pale.

CHAPTER 28

Take My Memories

Liam met me at the front door of Darkhaven. 'What are you doing here?' he asked. He looked so calm.

'Stephen called me. Surely you know about –'

With a furtive glance around, he pulled me inside before I could finish. 'Were you followed?'

I realised his "calm" was actually controlled tension. His eyes betrayed the fear under his neutral expression.

'Followed?' I'd put my phone in the Faraday bag.

Liam headed back towards the kitchen, mobile phone to his ear as he waited for someone to answer. Finally he said, 'She's here,' then hung up and turned me. 'Something is going on. I think you were right about your hunch that something bad is happening. But I can't see what it is.'

'Is this about Alex? Where's Stephen?'

He shrugged apologetically. 'I don't know. I'm sorry, Gabby. But you shouldn't have come here. Stephen thinks they might be following you somehow. You were meant to meet him at your Event location.'

Bubbling anger flashed over my body. 'How was I supposed to know that? You know my intuition is gone.'

Liam turned and placed a hand on my arm. 'It's okay. He's on his way back now.' His voice was gentle, but there was an edge to it I hadn't heard before. I shivered, despite the heavy heat.

We made a tense group in the kitchen. Donovan was on the couch, one leg crossed over the other, stoic as ever. Liam took a chair, and I sat down next to him. It felt like all I'd been doing since this whole nightmare started was sitting down at tables, but I couldn't think of anything else to do. Wander the streets? Knock on the Taskforce door? *Hi Sean, sorry to bother you, just wondering if you happen to have my uncle here. If I could have him back, please.* Yeah, right.

After fifteen minutes of wired silence, Stephen walked in. Taut lines of worry creased his forehead.

'What was the code?' he asked, bypassing "hi" completely. At least he wasn't mad that I hadn't understood his cryptic message about the meeting point. His gaze on me was heavy with compassion as he pulled out a chair and sat down.

Deflated and exhausted, I gave half a shrug and relayed the message. 'So nothing useful.'

'Except that the threat extends to your friends,' Donovan said darkly.

'What was the message you got about Alex?' I asked.

Stephen pushed his phone over to me. It was a single line from an unknown number.

I have her uncle – Sean

'What are we supposed to do with that?' I tried not to let panic rise all the way up my throat. 'Can we trace the number?'

Liam shook his head. 'It's just a pre-paid phone. We don't know how he has Stephen's number though.'

'What do we do?' I asked. The panic simmered at chest height. My ears started to ring, softly, insistently.

Stephen turned on his chair to face me. 'I might not have clairvoyance or a gift for it, but I still have some intuition. And it's telling me that we have to sit tight. He'll be in touch again.'

'How can you trust that at a time like this?' I asked, rising to my feet without really meaning to. 'Intuition! I trusted mine last time I was dealing with Sean, and it nearly got me killed!'

Liam reached a hand towards me. 'Gabby, Stephen's been intuitive for a long time. Trust me. He'd know if the feeling was gone.' His voice sounded empty.

I was not empty. Alex was in danger. One of my best friends could be dying on a bathroom floor and I wasn't there, and although I was still mad, fear for her writhed in the pit of my stomach. And for Cecelia. Keraun was gone, possibly never to return – why would he? Come back to Perth for some slightly superhuman girl who couldn't make a decision?

I was full of rage. My blood hissed, my ears rang, my vision sharpened to a harsh contrast and I channelled the anger. I threw my chair back.

'Trust you? You don't even know what's going on! I know when the feeling is gone, and I know why!' My voice rose to a roar. 'It's because I trusted every damn thing you ever taught me, and look where it's got me!'

Liam sat back down. Stephen sank his head into his hands. They looked defeated, but I wasn't done shouting. 'So you lost Luci! She was my mother! I was nearly murdered, and now my uncle is abducted and on top of all that you still want me to choose this!'

I picked up another chair and raised it above my head, ready to hurl it at something. Steel arms grasped mine, pulling them down and wrapping around me from behind, forcing me to let go of the chair. Donovan wrestled with me, containing my rage. I squirmed, but I was no match for her strength. She pinned me to her iron body until my blood cooled and the ringing stopped and I sagged. Then she lifted me by the shoulders like a rag doll and set me down on the sofa. She leaned against the wall, watching me. I sat and glowered until the silence started to close in.

'You know what?' I said, standing. Donovan made a move towards me, but I held up a hand motioning her to stop. 'When all this is over, I'm done. I'm going back. I'll have the Vicitretro. You can take my memories. I'd rather forget you all anyway.'

I stalked out of the room, down the hall and to the patio. Despite today's dampness, the landscape was drier than it had been when I first came here, the grass browning and the blooms on the tea trees faded. I leaned on the railing and gazed out as the gravid air finally caved under the weight of the water in it. The rain was sparse at first, but the drops were fat and heavy, and each fell to the earth with an audible *spaa-lop*. I took a deep breath, sucking in air, not paying attention to smells or sounds or even looking at anything other than the damp dirt.

'Petrichor.'

I turned. There he stood, this alien god, leaning against the wall like he owned the world and hadn't a care. He smiled, the colour of his eyes lifting to a faint yellow glow. Everything dropped away for a swift moment, all my worry and fear and stress, and it was just him and my heart, which was now somewhere near my knees. This must be how people swoon, a remote part of my brain thought. Their heart actually moves down a metre or so and knocks their knees out from under them with its pounding. Then reality crashed back on top of me, and I sank against the railing until I was sitting on the dusty floor. Keraun was at my side.

'What are you doing here?' I asked. He took my chin in his hand and turned my face to his as he leaned in. His breath was warm on my cheek. His eyes were so close to mine, I could feel heat radiating off them. They glowed, shifting from brown to liquid yellow as he closed them and moved closer and drew my face towards him and his lips met mine. My eyelids fluttered shut and my lips parted and again I forgot about everything except my heart now winging its way back up my legs and through my chest, past its usual resting place, past my throat and head until it soared out somewhere I hadn't even known it could go. Time almost stopped.

But it didn't. My breath caught in my throat. Keraun pulled back, eyes glowing, a gentle smile playing on his face.

'And you thought I wouldn't come back,' he whispered.

'I thought you couldn't read minds.' There wouldn't be much he could read now anyway – my mind was utter chaos.

'I can't. It was just that you looked surprised to see me.' He didn't take his eyes off my face. The intensity was soft and sharp at the same time. I looked away.

'I'm sorry,' he continued, 'I wasn't paying attention. What's wrong?'

'They've taken Alex,' I said, trying not to let the trembling take over my body. 'And Zenna's in trouble.'

Keraun squeezed my shoulders. Before he could say anything, Stephen stuck his head around the door, frowning. 'There's a new message,' he said.

I leapt to my feet and followed Stephen back inside, Keraun right behind me.

CHAPTER 29

Making Fakes

'I'd hoped you were gone.' Stephen glared at Keraun as we re-entered the kitchen, then gave me a questioning look.

Keraun smiled, genuine and dazzling. He held up his palms in supplication. 'There isn't anywhere else in the universe I would rather be.' But he paused just inside the doorway, giving Stephen and the others some distance.

Stephen turned back to the table, where someone had spread a map of Perth. He held his phone out to me. 'Sean wants that disk you took back in exchange for your uncle. We've copied it, although we can't decrypt the data, but he may as well have it back. He's given us two possible locations. Apparently you will know which one to go to.'

I stared at the map, then the phone, numbness spreading through my body. The locations were Cecelia's and Zenna's homes. The final words were *Gabby's choice*.

'He's playing games with us,' Liam remarked.

With shaking fingers, I dropped Stephen's phone back on the table as I realised. Sean must have hijacked my phone when he and his goons had taken me in to the Taskforce the first time. I hadn't even thought of it, but I'd saved Stephen's number.

'Which one is it?' Stephen asked.

I stared at the phone screen until it went dark. Before, my intuition had felt like an island that I'd simply swum too far away from. I had known it was still there. The water was clear blue with a sandy bottom, and I could maybe have swum back if I'd been able to understand myself. Now, I was in a riptide. Now, I was out in the deep ocean, nothing but black water below. 'I don't know,' I mumbled.

Donovan slapped a hand on the table. 'Well that's a whole lot of helpful.'

I ignored her. 'But he knows everything. He knows where Alex works.' I coughed to cover the crack in my voice. 'And where my friends live.'

'These are your friends' addresses?' Liam asked, concern filling his voice.

I nodded. Somehow Alex had found out and tried to let me know. And I'd failed. The best I could hope for now was that Zenna was bad enough to be admitted to hospital and Cecelia had stayed with her. Nausea turned in my stomach.

Stephen looked deep in thought. 'We will have to split up,' he said eventually.

Donovan scoffed, looking around the table at Stephen, Liam and me. 'What, four of us, split up? We couldn't take Sean and his henchmen down while securing hostages all together, let alone with only two. Although I'll give him a damn good fight.' She clenched her fists. I felt a slight – very slight – shift in sympathy. For all her faults, she was still on my side. Well, Darkhaven's side, which I supposed was my side. For now.

'It won't be two,' Keraun said, stepping forward from the doorway. 'I'm in. I'll come with you.'

'So will I,' said another voice before Stephen could raise an objection. Dr Whittaker appeared behind Keraun. Everyone stared. The doctor rarely left her lab and probably hadn't left Darkhaven since she'd come here.

'The Taskforce is threatening my home,' she said, as if that explained everything. 'I may not be a fighter, but I can still help.'

Donovan's eyes blazed. 'Well, six is better than four. Let's get this bastard.' She looked to Stephen. A subtle fire seemed to kindle in his face too.

'Wait,' Liam said. 'What about Gabby's friends? We need to make sure they are protected.'

I snatched up Stephen's phone and sent a text to Cecelia. It was so easy to remember numbers now.

She replied almost instantly. *Hospital. I think she hit an artery. Doctor with her now.*

'There's no one at Zenna's house,' I said, choking out the words.

'Will they stay out?' Stephen asked.

I nodded, swallowing the lump in my throat and banishing the image of Zenna's bloodied arm. 'I think so. At least for a few hours.'

'What about the other one?'

'Cecelia's out too. Her mum and sisters will be at ballet now, but they'll probably finish soon. I don't know about her dad. He might be home, if he's not on call.'

'Where does he work?' Dr Whittaker asked. 'I can make sure he's kept out of the house without raising suspicion.'

'Dr Robert Wilson. He works in emergency.' I gave her the hospital details.

'Okay,' Stephen began, pulling maps towards him and marking the locations. 'Donovan, Catherine and Liam will go to the Wilson house. Keraun, Gabby and I will take the other. Report back to Donovan or myself with any news. The aim is to secure the safety of Alex Whitehall. One group will have to take a fake disk.'

He placed a grey disk on the table. It looked a lot like the one I'd taken, except ...

'This is the fake?' I asked.

'Yes, a decoy to appear legitimate for long enough to make the exchange –'

'You are gambling my uncle's life with this and hoping Sean doesn't figure it out?' I was starting to tremble again, but this time it was with fury. I picked up the disk and turned it over. 'It hasn't got a holofoil. He's going to notice instantly if the disk doesn't have a holofoil.'

'She has a point.' Donovan stood. I turned and gaped at her. 'If his henchmen handle the exchange, we'll have time, but if Sean sees it first, he'll probably notice.'

Stephen's brow creased. 'What else can we do? We can't go with nothing, and we don't have much time. We have to assume that he's already in place, waiting for us. He'll know if we delay.'

'I'll make one,' Donovan said. 'I have a guy who can copy the holofoil. Close enough, at least.'

Stephen looked pained. 'How long will that take?'

'I'll message him now. I can be at the site in under an hour. All going well.'

'We'll have to head off without you then, make an appearance and hope you catch us in time. I can buy time at the second location by saying we sent the disk to yours.'

'You can't leave Liam and Catherine on their own, they don't have combat training,' Donovan said.

I didn't have combat training. How messy was this going to get? Presumably Sean knew our vulnerabilities. One shot to the head or heart with the right kind of bullet. Against that, combat training seemed almost pointless.

'I'll go to the doctor's house,' Keraun said.

I turned on him, worry churning in my stomach. Would a Taskforce bullet kill him too? I had no idea. 'Do you have combat training?' I asked.

He just quirked up one corner of his mouth like I was being funny. 'I'll buy you plenty of time if he's there. The rest of you go to the other location and take the real disk with you.'

Everyone stared at him. Donovan raised an incredulous eyebrow.

'Trust me, I know this guy,' he said. I was pretty sure he didn't know Sean at all, but then, no one else here knew what Keraun was.

'If I don't need to be on the approach team, I can also make sure the mother stays at the ballet studio,' Dr Whittaker said. I shot her a grateful smile and marked the studio on the map.

'Liam will go with you,' Stephen said to Keraun, with more than a hint of forcefulness. 'And when all this is done, you are going to explain exactly who or what you are, and what you want with my' – he paused, flushed – 'with Gabby.'

I hadn't picked Stephen for the possessive type. But he was working pretty hard to recruit me, so I suppose he counted me as his student. Or something. Something else nagged at me. The holofoil. 'Wait,' I said. Everyone looked at me. 'Why does Sean want the disk back?'

Stephen shrugged. 'Data control. He wants to make sure we don't disseminate it. Or lose it.'

I shook my head. Something Zenna had said popped into my head. 'You said you couldn't decrypt the data. What if the holofoil is the key? Like a cipher?'

There was a pause, then Donovan nodded. 'I think she's right.'

Donovan was agreeing with me way too much. It was unsettling. 'What do we do?' I asked.

She rolled her eyes. So not completely on my page. 'I'll make two fakes,' she said. 'We leave the original here. Catherine and I will take one to each location when I'm done.'

That was as good as the plan got. Doctor Whittaker and Donovan disappeared to their respective tasks. Liam and Keraun went shortly after to Cecelia's house. That left Stephen and I standing in the kitchen.

'I don't like this,' he remarked. 'We're back down to two people on each approach team, and one of those is a guy I don't know.'

There was nothing I could say to improve his trust in Keraun. Even if he believed me when I said the boy was an alien god, that would probably only heighten his suspicion. I let it go and followed Stephen out to the Corolla.

CHAPTER 30

Diversions and Decisions

Cecelia called while Stephen and I drove to Zenna's. When Zenna hadn't responded to her frantic hammering on the door, Cecelia had gone around the house and smashed in the bathroom window with a pitchfork from the garden shed. She'd found Zenna semi-conscious on the floor, blood flowing from a deep gash in her wrist. By the time Cecelia compressed the wound, the ambulance had arrived. She'd waited at the hospital while Zenna was taken through emergency.

'So unless you're going to let me help you, I'm going home to study,' Cecelia finished.

'Wait!' I said, a little too urgently.

'What? I have Chemistry on Monday. I feel bad for Zenna, but I can't spend all day in the hospital because of her life choices. I have my own future to look after.'

I winced at her lack of sympathy, but then Zenna's accusations about being a second-best friend whipped across my mind and my own rage flared up. Zenna was safe enough for now. I was pretty sure Sean was only after Cecelia to get at me, but if I told her that her home was unsafe, I could hardly expect her to sit idly by and do nothing while she worried about her own family. 'Cecelia, can you do something for me?'

'Sure. What is it?'

I glanced at Stephen helplessly. What could I ask her to do that would delay her? He was concentrating on weaving through traffic. My earlier explosion had waned, and without the anger fuelling me, I was hit again by the realisation I'd had in the Taskforce: this was my fault.

'I, ah, I need a library book. Would you mind picking it up for me? I won't get home before it closes.'

'A library book?' She sounded incredulous. Fair enough.

'Yeah, I lost my Human Biology book.'

'How? That thing is huge.'

'It fell in the bath.' I kept talking over her next exclamation. 'Can you please just get the library copy out for me?'

'They're old editions. You can borrow mine.'

'You know we won't have time to study together next week, you have a hundred exams to do still. Just get the book, and I'll come by for it tomorrow morning and explain it all, please?' I willed her to understand.

'Okay, whatever. But what's happening with Alex?'

'We're sorting it out. Honestly, Ceel, there's nothing you can do right now. Except help my exam stress by getting that book.'

We pulled into Zenna's driveway as Cecelia hung up. Stephen told me to wait in the car while he scouted around. I scratched at my neck, which had still refused to heal, and tapped my foot nervously. I thought about turning on the radio, just for a distraction, but figured it would be better if I could hear any activity. There was no sign of movement. I jumped when I saw the side gate open, but it was just Stephen. I got out of the car to meet him, earning a reproachful glare.

'There's no one here,' he said. 'And I asked you to stay in the car for your safety, you know.'

I ignored his rebuke as we got back in the car. 'So we go to Cecelia's.'

He shook his head. 'Liam will call to report. And Donovan is meeting us here.'

I opened my mouth to argue, but the look on his face caught my words. Layered over the strain and uncertainty was grief. After a few minutes of silence, he spoke.

'Do you really want to go back?'

'No.' I stared out at the huddled grey clouds. My heart felt torn. 'But I don't know what to do.'

'I know. It was too much to ask of you. Please understand, based on our previous case studies, I didn't believe there was a better way. But, well, I owe you an apology.'

I couldn't hold back a tiny smirk. 'I was right?'

Stephen's smile lifted some of the stress off his face. 'Not entirely. I'm not saying you did the right thing either. At some point, you are going to have to figure out what to do with yourself, but you don't have to do it now. Finish school and join Darkhaven if you like. We'll sort the rest out later.'

Did he mean what I thought he meant? I hardly dared to hope. 'So I don't have to leave everyone? But what about avoiding situations exactly like this?'

Stephen reached across the console and squeezed my hand. 'Gabby, this is not your fault. Even if your friends did believe you were gone, they could still be held hostage against you.'

I ventured a proper smile. 'Let me get this straight. I come and live at Darkhaven, and I can still visit Alex and have sleepovers with my friends?'

He nodded. 'At their houses, obviously.'

'Obviously.'

A thread of hope and happy anticipation rippled through the car, weaving with the worry and fear. All we had to do was make Sean's exchange, give him the disk, and all this would be over. I had something to look forward to next year. I didn't quite see the point of finishing school now, except that it would raise a lot more questions if I didn't.

My phone rang again. Cecelia.

'Is the book not available?' I asked, trying to sound disappointed. I knew my human biology book was sitting where I had left it after the last class, in the middle of my desk under some clothes.

'Um, I'm at home, Gabby –'

'What?'

'And Alex is here.'

Before I could yell any more, the phone disappeared from my hand. Stephen had it pressed to his ear, fingers clenched around it. 'Can you put Alex on, please?'

He talked tersely for a moment. I sank back down into my car seat and didn't bother listening to what was happening on the other end. If Cecelia was free to call me and Alex was on the phone and talking, it couldn't be that bad. Surely.

Stephen hung up, looking even more worried than before.

'Alex?' I asked.

'He's fine. So is your friend. Sean isn't there.'

'What? Why not? Doesn't he want the disk back?'

Stephen shook his head and pressed his fingers to his temples. 'I don't know. No. Wait. What if it was never an exchange? Shit.'

He threw the car into reverse as his phone rang. He reached for it, but nearly swerved into another car as he pulled out of the driveway. 'Can you answer it, please?' he asked, waving apologetically to the driver.

I picked up the phone. 'Donovan,' I said, putting her on speakerphone.

'Get back here,' she growled. 'It wasn't a ransom. It was a diversion. Darkhaven is under attack.'

CHAPTER 31

One Bullet

I thought the Taskforce didn't know where Darkhaven was.' I clung to my armrest. The rain had stopped, but the roads were slick with water and oil, and Stephen had abandoned any notion of driving legally.

'They've been hunting us for years. Guess they finally found it. Don't worry. We're prepared for this.' His tone didn't sound unworried.

'Even with half of the team out chasing diversions?'

Stephen drove faster.

We pulled up at Darkhaven behind Liam and Keraun. They jumped out and ran up the gravel incline to the steps, where five dark figures blocked the door. Men in suits. I recognised the one in the middle standing on the steps – slightly slimmer, with a stance that looked less like a brick wall than the those of the others. Sean.

Stephen parked further back. The air was sharpened with a smell like petrol and by the time we reached Sean, I was out of breath. The acrid smell seared my throat.

'Welcome!' Sean cried, voice full of mockery. I wanted to punch him. 'Inside, down the hall, to your left, you'll find your colleagues Esmerelda and Catherine. They're unharmed – for now.' He waved Liam towards the front door. Without hesitation, Liam rushed forward. Sean laughed and clicked his fingers. The suits stepped back and blockaded the door.

'Tell me, what is the point of all this intuition and foresight if you are just going to ignore it the minute one of your friends is in danger?'

Liam didn't answer, except to start pummelling the wall of men arrayed on the steps. It looked like he was hitting concrete.

Sean laughed again. 'You think you're the only ones with genetic enhancement? The difference is I refined mine to be more selective about the genes it activates. My subjects are loyal. They won't get cold feet and back out of the program, or burn the lab down if they have a change of heart.' He added a sneer to the last word. 'Sadly, these guys aren't going to live long. Made it an easy choice for me. I'll stay a regular human for now.'

Liam stopped attacking the suits, but as soon as he turned away, two of them whipped around and grabbed him in a stranglehold, hauling him back to the steps. Sean nodded, satisfied, then turned and stared at Keraun, who had beaten us to the door.

'Well, this is interesting. A god, in the flesh! I always hoped I'd meet one of you.'

Stephen shot me a sideways glance. 'A god?'

I nodded. The dark clouds overhead started to purple, forming a broiling mass that felt close enough to reach up and plunge my hands into. Thunder threatened from behind them. I couldn't see Keraun's eyes, but I was sure it was him.

'Weather control,' Sean said, peering at Keraun's eyes and then at the sky. 'Fortunately, my boss has met one of your kind, so I know how to deal with you.'

So Sean had a boss. In a way, that was good. He was just another henchman. But it also meant that getting rid of Sean wasn't going to break the Taskforce. Something shifted in my mind, a connection I couldn't quite make, but – hang on. Deal with Keraun? I leapt forward as Sean reached into his jacket. Too slow. He flicked something at Keraun, who crumbled onto the steps, huddled under what looked like a white film.

'What did you do to him?' I yelled, running to Keraun. Overhead, the clouds lightened and receded back to their foreboding grey, although the air kept its electricity.

'Don't worry, he's fine. I've just contained him. This has to be a fair fight, doesn't it?' He grinned at me, all teeth. I touched Keraun's arm. I couldn't feel the film, only see its shimmer. He stood, struggling to his feet as if he had weights on his shoulders, but he took my hand and squeezed it.

'So,' Sean began, addressing Stephen in his taunting voice. 'I've contained your muscle woman and your doctor. They won't be coming out. Your psychic was unable to see how you'd get into this situation, and he can't see your way out either. The god was a wild card, but not one we were unprepared for. Although, judging by your face, you weren't entirely prepared for him either. See, I don't need to be superhuman. I can read people no matter who they are. I knew Gabby would lead us here.'

He advanced down the steps, brushing past me as he went.

'Stephen May, the great ambassador for humanity's future. That is how you see yourself, deep down, yes? But you know the truth.' He stopped inches away from Stephen's face. I burned to jump down, tackle Sean, knock the viper away from

Stephen. Keraun kept a hold on my hand, only now it wasn't for reassurance. I could hear tyres on gravel and the quiet purr of an expensive engine. Someone was coming down the driveway, but they weren't visible yet and Sean couldn't hear that well. He continued with his speech.

'The truth is, you are nothing without her. And I am everything. But, and this is the problem, you are still between us. I love her, and I know she would love me, but she can't. Not while you exist. You will always be between us, until' – Sean pulled a pistol out from under his jacket – 'you are dead.'

Stephen glanced at the gun, but he didn't back away. I strained at Keraun's arm, turning to see a white Jaguar gliding to a stop behind us.

'What are you talking about?' Stephen asked, voice icy. Sean made a show of checking his magazine.

'Well, he has to be talking about me, but he's wrong,' a cold, familiar voice said from the Jaguar. I looked across. Luci had her red hair swept up into a twist and wore a slim-fitting black suit, all angles and sharp edges.

Stephen turned around. 'Luci?' His voice cracked.

A man got out from the back of the Jag. My gut twisted, twin shards of hope and mistrust twining. Dad. Maybe he'd got my message and come to help. Maybe he was siding with his work on this one. There was my nagging thought – *Dad* was Sean's boss. Had he met another Cyrean? Or was there someone else, someone higher up … Stephen's eyes widened as he stared at the couple standing next to the Jag.

Behind me, the sounds of scuffing from Liam's struggles stopped, and he took a sharp breath. 'Jan,' he hissed. Then, 'Gabby, go and greet her.'

What? I glanced back at him, tearing my eyes away from where Dad was standing behind Luci and Sean had a gun almost pointed at Stephen's forehead.

'She's your mother,' he said, not caring to be quiet. These genetically modified suits probably had advanced hearing anyway.

I stared at Liam. 'No way. She's a monster.'

'Just do it,' he said, but before I could demand to know why, Sean, already heading for Luci, turned back, watching Liam with narrowed eyes.

'There was a missing link,' Liam said, his voice low and urgent so Sean couldn't hear. 'But I see it now, and if you get to Luci, you can stop her. Gabby. Put your hand on her chest, her heart. And tell Stephen I'm sorry.'

I shook my head. 'I don't understand,' I whispered. Why did it sound like Liam was saying goodbye?

Liam implored me with his eyes. 'Just do it. I've seen –'

'The psychic knows,' Sean called. 'Jab him.'

I whirled back to Sean, but he wasn't the threat. In one smooth movement, the suit on the end produced a needle and syringe, stepped behind me and thrust it into Liam's neck.

'No!' I cried. Breaking Keraun's hold, I threw myself at the man's arm, knocking the needle out before he pushed the plunger all the way in. Liam tumbled down the steps as the suits grabbed me, one of them staggering into Keraun. I glimpsed the half-empty syringe rolling towards my foot across the concrete as I twisted uselessly against the suit's grip.

Liam sagged to the ground in Keraun's powerless arms. But he couldn't be dead. One type of bullet. That was all that could kill him. His eyes were closed, his face pale. I had no idea what he'd meant by putting my hand on my mother's heart.

Past Liam's crumpled form, Sean strode up to Luci, who leaned against the car, arms folded.

'You shouldn't have come here, dear. You're still weak,' Sean said, reaching for her.

She slapped him across the cheek. 'This is not how we said we'd do it.'

Just do it. Liam had figured something out, in the last several seconds. I had to trust him. I had to get to Luci. The half-full syringe lay beside my boot. I could hear the sounds of scuffles and fighting somewhere in the Darkhaven building – no doubt Donovan tackling an army of suits single-handedly. Sean was focussed on Luci, not looking back at Keraun and me. Half a plan formed in my mind, and I didn't second-guess it. With renewed vigour, I spun, elbow raised, smashing it into the neck of the man holding me. He staggered backwards and down, pulling me with him.

I grabbed the syringe, feeling movement around me as the remaining guards closed in. I lashed out wildly with the needle, stabbed it into a leg and pressed the plunger. The man behind me fell away as I pushed out of the crowd, making room for Keraun as he jumped into the fight, still shrouded in film. His movements were slow and cumbersome, but they were enough to distract the suits.

I got clear and leapt for Liam's limp form, praying he'd come to. Stephen approached the Jaguar.

'Luci,' he said, his voice hoarse. He dropped to his knees in the driveway as a sob wracked his throat.

A cool smile played across Luci's face. 'I see it now. You fools believed I was a prisoner. As if I'd give up what we discovered. With it, we control the world.'

Stephen shook his head. 'No. No. You have to stay here, continue our work together. Help us understand it.' His voice broke. 'You were the only one who could.'

I knelt beside Liam, putting my fingers to his neck. There was a pulse. A small part of my insides relaxed.

Luci smiled, if curling lips and exposing teeth could be called smiling. 'Stevie,' she cooed, cocking her head as if she were watching a puppy trying to pick up a toy too big for it. 'You've got it all backwards. It's magic. Real magic. It's not too late for you to join me.'

Maybe I shouldn't have stopped for Liam. Maybe if I had kept running, I would have reached them first, or delayed Stephen, or simply been in the firing line. Something.

Stephen's face was torn. I knew it was heartbreak writ across his features, not that he considered Luci's offer. But Sean was no such judge of character or emotion.

'No. She's mine.' Fury twisting his face, Sean turned, arm raised. A shot exploded through the damp, electric air. Stephen collapsed to the ground.

I screamed and launched across the driveway. Keraun grappled with the suits, fatigue dragging on his encumbered form. More of the men were pouring out of the building, with no sign of Catherine or Donovan. I skidded over the gravel to Stephen's side, all the air vanishing from my lungs as I took in his lifeless face and closed eyes. My arms longed to pull him up, hold him together so he could heal, so the wound in his chest would close over and the blood would stop seeping, but I knew it wouldn't. One bullet to the heart. Sean would take no chances.

CHAPTER 32

No Excuses

I had to trust Liam. I stumbled to my feet, but before I could reach Luci, the strike of a match sounded. I looked up as Sean tossed one to the ground on his left and another to his right. Now the petrol smell made sense. Like a wildfire, flames raced around either side, leaping high and surrounding the Darkhaven building – and all of us – in a wide circle. The spotting rain was not heavy enough to stop the dry scrub igniting. Luci and Dad and the Jag were caught outside the circle, blocked from my view by smoke and fire, and the only gap in the ring of flames was where Sean stood. A tongue of fire brushed his sleeve, singeing the fabric, and he stepped sideways. I slipped on the pebbly ground, landing hard on my knees in the gravel. I could feel them bleeding, stinging, then the skin scabbing over and healing.

'It's decision time, Gabby. See, I know you too. I know how you enjoy deliberating over the options. So you have a choice. These flames are not ordinary fire, not the kind that usually occurs on Earth.'

I heard the fight behind me stop. Keraun, his usually cocky voice filled with fear, whispered, 'Everfire.'

Sean's eyes glittered. 'Everfire burns too hot for even someone of Donovan's strength to survive. It needs fuel to burn like that, but your building is coated with it. You have about ten minutes to get them all out, or they burn to death. Even your god.'

'No!' I scrambled back to my feet. Sean held up a hand.

'Not so fast. You have to choose. Your friends – Cecelia and Zenna?' He said it like a question, but I was sickened. He had been playing me all along.

'Zenna has been asking for you. She's going in for surgery to repair an artery, in about half an hour. Did you know she's allergic to antibiotics? A pity her admission form doesn't say that.' He held up a copy of a hospital admission form with the allergy box circled in red pen. Blank.

'And Cecelia, she is a cold bitch, isn't she? Leaving your friend in a time of need. That put a small hole in my plans, but it's worked out for the better. I had meant for you to only have two choices and now you get three. After your people left her house, she did go back to the library for you. Alex took out my guard and went with her. I've had to rearrange some things to make sure one of my best men is waiting on the second floor. He is a creature of particular … appetites.'

I felt like someone had kicked me in the stomach.

Sean smiled. 'You can fix any one of these things. You can stay here and get your Darkhaven friends out of the everfire before it spreads. You can go to the hospital and speak to my anaesthetist there. Or you can rush to the library and intercept Cecelia before she runs into my man. He won't touch her if he sees you.'

My mind whirled. If I messaged Cecelia, and helped evacuate Darkhaven, then rang the hospital . . . how allergic was Zenna? Perhaps she had time.

Sean watched my expression. 'Before you start thinking you have time to do all three, stop. You don't. But I'm not completely unfair. I'll give you time to get to the location you choose. A ten-minute head start. But know that if you spend those minutes here, you will be too late to save either of your friends.'

'You can't ask me to choose,' I whispered. Sean knelt and lowered his face to mine. I recoiled from the personal invasion, screwing up my nose.

'That's not even the best part. See, I lied. It's a problem, I know, but I can't seem to help it. I didn't know where this place was. I put a tracker on you when you came to see me. That needle wound never did heal properly, did it?'

My hand went to my neck, which was still red and sore. I'd thought it was maybe a reaction to whatever drug they had been trying to give me. But it shouldn't have affected me at all. I should have healed. I kicked myself for not getting Stephen to check it.

Sean sighed as if he'd just realised something silly. 'And I'm lying now. Maybe this fire is perfectly ordinary, and your friends here can just walk through, or wait for it to die out. Maybe I haven't altered Zenna's paperwork. Maybe Cecelia didn't even go to the library. But one of them – one – is a real threat. You have to choose which one is real. Get it right, and you save them all. But if you choose wrong? Someone is going to die, Gabby, and it will be blood on your hands.' He leaned in close again, centimetres from my face, the corners of his mouth curling. 'Use your intuition,' he whispered.

He stood and folded his arms, waiting, smugness radiating from his whole body. Desperate, I reached in as far as I could, seeking that quiet place. But it was an unfathomable ocean, miles deep. I couldn't reach that far. My stomach roiled, nausea rolling up my gullet. 'Please. I'll give you the disk back. I'm sorry I ever stole it from you.'

Sean laughed. 'The disk. Luci wrote everything that is on that disk, and she has perfect recall. I'm just making sure you don't keep the encryption key. My men will take care of that.' He waved a casual hand at the crowd on the steps, all stopped to stare at the fire licking the edges of the building. 'Or the flames will.'

I despaired. It was almost worse, knowing that only one of the threats was real. I had to make the correct call. I wondered, as if I had spare brain cells to ponder any question other than "who do I need to save", what the point was. What did Sean want from me so badly that he would stage such an elaborate trap?

It didn't matter. I had to make a decision. And I was floundering, my mind sinking, unable to come up for air, unable to form rational thoughts. Smoke stung my eyes, and I pressed my palms to my temples.

Sean unfolded his arms. 'How about I give you a way out? Come and work for me, and I'll fix everything.'

'Never.' I spat at his feet.

'Then make your choice.'

'Gabby!' an impossible voice called.

I turned. 'Stephen?'

Stephen was propped up on one elbow, blood staining his shirt, his breathing ragged. Sean had shot him in the chest but must have missed his heart. My own heart lifted. Keraun took advantage of the momentary surprise to hit back at the suits, resuming his dogged battle, stopping them from getting to Stephen. One of them broke away, but there was a yowl and a flurry of grey fur. The man went down screeching as Savah clawed and scratched at his face. In shock, I stumbled and scrabbled up the drive to get to Stephen.

'Keraun, duck!' Stephen called. A magpie swooped low over the roof as Keraun dropped his head, talons extending and clutching at the middle of his back. It lifted away with the white film dragging from its curled feet. As soon as it was clear of Keraun's skin, the film evaporated into nothing. The bird cut a swift arc through the air and was joined by several more magpies, diving in and out in black and white blurs, slashing at the heads of the suits. Stephen's face was tight with focus.

With a crash, Donovan and Dr Whittaker emerged from the front door, sharp bruises already fading from both their faces. The doctor staggered down the steps and fell to Liam's side, shaking his shoulders. The birds swarmed Sean. Donovan pulled a gun on one of the remaining suits, then the next, and turned in time to catch another charging at her with a fresh syringe. A ragged suit broke away from the magpie flurry, launching at her back.

Keraun surged, a larger blur of black and white as he shoved the man aside. Donovan fired at the suit in front of her, then turned, her pistol clicking as it ran out of ammunition. She finished the last suit with a dull crunch of bones. The suits were all down. Keraun smiled at me briefly, then looked up, eyes glowing gold, and deep clouds developed over us. Fat drops of rain tumbled down to the earth. I supposed it wouldn't stop everfire – if it was everfire – but it might buy time.

I turned my attention back to Stephen. 'What do I do?'

'Do what Liam said. You'll know.' He spoke softly, so Sean wouldn't hear over the sound of flames roaring and raindrops hissing, half his attention still on the birds. Stephen must have heard Liam's instructions. *Tell Stephen I'm sorry.*

I swallowed. 'Liam said to tell you ...'

But he cut me off, placing a hand on my shoulder and meeting my gaze with serious grey eyes, giving me full focus. Magpies swooped away in my peripheral vision. 'It's okay,' he said. 'I'm proud of you, Gabby. Go get her.' He practically shoved me away.

Gritting my teeth, I climbed to my feet. Time to face Luci. Except she and Dad were stuck on the other side of the fire. I still had to get past Sean.

'Stephen.' Sean's voice was molten rage. The magpies had fallen back without Stephen's direct influence, but not before they'd ruined Sean's face. Shreds of skin were torn away, half an eyebrow dangled down the side of his cheek and his face ran with blood from brow to chin, dripping onto his shirt.

Reaching into his jacket, he pulled out his pistol again and marched up the driveway, his shoes munching the gravel. This was my opportunity to duck through the gap in the flames, to get to Luci, but I crouched just a metre away, transfixed, horrified, my feet cast in concrete, like some part of me knew what was about to happen.

Sean fired, point-blank, into Stephen's skull. The crack snapped through my eardrums, ricocheted off the bare walls of the Darkhaven building and faded away in echoes. A wordless cry escaped my throat, and the world went dizzy in front of me. Savah yowled.

A rough hand grabbed my shoulder.

'You!' I screeched, twisting in Sean's grip and clawing mindlessly at what was left of his face, my hands slickening with his blood. I stilled as gunmetal pressed into my temple.

'That's it, Gabrielle. You've had enough time. And the irony is, if you'd just made a decision earlier about school, about this' – he waved his hand towards the building – 'you and I might not even be here. But now you have to make a real decision. Who will you save?'

In my peripheral vision, I saw Dad step through the gap in the fire. 'Sean,' he warned.

'One.' Sean's voice was cold and metallic.

Dad stepped closer. 'Sean, that's enough.'

Sean didn't release me. I stared into the mud, mind in a blank panic, quiet place gone, drowning in the roar of flames and the stench of ash and the rain splashing over my skin.

'Two.'

Out of the corner of my eye, Dad raised his arm, reaching out to Sean. The clouds darkened to black.

'Thr—'

There was a shot, a flash and a searing, deafening crack. White fire engulfed me, but it was gone almost before my brain registered it, leaving me unharmed.

Sean fell to the ground, blood pooling around a small bullet hole in his forehead, hair and clothes blackened from the lightning strike. Keraun and Donovan looked at each other. Keraun's eyes were ablaze, but Donovan was still replacing her magazine. She hadn't fired. I looked around. Dad stood behind Sean, pistol still raised in his hand.

I climbed to my feet and stepped away from the body. Stephen had known. Liam had seen it, and Stephen had known he would die by sitting up and calling out. Whatever this was, it was more important than anything. As I felt the trust in him and in Liam, I felt my trust in myself build. The island of calm was on the horizon. I paused, sceptical, afraid that if I rushed to grasp it, it would slip away again. But it stayed there.

I walked through the gap in the flames. Luci still stood on the other side. I looked her in the face. She just stared at me, mouth open in slight surprise. I glanced at Dad, who met my eyes with inevitable sadness.

Before I could reach Luci, Donovan charged past, barrelling into Dad. She pinned him against the bonnet of the Jag with the barrel of her gun. 'Whose side are you on?' she growled.

'There are factors at play that you can't even comprehend,' he said, his voice calm, although his eyes flashed with annoyance. 'So I suggest you let me handle things as I must.'

In his awkward position, Dad's Taskforce swipe card had slipped halfway out of his pocket. Donovan kept her gun in place and flipped it over in her fingers. 'Jon,' she sneered. 'How many names do you have?'

A strange look flickered over his face. 'More than you know.'

'Donovan, let him go,' I said. I wasn't sure if I minded that she was beating him up, but I couldn't deal with anyone else getting shot today, let alone my dad.

She flashed me an unreadable glance, then returned her icy stare to the man lying on the bonnet. Donovan relaxed her grip and he stood, straightening his jacket. For a moment, it felt like time hung still in the air, giving us a moment to pivot. Pain still lanced through me as I thought of Stephen lying in the driveway, but I took a deep breath. Enough delayed decisions.

Now was the moment. If I was going to choose, I was out of time. Rainwater ran through my hair, down the back of my shirt and into my eyes, washing the salt and fear sweat away. I reached gently, deep, deeper than I'd ever reached before, to some dark foundation of myself that I hadn't known existed.

And I felt it. Certainty. Sean was lying. He was lying about the whole thing. He knew about Zenna in hospital and Cecelia going to the library because he'd tapped my phone. Things I hadn't seen when I was caught in panic sharpened into focus, and I realised I'd been in a state of panic since the fiasco at the Taskforce. If everfire was something that made even Keraun tremble, Sean would not have stood so close to it, so carelessly. Zenna would be in surgery long before I could get to the hospital. It seemed too convenient, but even if Sean had changed her medical records, it was already too late, and I'd have to hope the doctors had saved her. I didn't know what floor of the library Cecelia and Alex were on. But I knew, in this new foundation, that he was bluffing.

So I did nothing about Sean's dilemma. He was just a henchman, bigger than a pawn perhaps, but still another piece in the game the Taskforce was playing. I had the queen right in front of me and I knew, without knowing how, what Liam wanted me to do.

I reached out and put my hand on Luci's sternum, skin touching next to the collar of her blouse. Too late, she moved to block me. Her mouth opened slightly in surprise, and our eyes locked, but I didn't see her. I saw her DNA.

Like a code laid out before my eyes, in a language I could understand, I could read her DNA and see what she'd done to it as clearly as if I was reading a book. I could read her genome, and then some, information I'd had no idea could be conveyed by DNA, or perhaps I was seeing more than DNA. I could see her intelligence, her gift as a geneticist. I could see the gene that gave her physical regeneration. That was strong for her. I could see others, less strong, but I could understand how it worked, giving advanced strength, muscle growth, speed. Even a gene governing intuition and psychic abilities. I could see her DNA morphing too. The Praegressus program danced over her code like magic, swirling flashes of light ribboning before my eyes. But there was something changing in her DNA, even now, and it was impairing her physical abilities. That was what Sean had meant when he'd said she was weak. When – or if – she recovered, she would be stronger, closer to immortality than ever before.

There was a trace of another set of DNA too, a man's. There was something familiar there, but I couldn't quite place it. The entwinement suggested a partnership. I even saw events, marks on her DNA made by traumatic experiences, going back for generations.

Then I noticed an odd thing. There was a section that was somehow clumsily designed, like a piece had been cut out and the remaining ends forced together, leaving an ugly weld. I searched for what was missing.

Ethics. And empathy. Ingrained love for family. That was just the start. There should be compassion for humanity, and for the planetary system. Then life and the universe. A governing code of morality, shaped by her life experiences. It had been burned out of her. I recognised it because I knew what her genome should look like. She was my mother, and because we shared DNA, she couldn't break this connection. Somehow, I was in control. While I had my hand on her, she couldn't touch me.

Her driver punched me in the side of the head. Lights flashed across my eyes. I doubled over and vomited into the dirt.

The pain faded quickly, but the blinding light increased, filling the whole space. I realised it wasn't from the punch and turned to look for its source. A column of light was forming on the other side of the fire. Before Luci or her driver could grab me again, I rushed back through the gap in the flames. Tyres scrunched on the gravel behind me, but I didn't look back. Keraun stood at the centre of the light column, horrified. I was in front of him in an instant.

'What are you doing?' I asked, reaching out to him. Like the film Sean had put on him, I couldn't feel the column, only see it, but his shoulder was solid under my hand.

'I'm not,' he answered. His voice had lost all its velvet. It was hollow and sad, like water dripping onto a lost, undelivered letter. 'The Uzrun is taking me in.'

I glanced back at Sean's blackened form lying in the mud.

'But that . . . that was probably saving lives . . . and he's an evil . . .'

He grinned. 'Oh, I'm not apologising. But I might have to pretend at the trial. No excuses, remember?'

'Trial?' I asked, putting my hands on his shoulders. 'Where?'

'A long way from here,' he answered. 'Don't worry, I'll tell them I am sorry. They don't need to know that what I'm sorry for is leaving you.'

The rainfall slowed and the heavy clouds receded as Keraun's eyes dulled to normal brown. I gripped him. 'You can't go now!' I fought back the tears threatening to replace the rain washing down my face. I was not going to cry over this boy, not after one kiss. But the kiss. I bit my lip.

He took my wrists and pulled me close. 'I will come back for you,' he murmured. 'I'll even get a hybrid.'

'Keraun Thephyeu,' an officious voice said. Out of nowhere, a huge grey cube appeared, and two figures with translucent white hair and a third eye blinking on their brows stepped out of a door in the box. 'You are to be tried for the murder of a stage two human. Until the time of your trial, you will remain in confinement.'

Keraun let go of me and stepped back. The two officials flanked Keraun and escorted him into the giant cube as the light surrounding him faded. The box shimmered and vanished, and he was gone. The rain stopped. Tears like smudged ink rolled over my cheeks and dripped off my chin into the mud, and the fire kept burning.

CHAPTER 33

—

Expressionless Eyes

With an unusual lack of acid in her tone, Donovan offered to let me stay at her safe house for the night. I turned her down. I just wanted to go home, although I wasn't quite sure where that was right now. The fire raged through the bush behind the Darkhaven building. Dad and Luci had disappeared while Keraun's intergalactic magic beam was blinding everyone. After we'd retrieved Stephen's body, I helped Dr Whittaker save what she could from the burning building – fortunately the laboratory was at the end furthest from the fire. We filled the boot of the Corolla with boxes of files until even Donovan declared it too dangerous to continue dashing back into the escalating heat. I felt no need to test the theory that an Eventer could survive being trapped in a burning building. Some old shadow crossed Donovan's face when I ventured the question, and she didn't reply.

Once we were out, Dr Whittaker removed the tracking chip in my neck. It was so tiny I could barely see it in the petri dish she dropped it in. The fire brigade were on their way. Donovan had delayed the call until Dr Whittaker and Liam could get out unnoticed. Liam was unconscious, but Dr Whittaker thought he was stable, and she was now seeing to him in the back of the Corolla.

'Are you sure you don't want help?' I asked as Donovan, skin blackened with ash and clothes covered in grey mud, strode out of a small shed that had been spared from the fire, a heavy hose on one shoulder and a shovel in the other hand.

She turned to gaze at the Darkhaven building as the fire devoured the lab wing. 'There's no saving it, and the location is compromised anyway. I'll keep it contained until the firies arrive. If you're going home, go now, before your adrenaline drops and you crash.'

I nodded, grateful that she trusted me enough to let me go. I didn't think Stephen would have, although only because he would have been concerned for me. A pang sliced through my chest.

As I got into my car, Dad messaged to tell me he wouldn't be home and that he'd explain everything later. I was relieved. I didn't have the energy to confront him right now. While I flicked a text to tell Alex I was on my way to his place, Donovan set the shovel down and rummaged in her pockets. She held out my original, no-tracking-or-microphones bracelet and a small black case that fit in my palm. I had a horrible feeling about what was in the case. Thanks, intuition.

'You'll probably have to tell your uncle something about what happened. And your friends,' she said. There was a crackling and a bang as a burnt tree fell over on the other side of the driveway, sending a fresh load of sparks into the clearing.

'Shit,' she muttered, running back to put them out before the fire spread. I unzipped the case. In it was a small but intensely bright head lamp and three tiny blue syringes with little capped needles, the same as the one that was supposed to have had my amnesia drug in it, way back when this started. Now that I'd discovered this deep foundation of intuitive knowledge, it was like I couldn't lose it. I didn't need to read the slip of paper folded under the syringes to know what they did, and who they were for. One for Alex. One for Cecelia. One for Zenna.

Donovan was right about the adrenaline crash. I could feel my body sagging as I left the freeway and wound through the city to Alex's apartment. He met me at the door, opening it before I could lift my key to the lock and catching me as I stumbled over the threshold. For a long time, we stood like that in the doorway, his arms firm and comforting around my body. Cecelia padded down the hallway, and Alex extended one arm to pull her in too.

I didn't know how much Alex now knew about Netica, or if he knew at all, and I didn't feel up to explaining it to him. I begged fatigue and made for bed, via the shortest shower I'd ever taken just to get the smoke grit off my skin. Cecelia had already made up a camp bed in my room, then smothered it with textbooks, highlighters and notes.

'How have you been studying?' I asked as she came in with two mugs of hot chocolate.

'Here.' She handed one to me, set hers down on my dresser and tidied her books away. The thick, warm liquid was amazing, although no amount of chocolate could fill the Stephen-shaped void in my body.

'Thank you. But how?' I persisted, nodding at the books. I couldn't have studied if I'd tried.

'It's important to be able to focus. I was worried, but I had to spend the time somehow and Alex said there was nothing I could do anyway.' She packed everything neatly into her backpack.

'You really will make a great doctor.'

She smiled. 'Thanks. So how did you drop your human biology book in the shower?'

That question was innocent enough, but I knew she was getting to the real questions. I had no energy left to lie, but I couldn't tell her more than I already had. And I didn't want to talk about Stephen dying, or Liam being injured or the fact that my not-dead mother would probably not even understand the concept of a daughter by the time her transformation was complete.

So I lied. It twisted my guts, but when weighed against using the memory modification on her, lying was the best option. I made up something about a kidnapping and ransom because of Dad's work. This way, she still didn't know anything about Darkhaven or important names like the Netica Project. Well, she knew something was up with me, but she didn't really know what that entailed, and I hoped that knowledge wasn't enough to need modifying. And partly because she still thought I was withholding, but mostly because I had to tell someone, I explained what Keraun was and told her about the kiss. Her expression shifted from disbelief to dubiousness to awe within the space of a minute as I chose words I knew would best convince her my story was true. It was entirely likely that she thought I was having some post-traumatic psychotic break and was humouring me, but I didn't care. It just felt good to talk. She nearly dropped her mug when I told her about him striking a slow driver off the road. I reached out to steady her hand.

'Thanks. But what? A god? Like, created-Earth-and-humanity god? So all the scripture stuff is real?'

'Yes and no. Most of that is made up stuff to explain the gods' interactions with us, which used to be a lot more intense.

They step back as we evolve so we can learn for ourselves. Kind of like parents when a kid grows up, I guess. And the lazy ones like Keraun just figure out how to do less work.'

'He sounds about right for you,' she remarked.

'Oi!' I pinched her arm. 'I'm stronger than you now, remember?'

'You've always been stronger than me. Everyone in our year is stronger than me.'

'Probably not Dylan.'

'No, I could maybe take Dylan. Poor Dylan.'

We giggled. The feeling felt hollow, like tossing confetti into the void.

'Wow. We eventually do get to travel into space. Like, properly.'

'Yeah.'

'So what's happening with him? Are you official now?'

'It was one kiss, Ceel. And no.' My mood fell. 'He's gone. At the end, after my kidnapper wouldn't hand me over, Keraun struck him with lightning. He's not supposed to do that. He's been summoned back for a trial, or something.'

'Will he come back? Because I'm still not entirely convinced he exists, or that any of this could be real. You're going to have to introduce me.'

I shrugged, reluctant to dwell on it. 'He said he would. But I guess that depends on what happens in his trial. He might not have killed the guy. An agent shot him at the same time.'

'I don't think someone else murdering someone at the same time means you get off the murder charge.'

'He's not a murderer,' I whispered, feeling my eyes go hot. I hid my face in my mug.

'I didn't mean it like that,' Cecelia said, lying back on her bed. 'Just as a technical term.'

I knew what she meant. But it still stung to hear it, since that was what he was on trial for. I drained my chocolate. 'How's Zenna?'

'I called the hospital a couple of hours ago. She's fine. Well, not fine, obviously, but she's safe. You can visit her tomorrow.'

'Thanks, Ceel.' I yawned. She didn't answer. I looked down to see her eyes closed, softly sleeping. I lay back in bed, feeling the pillows receive my weight and stretched, feeling my tired bo—

I was asleep.

It was ten-thirty when I awoke on Sunday morning. Pretty early, all things considered, but Cecelia had already trucked her books to the library, preparing for her Monday morning Chemistry exam. I didn't have anything until Wednesday morning, so I felt like I could leave studying for later, especially now I was in touch with my intuition again.

Alex stuck his head in the door. 'Morning, secret agent. Breakfast?'

'Depends,' I said, rolling over and peering through bleary eyes. The Stephen-void loomed. I shied away from it. 'Are we going out, or are you cooking?'

'What's wrong with porridge?' It was his go-to breakfast: oats, water and salt, cooked to a smooth gruel. Sometimes, he got really crazy and added quinoa. It was edible, particularly after it had been heaped with honey and strawberries – or even better, Nutella – but it was still porridge. I groaned and went back under the covers.

'Fine, fine. Let's go to Lartte,' he said.

As much to throw myself away from the void of grief as to play normal for Alex, I made a great show of tossing back the covers, beaming falsely and leaping out of bed with my arms out like I was launching into a macabre song-and-dance with subtext: some terrible stuff happened, but look, it's fine. Except my foot caught on the muddy jeans that I'd thrown on the floor last night, and I stumbled into the linen basket.

Alex snickered. 'If they went straight in the wash, you know. You've got ten minutes to get ready. I'm starving.'

So was I, but it still took me fifteen minutes to find clean clothes, slap some makeup onto my pale face and decide on an alternative to my favourite black boots, which were also covered in mud and ash from yesterday. My hair reeked of smoke, but I didn't have time to wash it. I pulled it off my face into a scruffy low bun and sprayed some perfume around myself. I met Alex in the hallway, unapologetic in the face of his pained, dying-of-hunger expression.

Lartte was busy, but we found a table in the corner next to the postcard rack. We placed our usual orders (big breakfast for Alex, scrambled eggs for me with a side of hash browns) and waited for our orange juice. Once the waitstaff had delivered our drinks and left us alone, Alex set down his glass.

'Time to talk,' he said, joking gone.

I nodded, trying not to visibly squirm. 'What do you know?'

'Ah, that won't work on me. You've done enough hiding information, especially considering it's usually my job to know things others don't. Start at the beginning.'

Stephen had been right, in a way. There wasn't a way to be in this without the people I loved noticing that I was lying to them – that was the best-case scenario – or worse, ending up in danger because of me. I stared into my glass. I had tried to come up with a swallowable story about what had been going on all this time. Nothing was remotely believable. Hell, the truth wasn't believable. Maybe I should let him think it was all an elaborate lie. But I wasn't getting out of this. Friends I could put off or tell half-stories to, but not Alex, and at the heart of my hesitation was the tiny syringe secreted in my pocket. If I told him, I'd have to use it. And I couldn't. I couldn't do that to my uncle and know what I'd done.

'Gabby,' he said, voice gruff, as he reached a hand across to mine. His fingers brushed the bracelet. 'You can tell me anything. Anything.'

Fighting back the sob that threatened to close my throat, I took his hand and started talking. I didn't have a plan. At first words trickled, then they tumbled, and I told him everything. Well, I left out a few bits that I thought sounded too dangerous – details about the car chase at the beginning, for example. And, as when I'd told Zenna, I edited Keraun out completely, although for different reasons, more related to Alex worrying about things like sneaking out and sex. Cross that particular chasm if and when the alien god boy ever came back.

We paused as our breakfasts were set down, and then mine went cold in front of me while I talked. Alex didn't eat much either. I choked up when I explained Stephen getting shot. I finished with Luci disappearing.

He stared at me for a minute. I didn't feel the same relief I'd felt when I'd told Zenna. His eyes were distant, like he'd forgotten something important. To break the tension, I took a mouthful of egg. I was so hungry that, even cooled, the egg was like air after holding my breath for a minute. I took another bite. Alex followed suit, picking up his knife and fork, and we ate in silence. We ordered coffee and hot chocolate. The silence slowly faded from awkward to companionable.

'What happens now?' he asked, setting down his cappuccino.

I stared at the puppy face in my chocolate froth. 'I don't know,' I said. 'I still have to decide. Keep my abilities and work for Darkhaven or change back and live in the normal world.' I hadn't mentioned the details of the choice that was still before me: to stay at Darkhaven and remain a less-inspiring version of superwoman, I would have to cut ties with everyone. Or that in the process of reversal, I would have to forget everything that had happened over the past four months. Despite my outburst at Darkhaven that I wanted to forget them all, it wasn't true. But with Stephen gone, I wasn't sure if our agreement still held.

Alex didn't say much as we finished our drinks and walked back to the apartment, but when he looked at me, it was with a pensiveness, like he'd lost his little girl. Guilt hung in his face, cutting me to the depths of my being. I knew he felt he'd failed to protect me, but it should have been my guilt. I'd put him in this situation. And I knew then what I had to do.

He sat on the couch and flicked the television on to watch the rugby. I hovered behind him. The syringe felt hot in my palm. Then I perched on the end of the couch, hand hiding behind my leg, pretending to watch.

I got up, made tea and let it go cold on the kitchen bench while I stood, staring out the window. I rationalised my decision. If I didn't do this, Donovan would. The less time he had to stress about what he'd just learned, the kinder it was. But really, I just wanted to take it back, take the look of guilt and shame over his perceived failure out of his eyes.

I went and sat next to him. He gave me an odd glance – I made no secret of my lack of interest in sports. I angled my knees towards him and leaned back against the cushions like I was just sitting with my uncle because I was tired and stressed. He turned his eyes back to the game. His wary expression was justified, even if he didn't know it. After this, I would definitely not be his little girl anymore.

Taking a breath, I jabbed the needle into his neck. No turning back now. I depressed the plunger. He had a momentary look of alarm, then his face relaxed. It was unreal. His muscles slackened to the point where it was like all the quirks that made his face his were smoothed away. I shuddered. Inside the case was the list of keywords and gestures, but I remembered them all. I put on the head torch. A white room like the one at Darkhaven was ideal, but not necessary, according to the instructions.

'Darkhaven,' I began, lifting my fingertips to the point just in front of his expressionless eyes.

CHAPTER 34

A Bittersweet Ache

I'd meant to go and visit Zenna that afternoon, and that's what I told Alex I was doing, although he was barely aware of me talking as he sat, unfocussed eyes vaguely following the men chasing the ball on the screen. But as I closed the front door behind me, the reality of what I'd just done sank right in. I couldn't do it to Zenna too. Not yet. If she was awake, she'd ask. If not, well, she wouldn't know I'd visited anyway. And another little – okay, large – part of me was still mad at her for what she'd done, and I knew neither of us could handle a conversation about that at the moment. I was relieved when Donovan messaged to say they were having a service for Stephen that evening.

I had been right, at least, about the fire not being everfire, but it had still been fierce. Keraun's rain and the firebreak had protected the neighbouring land, but the building was gutted and most of the Darkhaven bush been destroyed, including Liam's pergola, which was where Donovan had built a pyre that smelled faintly of diesel. At least it wasn't petrol. That scent had already haunted me when I fuelled up the Mazda on my way here, the smell hitting my nose and triggering a detailed recall of kneeling in the gravel before Sean's sneering face.

The smoke hung heavy in the air, and I pushed back the waves of memory threatening to replay the day before. I stood alongside Dr Whittaker in the cluster of charred stumps and blackened furniture where the pergola had been, kicking up bits of ash and dead leaves with my toe and watching them drift back to the earth in the late-afternoon light. My chest was still, hollow. Stephen would never sit out here under the jasmine again, sipping tea with Liam and watching fairy-wrens play in the fountain while Savah swished her tail. The feeling swelled like saltwater tide when I realised I'd never again chat to Stephen over the comfortable hum of a car engine or get to work with him if I joined Darkhaven.

I glanced at Liam, propped up in a chair, while Donovan fussed about Stephen's body. Liam looked exhausted. Sean's injection had turned out to be Viciretro, the "cure" for the Praegressus program that Keraun had discovered, intended to return him to ordinary human gene expression. But I had knocked the needle out before the full dose had been delivered, and we weren't sure yet if the change would be permanent.

Dr Whittaker had cleaned Stephen up, wiping away the blood, dressing him in fresh clothes and placing a bandage over the bullet wound on his head, a stark white reminder of why we were here.

We didn't talk. The doctor stepped up first and laid a small handful of daisies on Stephen's chest. She offered her arm to Liam. I took his other side, and he hobbled, as if every cell in his body hurt, to the edge of the pyre. He set a long black feather next to the daisies. We escorted him back and eased him onto his cushion before I turned back to the pyre. I reached into my pocket. I'd forgotten to return the tracking bracelet before my exams, and then I hadn't had a chance. It flashed in the light. Sean had cut away the *Jeans* when he took the GPS out, so it simply read *Superhuman*. I laid it on Stephen's chest. 'Thank you for looking out for me,' I whispered.

Donovan stepped up and placed a coin next to our tokens. I couldn't see what was on it. We formed a line beside the pyre, then Donovan cleared her throat.

'*Lovely is the night*,' she began. '*A hiding place, fit for the most beautiful dreams.*'

She recited the poem by heart, one I'd never heard before, and for an inane moment I wondered what Mrs Johnsen would have made of it.

'*But wait for the night*' – Donovan's cadence brought a finality to the air around us – '*and our salvation.*'

We stood in silence. In the distance, a magpie warbled.

'Peace in the dark,' Donovan said softly.

'Peace in the dark,' Liam and Doctor Whittaker echoed. I let my lips form the words. The phrase had the weight of long tradition, one I wasn't quite part of. Not yet.

Donovan stepped forward with a lighter and the pyre whooshed into flame as the accelerant caught. We stood and watched the fire dance until it became too hot to bear, too much like yesterday, then we retreated. Donovan stood a little way away and stared at the flames, her expression closed. Doctor Whittaker helped me settle Liam on the blackened patio steps and disappeared to her own reflection.

Movement at the side of the building caught my eye, and I peered around to see Savah picking her way through the ash and charred sticks. Liam smiled and extended a hand. She rubbed her face on his fingertips, then brushed past his legs to sniff my boot. She was covered in soot, but otherwise seemed unharmed.

'We worried she'd died,' Liam said. The cat purred as he stroked her spine.

I watched them both, feeling into my intuition to see if Liam would prefer time alone, but it felt right to stay. I perched on the steps next to him, feeling like a shattered pane of glass held together with sticky tape. But I also had an unexpected sense of peace.

Maybe Liam had known what I was about to ask, although he claimed that his clairvoyance was no longer working for him. Maybe it was just the look on my face as tears crept out of my eyes and my mouth lifted in a smile while a magpie warbled from a burnt branch above our heads.

'It's part of the transformation,' he said. 'A deeper understanding of how life works, even if you can't quite comprehend it up here.' He tapped his temple. 'We have made these advancements so quickly, by rewriting DNA. The human mentality is very strong, and it takes a lot to make it see new possibilities. Eventually, you'll know that death itself is a beautiful thing, a transition, not an ending. But for now, your reality still tells you it's a permanent loss.'

I toyed with the zipper of my boot. I couldn't quite get it. But I did. It was muddling. 'I'm still sad, though.'

He nodded. 'That's part of the beauty.'

Beautiful sadness. I sort of smiled. 'What about you?'

'Catherine says it might all come back, she can't quite tell yet. My body isn't healing properly, but when it does, it might kick the Viciretro.'

'What if it doesn't?' I tried to imagine going back to being normal. Sure, life would have been a lot less stressful if I hadn't been through what we were now referring to as "Sean", which encompassed the entire day's drama. I could probably extend that window of stress back to my Event, actually. But the deep feeling of certainty I had now that I'd regained my intuition was nice. It was hard to imagine giving that up.

Liam smiled. 'Don't worry. I'll be beating you at poker again before you know it.'

'Not a chance,' I said. 'My intuition is better now.'

'Then I might have to teach you a new game to even the odds.'

We laughed gently. The sound fell about the burnt bush in soft, surprised echoes.

'I liked Keraun,' he said. Before I could ask him to elaborate, Doctor Whittaker reappeared with red-rimmed eyes and Liam nodded, reaching up for her hand. I helped her get him into the car, bundling Savah in after him. As I shut the door and turned away, the doctor caught my arm.

'Thank you, Gabby,' she said.

I wasn't entirely sure what for. Watching Liam, so she could have her own moment? Something else? It didn't matter. 'You're welcome, Doctor Whittaker.'

She smiled. 'Call me Catherine.'

I nodded, and then they were gone, a trail of dust settling over the gravel drive.

Donovan said I didn't have to stay, which I interpreted to mean she didn't want me to stay, so I left her beside the smouldering pyre and went back to the city.

Alex seemed to have recovered and greeted me with his usual reserved demeanour from the kitchen, where he was making his surprisingly good vegan pizzas. Dad was due home on Tuesday – I was suspicious he'd even left – and Alex would fly back to Canberra. Everything was normal. For him, at least. I'd gotten the message from Dad too and was torn about whether I should go home and find out where his loyalties really were or beg asylum from Donovan and avoid the awkward conversation. The mission he'd been called away for on Saturday was obviously the Sean attack. I was quiet through the meal, but I brushed it off as exam stress. Alex was relaxed and happy, and that was good enough for me.

The next evening, I knew I couldn't put it off any longer. I went to the hospital and asked for Zenna's room, only to be told that she'd gone home that afternoon.

'So soon?' I asked.

The nurse was already gone, bustling off down the hallway. I followed the colour-coded stripes painted on the walls back to the elevators and went to Zenna's house. In a way, I was relieved – it would be less awkward than a hospital room.

Zenna's mum met me at the door, smiled thinly and showed me inside. I declined her offer of tea in case the harpy was about and knocked on Zenna's bedroom door.

'Hi, Zenna,' I said when she opened it, clutching a sheaf of paper. She went straight back to sit on her bed, legs drawn up to her chest and arms wrapped around them. White bandages covered her left arm from the elbow down. I turned her desk chair around to face the bed and sat down.

Silence.

'Do you want tea, or something?' she asked.

I shook my head. 'I went to the hospital first. I'm glad you're home. How are you feeling?'

'How do you think?'

Heat rose in my face. 'Well, I don't know, I've never –' I caught myself before I said it. Don't start anything, Gabby.

'Never tried to top yourself?'

'I'm sorry,' I began.

Zenna gave me a black glare. 'Sorry for what?' Her voice was a vicious jab. 'Sorry you weren't there for me when I needed a friend? Sorry you ran off to deal with your shit while I was bleeding out in the bathroom? Sorry you took so long to visit me that I wasn't even at the hospital by the time you showed up? Or are you just sorry you came here now? Sorry you have a friend who is so screwed up?'

I stared at her, meeting her gaze with burning defiance. There was something off about her eyes.

'Fuck you,' I said, surprising myself with my aggression. 'You have no idea what I've been through this year, and you throw all this crap in my face.'

'No, you have no idea what I've been through. Everyone has shit going on, Gabby. Your uni decision isn't the biggest thing in the world. I just needed someone to hear me. And even when I cracked apart right in front of you –'

'You mean, sliced up your arm and shoved it in my face, then told me it was my fault.'

'I mean, when I was out of my mind with desperation, you turned your back. So fuck you too.'

The door, which I'd left ajar, moved. Zenna's cat, a scruffy brown and white fluffball, nosed the door open, wound itself around the corner and jumped up on the bed. It settled on Zenna's papers and stared at me. I looked away, out the window, watching the jacaranda next door waving its delicate lavender blossoms against the evening sky. A crescent moon flashed in and out of view. Something nagged at me. The way she'd said "everyone has shit going on".

'Zenna, do you remember what I told you? About the lightning?'

She bit the words off harshly. 'What are you talking about?'

The question whipped me in the face, along with an intuitive knowing, and guilt pressed like granite stones in my stomach. Donovan had got to her. It was supposed to be my job and I hadn't done it. I imagined Donovan's criticisms about irresponsibility and weakness of character as she took care of Zenna for me. And it was my fault for telling her in the first place, when I should have known better. I suddenly longed to leave, to find a quiet, dark place where no one was accusing me of anything. 'Maybe we should talk later,' I suggested.

'There won't be a later.'

I regarded her face, trying to intuit her meaning. 'What are you saying, Zenna?'

'Mum and Dad are sending me away.'

'What? Where?'

'A place down south, somewhere near Yallingup.'

'What, like a mental hospital?' I blurted. Whoops. 'Sorry.' I looked down at my hands, toying with a loose thread on the cushion of her chair.

'Your bluntness is the one thing you don't need to be sorry for. I like that about you.'

I met her eyes. We almost smiled at each other.

'It's a meditation retreat for teenagers with issues, I think. Lots of stupid hippie shit. Yoga and art classes and group therapy.'

'How long?'

She shrugged. 'I think a month or two is normal.'

I stared back out the window. 'How are –'

Her shadowed eyes flashed in anger. 'God help me, if you ask me how I'm feeling one more time, I will kill you.'

Maybe Zenna was the one with a gift for intuition. I was royally screwing this up. 'I'm sorry, I'm just trying to . . .' Even I didn't know what I was doing. Making up with Cecelia was so simple. Zenna had never been one to forgive easily. And if I was totally honest, I was equally unwilling to move towards the forgiveness table. A large part of me still felt like she should be apologising.

'Stop being sorry when you don't know what for.' Zenna stood, her arms folded across her chest. The cat rolled off the paper and curled up to sleep. I glanced at the document, and staggered. The handwriting at the top was familiar.

Don't let them take you.

'Zenna,' I began, unsure how to bring it up, since she now had no idea about any of this.

'Please go. I'm tired.'

I hovered. 'Can I ...' Can I what? Read your private paperwork about your mental state?

'Get out.'

'Okay, fine,' I said, standing and walking to the door. Maybe when she got back I could ask her, follow the lead. 'But if you want friends to be there for you, you have to actually let them be there. Even when they're not saying all the right things.'

'You should hear yourself. Bye, Gabby,' she said, closing the door as soon as I was a centimetre out if it. The air displacement blew my hair past my face.

I let myself out of the Robinson house, slammed my car door and drove away, angry tears filling my eyes. Then I thought about how much of a verbal klutz I'd been, and they turned to frustrated tears. I was losing one of my best friends, and nothing I could say worked. Then *Hey Jude* came on the radio and the tears turned sad, then expanded into giant, uncontrollable sobs. I turned up the music so I couldn't hear my gasps and hoped no one would pull up alongside at the traffic lights. We'd be okay. I thought. I hoped.

But the tears didn't stop, not while I drove home, and not while I cleaned my teeth, which was pretty messy while crying, and not until long after I went to bed. I cried for Zenna. I cried for Alex. I cried for Stephen. I cried for meeting my mother and finding out there was no love there and never would be. I cried for Keraun being snatched away to face trial for a murder he'd committed for me. Finally, I cried for myself until I fell asleep.

CHAPTER 35

Stupid Cute Puppy

I awoke the next morning feeling ... no. Couldn't be.

I rolled out of bed and went to the bathroom to check myself in the mirror. I looked the same. My roots needed attention and my final exam still loomed, but ... optimistic? When did I ever feel optimistic? Yet somehow, all the anguish and guilt and despair seemed to have drained away.

Almost all of it. My conscience still twinged when I saw Alex eating his quinoa porridge. I supposed he was happy enough. At least this way I would carry the guilt, not him. And with Luci still at large, he was safer if he didn't know about Darkhaven. I drowned some wholegrain rice puffs in milk and sugar and joined him at the table. He gave me a hug goodbye, wished me luck for the exam and said he'd make sure to come home for my graduation.

I lingered in the kitchen. The exam was tomorrow, but Donovan had messaged requesting me to meet at the safe house for a briefing, and I was happy to oblige, since the alternatives were sitting in my room reading about the human cardiovascular system or feeling anxious about not sitting in my room reading about the human cardiovascular system.

I parked next to the GT-R at ten minutes past eleven and found Donovan, Catherine and even Liam propped up on some pillows, waiting in the cramped kitchen.

Donovan looked at her watch. 'You're late.' Her tone suggested I wasn't supposed to respond. I took a seat next to Liam, who was gaunt-faced. Silence fell across the table.

'I suppose,' Donovan began, with knives edging into her voice, 'we need to talk about Jan.'

'Don't you mean Sean?' I asked.

'Sean was a foot soldier. I mean Jan, as in the filthy vermin who ratted us out last time and is now apparently continuing the Netica Project, if your reports from your foray into the Taskforce labs are any indication. Luci isn't working alone.'

She gave me an appraising look, like I might have got it all wrong.

I glared back. 'What are you talking about? I thought Jan died in the lab fire seventeen years ago.'

'So did we,' Donovan replied. 'But then he showed up on Saturday.'

'He showed up? When?' I asked. Everyone looked at me like I'd sprouted the ears of a cat. A sinking feeling crept into my gut, hooking into my earlier optimism and dragging it down my legs, through my feet and out into the cracked linoleum floor.

'With Luci. The bastard,' Donovan grumbled, her fingers clenching into fists.

With Luci. They'd had a driver, her and Dad, but I knew Donovan wasn't talking about the driver. I was more tangled in this than I'd realised. It wasn't just my mother who'd volunteered me for the Netica Project. Dad didn't administer the

Taskforce from afar like it was simply another part of his work, unaware of its true scope. He was up to his bald pate in it.

Dad – first name Jon – was Jan.

'That was my dad,' I said, staring at them all. They stared back in varying degrees of shock. Liam's face melted in sympathy. Catherine's lips parted. A strange look of understanding flashed over Donovan before she steered the meeting on.

I reeled as the conversation circled back to how Liam, who previously could foresee things concerning Darkhaven and its inhabitants, hadn't seen any of this coming. His theory was that he'd believed Jan was dead, and since the whole set-up and attack on Darkhaven had been masterminded by Jan, Liam couldn't perceive it.

'That makes sense,' Catherine said. 'So Sean hit you with Viciretro because once you realised, you would be able to give us an advantage and spoil the trap he'd set for Gabby.'

'Can we trust him?' Liam asked. 'Jan? He is Gabby's father.'

'No.' Donovan cast a glance at me. 'But we can't avoid him, so we'll just have to play it smart.'

I drifted in and out of attention while Donovan discussed finding a new venue for Darkhaven, and tuned out completely during the talk of rehabilitating the old grounds for sale or lease. We'd lost the disk and the holofoil in the fire, although Donovan had, while making the copies, figured out some of the data: the list of subjects from the first cohort. I shivered. My name would be on that list. There were five more potential Eventers still out there.

My thoughts turned to Keraun. Where was he? On his planet, but in a jail? Or at home? Did they have trial by jury, or hear from witnesses? I thought someone who had been here should be a witness. If he hadn't killed Sean, who knew how many more of us would have died? And then there was the matter of who killed Sean at all, because if Dad – Jan – had landed his shot a fraction of a second before . . . all of this was really just a preamble to what I wanted to think about, which was the kiss. And at the same time, I was trying desperately not to think about it, because it was trouble, like Keraun was trouble, and he was an alien god and definitely not boyfriend material, or anything else, but I wished I could get in touch with him somehow –

'Gabby?' Donovan's sharp voice intruded on my thoughts. 'I didn't ask you here just so we could look at your pasty face.'

For a moment I regretted coming to the meeting. Not having Donovan in my life was a plus in the Option B "leave the Netica Project forever" column. 'I'm sorry?' I asked, not sorry at all.

'Is Luci's genetic modification going to work?'

'I don't know. Right now, she's weak, so whatever she's done is messing with her healing. If it works, she'll be smarter and stronger and harder to kill than before. But it might not.'

Donovan drummed the table with her fingertips. 'My scouts say she hasn't returned to the Taskforce, and there's surveillance footage of her at the international airport. I should go after her.'

'Are you sure?' Catherine asked. 'It's a problem that might take care of itself.'

'Or it will be a problem we cannot fix later. She's weak now.'

Liam shifted, rearranging his pillows. 'So are we. We need time to mourn and figure out how to work without Stephen. We need your help, Es. I have to get better. And Gabby has to finish her exams and decide what she wants to do. It'll be worth waiting, in the long run.'

For some reason, Donovan flinched. 'So I just let Luci go. And Jan.' She shook her head, jaw clenched. 'This isn't going to be the end of it.'

'That is what we'll count on,' Liam replied. Then his eyes fluttered, and he collapsed bonelessly onto the table.

Catherine carried him back to his room, Donovan and I hovering at her heels. After a brief moment of observation, she declared him fine, just exhausted and in need of rest. Then she kicked us out, saying she'd let him up again tomorrow.

Donovan followed me to the door.

'My exam is tomorrow,' I said. 'I'll call in on Thursday.'

'I don't think I need to tell you how important it is that we catch Luci before she becomes unstoppable,' she said, voice low.

I didn't turn back to face her. 'You don't.'

'And we can't do it with a team of three, when one of them is a doctor with no interest in field work and the other can barely sit up.' She grabbed my shoulder and pulled me around.

Nice how she presumed *I* would be interested in field work. I was intrigued, kind of, but still. I squared my feet and shrugged free of her grip. 'I didn't sign up for Netica.' I'd made my decision. Stand in your power, Gabs. 'I am no more responsible for Luci than anyone else out there, and I won't be bullied into this.'

Donovan straightened up. 'Look who finally grew some balls.'

I suppressed a smile. I didn't want to ruin my newfound assertiveness. Instead, I glared her in the face.

'Well, get out then,' she added, turning back inside.

Take the victory, Gabby. Walk away, Gabby. Let her sweat before you tell her what you're going to do.

Ah, hell.

'Donovan?' I called. 'Sean had balls. I don't. But I am joining Darkhaven, and I'm taking time to make the transformation. Let me know if you need help moving.'

Donovan spun towards me. Before I could say anything else to anger her, I bolted out the door.

I drove back to the city and stopped to pick up an iced chocolate from Lartte on my way to Alex's. I still hadn't packed my stuff. I didn't want to – the idea of playing nice with Dad while I knew he was working with Luci, even if he was on our side, was unfathomable. I could just stay at Alex's. It wasn't like I had to get to school every day any more, and I had my own car now.

Dad had sent me another message, this time a text-novelette assuring me I was safe at his place. He claimed he was working undercover at the Taskforce and had to go along with Sean's plan at Darkhaven, and he'd been delayed but would be home tomorrow night. I could sense something was up with his story. I knew I was safe; he genuinely had no intention of hurting me that I could intuit. But he'd been involved since before I was born, and I just didn't want another horrible conversation. I sent Cecelia a text asking if I could stay for the night.

While I waited for my iced chocolate, a couple on bicycles approached with a Border Collie puppy in a basket. It bounced excitedly, escaping from its owners and scampering into the cafe as they stacked their bicycles against the wall and fiddled with bike locks. I smiled at its effervescent enthusiasm.

'Oh, he's so cute!' the waitress gushed as she came towards me with my drink. Tail wagging, the puppy jumped up on her leg, catching her foot as she took her next step. She fell. I could save one thing: the waitress from crashing into a table, or the iced chocolate from hitting the floor. I caught the girl by her shoulders.

'Thanks,' she said. The puppy retreated and sat, all innocent eyes, then gave a high-pitched little woof. 'I'll clean up and make you another one.' She bustled off. I knelt and looked at the young dog with its disproportionate feet and downy coat. It stared back, suddenly serious, cocking its head to one side. I ruffled its ears.

The owners rushed in, apologising profusely. I left them to it. My drink arrived – again – and I wandered out, sipping on chocolate milk, something clicking. Probably something to do with my returning optimism. I had a plan.

CHAPTER 36

Sounds Like Stealing

Cecelia allowed me to stay, but she would not be distracted from her revision. I hadn't even brought any study notes with me, but I had other research to do. I asked to borrow Nancy's laptop and kept out of Cecelia's reproving-glare range. Plan settled, I went to bed before she did, feeling content for the first time in a long time.

In the morning, while Cecelia was still working (had she even gone to bed? I asked her, and paid for that mistake by having my head bitten off) I took a drive and cruised past Dad's house. He wasn't back yet. Good. I let myself in and went to his office, rummaging around in his desk. He would notice of course, but by then it would be too late. I took what I needed and snuck back out, pausing in my bedroom to retrieve the TISC handbook from the floor and throw it in the bin. It was a token gesture, since I was pretty sure I'd missed the deadline anyway, but it felt good. I arrived at the exam with ten minutes to spare.

Somehow, I did okay with human biology, although my textbook was still sitting where I'd left it a week ago, under the clothes on my desk at Dad's. Having my intuition back helped. So did having tossed the TISC book and all that stress in the bin. After the exam, I ushered Cecelia into the car to enact my plan. She was still going over questions.

'Section A was fine, I mean, multiple choice, that's not even really a test. And Section C was easy, the essay questions on the endocrine system were good. But I think there was some stuff in B, the Krebs cycle, that I missed.'

'Cecelia.'

'Question two was ugly, it –'

'Cecelia!'

'What?'

'It's over. The exam is over. High school is over,' I said. 'We need to go and celebrate.'

Cecelia pouted. 'Well, I don't know, I need to come up with a plan to stay sharp over the summer, uni is like, five months away, and it's easy to forget everything.'

I suppressed my grimace. As easy as a jab with a miniature needle. 'Well, you can start your summer revision program to-morrow. Today, we forget about school.'

She relented. 'Milkshakes at the Shack?'

I shook my head. 'Surprise.'

I refused to answer her questions, or talk about the exam, as I drove us across the city. Driving was easier now, with my intuition back. The day was hot and sunny.

'Oh!' Cecelia exclaimed as we turned down the driveway of Perth Creature Rescue.

I grinned as I searched for a car park. 'I figured you weren't up for drinking at the beach with the rest of our year group, so I thought you could help me choose a puppy.'

'What?' Cecelia exclaimed, eyes dancing. 'You never told me you were getting a puppy! Where are you going to keep it?'

'Dad's place has a big enough yard. School's over, so I have heaps of time for training and puppy classes. I've been thinking about it for a while, and you know I've wanted a dog for years. I feel like now is the time.'

Cecelia looked suspicious. 'Do Jon and Alex know about this?'

I smirked as I switched off the engine. 'Not exactly. But I deserve it.' I pulled Dad's credit card from my pocket. 'Dad has kindly agreed to fund it.'

Cecelia's face darkened. 'That sounds a lot like stealing, Gabby.'

'Oh come on, don't be like that. He's always felt bad about being away so much, and he said if there was anything he could do to make it up to me, I just had to ask.'

'Yes,' Cecelia folded her arms. '*Ask.*'

'Well, then he flew to Canberra, so I'll ask later. He'll say yes.'

She hesitated, uncomfortable at the edges of her well-defined ethics, but her arms unfolded and her face lit up. 'Fine, let's go. I'm getting cat cuddles!'

Cecelia jumped out of the car and skipped to the door. I walked. A dog had been in the back of my mind all year. Dad had never let me get one because he thought that as a kid, I couldn't handle the responsibility of moving it between two homes, and as a teenager, I needed to focus on high school. But those two excuses were now moot. The idea of bringing a dog with me to Darkhaven made the whole move much less daunting. After ten minutes of deliberating over asking the bitch anything, I had sent Donovan a text that morning.

Do you know much about dog training?
Absolutely nothing.
I was thinking about getting a puppy.
Talk to Cat. Her parents were breeders.

Catherine had agreed to help me train a puppy. Of course Cecelia didn't know about Darkhaven or the other people in my life. She hadn't asked about Alex or how I was feeling, and I suspected Donovan might have gotten to her too, although it was entirely possible that exam stress and study had simply pushed all other information and events out of her brain.

We visited the cat section first. Rows of boxes lined the walls, Perspex panels allowing the cats to watch the activity outside, and cat-sized doors in one side of the box led to private burrows the cats could hide in. The boxes had their own central ventilation system. At least half of the Cat Hotel was occupied: cats that had been found on the street, or given up, or seized by animal welfare officers. Cecelia found a big fluffy calico with ginger patches and asked to pet him. He smooched and purred, rubbing his head against her hand.

'He likes you,' the girl showing them around observed. 'I can get some forms for you if you like.'

Cecelia sighed. 'Oh, I'm sorry, I can't, my dad is allergic.'

I reached towards the Perspex front of a box containing a short-haired black cat, whose name was Thunder. The cat shrank back, hissing, then disappeared through its escape hatch into its private box, where I could just see a glint of green eyes.

Some of the dogs were friendlier, but a lot of them were timid and cowered away from a group of approaching humans. There weren't many in the Dog Resort. Apparently they'd had a big adoption drive last week, so most of the dogs who were ready to move to new homes had gone.

'What sort of environment are you bringing the dog to?' the girl asked. 'Will it be noisy, quiet, have kids, other pets, lots of space?'

'Um, no kids,' I said, glancing around. Cecelia was still in the cat area. 'A cat, a few people and, um, possibly noisy activity. So I guess it has to be good with that.'

The girl gave me a puzzled look. I regarded the dogs one at a time, feeling into my intuition. Some of the faces were cute, but I sensed that none of them were a good fit for me. I had no idea what I would be doing at Darkhaven next year, but I suspected it wasn't going to be entirely quiet and peaceful. 'I probably need something pretty resilient,' I admitted.

'You're best with a puppy then, so you can socialise it,' the girl said. 'We don't have puppies around for long, they're popular. But we did have a litter of Maltese/Shih-Tzu's come in yesterday. You could select one and pick it up next week.'

'They're tiny, right?' I asked, to be polite. No way was I having a yipping pom-pom for a dog. That was almost as bad as a cat.

She nodded. 'Small dogs. Quite fluffy, very cute.'

I stared at the fearful brown eyes of a brindle bitza huddled into her bed. My heart ached, and I although I didn't know exactly what my future held, I sensed she wouldn't cope with it.

'Oh, I know,' the girl's eyes widened. She reached into her pocket for her phone. 'I have a friend who picked up a puppy last week and found out this morning that her husband is getting transferred interstate and they can't keep him. He'll be a handful. And big. Do you have experience training dogs?'

'My housemate used to train huskies,' I told her. Close enough.

'Perfect! I can fix you up with everything you need,' she said, already bouncing back to the front shop where she started to fill a basket with food supplies and poop bags.

'This is great, she was worried she wouldn't find a home for him. Malamutes get dumped all the time.'

'What gets dumped all the time?' Cecelia asked, wandering back in from the Cat Hotel, her blue blouse covered in white fur. I just grinned.

Salt was a ten-week-old German Shepherd/Alaskan Malamute cross with a fluffy white coat, a wolfish head and what would eventually be a plumed tail arching over his back. I'd heard malamutes were difficult and hoped he had a good dose of shepherd obedience or whatever it was that made them ideal police dogs.

Despite my concerns, I sensed that we would be friends for a long time. I was free to name him however I liked, but Salt – a nickname from his breeder, not because of his white coat, but because he'd snuck into their kitchen and smashed the salt shaker on the floor, twice – suited him. He had slightly darker fur around his ears and eyes, humongous paws and a cute little grin. The previous owners agreed to give him to me for a donation to the animal shelter, happy just to have found him a home. I was generous with Dad's credit card.

I took the twenty-page instruction booklet that the breeder had provided and loaded the car with the crate, puppy pen and a box of toys, food and other paraphernalia, grateful that I had a hatchback. Salt sat on Cecelia's lap on the way home, sticking his little black nose out the gap in the window and leaving slobber all over the glass.

Dad called while we were driving back to the city. 'Hey Gabby, how are you?'

'Driving,' I replied.

'Hands-free?'

Nope. 'Yep.'

Cecelia rolled her eyes.

'Are you coming home tonight? You know you still have to stay with a legal guardian.'

'There's no law about that,' I said. Or maybe there was. 'Anyway, I'm coming home. I have a surprise to show you.'

'Does this have anything to do with my missing credit card?'

I gave him a cheeky 'maybe' and hung up. Grinning like a maniac.

'Will he be mad?' Cecelia asked, now holding up Salt's head because he wanted to snooze but also have his nose on the window ledge.

'Nah. Dad is pretty good with this stuff.'

'You know you're going back to school next year? Uni is school.'

'I'm not going to uni,' I said, not looking at my friend.

'Of course you are! You can take a gap year – I'll let you do that – but then you'll have to get a job, and you'll have even less time.'

I elbowed her, causing me to jolt the steering wheel. 'You'll let me take a gap year? How generous.'

'Stay on the road!' she cried, clasping Salt a little tighter, but she laughed. We fooled around all the way home. Salt melted Dad in about thirty seconds, and a minute later had Dad whipping up a homemade puppy treat in the kitchen.

Cecelia and I flopped on the couch. I finally let her vent about all the injustices in the exams, which she had no doubt passed with high nineties anyway, and considered how grateful I was that I had a friend who would trust me, and not pressure me. Well, except for my studies. That one wasn't going to let up. She looked tired though. Dad noticed that too and, after Salt had been set up with gourmet treats for a week, made his apparently famous world's-most-nourishing chicken soup for dinner, with crusty bread.

After dinner, Cecelia crashed in the spare bedroom. Salt was asleep in his bed, which had come with him so something would be familiar, arranged on the living room floor with a bunch of toys in his new pen. Dad and I stayed up, sitting on the rug next to the pen.

'Exam stress hasn't hit you so much?' he asked, sipping at a mug of peppermint tea.

I shrugged. 'They weren't great. But I had other stuff going on, *Jan.*' I let that hang. He was quiet, looking at the carpet. I gave him time.

'I have to keep up appearances,' he said. 'I'm sorry I couldn't help you more at Darkhaven. But if I stay in Luci's inner circle, I can help you now. I'll find out where she is.'

I nodded. I didn't like it, but it made sense. I suspected he was withholding something, but my intuition suggested that he was genuinely on my side of things. In his mind, at least.

'What does Alex know?' he asked.

'Nothing,' I said, voice flat.

'What's the cover story?'

'There isn't one.'

'Oh.' I knew he knew what I meant, despite my not being able to say it. 'Well, that's good.'

'Is it?' I met his gaze, desperate, anguished.

'You did the right thing. It's always hard when it's family.' He drained his tea. 'I'm off to bed. Goodnight, Gabby.'

He left me staring at my hands as they absently rolled a puppy toy around and wondering which family members' memories he'd modified. Finally, I went to bed, even though the evening hadn't cooled and it was too hot to sleep.

Salt started crying the moment I left, so I pulled the sheet off my bed and stretched out on the couch. He settled, but I lay awake. What kind of world was I in, now, where that conversation could even happen? However nice Dad was being, there was a distance between us that hadn't been there before. But I'd made it through the school year, I still had my friends and I'd made a decision about Darkhaven. I could only hope that Donovan would honour Stephen's offer for me to keep my friends and family, but I had to follow through regardless. Luci was still out there. And now Zenna was tangled up in something connected to my Event, even if she didn't know. I turned over, trying to get comfortable, and stared out the window. There was no moon tonight, and the stars seemed brighter than usual, sparkling across the sky like magic dust. Despite my grief and worries and questions, I still tingled with my earlier sense of optimism. High school was over. TISC decisions were done. I was joining Darkhaven, discovering more about human potential than I'd ever imagined.

And it was quite possibly magic.

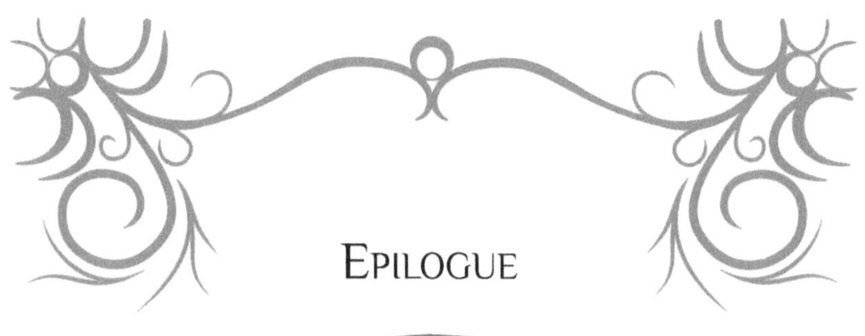

The Book of Love

A blinding light flashed in the room. I rose, heart thumping. Salt sat up too, ears pricked towards a golf ball–sized orb of light hovering just above the coffee table. I climbed off the couch and knelt in front of the table. As I edged closer, an excited bubble expanded in my chest, coupled with a sensation of longing, as eyes burned close to mine and lips brushed . . . I pushed Keraun's kiss away. It wasn't helpful to dwell on it. But the feelings grew as I peered at the light. There was something familiar about it. Nothing sinister, so I reached out and touched it.

It expanded, engulfing my hand. I didn't hear anything, but I knew. I knew it was Keraun, and it was a message. He was thinking of me. No. He was communicating with me.

My heart jumped, flying around somewhere outside of my chest, leaping about the room. He was alive, and not imprisoned beyond reach.

There was more, but it was tricky. If I focussed too tightly, it slipped away. I took a breath, relaxing.

Hi? I ventured.

Hey. It wasn't really a word, just a sense of acknowledgement. I paused for a moment, caught in the strangeness of whatever kind of intergalactic telephone call this was.

Where are you? I thought. Again, not words, just a wondering about where he was.

Cloudlight. It's a facility closer to Abell than Earth. He was reluctant to tell me, but he didn't seem to be able to hide it, despite being practically on the other side of the universe. He was confined to a strange room. Safe, comfortable enough, but not home. And he felt embarrassed.

Jail?

He laughed at my idea of jail. *Nothing so crude as what you know as jail. But I suppose it's the closest comparison you have.* He hesitated. *There's been a complication. It's taking them a while to figure things out.*

I wondered about his embarrassment, not intending to ask about it, but he answered anyway.

My family have a long connection to the Uzrun. I've caused them quite a bit of trouble. And all for the love of a girl.

He definitely hadn't wanted me to hear that. His thoughts were sticky with reluctance.

It's the telorb. The communication orb. You have to be honest. A rueful sigh. *Whatever you ask, I'll have to answer.*

Without meaning to, my months-ago realisation sprang to mind – how Keraun had met me before the lightning strike, in the school office. If he had pursued me because of the accidental lightning strike as he'd said, how had I met him before my Event even happened?

I didn't even have to think the question aloud. Without a word, I felt as if I dissolved into some other space. It was Keraun's mind, his memory. I sensed more strongly that he wasn't entirely volunteering this information. I smiled to myself as he squirmed.

Keraun – I knew it was Keraun, although it didn't really look like him, rather it was a dreamlike, featureless apparition that I simply knew was him – stepped through a silver door. He was alone, but I sensed his caution. The room was circular, and darkened, lit only by tiny spheres of silvery light that seemed to hover around the perimeter of the area like lanterns on an invisible festoon. They rippled as he ventured deeper into the room, heading for the centre.

As he approached, a pedestal appeared before him. Its blue luminescence grew as he came up and stood before it. On the pedestal was an enormous, ornate book, bound in leather with gilded pages and metalwork adorning the spine and corners of the cover. It had an embossed title, glowing in the shimmering light: *MaDala Nezima Ku-hubar*. Keraun didn't bother trying to pronounce the title; he simply referred to it as the "Book of Love". Through the memory, I rolled my eyes at his tendency to oversimplify the complexities of the universe. The pressure to turn and run pressed down on him, as if the spheres lighting the room would at any moment turn on him and devour him for his trespass. But his curiosity burned brighter than the lights. With a general lack of reverence, he reached out and flipped the book cover open.

A burningly bright light shot down from the invisible ceiling, high above. I half-expected it to set the book on fire, but it illuminated a blank page. Keraun turned it. Page after blank page he turned, for what felt like an age, until finally he turned to a page that had text on it. I couldn't read or understand the language. But I understood Keraun Thephyeu's comprehension. The name of the greatest love of his life was Gabrielle Adele Whitehall. Keraun's hands felt warm, then hot, and flames started to curl around the corners of the book, bordering the forbidden knowledge on the page. Keraun slapped the volume shut and fled from the room as the book burst into fire and the spheres emitted a wailing shriek, descending on him. He slipped back through the silver door just in time, but not before glancing back at the pedestal, where the Book of Love sat, gently illuminated and unblemished.

The memory dissolved, and I found myself firmly back in my own mind. I could sense Keraun's sheepishness at finding me by reading a book of knowledge off-limits even to his advanced race of humans.

So you're really not an omnipresent being who knows all things, I thought to him. I mean, he'd told me he wasn't, but he seemed to read me so well I'd never quite believed him.

Not even slightly. Except for weather. I know all things concerning your solar system's weather. Even in thought, I could hear his droll tone.

Are you still controlling the weather here? What a random question.

More embarrassment. *The Sol Group are taking care of things. But I still know what is happening. I can't not know. It's like how you know your heart is beating.*

So you can't fix this weird rain? I asked, trying not to reveal my cheeky trick. We were actually in the middle of an oppressive heatwave. Unfortunately for me, the honesty thing worked both ways.

He smirked. *Good try.*

I'd have to ask him one day how he'd even gotten to such a place as the circular room with the book. I knew, somehow, that it wasn't anywhere on his world, or even connected to his race. There was a whole other level to this evolution thing.

What happens now?

Keraun's demeanour shifted. *I await my trial. Eftychi thinks I have a good cha—*

Salt's soft whine cut into my awareness. I had a sudden jolt of alarm, like I'd been sprung sneaking into the pantry before dinner, and the telorb vanished into a fading mist of tiny glittering stars that I'd seen once before: the mysterious envelope in Dad's jacket, before I'd gone for a walk in a thunderstorm.

Despite the abrupt ending, hope fluttered in my heart. Keraun cared enough to call me from the other side of the universe. And he had a chance. Salt curled up on his bed, quiet again.

I lay back and gazed at the stars.

Thank you!

Hi! Kel here.

I'm so glad you read and hopefully enjoyed Darkhaven! If you'd like to see more, there are two great things that make that happen: leave a rating or review, and join my newsletter!

Head to wherever you bought this book and leave a review. The book is also listed on Goodreads and Storygraph. Reviews really do make all the difference to the success of a book and I will be eternally grateful.

Join the newsletter and get a free story!

Visit kelefox.com, sign up to my newsletter and get *The Inheritance Experiment*, a short story prequel to *Darkhaven*. You can follow me on socials too, but the newsletter is where the VIPs are at. For even more special treatment, or if you'd just like to contribute to the process, you can also become a patron for a small monthly amount. All details on the website!

See you somewhere soon.

Acknowledgements

Hello, reader friend! Thank you! I'm honoured. I presume you liked the book, because you're still here. (Bear in mind this is the part where the house lights come up and the credits roll. 99.95% less interesting than the last several hours. But if you've still got some popcorn left, hey, stick around.)

To my partner, Joel: my utmost love and gratitude for being my sounding board, my first reader, my reassurance, and for holding up practicality while I chase this dream. And for the dancing. Always for the dancing.

To Mum, the deepest thanks for her lifelong support and encouragement, for beta reading mismatched chunks of book (Me: Mum, hi. Where are you up to? Mum: Umm. Chapter six. Bruce and Gavin are going surfing. Me: Ah. That's all wrong. I'll send you a new version. Don't read any more. Don't read any more!) and for all but shouting about my book from the rooftops.

To Dad, for helping to put me through uni, for not raising both eyebrows at my choice of major, for supporting my ambitions, and for helping me write a poem about guinea pigs when I was ten.

To Rolf and Ashlea and Nic, for being excited about having an author in the family. And for joining the hunt for sneaky typos!

(Friend! You're still here. You must be out of popcorn. Just so you know, this is where the credits music, which was a groovy song in theme with the movie, has now changed to some random orchestral B-side that has nothing to do with anything. But it is a stirring piece. French horns are soaring!)

S.M. Isaac has only recently joined my writing journey, but I have a feeling she'll be here to stay. Thank you for jumping in with so much enthusiasm, providing helpful suggestions and just bringing joy to the writing process.

To the Coffee & Cats Fantasy Writers' Circle, thanks for being a safe and fun place to talk about all the trials and triumphs that go with crafting stories.

(Timpani! A gong! Trombones singing! The only popcorn left is on the floor!)

To my editors, Mandy Ballard from Salt and Sage and Justin Dill from Royal Editorial: thank you for being excited about my project and showing me so many ways to be better (so many ways). I look forward to the next one!

To Marilyn, my first patron, and the Moonlighters . . . this one's for you! Your unanimous encouragement was one of my cornerstones, that point where I started to truly believe the dream was real. I can't wait for the next book club meeting and hope you all enjoy the sequels just as much.

(Strings, diminuendo . . .)

These people will likely never find this, but I am grateful to be part of several professional bodies, most notably the Alliance for Independent Authors (ALLi), and the 20Books group. ALLi has provided me with fantastic resources, and Craig Martelle is a legend. Thank you to both.

(Hey friend. FYI, there's a youth with a vacuum cleaner coming up the aisles. The music has finished, but I look forward to meeting you again in the next book!)

(P.S. I hope you didn't eat any of the floor popcorn.)

About the Author

Kel E Fox was an apothecary in a past life, a stage technician in the theatre in this life and hopes to be a wizard in the next. Right now, she is the author of all sorts of fantasy short stories and poetry. Her first published short story, 'The Inheritance Experiment', won an editor's choice award in 2018.

Darkhaven is her first novel, kicking off the epic Lightless Prophecy saga, some six books and a number of short stories, which she will publish over the next few years.

Kel lives in Perth, Australia, with her partner, two lazy cats and a wilful Alaskan Malamute named after Nighteyes. She loves ballroom dancing, art, playing Magic: the Gathering, and of course, reading fantasy.

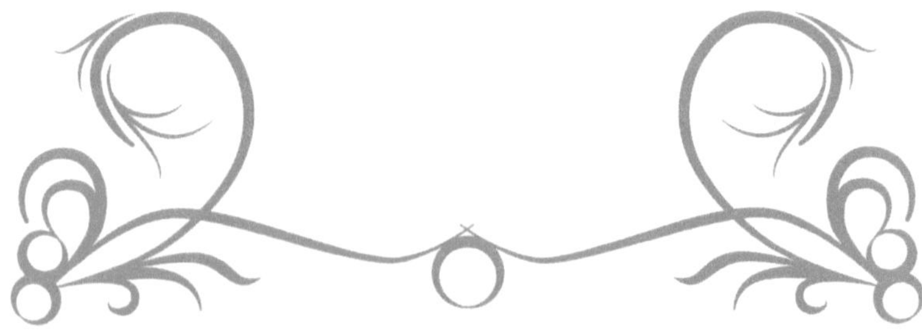

9 781922 731012